# THE LAST CRUSADER

Louis de Wohl

# THE LAST CRUSADER

## A Novel about
## Don Juan of Austria

IGNATIUS PRESS    SAN FRANCISCO

Originally published by J.B. Lippincott Company
© 1956 by Louis de Wohl
Reprinted with permission of the
Society of Jesus, British Province,
on behalf of the Estate of Louis de Wohl

Cover art: Christopher J. Pelicano

Cover design by Riz Boncan Marsella

Published in 2010 by Ignatius Press
ISBN 978-1-58617-414-9
Library of Congress Control Number 2009930110
Printed in the United States of America ∞

DEUS LO VULT

*All the leading characters in this novel are historical,
and the author hopes and trusts that
any similarity between them and their originals
is not purely coincidental.*

# CONTENTS

# BOOK ONE

A.D. 1554–1559

THERE WAS NO ROAD to Leganés, just a narrow, muddy path marked by occasional imprints of naked feet and strewn with stones—irregular, ragged, and discolored like the teeth in an old man's mouth. The village itself, perched on a cluster of hillocks, was brooding wearily in the early afternoon sun.

When Charles Prévost saw it through the window of his carriage, he shook his large, gray head. They might have chosen a better place, he thought. But then that man Massy had been a viol player, a musician, and there was no way of understanding such people. He could have settled down in Valladolid or even in Madrid itself, though of course life there would have cost more; moreover, in the cities there was a far greater danger of meeting people who might ask questions, or worse still, get a glimpse of the—the secret. And that . . .

A sharp knock interrupted his chain of thought—something had hit the carriage.

Charles Prévost heaved his large, fleshy body nearer the window and peered out. And then he gasped. There was an arrow sticking in the leather curtain. An arrow!

Glancing about he saw at some distance a turbaned head—and another and a third. Moors . . .

For one wild moment Charles Prévost felt himself whirled back in time to the siege of Tunis, trumpets blaring, banners streaming in the wind and the Emperor himself roaring commands as only he could.

But then he saw that the faces under the turbans were boys' faces and very frightened ones at that. Boys playing

Moors and shooting at his carriage! His face flushed and he pulled at the silk cord the other end of which was tied to the coachman's little finger.

The carriage came to a stop.

"Just you wait", said Charles Prévost grimly. He began to fumble at the door.

"Don't do that", a young, clear voice said sharply. "Please!"

The heavy man turned around. A boy was looking into the carriage from the other side, a boy perhaps seven or eight years old, fair-haired, with a pale, eager face. He was dressed in rags.

"What do you mean?" Prévost stared at him, goggle-eyed.

"You were going to interfere, weren't you?" The boy sounded impatient. "They didn't shoot at you—your carriage just ran into their line of fire."

"Vaya ...", Prévost began to splutter. "Go away! I never ..."

"It was bad shooting", admitted the boy hastily. "But if you'll stay in your carriage, I'll avenge you."

Prévost's eyes narrowed. Blue eyes. Blue eyes and blond hair.

"Who are you?" he asked hoarsely.

"I am the 'Christian' leader", the boy said gravely. "And this is my chance to win the battle. Stay in your carriage, please! You'll see, I'll win it." He turned away and let the flap drop behind him.

Prévost blew up his cheeks. Mechanically he drew out a large silk handkerchief and dabbed his forehead. Then he lifted the flap. The "Moors" were still there—in fact there were more of them now, six, seven, a whole dozen, boys between seven and twelve, beturbaned and armed with wooden swords, slingshots, and bows and arrows.

Still more were coming up and all of them were gaping at the carriage. Maybe it was the first they had ever seen.

The countryside was poor here. A man was considered well-off if he had a donkey, and rich if he owned a mule. A carriage with two outriders, a liveried coachman, and groom was doubtless a sensation and of far greater interest to them than their game.

Prévost began to tell them what he thought of a flock of snotty-nosed urchins trying to impede his progress by shooting at his carriage, and they listened, wide-eyed and respectfully.

From somewhere a clear, sharp voice yelled: "Santiago!" and they looked up, startled, and tried to get into some kind of formation.

It was too late. A compact little troop of boys attacked them from the rear and almost as soon as they had come to grips with them a second batch came straight at them from behind the coach, led by the fair-haired boy. The "Moors" broke and ran, hotly pursued by the "Christians".

Charles Prévost began to chuckle. Then he pulled twice at the silk cord and the carriage rumbled on toward Leganés. After a few minutes the first houses stared at it with the eyes of all their inmates. Doors began to fill. Dogs barked madly at the horses.

When Prévost saw an old priest passing, he leaned out of the window and took off his hat. "Good morning, Reverend Father", he said courteously. "Will you tell me where I can find the house of Señor and Señora Massy?"

The priest was at least eighty years old, and his cassock not very much younger. He looked like a scarecrow, but he bowed like a grandee.

"I am Padre Bautista Vela, at your service. Señor Francisco Massy died some years ago. I closed his eyes. May God rest his soul."

"Amen", said Prévost, crossing himself. "And the Señora?"

"I shall lead you to her house. If you will kindly order your coachman to follow me . . ."

"Why don't you ride with me?"

The old priest gave the horses a worried look. "If you will forgive me, Excellency, I would rather walk. It is only a stone's throw away."

He walked on, a long, lean, wobbly figure, a shadow with a life of its own.

The house of Señora Massy was a ramshackle, sun-baked building. A few hens fled, cackling, as the carriage approached. The street began to fill with people, quiet, solemn-faced villagers who gaped at the unusual sight just as the "Moors" had done.

A woman appeared in the door. She was in her late forties, but her face showed vestiges of former beauty and her simple dress was clean. She paled and began to tremble. The priest went up to her and mumbled something. She did not seem to hear. She stared at the carriage and at the large man now dismounting with the help of the groom.

No one here had ever seen such a man before. The villagers gazed enraptured at the flowing white moustachios, the carefully kept, pointed beard and the glorious bottle-green of his dress.

"Señora Ana Massy?" asked Prévost, and once more he took off his hat. "I am Charles Prévost, a servant of His Majesty the Emperor."

The woman bowed her head. Perhaps it was a gesture of respect, but it looked more like the acceptance of a sentence. She beckoned the visitor to enter the house. After a moment of hesitation the old priest followed them and closed the door behind him.

The house was no better and no worse than any other in Leganés. Prévost was offered the best chair and a tin goblet

14

of wine. He accepted both, took a cautious sip, and cleared his throat.

"Señora Massy, I suppose you know why I have come."

The woman said nothing.

Prévost pursed his lips. He drew a document from the inner pocket of his coat, unfolded it carefully, and began to read, very slowly, in a dry, businesslike voice.

"'I, Francisco Massy, viol player to His Majesty, and Ana de Medina, my wife, acknowledge that we have received a son of the Señor Adrian de Bues, groom of His Majesty's chamber, whom we have taken at his request that we should bring him up as if he were our own son, and that we should not tell any person whomsoever whose son he is, because the said Señor Adrian desires that neither his wife nor any other person should by any means know of the child, or hear him spoken of. Wherefore, we swear and promise that we will not tell or declare to any living person whose the said child is, until the said Señor Adrian shall send us a person with this letter or come in person; and we acknowledge to have received from the said Señor Adrian for the first year the sum of one hundred crowns. And henceforth the said Señor Adrian is to give us fifty ducats for every further year of the boy's maintenance. Done at Brussels on the thirteenth day of June, Anno Domini one thousand five hundred and fifty.'"

Prévost carefully folded the document and returned it to his pocket. Only then did he look up. "I trust this will suffice to establish my identity and the purpose of my visit to you. Where is the boy, Señora Massy?"

"He ... he'll be home soon", stammered the woman. "It'll be time for his evening meal." She gulped. "You have come ... to inquire about his progress?"

There was little hope in her voice. When the blow fell, it was no more than the confirmation of her fears.

"I have come to take him with me. What he must learn now, he cannot learn here."

Ana Massy began to cry softly. The old priest patted her shoulder. His hand, crippled and deformed by arthritis, was like that of a mummy.

Prévost produced a small silk bag. "I've brought another year's payment in recognition of your services", he said not unkindly. "Fifty ducats."

Her eyes lit up. "So you won't take him away at once, señor—you will leave him with me for a time ... a little time ..."

"No, señora. He must leave today."

She pushed the bag away. "I don't want your gold." She turned away. "He's been ... like a son to me. It would be like ... selling him."

"Selling him?" Prévost was outraged.

"He's all I have left", she said in a trembling voice. "My husband—"

"I heard about your loss", Prévost interposed quickly. "The good padre told me. I am sorry to have to add to your troubles, but I am under orders—we're all under orders."

Even now she would not accept defeat. "Surely, if his father could do without him all these years, it should not matter to him so very much if the boy stays a little longer with me."

Prévost rose majestically. His enormous, obese figure seemed to fill the room. "Señora Massy, you do not realize your position. Adrian de Bues is a personal servant of the Emperor and my mission has been entrusted to me by the puissant Don Luiz Méndez Quixada himself, Majordomo of His Imperial Majesty. You will not presume, I trust, to resist his explicit orders."

This time she gave in completely, with a fluttering, helpless gesture of both hands, and Prévost, not unaffected by her misery, took out his handkerchief and blew his nose. "Come, come, my good woman—it's only for the boy's good. Where *is* he?"

"Jerome is just behind you, señor", stammered the woman. "He slipped in a moment ago."

Prévost turned round. Seven or eight years old. Fair-haired. Blue eyes. The "Christian" leader, carrying a little harquebus.

Prévost realized that he had suspected it all the time: a boy of seven or eight—leading all the others, some of them years older and twice as strong. He smiled.

"I have come to take you with me on a journey."

The boy looked at him from unblinking eyes. "I won the battle", he said. "Did you see me win the battle?"

"I did."

"Good", said the boy. "I will come with you on the journey, but first I must eat. I am hungry."

If Prévost was amused, he did not show it. He stalked to the door, opened it, and barked orders. The groom and one of the outriders appeared with tablecloth, linen napkins, silver, and a well-filled hamper. Prévost supervised the laying of the table and then turned once more to the boy. "The meal is served", he announced.

The boy sat down and began to eat, as if a roast partridge, white bread, and delicious honey cakes had been his daily fare for years. But after a bite or two he asked: "Is Señora Massy not going to eat?"

Ana Massy started crying again, and at once the boy got up and walked over to her. "He said it was for my good, didn't he?" he asked. "Why do you cry then?"

"It's all right", sobbed the woman. "Qu-quite all right, Jerome. Just eat your nice food."

He obeyed without too much eagerness. Prévost carved the partridge for him with experienced hands and later changed the plates. When the boy had finished, Prévost sent the groom with silver and linen back to the carriage. "Now we must leave", he announced quietly.

The boy nodded. Ana Massy rushed up to him and threw her arms around him. "Jerome, my sweet little Jerome ..."

He was embarrassed, but he was moved, too. There were tears in the blue eyes. He kissed the woman's cheeks and he bowed to receive Padre Vela's blessing. Then he picked up his harquebus.

"No need to take anything with you." Prévost smiled.

But Jerome marched on with his harquebus. When they emerged from the house, the street was packed with people. The whole village had assembled.

Jerome went up to a boy almost a head taller than he and pressed the harquebus into his hands. "Take it", he said with great dignity. "It shoots fairly straight, but you must allow for the wind, of course."

The leader of the "Moors" stood fingering the weapon. He muttered his thanks and received a quick smile in exchange.

Then the boy stepped into the carriage and Prévost followed him. The groom closed the door with a bang and rushed round to take his place beside the coachman. The whip cut through the air and with a jerk the carriage began to move, followed at once by both "Christians" and "Moors" in noisy unity.

Ana Massy rushed out of the house in a frenzy, her hair disheveled.

"My son! Jerome ... Jerome ... my son! ..."

Some of the villagers laughed, but many looked at her with compassion. The old priest caught up with her. "Control yourself, my daughter", he murmured. "He is not your son. Do not persuade yourself that he is; it will do you no good."

She pushed the hair out of her face. "You're right, Padre Vela. He isn't my son. He never was. I am just a foolish woman. But, mark my words: he isn't the son of Adrian de Bues either."

Padre Vela stared at her. "What do you mean?"

She laughed hysterically. "Don't pretend, good Father. You've seen the way that man treated him—with respect, with more than respect—with deference. Jerome isn't the son of Adrian de Bues, the son of a lackey. Shall I tell you who I think he is?"

The old man was afraid now. "Don't shout, my daughter. People will hear you and . . ."

"I don't care." But she dropped her voice. "He is no ordinary boy, Padre. I think he is the son of a great nobleman—and from what Señor Prévost said today, I think he is the son of Don Luiz Méndez Quixada himself."

"You have no right to accuse anyone." For the first time the voice of the old priest sounded firm and strong. "Whoever the boy's father was, he was first and foremost a sinner and needs God's mercy."

The carriage had left the village behind and was rumbling down toward the plain.

Prévost looked at the boy who was sitting beside him, erect, silent, with great, luminous eyes. "You don't seem surprised about the turn your life has taken."

"I'm not."

"No!" Prévost frowned. "What do you know about your birth?"

"Nothing."

Prévost tried again. "How is it that you are not surprised?"

The boy looked straight ahead. "I always knew this would happen one day."

## CHAPTER 2

"Ask Señor Prévost to come in", ordered the prior.

The barefooted friar went down on one knee, rose again, and walked away, over the hot stones of the courtyard.

The prior smiled wryly. They were getting accustomed to it now. It was only a few years ago that the Padre Provincial stiffened the rule and they all had to take off their sandals. Some had even been wearing soft shoes. They had groaned and sighed a good deal, poor things, but the Padre Provincial was adamant. "It was good enough for St. Francis—it should be good enough for us."

Well, he asked much less from others than he demanded of himself, one had to admit that. He had whittled down his sleep to a couple of hours and took food only every third day. He had made it known that he would never demand that of anybody else, but the fact that he himself was doing it, evoked something very much like a bad conscience in others—in some of the others anyway. It was a wonderful thing to have a saint as one's superior. It was also rather uncomfortable.

The prior sighed. Pedro d'Alcántara, the Padre Provincial, had been away many months and yet it was impossible to relax; it was as if he might come round the corner at any moment with his short, halting steps, seeing everything, even the thoughts that were creeping through a man's mind, the good and the bad alike. He would not say anything. Perhaps that was the most astonishing thing about him. He would never speak, unless spoken to—like the humblest of the serving brothers. But every man felt the urge to address him, to ask him questions. It was an irresistible urge. And then he would answer—in that blunt, terrifying language of the heart so few men could bear. Human friendliness was warm and comforting, but divine love was white hot.

Now who was the fat man with the boy at his side? Prévost, Prévost—French? Flemish? Flemish, more likely, judging by his moustachios. Not a man of rank. Some kind of superior servant, court atmosphere all around him— yes, Your Highness; at once, Your Highness; without fail, Your Highness. The boy—that was less easy. Dressed in rags. No trained movements. A little village boy, almost a little savage, but with the face of one of noble blood. *Sangre limpia*, without any doubt. Not a Spanish face. Northern. Northeastern. An enigma, a riddle, perhaps a mystery. Ah well, human mysteries usually revealed their explanations pretty quickly, and they were usually profane. The illegitimate child of some nobleman, perhaps— another one. All too often the spirit was weak and the flesh all-powerful. . . .

Prévost took off his hat. "Reverend Prior, I beg you to forgive this intrusion. . . ."

"If there were anything to forgive, I have already done so by asking you to come in, Señor Prévost", the prior said affably. But his eyes were on the boy. "Not your son, surely."

"Oh, no, Reverend Prior, oh, no. The son of one Adrian de Bues, a servant of the Emperor. Don Luiz Méndez Quixada would be grateful, if you could give him hospitality— just for a few days", he added quickly, as he saw the prior lift his brows a little. "And maybe not that long unless—I had better speak to you alone, Padre Prior, if I may."

The prior bent down to the boy. "What is your name?"

"Jerome, Reverend Prior."

"An excellent name and a great saint. Do you know anything about him?"

"Yes, Reverend Prior. He translated the Bible into Latin and he was very rude to St. Augustine."

"Was he really?" The prior managed to remain serious. "Well, I hope you won't imitate him in that. Now you run along and look at our garden out there, and if you can find any ripe oranges, help yourself."

"Thank you, Reverend Prior."

Good bone structure. Good wrists and ankles. Breeding, but no training. Don Luiz Quixada, eh? The mystery seemed to be cleared up, although the explanation was rather surprising. Don Luiz, of all people! Now the boy was out of earshot.

"Very well then, Señor Prévost; what does Don Luiz want of us? I didn't know he was back."

"He is not. I left him several weeks ago in Flanders—in Flushing, to be exact. May I ask whether Padre Pedro d'Alcántara has yet returned? He went to Rome sometime ago, Don Luiz said."

"He walked there, barefoot, yes. And he'll come back the same way." The prior could not help saying it, although he knew that the Padre Provincial would not have been pleased. "He may be here any day now."

Prévost rewarded him with clucking noises of astonishment and admiration, but he seemed disappointed. "You see, Reverend Prior—Don Luiz ... the boy ... Don Luiz would very much like to know whether the boy would be suitable for the religious life."

"Surely he is a little young. . . ."

"Oh, there would be no question of making a decision now. All Don Luiz wants to know is whether there is any kind of indication that way. It would influence the boy's further education."

"I see." It was understandable that Don Luiz wanted the judgment of the Padre Provincial himself. It also went to show that the matter was important to him. "Very well, Señor Prévost; we shall keep the boy here for a short while. What about yourself?"

"My orders are to take him from here to the castle, as soon as Your Reverence has given judgment."

To Villagarcía! The enigma deepened again. If the boy was Don Luiz' son, would he let him be taken to the castle, where his wife resided? Doña Magdalena was a jewel among women, but there was a limit to what any woman would put up with.

"If you will take quarters with the brothers, Señor Prévost, you will be very welcome, though I'm afraid you won't find our fare comparable to what you are, no doubt, accustomed."

Prévost bowed.

"As for your carriage," the prior went on, "my friars will look after it."

"There is no need for that, Reverend Prior. I left it outside the town, near the Balboa Gate. I thought it would be better to enter the town on foot. The streets were so full and . . ."

"Ah yes—there are many activities these days. Don Philip is here on a visit to the Princess Regent, and they drove in state through the main streets today—didn't you see them?"

"Well, no, we—we must have missed them somehow."
The fat man was obviously ill at ease.

"Missed them? What a pity for the boy! I'm sure he would have enjoyed the sight."

"Perhaps", Prévost said. His face was without expression.

Could it be that the fellow did not *want* the boy to see royalty? Or—or was it that he did not want the boy to be seen? What was all this about? The prior felt oddly annoyed. It was absurd to go on guessing about this sorry matter, more absurd still to bother about a servant, however superior, who was trying to be mysterious.

History was being made in Valladolid today. Don Philip, Prince of Asturias, had come to bid farewell to the Princess Regent Juana before setting out for England, where he was to marry the Queen. It might be, it very likely was, the beginning of a glorious new era, for Spain, for England, for the world.

"Señor Prévost, you will find the brothers' quarters in the left wing of the main building. If you will excuse me now ..."


The oranges were good, much better than the ones in Señor Álvarez' garden in Leganés. But then, everything seemed to be better everywhere than in Leganés. He would never go back there.

The palace of the Princess Regent must be the most beautiful thing in the world. He had had only a quick glimpse of it—Señor Prévost seemed to be in a great hurry to pass it by. So many people in the streets were beautifully dressed, even more handsomely than Señor Prévost, although *his* coat was of a material as soft as Aunt Ana's cheek when he kissed her good night. She always wanted him to call her Aunt Ana, but she wasn't a real aunt. It wasn't true that only children wanted to play games, the grown-ups did too—or some of them. Señora Massy played "Aunt" as the boys played "Christians and Moors". She was a good woman, of course, just as Ramón was a good boy, although he always had to play the Moorish chieftain, because his skin was rather dark. If only he handled the harquebus right. It was a good weapon and it hadn't been easy to make.

Enough oranges. Only the first two tasted really good, or the first three. The others were like—like the common soldiers, following their officers.

"Hey, boy . . ."

There was a friar approaching him, a young man with a broad, smiling face. "We're going to sing Vespers now. Want to come? You don't have to, unless you feel like it."

"I'll come, Padre."

The church was cool and quite empty. The friar hastened away to join the others for their solemn entry.

Jerome knelt down at one of the benches in the back of the nave. He prayed a little—for Ana Massy, for Ramón, for Padre Vela, because the old man often asked him to pray for him. For Señor Prévost who was showing him a new world full of beautiful people and buildings. For the prior, who was giving them hospitality.

Just as he started praying for himself, the friars filed in, took their places in the choir, and began to chant, and it was as if his words were taken up bodily by the singing and carried up to the roof, where God was waiting to receive them.

He could never quite get away from that idea of God waiting on the roof of a church. He had told it to Padre Vela once and the old man shook his head. "God is not on the roof; that's silly, boy. God is in the tabernacle, as I taught you."

"I know *that*, Padre. But I was praying to God the *Father*."

"God the Father is everywhere."

"If he is everywhere, he must be on the roof, too, mustn't he, Padre?"

Padre Vela had given up.

God on the roof had to listen to a great many wishes and thoughts. It was just as well to have prayed for the others first, otherwise he would never have gotten around to them.

The chanting went on and on, like birds released to fly up not only to the roof but to the throne of God himself.

It should be beautiful to sit among these friars and sing with them every day of his life, to the honor and praise of God and the Blessed Virgin. No one was as powerful as a priest, Padre Vela said. For a priest could make God descend to earth every morning that God made.

Suddenly and for no apparent reason Jerome turned his head. An old man was sitting behind him, and for one moment he really thought that it was God. An old man with white hair and a white beard. He had the largest eyes Jerome had ever seen, and he smiled with them. He was dressed exactly like the friars.

Jerome gave him a respectful little bow—it was difficult to bow with one's head turned—and the old man returned the courtesy with a kind of grave hilarity, but made a little sign as if to say: "Don't you think you'd better look back toward the altar?"

Jerome obeyed. A few minutes later the friars rose and marched out in twos, with the prior bringing up the rear.

When Jerome rose too, and turned to leave, the old man behind him was gone.

He went back into the garden and lay on the grass, looking up into the mellow blue sky, till the young friar with the cheerful face came to summon him to the refectory. They arrived there just in time to join in the responses to the grace said by the prior.

Supper was good: a little fish, vegetables, bread, cheese, and even a goblet of red wine, mixed gradually with water and more water, so that it changed from the color of blood to that of the small amethyst Señora Massy used to wear on feast days.

Señor Prévost was present, too. But nowhere could he see the old man who had been sitting behind him in church.

He felt a little shy at first, but the friars sitting on his right and left soon dealt with that and he ate heartily.

Talk was not permitted during supper. Instead, one of the friars who had supped half an hour earlier read from the writings of a saint by the name of Bonaventura. Jerome listened, but he did not understand much of it. Once or twice he felt the prior looking at him intently. Was he eating too much?

When the meal was over, the prior said the closing grace and then the friars began to sing a cheerful hymn of thanksgiving. Still singing, they trooped out of the refectory and along the long corridor leading back to the church.

The prior laid his chubby hand on Jerome's shoulder. "Time for Compline", he said. "I don't suppose you feel like coming with us, do you? You could go to the cell where you'll sleep tonight—it's the one over there, the second on the right—and chat a little with Señor Prévost. After all, you're not a friar." He walked on to rejoin the others.

Compline—that was the last prayer of the day. He knew that, although he had never assisted at it before. He liked the cheerful friars and their singing. And perhaps the old man would be in the church. He wanted to see him again.

He walked on, passed the cell where he would sleep, and slipped through the door into the church.

It was quite dark now, and he did not know his way. Even if the old man were around, he would not be able to see him.

The friars were singing in the choir and he listened. It sounded sad, almost plaintive this time. Night had fallen, and only by the grace of God would there be another day. As he tiptoed around a large pillar, he could see them, looking like ghosts in the dim light of a few candles. But after a while they rose and trooped away, not out of the church but past the main altar to the Lady Chapel, and once more he followed.

For the last time this day they sang.

"*Sal-ve Regi-na*—"

The greetings to the Queen of Heaven, the highest of all beings only human, the Mother of Christ, and, since Golgotha, the Mother of all mankind.

"Mother", said Jerome slowly and respectfully. "Mother."

" '—turn then, most gracious Advocate, thine eyes of mercy toward us and, after this our exile, show unto us the blessed fruit of thy womb, Jesus . . .' "

If only he could see her just once, just for a glimpse as brief as the one he had had of the Princess Regent's palace. But for that he would have to wait till the end of his life on earth. Only saints, and not even all of *them*, saw her before they died.

Everyone else had to be satisfied with his earthly mother— everyone who had an earthly mother.

Jerome pressed his lips together. He had no mother but the Queen of Heaven.

" 'Pray for us, O holy Mother of God, that we may be made worthy of the promises of Christ.' "

The imperial service entailed many hardships, but a monk's life was considerably worse. Prévost's bed was a wooden plank with a thin layer of straw on top; the water jug in one corner had to serve both for drinking and washing;

and bells woke a man up in the middle of the night, just when he had found sleep after hours of tossing and turning. No bugs, though. That was something. And breakfast was not too bad either, at least not for guests of the monastery. But there must not be another night here; he made up his mind about that.

Luckily, he caught the prior in the courtyard, and after a little bowing and scraping he asked him for his verdict.

The prior shrugged his shoulders. "It is still too soon, Señor Prévost; you must realize that. Even so—but I wish you could tell me just a little more about the boy. No, no, I'm not trying to pry into secrets. Why so crestfallen, my good señor? It is fairly obvious that there is *some* secret, is it not? All I want to know is: What spiritual education has he had so far? He must have had a good teacher."

"Just an old parish priest. I couldn't see anything particularly impressive about him. I don't know about such things, of course. . . ."

"The boy is extremely devout", the prior said thoughtfully. "I watched him yesterday at Vespers. And at supper, I told him he need not attend Compline, but he came anyway. I watched him this morning at Mass, too. He stayed for the thanksgiving. Not many lay people do and scarcely any boy of that age. And just a few minutes ago I saw him slip back into the church."

"Again?"

"Yes, again. I don't know how well Don Luiz knows him . . ."

Prévost raised his brows. "Don Luiz saw him last six years ago, and the boy wasn't much more than a baby then, of course."

"All the more astonishing then that he thinks the boy may have a vocation. You see—he may be right. I can't say for sure yet; mind you, the boy hasn't been here for even one full day and I never make a decision of such gravity, before I've made a very thorough—" He broke off.

"He can't hear you surely", Prévost said.

But the prior was not looking at the boy just coming out the church door. He was looking at the tall, white-bearded friar with him, holding the boy's hand.

"The Father Provincial ..."

The unequal pair approached.

"Father Provincial, Father Provincial. ..." The prior was excited. "If only we had known ... we had no idea that you were back. ..."

The old man smiled. He said nothing.

Prévost could no longer contain himself. "Most Reverend Father, permit me to introduce myself. I am Charles Prévost, servant of His Imperial Majesty, and I am here by order of Don Luiz Quixada, who will be very pleased to learn that I was able to see you. Don Luiz is asking you for a great favor. He would like to know whether or not— Jerome, I am sure you will be allowed to pluck a few more oranges in the garden. ..."

But the old man did not release the boy's hand. "He will live in the world", he said, beaming. "He should do well in the world, when the time comes." He nodded to the boy, gently withdrew his long, thin fingers, and shuffled off, with the weary little steps that had carried him to faraway Rome and back again.

He has grown old, the prior thought. Very old. Perhaps his judgment is no longer what it used to be. After all, he had only just set eyes on the boy.

But Prévost stammered: "Live in the world? Live in the world? How could he know what I was going to ask him? How could he decide it so quickly? You said ..."

"The Father Provincial has his own ways." Was there a tinge of bitterness in the prior's voice? "Well, anyway, you have your answer—and much sooner than you could have had it from me."

From beyond the courtyard came a sudden blare of trumpets.

The boy raised his head. With a few leaps he reached the wall. He climbed it with the agility of a monkey.

"What are you doing?" cried Prévost.

"You'd better come down, my boy", said the prior.

Jerome did not hear them. Sitting on the wall, he was staring with rapt attention at what seemed to be a long column of slowly moving towers. Towers of glittering, sparkling steel, immensely powerful, invincible—the Guards, the Royal Guards of Castile, heavily armored and riding the largest horses in the world, armored too, so that rider and mount looked like one being. He remembered Padre Vela at school, telling the story of Don Francisco Pizarro, who had conquered Peru for Spain and the Faith. How in battle the Indios valiantly fought the Spanish knights, undaunted by the fact that their arrows and clumsy lances could not pierce the Spanish armor; how their vastly superior numbers threatened to decide the day. Then one of the knights was unseated by a lance thrust. He fell, but he picked himself up again. That was too much for the Indios. The terrible creature, scaly as an armadillo, had been split in half and yet both halves went on living! It was sorcery, witchcraft. The Indios shrieked with fear and ran—and the battle was won. Surprise, the appearance of something new, something not understood could be decisive in battle! Exactly for that reason Ramón and his Moors were beaten, when surprise came in the guise of a carriage. . . .

Here they were, now, the sons and nephews and younger brothers of the knights who had conquered Peru, each man a little fortress, moving majestically, inexorably.

Silver trumpets! The plaza was black with people, every balcony was crammed, every window, every roof. The women were throwing flowers and waving their fans and handkerchiefs, their treble voices mixing with the roars of the men. Twenty-four trumpeters in coats of yellow and red; the halberds of the German Guards, the halberds of the Spanish Guards, Jerome knew all the uniforms; Ramón's father had a book with pictures of all of them. Officers—high, very high officers, all on horseback, glittering with gold and silver.

Then one lone rider on a wonderful, white charger with long-fluttering mane and tail. He was dressed in purple and cloth of gold; his face was pale; his hair and the short beard were fair. But no one would dare to tease *him* because of that, as they had teased the one boy in Leganés who had fair hair. The people all clapped their hands instead and roared and shouted; it made one feel quite dizzy. A prince, that's what he must be, a royal prince. It could not be the Emperor; everybody knew that he was an old man. A prince . . .

Down in the courtyard the prior smiled wryly. "The Father Provincial is right, as usual, Señor Prévost. Better let the boy become a soldier."

The din outside was such that Prévost could hardly hear him. "What is going on there, Reverend Prior?" he shouted.

"Don't you know? Don Philip is passing by—the Prince of Asturias."

Prévost became deadly pale. He rushed to the wall, managed, with a wild jump, to grip the boy's legs and drag him down, a thin, struggling bundle. "You mustn't", he gasped. "You mustn't . . ."

As soon as Jerome had his feet on the ground, he turned on the fat man like a young tiger. "How dare you! I want to see him! He's a prince! How dare you do that to me!"

"Easy now, my boy", said the prior, and Jerome stepped back at once, but with his fists still clenched. The prior patted his shoulder. "A soldier, Señor Prévost", he repeated. "And ... he may go far, you know...."

## CHAPTER 3

"He'll be here any moment now", said Doña Magdalena, breathlessly. "And I don't know what to do. I wish you could help me, señor brother. I know you can't. No one can, and I shouldn't have asked you to come; it isn't fair to you...."

"The only thing that is not fair is that you are making me giddy", said the young man in the austere black-and-white habit of the Dominican Order. He smiled. "I do wish you'd stop walking up and down. The tower room is too small for such exertions. Why must we stay up here?"

"Because it's the only place from which I can see them arrive."

"Gómez will sound his horn, surely. You don't have to be your own watchman." The young friar shook his head and his smile broadened. "You haven't changed much, have you, Magdalena? Even as a little girl you always felt you must do everything yourself."

"As a little girl I wasn't allowed to do *any*thing myself and you know it." But she could not help smiling, and the resemblance between the two became unmistakable, with their eyes crinkling up as they both lifted their heads and stuck out their chins at each other, the determined, round chin of the Ulloas. But the young woman's smile faded and was gone even before she had turned back to the window.

She would have been a wonderful nun, Fray Domingo thought. If she had known that she would never have a child of her own, perhaps she would not have married Quixada. Or would she? Well, this was not exactly the moment to ask her such a question. And Quixada was a great caballero, and the marriage, up to now, had been exemplary—if one could call a marriage exemplary in which the husband had to spend so much time away from his wife, in the field, at court, on official missions. . . .

Magdalena seemed to know what he was thinking. "Five years," she said, "five years of marriage—and not one of them that we could spend together from beginning to end, not one when he was not called away after a few months. . . ."

"The Emperor is the rival of many wives", Fray Domingo said. "If you had married a simple country squire instead of His Majesty's right hand . . ." If she wanted to talk, she would talk now.

She did. "God and His holy saints forbid that I should not give the Emperor what is the Emperor's—even if it is the most precious thing in my life: the presence and well-being of my husband."

He nodded. "A noblewoman is noble first and a woman afterward."

"Oh, certainly." She gave a despondent little shrug. "It's easy enough to fulfill the requirements, señor brother—when one knows that one has no choice in the matter. I wasn't complaining about the Emperor. But when a man is away from his wife so often and so long there may be . . .

34

other rivals. And toward those I am a woman first, and nothing but a woman."

I was right, he thought. He was thirty-two years old—three years older than his sister—and he had been a priest almost as long as she had been married. He had heard confessions by the thousand, and when one had heard the first thousand, one had heard them all. It was always the same dreary song, the same thoughts, words, actions, and omissions, the same motives, wave after wave of brackish water, and the same reactions. He knew, of course, that all this was in his own nature too, but he despised himself for it and thus found it difficult, at the beginning, not to despise the others—a grave sin in itself—instead of being the instrument of regeneration whose thoughts were of value only inasmuch as they helped the sinner to clear his mind.

"On our own", he said gently, "we are a sorry lot. But we needn't be on our own, you know."

She swung round. "You know what I am thinking, then?"

"My dear, it is as obvious as it could possibly be. Your husband sends you a letter from Brussels—"

"There! There is the carriage!" Her pointing finger was trembling. "Oh, what shall I do? What can I do? I must—"

"Wait", he said. "They haven't even reached the village yet; it'll be almost a quarter of an hour before they reach the main gate. I know you only asked me to come here today because you didn't want to be alone; you didn't expect me to be able to help you, not really. But now that I'm here, I'll try and do the best I can. Let me have that letter again, will you?"

She said nothing. She went on staring at the tiny, toy coach rolling along the dusty road toward the first houses of Villagarcía.

"Give it to me, *chiquita*. . . ."

35

She pressed it into his hand. The coach disappeared behind the house of the widow Fuentes, which needed a new roof badly—she must talk to Valverde about it.

"Charles Prévost, a very trustworthy man, will arrive at Villagarcía with a boy about eight years old", Fray Domingo read aloud. "'In the name of my love for you and yours for me I beg of you to take care of the boy and to give him your motherly protection. . . .'"

Doña Magdalena's body stiffened, and she bit her lip.

"'The boy is the son of one of my best friends'," her brother read on, "'whose name I am not permitted to reveal but whose nobility and renown is beyond questioning. The boy Jerome must receive the education due to the son of a caballero, but it is his father's wish that he should not become too ambitious and that his way of dressing should be kept very simple.'" He refolded the letter carefully. "A boy about eight years old", he repeated. "That means he was born three years before you met Don Luiz."

"Yes."

He smiled compassionately. "One of the greatest boons of being a priest, a friar, is that one can have implicit faith in one's Master. But until now I'd always thought that your husband was beyond reproach. Of course, it is always easy to have faith, as long as it isn't tested."

"I will ask the priest, the friar, a question." Her voice was brittle, and she still looked at the distant village, where nothing was moving now. "Why should it be God's wish that I cannot give Don Luiz a son?"

He took a deep breath. "I don't know, *chiquita*."

"At least you're honest."

"It's not much use speculating, of course", he said slowly. "But it might be—it just might be that God wants you to extend all your love to the boy out there."

She turned around at last. Her lips were white. "It's not much use speculating, as you say. And I can only hope that such is not God's wish. For I find it very difficult not to hate him even before I have met him. And now I think we had better go down."

She swept out and began to descend the narrow staircase. Fray Domingo followed in silence.

He was standing behind her in the first floor passage when she clapped her hands to summon the servants. The two dueñas, Doña Isabel and Doña Petronila de Alderete, all in black with large white caps; the valets, Diego Ruiz and Juan Galarza, both veterans of the war against the infidels in Tunisia; Pedro, the majordomo; Valverde, the almoner, who could both read and write; the three pages and two of the maids, Luisa and La Rubia of the red tresses and thousand freckles. From this first floor, broad stairs went down to the courtyard with its well and the carefully clipped shrubs Don Luiz was so fond of.

They formed a compact group at the head of the stairs. Fray Domingo smiled wryly. She is not receiving a guest, he thought. She is warding off an attack. He had never seen her like this. Perhaps it was Don Luiz' boy. This kind of thing had happened before—though Don Luiz— ah, well, even the best and most upright of men could make a slip. But if it were so, you couldn't blame the boy. Even the best and most upright of women didn't have much sense of justice when their emotions were involved. And if, for some unknown reason, a woman unable to conceive herself had another woman's child thrown into her lap, a living reproach to her barrenness ... Don Luiz shouldn't have surprised her like this. If he had prepared her properly ...

The iron-studded gate was opening and now the carriage came in, clattering and creaking past shrubs and well and shrubs again, then turned left and came to a halt.

From the corner of his eye Fray Domingo saw his sister's face at an angle, taut and white. He could not see her eyes.

A stout man with luxurious moustachios emerged from the carriage, looked up, removed his hat, bowed, replaced his hat, turned, and saw that the companion whom he wanted to help alight had already done so.

A slender little boy, fair-haired, blue-eyed, simply dressed, was standing at the foot of the stairs. Seeing no one, he looked up and then slowly began to ascend.

Except for his light steps there was no sound.

He was looking straight at Doña Magdalena. Halfway up the stairs he paused. Perhaps the stout man had told him that he was going to meet a great lady. Perhaps he remembered what Ana de Medina had taught him about the right way to greet the greatest lady of all. He went down on one knee and raised his hands, palms pressed together.

There was a flurry of black velvet and lace and gleaming white ruffs, and the Lady of Villagarcía bent over him, drew him up, and took him into her arms.

Fray Domingo murmured a very cheerful little prayer as he, too, descended. Still pressing the boy's tousled head to herself, she lifted a tear-stained face. "What a pity", she murmured. "What a pity I'm not the mother of this angel."

Fray Domingo grinned so broadly she almost became angry again.


Latin was bad enough, but Greek must have been invented by the devil.

Jerome suggested this gravely to Padre Guillen Prieto, who was teaching him both languages; and Prieto, an amiable, roly-poly young man with a shock of unruly black hair, pointed out equally gravely that if that were so it would still be a good idea to learn Greek. "If you wish to beat an enemy, make sure that you know all his tricks." Jerome looked at him a little doubtfully, but decided to concede the point. But when Padre Prieto told the story to Padre García Morales, the principal chaplain of the castle, the older priest shook his head. "A dangerous argument indeed. On the basis of it the boy could think himself entitled to study anything forbidden; why, he might even study the black art itself!"

"He won't have much opportunity for that in Villagarcía", Padre Prieto replied cheerfully.

"Maybe not. But he won't stay here all his life, and he may remember your teaching when he meets the forbidden at some later stage. You should have told him that Greek could not have been invented by the devil, since the Church uses at least a few Greek words in the Mass."

"*Kyrie eleison.*" Prieto smiled apologetically. "I'll tell him that—when he has learned the irregular verbs."

He did not add that this would probably take years. Little Jerome was quick only when he liked what he was learning.

Juan Galarza, who was teaching him swordmanship, the use of the lance and of the crossbow and the art of riding, had no cause of complaint. The two had made friends quickly, and many a time the maids giggled when they saw the odd pair walk off to the small courtyard Galarza preferred as a training ground—the slender little boy and the stocky old warrior with his grizzled beard and the long scar on his left cheek.

"Giggle, La Rubia, giggle!" Galarza said. "Nothing better can be expected of you. A few more lessons and the young man here will be able to prick every single freckle on your nose—though of course he may get tired of the game after the first few hundred." He grinned at Jerome. "Women", he said. "Never let them get uppish."

"Scarface", shrilled La Rubia. "Old scarface!"

Galarza pointed with his thumb. "She thinks that should make me angry." He chuckled. "A scar is an honorable thing", he said very loudly. "But freckles grow on a girl's face one by one for every sin she commits. Me, I don't envy the recording angel who has to count 'em in this case."

But Jerome was not interested in his teacher's duel with La Rubia. Rubbing his own soft cheek he said thoughtfully, "You must have parried that one badly."

"Think so? Well, maybe I did. But a fellow has only two arms and when that circumcised dog of an infidel lunged out with his curved sword I was holding a shield over Don Luiz with my left and warding a lance thrust off with my right. What would *you* have done?"

Jerome thought it over. Frowning, he asked, "What is 'circumcised'?"

Galarza cleared his throat. "Something the Turks do. They cut off something. Now on that day—"

"Where do they cut it off?"

"In Tunis", Galarza said emphatically. "It all happened in Tunis and what a day it was, by Santiago. As I said, I was covering Don Luiz. He's the greatest fighter you ever saw."

"As great as the Cid?"

"As great as the Cid."

"Then why didn't *he* cover himself?"

"That's an easy one", Galarza said. "He couldn't cover himself because he was covering the Emperor." He lifted his cap perfunctorily.

"O-oh", said Jerome. "Was he there too?"

"Was he there? He was our commander-in-chief, boy! He was our *jefe* and there's no better one, not in this world there isn't. They say he's old now and his health's no longer what it used to be, but in those days he could kill a Turk with a crossbow at more than a hundred paces. I've seen him do it. Ah, yes—the times are gone when noble knights could turn up their noses at the crossbow and say it wasn't a fair weapon and only good enough for the foot-slogger."

"Did they say that?"

"They did. Gave the common man too much of an advantage. The bolt from a crossbow pierced their armor. Took much of the fun out of fighting, I'll admit that. A knight was practically invulnerable before the crossbow came. Upsetting thing. Now my grandfather told me that a long time ago, when Innocent the Third was Pope, he banned it. Said it was a weapon unfit for the use of Christians and hateful to God."

"Your grandfather banned the crossbow?"

"No, no, the Pope did. So he never became a crossbow-man, wouldn't touch it. He used the halberd instead. Well, it's not a bad thing either, of course, but—"

"The Pope used a halberd?"

"No, my grandfather did. What's the matter with you?"

"But if the crossbow is forbidden, how could the Emperor use it?"

Galarza rubbed his ear. "Maybe the Pope changed his mind later—he or another pope. Anyway, the Emperor used it against infidels. Now will you stop asking silly questions? Take up your crossbow and load it. You can use the same target as yesterday."

Jerome obeyed mechanically. His crossbow was not, of course, the one used by a regular soldier. Galarza had made it for him—as he had made those for the four grown-up crossbowmen guarding the castle—of wood, horn, steel, cat-gut; he had made the bolts as well and given them the right feathering, and he had oiled the groove and the revolving nut. It was a lovely weapon. All the same, if the Pope had forbidden its use ... But then he remembered Padre Prieto. It was good and necessary to know all the tricks of the devil. His face brightened; he raised the crossbow, took careful aim, and pulled the lever.

"That's one Turk less." Galarza beamed. "Pity Don Luiz didn't see it."

Don Luiz. Everybody in Villagarcía spoke of him the way Padre Vela in Leganés used to speak of God. "If you want to please Don Luiz, you must learn more Latin words." "When Don Luiz comes he'll want you to show him how well you can ride." "Don Luiz won't like it if you go around with spots on your coat." "Don't put your elbows on the table; sit up straight—Don Luiz hasn't much patience with a boy who doesn't mind his manners."

He was not at all sure that he was going to like Don Luiz. They all did here, though, even if they didn't say so in so many words. He could always tell whether people liked the person they were talking about or not. When they did, there was a sort of softness in their voices, even in Juan Galarza's voice.

Tía loved Don Luiz, of course, but that was only natural, as she had married him. He had called her Doña Magdalena at first, as Señor Prévost told him to, but she said at once he could call her Tía. It was wonderful to have her as an aunt. Once, when he was not quite well—the first fresh figs had come in the day before—she put him to bed and nursed him. Her hands were cool and white and smelled of flowers.

"Tía ..."

"Yes, Jerome?" She never called him "*chico*" or worse still "*chiquito*" as some stupid people did—as if he didn't know that he was not very tall for his age.

"Tía, I'm awfully rich, aren't I?"

"Why, what do you mean, Jerome?"

"Most boys have several mothers and several aunts . . ."

"Several mothers?"

"Of course. Their own mother and the Mother of God. That's two and two is several, isn't it? Well, I haven't. I have only one mother, but it's the Mother of God; and I have only one aunt, but it's you!"

He looked at her very sharply, but she did not laugh; she did not even smile. She said, "That was a very sweet thing to say, Jerome; thank you very much."

There was no one like her, and no one good enough for her. Not even Don Luiz.

She was good, too, as good as a saint. She went to Mass every day in the chapel, and afterward he had to tell her how many poor had arrived and she went to fetch two bags of money for them, silver and copper. She knew *all* the poor by name and where they lived and who their relatives were, everything. From the third day onward she let him pay out the money for her under her supervision, never less than twenty maravedís each and often much more. There was one old man, old Pablo from Tordehumos, whom no one liked, and it was easy enough to see why. He was terribly dirty, and his hands were ugly and deformed and covered with warts.

When his turn came, Jerome pretended to drop the silver coin by mistake, and the old man bent down to pick it up. But Tía was quicker. She stopped him, picked the coin up herself, and before she gave it to him she kissed his horrid hand.

Jerome's face was burning. She did not even look at him. He went on distributing the money, but his hands trembled. When it was done and they returned to the hall, she did not say a word and he did not dare to speak. Later he missed the target twice with the crossbow, and he rode so badly Galarza had to shout at him.

Three days later the old man was back among the petitioners. Jerome knelt before him, kissed his hand, and, still kneeling, gave him his silver piece.

When he saw Tía's face he knew that all was well again.

## CHAPTER 4

DON LUIZ WAS COMING. The news seemed to have changed everybody and everything in the castle. Tía walked about as if in a dream. When Jerome asked her a question she more often than not forgot to answer or else answered something that had no bearing on what he had said.

Galarza was polishing all the arms; the maids were rushing about, cleaning and dusting and scrubbing, even La Rubia who did not care much for working. An entire wing of the castle was refitted and put into service again, carpets were laid, and furniture polished.

Jerome felt forgotten. The servants would not even let him enter the new wing where they were so busy. They were nervous and tense.

And because they were nervous and tense they forgot to lock the main door to Don Luiz' study, and when the servants were all having their dinner he slipped in to have a good look.

It was a beautiful room and very large, with stained-glass windows as if it were a church. There was a large, heavy desk, upheld by strange figures of honey-colored wood, with chairs that matched it, and many-colored carpets covered the floor. They had put flowers in the room—so Don Luiz would arrive today. Books—one, two, three—six books. He had never seen so many books in one room, and all of them bound in beautiful leather encrusted with silver ornaments.

There was a large painting hanging on the wall: Tía. Tía, in a dress of black and gold and smiling a little. Surely the man who had painted this must be a sorcerer. It did not just look like Tía; it *was* Tía. It was as though she were going to speak at any moment.

The windows were open and he could see the trees outside moving gently in the wind and sighing a little.

Then he saw the thing on the other wall, the wall behind the desk, and his eyes widened. It was a crucifix, a wooden cross with the figure of Christ nailed to it. But . . . but . . . it was half burned.

It frightened him. Who could have done that? Perhaps one of the maids? Did Tía know about it? Now, if they found out that he had been in the room, they might think that he had done it. . . .

The thought alarmed him. He turned—and stood face to face with Tía. He gasped. He tried to find words to explain why he was here, that he had not done anything, that it was not his fault. Then he saw that she was not looking at him, but at the crucifix. There was an expression on her beautiful, pale face he had never seen before and whose meaning he did not understand. Sadness was in it, and humility and yet also joy and pride. After a while

45

she said, "Of all the things in the castle this is the most precious." She stepped forward and laid her hand on his shoulder. "I'll tell you why, Jerome. Juan Galarza has told you, hasn't he, that Don Luiz accompanied the Emperor on his crusade against the infidels of Tunis. Tunis was a nest of pirates then, no ship, Christian or otherwise, was safe from them; and there was the suspicion and more than a suspicion that they were in secret communication with the Moriscos in the south of our own country, people who professed to be Christians and went to Holy Mass, but secretly at night reverted to Islam and invoked Muhammad. Before Don Luiz joined the fleet he traveled through the Huerta de Valencia and somebody told him of a certain house where Moriscos came together for secret meetings. He disguised himself and took quarters in an adjacent house. On the second night he saw there was a fire burning in the court-yard of the Morisco house. He climbed the wall, careful not to make any noise, and there were about sixty Moriscos sitting around the fire and praying on their knees, bobbing up and down as they do."

Jerome felt her hand tremble a little.

"Then the door of the house opened," she continued, "and two more men came out with a crucifix attached to a long rod. It was obvious that they had stolen it from a church. And all the Moriscos stopped their praying and began to curse instead, and one of them tore the crucifix off the rod and threw it into the fire. That was too much for Don Luiz. He jumped off the wall and into their midst and drew his sword and laid about him. He has fought in many wars and in many battles, and his name as a fighter is second to none in the kingdom, but never was he aroused so terribly as he was at that moment. The Moriscos must have thought that he was not a man but one of their demons—*afreets* they call them—for how could one man dare to fight them all? Or perhaps they thought that he must have many men outside who would come to his aid in a moment. Anyway, they ran. But Don Luiz jumped straight into the fire and kicked the logs away till he had found the crucifix and seized it, burning hot as it was, and carried it away. His clothes were on fire, and he had to tear them off; his beard and eyebrows were singed, his hands covered with blisters, but he lifted the crucifix up high and, sword in hand, he marched out, straight through the door by which the Moriscos had fled and out of the house and into the street, and no one dared to stop him. And that is how this crucifix came into our possession."

All the while she spoke, she kept her eyes on the crucifix, almost as if she were reading words from the charred, mutilated wood, the words of a simple, artless poem.

"I want to be like him!" The boy's voice startled her. She turned toward him. His little face was white, his eyes were sparkling, the hands had become fists.

"I want to be like him!" Jerome repeated. "Mother in Heaven, let me become like him—please!"

"Like our blessed Lord?" Doña Magdalena asked.

But he shook his head. "Who can be like God," he said, "when it's almost impossible even to be like Don Luiz?"

To his utter astonishment he saw that there were tears in her eyes. "What is it, Tía? Have I said something wrong?"

"No, no . . ." She took his face into her hands. "I hope you will be like him", she whispered.

Two hours later the horn sounded from the northwest tower and there was a flurry of excitement. Then the bells of San Pedro, San Boil, and San Lázaro began to ring, and the harquebusiers of the village fired off a ragged salvo.

47

Everyone in the castle assembled at the main gate, except for Juan Galarza, who had climbed the northwest tower and stood in readiness. For at the exact moment when the lord of the castle crossed his own threshold, the blue and silver flag of the Quixadas must be raised.

Jerome, standing beside Doña Magdalena, held a cushion with the keys of the castle.

Outside the walls, the entire village was shouting, screaming, dancing, and clapping hands as the cavalcade arrived.

Don Luiz was riding at the head of it—only for him would the main gate open—and Jerome saw a tall, athletically built man with a stern, bearded face under a light linen beret, wearing a long, silk coat now fairly dusty from the long ride; he was riding a noble Andalusian mule with a glossy white coat; its trappings lavishly adorned with silver. Behind him came a bevy of officers on horseback and a train of twenty mules packed with luggage.

As he had been instructed, Jerome knelt down to present his keys.

Don Luiz dismounted. But instead of picking up the keys he went straight up to Doña Magdalena and, taking off his beret, embraced her, kissing her on both cheeks. Only then did he turn toward the kneeling boy, take the keys, and with a courtly little gesture make him rise. For one brief moment Jerome saw the face of the hero of the Huerta de Valencia very close—bushy black eyebrows, a strong, aquiline nose, a black, pointed beard with only a little silver in it. There was an indefinable expression in Don Luiz' dark eyes, and he did not smile. The next moment he had gone, had vanished in the midst of cheering, shouting people; a band assembled at the foot of the main staircase broke into the strains of the Quixada song; Juan Galarza hoisted the flag, and Jerome, the empty cushion

48

in his hands, felt suddenly alone in a scene of triumph in which he had no part.

He was sent to bed early that day, and out of sheer loneliness he lay awake for hours, listening to the thin strands of music wafting in from the great hall. Perhaps from now on it would always be like that. Don Luiz was here, and there was no room in anybody's thoughts for anyone else.

He saw him again in the morning at Mass and at breakfast, but the officers were there as well and there was a good deal of talk about politics in Flanders and in Germany, involving dozens of names that meant nothing to him. Tía had given him a fleeting kiss on the forehead and gone on looking after the needs of the guests. Then Padre Prieto rose and gave him a little nod, and he followed him back to the padre's room for the usual lesson. "Translate into Greek: 'When the messengers of the Persian King told Leonidas their number was so great that their arrows darkened the sun, the King of the Spartans replied: so much the better; we shall fight in the shadow. . . .' "

The Latin lesson followed and after that the French lesson. They were making a monk out of him, or almost.

He felt better when Juan Galarza appeared to fetch him for the riding lesson.

"Nothing new today", Galarza declared. "Let's just see what we have learned so far." For the better part of half an hour he took his pupil through all the exercises—trotting, galloping, jumping, and the thrust of the lance at a man-sized target. "That will do. Now let's see what we know about fencing." The rapier, the sword, the combination work with rapier and dagger—the deadly point of the weapons made harmless by a small ball of leather.

"That will do", Galarza said again. Strangely enough he did not add any criticism this time, although Jerome knew that he had made a few mistakes, especially in the combination work.

The hour of the midday meal was approaching, and he went back to his room to change clothes and to wash. Just as he was leaving for the hall, La Rubia came to tell him that Don Luiz wanted to see him in the study.

Don Luiz . . . in the study . . . he gave the girl a casual nod and went to the study. His steps seemed to become shorter and shorter, and as he knocked at the heavy door his knees seemed to have a will of their own and became all wobbly.

A deep voice asked him to come in and he obeyed, closing the door behind him.

Don Luiz was sitting at his desk, under the crucifix for which he had battled sixty Moriscos. "Come nearer, Jerome", he said, neither kindly nor unkindly. "I wish to tell you that on the whole I am pleased with your progress. Greek doesn't seem to be very interesting to you, and I regret that. It is the only language whose beauty can match that of Spanish, and there is much pleasure in reading Homer, Thucydides, or Euripides in the original."

Padre Prieto had told him the same thing, of course.

"You are doing a little better in Latin, and I like your pronunciation of French", Don Luiz continued. "You must become perfect in both. Latin is *the* language, and God speaks to us in it through his Holy Church. French is the language of our Christian enemy, and we must be able to understand him. You won't have to learn either Turkish or Arabic because the only language in which we speak to Turks and Arabs is that of the sword. You are learning that now—I watched you."

Jerome flushed.

"You will never become a large, heavy man", Don Luiz said. "Therefore you must try to increase your muscular strength. I shall talk to Galarza about that. Your riding will improve when you have learned to treat your mount as a friend, and more than that: as part of yourself. In your sword work remember that you must control your temper. The cool fighter will always triumph over the hot one in the end, when strength, skill, and quality of weapon are equal. But on the whole, as I said, I am pleased."

"Thank you, Don Luiz", Jerome said a little breathlessly.

"There is one more thing—" Don Luiz rose. "Doña Magdalena has told you the story of the crucifix here." He took it down and held it in his hands reverently. "Take it", he said quietly.

He had to repeat that before Jerome summoned enough courage to obey. The boy's fingers trembled as they closed on the sacred wood.

"It is yours", Don Luiz said.

Jerome gasped. "M-mine?"

"Have it placed over your bed—and guard it well, as he whom it represents may guard you."

His eyes full of tears, the boy kissed the charred feet of the Crucified. He could not speak. Secretly he prayed that God would allow him to die for the master of Villagarcía.

Why? Why should Don Luiz honor him like this? He had done nothing to deserve it; he had done nothing at all yet for either God or the Emperor. But then, of course, everybody prayed at Mass, "*Domine non sum dignus....* Lord, I am not worthy"—and then went to the altar rails all the same; it was sheer impertinence, really, but God didn't seem to mind. And emperors were supposed to imitate God as best they could, and noblemen were supposed to imitate the emperor as best they could and perhaps that was why they sometimes gave honor to a subject before he merited it. Even an ordinary soldier was given a silver real before he put on his uniform.

But this crucifix was more than that, more than any honor one could think of. Tía said it was the most precious thing in the castle; it was a relic, a holy relic, and it was given into his care. Only yesterday he had felt that he was nobody, that no one cared for him, and now he was the guardian of the most precious thing in the castle. Don Luiz even said that it was *his*; but that could not be. No one could *own* this, like a cap or coat or horse or house. No one could own a thing that was sacred.

He would guard it with his life. And he would learn the irregular Greek verbs, all of them. And Latin and French and everything.


Padre Prieto reported that his pupil was making the most amazing progress. Juan Galarza reported the same. "He's as agile as a cat. What he lacks in sheer strength he makes up for by speed and subtlety. If he goes on like this . . ."

Don Luiz nodded, but made no comment. Instead he asked Jerome to come and help him look after the armory. Like many nobles of the time Don Luiz was his own armorer. Diego Ruiz, who held the post officially, was in charge only when Don Luiz was absent. "When I'm here myself, he still looks after the arms and ammunition of my men, but he's not allowed to touch my own things. I can only advise you to do the same, once you carry arms. Your life may depend upon a little speck of rust, a gun not oiled well enough or the whetting of your sword."

He began to clean a hunting gun. Jerome had to give him the parts, one by one. It was a thing very different from the little harquebus back in Leganés, and he studied the parts with great interest.

Don Luiz saw it. "Do you think you'll be able one day to fire a gun like this and hit something?"

Up went the boy's chin. "Not only that, Don Luiz."

"No? What else, then?"

"To wait for the enemy's salvo, as you did in the battle of Thérouanne."

Don Luiz gave him one of his rare smiles. "Old Juan Galarza told you about that, I suppose."

"Yes, sir, he did. And about the battle of Goletta and of Hesdin and of Landrecies, when the Emperor gave you the flag and told the squadron of bodyguards . . ."

"'This is your day of honor'," Don Luiz quoted. "'Fight like the caballeros you are. And if you see my horse go down under me and Luiz Quixada's flag fall—save the flag first.' "

The boy's eyes sparkled.

"Maybe you will be a soldier", Don Luiz said slowly. "You have given me a soldier's answer today anyway. Very well then . . ." He laid the gun aside and went over to the rack of swords. He selected the smallest, drew it from its sheath, and tested its elasticity over his knee. "Here", he said, sheathing it again, "take this. It's yours. You may wear it whenever you leave the castle."

CHAPTER 5

DOÑA MAGDALENA COULD NOT SLEEP. She knew quite well what was keeping her awake. Although it was past midnight her husband had fallen asleep more than an hour ago.

He could sleep at will—or so it seemed. They said that most men could when they had been soldiers a long time, and Don Luiz had been a soldier all his life.

He was breathing deeply and regularly, and she knew without looking that he lay stretched out straight, with the end of his beard pointing upward and his hands folded over his chest, as if he had been laid out on his deathbed. He always slept like that, the saints protect him.

She knew him so well, his movements, thoughts, ideas, loyalties—not fears, no, for he did not have any—but everything else, everything, except that one thing. . . .

There was a secret. For the first time in her marriage there was a secret between them, and it was a thing of terrible power.

Six years ago a marriage contract had been drawn up between Doña Magdalena de Ulloa Toledo Osorio y Quiñones, daughter of the Lord of la Mota, San Cerbrián and la Vega del Condado and of Doña María de Toledo, sister of the Marqués de la Mota, closely related to the ancient family of the Condes de Luna, and Don Luiz Méndez Quixada Manuel de Figueredo y Mendoza, Lord of Villagarcía, Villanueva de los Caballeros and Santofimia. On February 29. How well she remembered. In Valladolid. Neither bride nor bridegroom was present. The bride was represented by Don Diego de Tabera, Councillor of His Majesty and member of the Inquisition, the bridegroom by his uncle, Don Pedro Manuel, Archbishop of Santiago, by Don Gómez Manrique and Don Pedro Laso de Castilla, master of ceremonies of the Archduke Maximilian of Austria.

In the contract the Marqués Rodrigo de la Mota undertook to give his sister a dowry of ten million maravedís: five thousand duros in money, two thousand in jewelry, and the rest in land; the bridegroom undertook to pay four thousand ducats and guaranteed that amount, as well as the dowry, with his estates of Villanueva and Santofimia.

The contract was approved by the Emperor. The bridegroom then gave his brother Álvaro de Mendoza written powers to marry Doña Magdalena in his name, and that ceremony was performed on November 27, 1549. Don Luiz himself was in the field with the Emperor.

A full three months later he was granted leave and hurried to Valladolid to meet the girl he had married by proxy. And he met her for the first time in his life. There was nothing very unusual about that. After all he had seen a painting of her, and her uncle had given her a good description of him, as he had never had the time to sit for a painting.

By the grace and goodness of God there was no need for them to learn to love each other in the course of time. They fell in love at once, and after a few days felt they had known each other all their lives. He thought she was far more beautiful than her portrait and told her so in a voice that came straight from the heart; she discovered that no description, however eulogistic, could do justice to him. He was noble in every way, magnanimous and upright; despite his being in constant touch with the Emperor, there was nothing of the sleek courtier about him. He was a man a woman could look up to, without fear but with deep respect.

Young noblemen in these modern times all seemed to be driven by a new spirit of adventure, of enterprise and conquest combined with an insatiable greed for riches, evoked, perhaps, by the incredible wealth of the newly discovered countries. Don Luiz, middle-aged, was different. He, too, was ready at all times to meet danger and risk, but only in the service of the two great causes sacred to anyone who wanted to be worthy of the rank of knight: the cause of God and the helpless—and the cause of the Emperor and of the country.

His rank and station had led him away from her side time and again, and each time she had given him a smile when he left and kept the tears for herself, and the day he returned was a feast day and the joyful renewal of a state of bliss.

But now there was a secret.

She knew that everybody in the village regarded Jerome as Don Luiz' natural son. To them there was no mystery and no doubt, and probably there was no one who had not counted on his fingers at least once to figure out whether or not the boy had been conceived and born within the time of their marriage. In the castle the same thing happened, of course.

La Rubia, impudent enough, let her eyes wander from Don Luiz to the boy, backward and forward, drawing her comparisons for everyone to see. And Luisa, good, fat, stupid Luisa, when asked the other day where the master was, blurted out: "He's in the armory with his son", and then became as red as a peony.

Was Jerome his son?

She could not find any resemblance in figure or features. Don Luiz was tall and heavily built; Jerome was slight for his age. Don Luiz' eyes were dark and so was his hair, what was left of it, and his beard; the boy had blue eyes and fair hair. But he might take after his mother. Perhaps he was the very image of his mother and conjured up that image every time Don Luiz looked at him. Perhaps she was still alive, most likely she was, perhaps Don Luiz was still in love with her—no, that was impossible; he was not the man to enter into a marriage with the picture of another woman in his heart, though they said that most men were quite capable of that and worse.

He loved the boy, she knew that. The first day after his arrival he had spent hours sitting behind a curtain and listening to the boy's lessons. He had watched him from the window, when Juan Galarza had him ride and fence. He had given him the crucifix and a little sword of his own; and the boy worshipped him, of course, that was only natural.

If Jerome was his son, why didn't he tell her? Why tell her that story of his being the son of one of his best friends—unless, of course, he thought she would understand what even that goose of a Luisa understood; unless this was his courteous way of telling her what he could not tell in any other way without making a confession that ought to remain reserved for the confessional. . . .

It was not surprising that he loved the boy—one couldn't help loving him; she herself couldn't help loving him, whomever he might resemble. Perhaps, if she suggested to Don Luiz that he adopt the boy he would tell her—no, it was not right, the idea was not born, not wholly born of love, it was not right. She might just as well ask him point-blank: Is the boy your son? An impossibility. If he wanted to tell her he would have done so. To force his hand was grave discourtesy, and it would be the first that had ever been committed by either side.

Also it was quite obviously not Don Luiz' wish to adopt the boy. Why else should he have asked her to see to it that he did not become too ambitious and that he should be simply dressed?

On the other hand, if he didn't wish the boy to become too ambitious why had he given him the crucifix to guard—and why give him a sword at such an early age?

The whole thing was full of contradictions, only Don Luiz had the key to the riddle and surely he knew that she could not ask him for it, that it was for him to tell her, to honor her with his confidence. That was it—the lack of confidence he showed, that was what was so upsetting. It was so unlike him to be sure she would not ask the question to which everybody else in both castle and village seemed to have found the answer.

From afar came the thin bell of San Lázaro. Two o'clock.

Don Luiz was sleeping peacefully—his folded hands rising and sinking as regularly as ever; his face relaxed and dignified even in sleep, where most men were said to look helpless and even a little ridiculous. He was in complete harmony with the night, this night which to her seemed endless, restless, dreadful. . . .

The corrida de toros at Villandrando was not, of course, a big affair, and aficionados from Valladolid, Cordova, or Seville would have shrugged their shoulders (although, of course, they would have come all the same, provided there was no other bullfight). Nevertheless almost the whole of Villagarcía was there, and at least four other villages were sadly depleted when the show started, as usual at five o'clock in the afternoon and as usual on time, because no one, whether nobleman, mayor, or whatever else, could afford to let the crowd wait for what Padre García Morales called "their accursed, stinking, gory heaven on earth".

Also, if the matadors were decidedly third rate, the banderilleros either too young or too old, and the entry through the cuadrilla gate not exactly impressive, the toros at least were good, sturdy, black animals, bred to kill or be killed and tested for bravery on the ranches.

The ladies at the windows overlooking the plaza noted with interest that a number of servants from the castle were there and, sitting apart from them, a boy, no less than eight, no more than ten years of age, with fair hair and blue eyes— yes, it was he, no doubt about it; my *dear*, haven't you heard? *Everybody* knows . . .

Eyes narrowed, tongues wagged, fans moved; this was a show within the show.

Fat Luisa woke up with a start to find that La Rubia was shaking her. "What's the matter", she moaned. "Can't a girl have her sleep? Is somebody ill? What's happened?"

"Wait till I tell you, just wait till I tell you." La Rubia's voice was tremulous with excitement. "The third bull . . ."

"You and your corrida." Luisa yawned prodigiously. "I'm glad I didn't go, and I don't want to hear about it. You better go to bed yourself. And I wish you hadn't waked me."

"I know you're not an aficionada." La Rubia's eyes sparkled. "I'm not going to tell you about the fight, you wouldn't understand anyhow. But you just wait till you hear what's happened . . ."

"Well, what happened? Somebody fallen in love with you?"

"Most likely, but what chance would he have, with old Inez at my side all the time . . ."

". . . because if she weren't, you'd make eyes at every-body with hair on his lip. I do wish you hadn't waked me."

"It's not my fault if I'm pretty, Luisa dear. We can't all have a nose like a Flemish dumpling and cheeks and bosom to match. . . ."

Luisa sat up. "Now listen, you . . ."

"Have I got you wide awake at last? Then *you* listen: the third bull was a mad one; he slit up the matador, Porreno—he never was much good—and then he attacked the tribune and jumped it; you never saw such excitement, everybody running in all directions . . ."

"I *told* you I don't want to hear about the stupid fight . . ."

". . . everybody except the master's son, that is. *He* didn't run."

The fat girl gaped at her. "Dios! Has anything happened to him?"

"He stayed just where he was", La Rubia went on. "And he drew the little sword the master gave him last week."

"That tiny thing—against a bull?"

"Yes. And it was a real bravo, that one, you should have seen the horns, and there it was, drawing itself up to get its hindlegs over the tribune too, and everybody shrieking, and the little man just lunged out and stabbed it in the neck, just the right place too!"

"Santa Madre—did he kill it?"

"Who's getting excited now?" La Rubia grinned like an urchin. "No, he didn't kill it, stupid, not with that plaything of a sword and with the bull in that position. But he hurt it. He hurt it enough for it to grunt like a damned soul and shake its big head and slide back into the arena, and after that it wouldn't play anymore, whatever they tried. You should have heard the shouting that went up, especially when the master's son drew his sword back and looked at the blood and wrinkled his little nose and wiped the blood off with his handkerchief and sheathed his sword again as if he did that sort of thing every day. They threw flowers at him, of course, and then Juan Galarza came up at last . . ."

"He should never have allowed it to happen. The master . . ."

"He couldn't help it; his seat was way behind, and he had to clamber over people to get there. Dios, how excited he was. If anything had happened to the boy, the master would have bitten old scarface's head off and he knew it. We brought the boy back in triumph and old scarface told the master and he said, quite calmly, 'Well done, Jerome! Better go to bed now, it's late.' Didn't want the boy to get too puffed up about it, I suppose, but *I* could see how pleased he really was and the lady smiled and I'm not sure whether the smile wasn't a bit pinched, you know what I mean. . . ."

"I wouldn't have you say anything against her, I . . ."

"Who is saying anything against her? I'm simply telling you . . ."

"You and your loose tongue. I'm going to sleep now."

"Oh, are you? You haven't heard half of it yet. Do you know what the master did when the boy had gone? Went to his study and wrote a letter on his very special paper, the one he uses only for the most important documents. It's on his desk now, sealed; Secretary Álvaro has seen it, but the fool didn't look at the address."

"What can it possibly matter . . ."

"Goose! Don't you understand? No, of course, you don't. *If* the letter is addressed to some of the excellencies in Madrid, that means the master is going to adopt the boy—what else *can* it mean?"

"Well, what if he does? We'll know in due course."

"Santísima! I want to know *now*. I'm going to have a look."

"You can't go into the study! Why, if the master . . ."

"He went to bed right after I came in. There's nobody in the study now."

"But . . . but . . . you can't read! How will you know . . ."

"Ah . . . you *think* I can't read. I've had lessons, and here in the castle, too."

"You're just lying."

"I'm not. I always wanted to learn how to read, and write, too. And Señor Álvaro was good enough to give me lessons."

"Really?" For some reason Luisa was upset. "And was Inez present when he was giving them to you?"

61

"I'm sure I don't know what you mean." La Rubia tossed her head. "Will you come with me to have a look at that letter?"

"You forget that Señor Álvaro didn't give *me* any lessons", Luisa said pointedly. "And you don't really want me to come with you, do you? I'm sure you're just going to have another lesson ..."

"Listen to the impudent one! Come with me and you'll see for yourself where I'm going! I ... I don't want to go all the way to the east wing alone in the dark."

"Neither would I, if I had a bad conscience", Luisa retorted. "And now I will sleep, and so will you if you know what's good for you."

After a moment's hesitation La Rubia shrugged her pretty shoulders. "Oh, very well. Good night." She began to undress, too, although she did not seem to be in a great hurry about it.

A few minutes later she could hear the familiar sound of Luisa's stertorous breathing. The fat girl was asleep.

La Rubia watched her for a while. Then she slipped on her dress again. She lit a candle stub, shading the light with her hand, although there was really no need for such precaution: when Luisa was asleep she was asleep. It had been difficult enough to wake her, and La Rubia now regretted she had done so, and even more that she had told her anything about the letter and about going to the study. Was it possible that the fat girl had an eye on Señor Álvaro herself? Ridiculous, with that nose and that figure! But it might be just as well that she knew nothing more; she was quite capable of telling old Inez or even the lady.

La Rubia stepped into the corridor, closed the door softly behind her, and went on her way. Tiptoeing past the servants' quarters she reached the hall and once more shaded the light of her candle, in case the sentinel was just passing by. Up the staircase, and slowly, some of the stairs were creaky; along the upper corridor and across the big reception room. Here she had to go on tiptoe again; there were no carpets and their lordships' bedroom was near. Once she stopped in deadly terror and almost screamed. But the giant shadow on the wall was her own: she waved at it and it waved back awkwardly and was gone, as she reached the other side and the door to the little corridor, flanked, right and left, with the armor of Don Luiz' ancestors, blind watchmen whose stiff silence seemed to indicate disapproval. Visors and cuirasses gleamed angrily in the candlelight.

The study at last. The door would not creak; she had oiled it herself not so long ago. The desk—and there was the letter and she began to study the address. It took some time; Señor Álvaro's lessons, though not few, had not been entirely dedicated to the noble art of reading and writing: and the address was long and full of titles. She was only half through when she heard footsteps. Footsteps approaching the study.

She knew it was too late to leave by the main door. There was a panel door in one wall, and she rushed there. It would not open. The steps grew louder and louder. She pressed and tore at the door handle with both hands, and now it opened quite noiselessly and she stumbled out on another corridor. It was pitch dark. She had lost her candle, either when she tried to open the panel door or when she closed it behind her. She had to make her way back without it and quickly, now that she knew somebody else was awake, and most likely Don Luiz himself.

She fled along the corridor and, with some difficulty, found the door to the small staircase at the other side of the reception hall. Once she had closed that door behind her she was safe.

The candle-end had rolled under a heavy cupboard; its tiny flame flickering weakly. Almost it went out. But it met the corner of the carpet and began to lick it, first cautiously, then greedily.

The sentinel gave the first alarm on his horn. Juan Galarza, waking up, seized sword and helmet and raced to the northeast tower for which he was responsible. Halfway up he became sufficiently conscious to remember that Spain was not at present at war with anybody and that the sentinel's horn must mean a fire. At the same time he became aware of the smell of smoke. He raced back. From the bastion at the rear of the tower he could see a pall of smoke overhanging the east wing. Roaring like a bull he ran in that direction.

The castle came to life. There was a good deal of shouting and the first lanterns appeared.

Doña Magdalena woke coughing, and almost at the same moment Don Luiz jumped up. In three steps he reached the door and opened it. Thick black smoke rolled in. "Wait for me", he shouted to her and rushed out. Hastily she slipped into a long cloak. Somebody down in the courtyard yelled: "The whole castle is on fire!"

The smoke was terrible; she could hardly breathe. She poured the goblet of water on the table beside her bed over a kerchief and held it over her mouth and nose. Now she could hear the crackling and hissing of the flames. Where had Don Luiz gone? He had told her to wait for him, but the fire seemed to be coming nearer. She went to the door.

To her horror she saw that the fire had reached the heavy curtains of the reception hall—a few more minutes and the way to the main staircase would be cut off.

The small corridor was full of smoke.

Jerome, she thought. María! I must wake the boy at once.

Then she saw her husband rushing up, dishevelled and blackened.

"Magdalena! Are you all right?"

She managed to smile at him. "The boy", she said. "Where is the boy? I must . . ."

"He is safe. I carried him out. Now come, quickly, before the roof falls in." But after a few steps she staggered.

"I . . . I can't . . . the smoke . . ."

He lifted her up bodily and carried her through the reception hall now ablaze and so hot that she moaned with pain.

Only a few moments, and they were in the air again. The main staircase was still intact. Valverde and Galarza came up to help, but Don Luiz pushed them aside. "You must get the men together—form a chain—let the women bring pails of water", he ordered curtly. "I'll be with you in a moment." He would not let her go till he had got her outside. Fresh air. Isabel de Alderete turned up seemingly from nowhere; she was carrying a lantern. "Here", Don Luiz said, putting his wife down. "Look after her till I come back. Is your sister with the boy?"

"Yes, Don Luiz."

"Keep him where he is", he ordered. "You three are responsible for his safety." Then he ran back to the castle.

Within a quarter of an hour he had organized the fire fighting, and two hours later the fire was under control. When dawn came the castle was safe. Only the east wing had suffered badly. La Rubia, in hysterics, denounced herself, and Don Luiz spoke sternly to her and dismissed her from his service. She was to go back to her parents in Alcalá. There was no other punishment, much to Juan Galarza's disgust. "At least you should send her back with her hair cut off, sir."

Don Luiz shook his head. "It is not my way."

"But look at all the damage she's done, sir! Furniture, panels, carpets, curtains . . ."

Don Luiz smiled wanly. "Nothing of all this can be replaced by a servant girl's hair."

Juan Galarza walked off, shaking his head.

An hour after dawn Don Luiz entered the room in the west wing, where the two dueñas had made Doña Magdalena as comfortable as possible. She was wide awake. "At last", she said. "Oh my poor dear, you are exhausted. Let me help you with your clothes." But instead of helping him she embraced him spontaneously. "I love you", she said. "I love you. I love you. The boy is asleep. Soundly. Oh my dear, my dear, I wish I could tell you how much I love you. And I am so proud of you."

"You are?" He kissed her. "Why?"

To his utter astonishment she went down on her knees. "Before I tell you, I must ask your forgiveness."

He looked at her, bewildered. "Why? What for? Please do not kneel . . ."

"It is fitting—" she smiled—"to kneel in the confessional. And I am confessing to you that in my heart I accused you of sin—quite wrongly. It was a thought unworthy of me—and, much worse, greatly unworthy of my love and respect for the best, the finest husband a woman can have."

"Whatever it is, I forgive you gladly." Don Luiz did not quite know whether to be touched or amused. He helped her to her feet.

"It was awful", she went on. "I'd give every jewel I have if I didn't have to tell you. . . ."

"You don't have to tell me, my dear."

"You know it, then?"

"Frankly—" he smiled—"I haven't the least idea. But why should you torture yourself with it? Banish it from your memory."

"No", she declared emphatically. "I will have no secrets from you, just as you have no secrets from me—as long as they are *your* secrets. You know, don't you, that everybody in Villagarcía is convinced that Jerome is your son."

He frowned. "It did occur to me they might think so."

"Well, in the end ..." She gulped, but went on courageously. "In the end I ... I almost believed it too. And it was a very small 'almost'. I didn't mind that so much, I think—but I did wish you'd have more confidence in me, even if you couldn't mention the name of his mother; then I thought you took it for granted that I knew—and then again that you thought me very stupid, and it hurt my vanity, and altogether it was terrible."

"My poor dear", he said.

"The worst was that it was a secret", she continued. "The first secret between us. Oh, how I bless this fire. . . ."

"Bless the fire? What are you talking about? My dear, you are ill, overwrought. . . ."

She smiled, with tears in her eyes. "On the contrary, at long last I am well again. I bless the fire because it has given me proof that I was a wretched fool to doubt you for a single moment. Now I know Jerome isn't your son."

"You do?" He looked at her searchingly. "How is that?"

"I love you", she said. "And you love me. In my life you come first. In your life I come first. If Jerome had been your son, you would have saved me first—and then him. But you didn't. You asked me to wait, and you went out and saved the boy instead. Only then did you come to fetch me. Therefore this boy has been given into your care by someone else—and to this someone you have pledged your honor—"

"I forbid you to go on", he interrupted. "I forbid you even to guess who he may be." But he looked at her with fierce pride. "You are right", he added. "And you are a queen among women."

## CHAPTER 6

THE COURIER CAME at night and Juan Galarza told Jerome that the courier's horse was in very bad shape and might not recover. "When you ride for the Emperor the only thing that matters is to get there quickly. There are many horses in Spain, but there is only one emperor."

There was a good deal of whispering about the message that the courier had brought in such a hurry, but for a while no one knew anything for certain, except that the man had come from Yuste, where the Emperor now resided. Valverde knew that Yuste was not a town but a monastery—a cousin of his was a monk there—and Jerome remembered a few words Don Luiz had exchanged with Tía on one or two occasions, about the Emperor having been retired there "for some time". He could not quite imagine how this was possible. He remembered the monastery at Valladolid. Did the Emperor sleep in a tiny cell? And what happened to all the grandees of the court, the generals and admirals and statesmen, and the ladies! No lady could enter a monastery.

Álvaro, the secretary, thought perhaps the Emperor was dead, but Galarza only laughed. "Surely in that case Don

Luiz would have told us, and the flag would be flying at half-mast now. What you say is ridiculous!"

The secretary raised his eyebrows. "After all, Señor Galarza, the Emperor is an old man. . . ."

"He's not much older than I am", snapped Galarza. "Do I look like dying to you, Señor Álvaro? Take up a rapier or a sword and we'll see which of us two is more of a corpse than the other."

Álvaro was wise enough to remain patient. "We all know you are a very strong man, Señor Galarza, and my only weapon is the quill. I never said you were dying. I said . . ."

"I heard what you said. But next to Don Luiz I am the man here who knows the Emperor best; God bless him and give him a long life. . . ."

"Amen, amen", said Álvaro hastily.

"I have fought at his side many a time, Señor Goose-quill, and I tell you this: the day he dies will be like an earthquake, a catastrophe, shaking the whole world, and we won't be sitting here, as we are, having breakfast."

In the afternoon orders came from Don Luiz to pack a great number of things: furniture, paintings, carpets, silverware; to buy a dozen more mules; to inspect all the carriages. And now Tía told Jerome that they would travel to Yuste, or rather to the village of Cuacos near Yuste.

"The Emperor wants Don Luiz near him, and as he knows that it will be for a long time, he has graciously given permission for us to settle down there." There seemed to be the slightest bit of reluctance in her voice, and, if such a thing were possible, one might have suspected that she did not really enjoy the idea.

Jerome was radiant. Such was the upheaval in the castle that there was no time for further lessons; Padre Prieto had to pack his own things, as he was to be the family chaplain in Cuacos, Padre Morales being too old and frail for the journey; and both Juan Galarza and Diego Ruiz were sorting out arms in the armory and supervising the packing of some and the distribution of others, and they did not object to a boy's help. Was there anything more beautiful than arms? The smooth, deadly lines of a crossbow, the steely seriousness of the battle sword, the arrogant pomp of the court sword, all gold and precious stones and dainty crenelation; even the vulgar cutlass had a beauty of its own, and so had the Arabian khandjar and the Turkish scimitar bent like a half moon and sleek and glittery as a serpent. And the guns, three, four, six different makes of them, the wonder weapons that had subjugated the New World, feather-clad Incas and Aztecs—and all that in the service of the Emperor, the ruler of the worlds, both old and new, whom he would soon see.

There was no doubt at all in his mind that he was going to see him. After all, Cuacos was quite near Yuste, and the walls of Yuste would have to be very high to prevent him from having a look at some time or other. Don Luiz, of course, would see him frequently. The Emperor *wanted* to see Don Luiz. If anything could increase Jerome's hero worship, it was that even the Emperor quite obviously could not manage without Don Luiz.

This was a very different journey from the one with Señor Charles Prévost. Jerome was allowed to ride his little mule at Don Luiz' side in the vanguard of the long caravan.

"We are taking exactly the same route the Emperor himself took when he set out for Yuste", Don Luiz explained. "From Valladolid on, that is. He left there after the midday meal. No one, except his personal servants, were allowed to accompany him any farther than the gate del Campo.

The military escort consisted of a detachment of cavalry and forty halberdmen. We made the first rest at Medina del Campo."

"You were with him then, sir?"

"Yes. We stayed overnight in the house of a rich man, one Rodrigo de Dueñas. Like most men who acquire riches within their own lifetime he was vain and money proud. It was in November and fairly cold. So he put a heavy gold pan into the imperial bedroom, filled with precious cinnamon from Ceylon instead of coal—just to show off. It made the Emperor cough. Besides, he dislikes boasting. So he had the pan carried out, and in the morning he gave orders to the marshal to pay for all the expenses de Dueñas had incurred. Do you understand why he did that?"

"I think so", Jerome said hesitatingly. "He did not wish to honor the man by having been his guest. He treated him as an innkeeper."

"Quite right."

A few days later they reached Tornavacas and, again as the Emperor had done, took the shortcut across the pass of Puerta Nueva.

The ascent to the pass was not easy. There was nothing like a real road, and the mules, horses, and carriages had to make their way through thick, dark forests of chestnut trees, across wildly rushing mountain brooks, and through deep gorges.

"A few more hours", Don Luiz said, "and we shall be richly rewarded for our pains." He gave his wife an encouraging smile. He rode beside her carriage through the difficult terrain, and many a time he dismounted, gave the reins of his mule to a servant, and he himself led the mules drawing Doña Magdalena's carriage, which greatly disturbed her coachman.

The last two hours before they reached the pass itself were the worst of all. Slowly the long caravan climbed the mountain, until the gorges they had left behind looked up to them like baleful eyes, and the chestnut trees grew scarce as if they feared to go any farther.

As they were nearing the summit, Don Luiz rode up to the vanguard again. Jerome did not seem to be tired at all; he was sitting on his little mule as perkily as if they had just left Villagarcía. His precious crucifix he had tied very carefully to his saddle, and his tiny sword dangled from his belt.

Don Luiz thought of the night of the fire. When he rushed in to save the boy, Jerome had struggled free, seized first the crucifix, then his sword and only then permitted himself to be led to safety.

Slowly he rode up to him. "A little to the right now", he said almost gruffly. The boy obeyed. They passed a number of harsh rock formations and then they both stopped.

Far below them extended a large, beautiful plain, wavy with hills and sweet with orange and olive groves.

"La Vera de Plasencia", Don Luiz said softly. "Spain at her most peaceful and beautiful."

At the far horizon, above the fertile valley rose a hill, green with fruit trees and upon that hill white, shimmery buildings topped by a church.

"Yuste", Don Luiz said. "We shall be there the day after tomorrow." After a while he added, "You are now exactly where the Emperor was sitting. He had been carried up on a portable chair, and I was standing at his side. He said to me: 'There will be only one more pass for me to cross: that of death.'"

Jerome gasped.

Don Luiz looked at him strangely. "The Emperor, my dear Master, is an old man", he said gently. "Much older than his years. Even a titan becomes weary when he has carried the world on his back for so many years. Pray for him, Jerome. Pray for him every day."

"I will, sir", said the boy in an awestruck voice. For the first time he had seen tears in Don Luiz' eyes.

Then they began the descent.

Life in Cuacos was a disappointment. Perhaps the main trouble was that no one had any time for him, or at least very little. There was no castle here—obviously, as even the Emperor himself had to live in a monastery—and they were all living in a large, somewhat ramshackle house that was really three houses which lots of craftsmen and peasants and dayworkers had been working on for months until it was some sort of *one* house. Don Luiz was not satisfied with it at all, and he conferred with some of the craftsmen and drew up plans and ordered changes and then had to rush off to see the Emperor in the monastery. The craftsmen passed his orders on to the peasants and the daylaborers, and they all went to work again. When Don Luiz came back in the evening, he found that they had misunderstood him completely and that it all had to be done over again. There was constant hammering and sawing and tearing down and building up, and while this was going on Don Luiz had to receive a great number of guests, great gentlemen with wonderful white ruffs and glittering decorations, archbishops and bishops and abbots, and always he had to make a little speech, apologizing for the state of his house, and each time the guests praised him for sacrificing his comfort and ease for the sake of the Emperor.

They had no use for a boy, and Jerome had to try to kill time. Kill time! Don Luiz, Juan Galarza, Padre Prieto, even Tía, his gentle Tía, kept telling him about the terrible state

73

the world was in, what with the French and the Lutherans and the Arabs and the Turks and the never-ending hatred of the Moriscos and the English pirates robbing the empire in the New World and the strife in the Netherlands and so many other places, and here he was—eleven years and four months old, going on for twelve years, one might say, and all he was allowed to do was to kill time, running about with a small crossbow of Juan Galarza's make and killing birds and squirrel as if he were still seven.

He was still helping Tía to give money and things to the poor, for Cuacos had its poor too, but it was Tía's money and he always felt ill at ease when they thanked him and tried to kiss his hand, as if it were he who was their benefactor.

Who would have thought that one day he would actually long to go on with his Greek and Latin lessons as well as with geography and history and everything! But Padre Prieto was not ready for that. Many a time he accompanied Don Luiz to Yuste, and at home the constant hammering and sawing made regular lessons almost impossible.

The one thing Jerome really wanted to do was to go to Yuste and have a good look at everything, which with a little luck might include the Emperor himself. But that Don Luiz had strictly forbidden, and however he might be tempted to do so secretly, there was no hope of doing so without being found out. Too many people were around who would see him at some stage of the way. The one great, thrilling experience was only a third of a league away, a few minutes walk—and he could not get there.

There was little compensation in the new suit Tía had had made for him, a suit quite different from the simple things he was used to, quite short and puffed at the arms and around the thighs and of a material almost as soft as the stuff in her own dresses. The costume of a page, Tía said, and the word enchanted him. "I love to be your page, Tía. I'll always be your page."

New shoes, too, and of silk instead of leather! And endlessly long stockings. When the suit was finished and he put it on, he could scarcely tear himself away from the mirror. "I'm a page", he said proudly. "I'm Tía's page."

Doña Magdalena was pleased, too. The boy was extremely good-looking; he moved with an easy grace and yet there was nothing in the least girlish about him, despite his obvious vanity. "Pleased with yourself, are you?" she asked lightly. "Well, let's hope the Emperor will find you pleasing, too."

Jerome turned around with a jerk. The mirror was forgotten. "The ... the Emperor?" he asked. "Why, do I ... shall I ..."

"I am having an audience with the Emperor tomorrow", she told him. "And you will come with me, as my page, and offer him the little present I have for him and which I hope he will deign to accept."

Jerome's head whirled. "But, Tía dear ... I ... I don't know what to say to him! I'll say all the wrong things. I ..."

"You will say nothing at all. You will wait till he addresses you—if he does so at all, which is by no means certain. And when he addresses you, you will simply answer, in a quiet, even voice. He won't ask you anything that you cannot answer. You will call him Your Majesty, of course, as everybody does. That is all you need to know."

He slept fitfully that night, worried about committing some appalling blunder; perhaps his new stockings would fall down, or he would drop the present—beautifully embroidered lace handkerchiefs—or he would stutter and stammer and go all red in the face when he had to answer the Emperor's questions. The Emperor! The victor of Muehlberg, of Tunis, of Pavia, the greatest conquerer of the time, the ruler of almost all the Christian world and of all the millions of heathens of the New World, would ask him questions! Now if it came to his head to ask him about the irregular Greek verbs, for instance . . .

He jumped out of bed, managed to light a candle, rummaged till he found his list of Greek verbs, and went through them, one by one. The valet who came to wake him in the morning found him fast asleep at his table with a candle burning dangerously near his curly hair.

The valet shook him gently back to consciousness and was rewarded with a flood of Greek verbs. He ran away, bewildered, and reported to Doña Magdalena that the boy must have had a nightmare unless it was worse and he had lost his reason. However, when she arrived to see what had happened, Jerome was already having a very thorough wash, with water flying in all directions, and she withdrew, much relieved. Everybody knew that people who had lost their minds never went near water, except sometimes to drown themselves, which was obviously not Jerome's intention. It was an open secret that the Emperor's unfortunate mother, Queen Juana, hated washing all her life and, when her madness was fully upon her, would attack anybody approaching her with a basin of water.

A little later Doña Magdalena carefully examined her page in all his new finery and gave a nod of satisfaction. "We are leaving at three o'clock", she said. "See to it that you are as clean then as you are now."

Don Luiz left for Yuste in the morning, as usual. He saw Jerome and exchanged a few words with him, but made no remark whatever about his appearance.

Time in its approach to three o'clock seemed to ride a snail. Padre Prieto, who had not gone to Yuste that day, was fairly bewildered when Jerome visited him in his room and grimly insisted on being given another lesson in Greek. Later he told Don Luiz: "I was absolutely amazed. Every other boy would have had thoughts only for that audience with the Emperor. I have never seen such determination."

At the midday meal the boy ate very little. Doña Magdalena was not present, as she was still busy dressing.

However, like all women who had been at court, she was punctual. As the bell from Yuste sounded three o'clock she came sweeping down the stairs, and her page, spotlessly clean, opened the carriage door for her.

"Do I walk beside the carriage, Tía, or shall I get my mule?"

"Neither, of course." Doña Magdalena was horrified. "Do you think you can appear before His Majesty with your shoes and stockings all dusty from the road, or, worse still, reeking of mule? You'll ride with me in the carriage." She entered it, magnificent in rustling black silk and shimmery white ruff. He followed her meekly; a groom closed the door, and the carriage began to move.

Suddenly Jerome jumped up. "The present, Tía, we have forgotten the present!"

"Sit down and calm yourself", Doña Magdalena said serenely. "We have forgotten nothing." She showed him a small velvet cushion and a tiny bundle. "Everything in its time."

"But ... will the Emperor be allowed to use those handkerchiefs?" asked Jerome doubtfully. "I thought in the cell of a monastery ..."

"The Emperor doesn't live in a cell. He is not a monk." And now at long last he was told the answers to a question he had never asked because he did not want to be laughed at.

"They have built a new wing for him—it's almost like a small palace; he has his own garden, too, and fifty servants of his own; besides, there are fifty-three monks of various abilities who have been sent to Yuste from other monasteries. They live according to the rule of their Order, of course, but they have the special mission to assist His Majesty in those matters for which they were specially trained."

"Then he is living in a palace after all?"

"If you can call a house with eight rooms a palace, yes. Don Luiz says he has had some of his Flemish tapestries put in there, a great many beautiful pictures and other precious things, but of course, there is little room. The valets, barbers, cooks, bakers, and his trusted old watchmaker Juanelo have to live in another part of the monastery. The learned Doctor Mathys, his physician; Señor Overstraeten, the apothecary; and the special beer brewer Dugsen are staying in the monastery hostel, and Secretary Martín Gastelu and Señor Morón, the Master of the Wardrobe, are staying in Cuacos, just as we are. Now, are you satisfied?"

The carriage came to a stop and a black-clad servant opened the door. Jerome clambered out and helped Doña Magdalena to descend. Only then did he see that they were in front of the monastery church.

He looked questioningly at Doña Magdalena, but she calmly unwrapped the little bundle, took out the handkerchiefs—small miracles of gossamer lace—and put them on the cushion. "There", she said. "Take it and follow me." He obeyed mechanically, as she walked up the steps and into the church. He had to shift the cushion to his left hand, to receive the holy water her slender fingers offered him. On she walked toward the high altar. She genuflected at the communion rail and so did he, carefully so as not to drop the cushion; he suddenly remembered Don Luiz' words and prayed that the handkerchiefs would give pleasure to the Emperor, who could no longer carry the burden of the world.

Then he saw Doña Magdalena walk on, still toward the high altar, and his eyes widened; but now she turned to the right, and as he followed he saw the glass door and beside it another servant. The man bowed deeply and opened the door.

As if in a dream Jerome entered a room. It was a bedroom, simple and austere, with the bed so placed that it was possible from there to watch what was going on at the high altar outside.

Doña Magdalena turned to him. "You see," she said in a whisper, "His Majesty can participate in the Mass even when he is not allowed to leave his bed. And the celebrant comes in here to give him Holy Communion."

Jerome nodded. His throat was suddenly so tight, he could not even whisper.

She pointed to the picture of a Madonna, beautiful beyond words. "His favorite painter did this", she said. "His name is Titian."

Jerome bowed instinctively, he did not quite know whether to the Madonna or to the genius of the artist.

Two more servants were guarding the next door, and a third, much more richly clad, drew back a velvet curtain with a courteous gesture.

They entered darkness. The room was black, as black as the livery of the servants. Black tapestry, black curtains, a black canopy, black covers on six heavy chests; six beautifully carved chairs of walnut, covered with black leather. A large table with a covering of black velvet and next to it . . .

Poor man, Doña Magdalena thought as she sank down in a deep curtsy. Poor, poor man. She knew that the Emperor had ordered all that black because his mother had died just before he was settled down in Yuste. Juana, La Loca, the Mad One. Her death, at last, after so many years of cruel torments of the spirit, must have come as a relief, and not only to her. The Emperor went into mourning, of course— but now the official time of mourning was long past. Yet he kept the room like this. Was it that he wished to take part in her past sufferings by surrounding himself with a night as black as that of her mind?

Drawing himself up after a deep bow into nothingness, Jerome saw in all that world of blackness one white, irregular spot, the face of an old, old man with a feathery, white beard. He was sitting in a wheelchair, propped up with cushions, his legs covered with a thin, silk rug. Next to him, on the table, was a cage with a strange bird in it, a very large bird the like of which he had never seen before: its feathers were of the most wonderful blue on head and back and wings, but the breast was yellow and around its eyes were large, white circles.

Two small cats were playing at the Emperor's feet, and they too were quite different from other cats: their fur was like deep ivory, except for their faces, which were pitch black, as if the devil had touched them to spoil their beauty.

As Jerome's eyes became accustomed to the darkness, he could see, near the wall, the shadowy figure of Don Luiz, strong and upright, but though he wanted to, he did not dare smile at him.

The wheezing, asthmatic breathing of the Emperor was the only sound. The heavy eyelids rose, and he looked straight at the boy.

Jerome began to tremble. The Emperor's eyes were like blue ice, hard and sharp and overwhelming; all that was still alive in him seemed to concentrate there. And yet there was an expression of great sadness in them, a strange, painful riddle, impossible to solve.

Barbara, thought Charles V. Little Barbara. That day in Regensburg, Pietro Columna was there and the Landgraf of Leuchtenberg—he no longer remembered what they wanted of him; there was so much trouble, O God, with Contarini tugging for Rome and Granvella seconding him and no idea what the Saxon would do if there were war. The end of April it was or the beginning of May, but cold, always cold; they had to light fires every day three and four times in that inn; what was its name? Dem Goldenen Kreuz, that's right, the Golden Cross. And outside, the good citizens of Regensburg gaping at the windows to catch a glimpse of the Emperor. The Golden Cross: just the right name for the time, with everybody out for gold and forgetting the cross—except the kind of golden cross they could wear on their breasts or around their necks, the fools, when the one Cross that ever mattered was carried on the back. But the boy looked like Barbara. And he had blue eyes. By what miracle of God did children inherit the traits of their parents? The wisest and the most erudite physicians did not know, and if they did learn, it would still be as much of a miracle as it was before. Titian could make a good likeness of me, but only God could make Titian—and me. And me. And this boy. Except that God's will was not done in the case of the boy. Who was it, what was it, that led little Barbara to the Golden Cross? She sang for him there—one of the choir boys had fallen ill, was that it? It was his sister's idea to get that choir to cheer him up; bless her, Joan of Hungary, the only one of all his relatives who was cheerful—at least she had been so in her youth. And she knew how much he loved music. Music was a concentrated form of life; it could lead to heaven and to hell, to ecstasy and to despair; a man must know what he can bear or he could be carried away, and then ... then one wants to know who the singer is and Quixada had to go and fetch her and she was youth, youth itself, a spring of youth, simple and cheerful and not at all overawed and yet not disrespectful ... a pity she behaved so badly later, he was furious about it at the time ... just as well he had kept her short of money, God knows what she would have done if he had given her all she wanted ... "You can't tear a boy away from his mother—it's cruel; it's inhuman", ah well, they probably all thought so and a few years later the boy would tear himself away if he was worth anything. A few furtive days in Regensburg, confessed so long ago—and the end of Charles the man, the end of Charles the private person, though *she* could not know that, thinking only of herself and even of the child only as her possession. Confessed so long ago, and here was the sin, alive and the very image of his mother; no need for Quixada to give him a little nod, no doubt about it in any case, we still have eyes to see. He must talk to Philip about it. In the meantime Quixada had done well, or so it seemed. Adiós, little Barbara ...

Doña Magdalena had waited—it was just possible that the Emperor wished to say something. When he remained silent, she gave Jerome a slight push and the boy clenched his teeth and marched forward toward the terrifying old man and knelt down before him, offering his lady's gift. A crippled hand, the color of old ivory, stretched out, took the handkerchiefs, and dropped them on the table; then it touched the boy's head. Was it a blessing?

Jerome saw the old man close his eyes, and at the same moment a voice, scarcely recognizable as that of Don Luiz, said gently: "You have permission to withdraw."

He rose and walked back to Doña Magdalena. Together they left the presence by the same way they had come. The

Emperor's bedroom. The glass door. The church. Unconsciously they walked without making a sound.

Outside, in clear daylight, the carriage was waiting. But Jerome tugged furtively at Doña Magdalena's dress, and as she turned toward him, he threw himself into her arms, sobbing his heart out.

"What is it?" she asked. "What is it, my dear?"

"I don't know", Jerome sobbed.

Over his head she suddenly saw her husband standing in the portal. He was looking not at her, but at the boy. His strong, severe face was strangely drawn, and his lips trembled a little.

Doña Magdalena's hand, caressing the boy's head, stopped in midair. But a moment later she resumed her caresses. She knew she must keep to herself the knowledge that had suddenly come to her.

CHAPTER 7

THE NEWS OF THE VICTORY of Gravelines was brought to the Emperor as he was sitting in his wheelchair out in the garden, fishing in the blue-tiled pond. He was having one of his better days, and he savored the message like a succulent tidbit. Luiz Quixada had to give him all the details that were known

"Egmont, eh?" The old man was positively cheerful. "I always liked that boy. One of my best pupils; he and William of Orange and Alba, my best pupils. I did see to it that Philip has some good and able servants, Egmont and the English fleet, you say? I was right about the English, too. That's something my brother will never understand; he cannot think in terms of the sea, yet he must, if he wants to rule an empire. They can build ships in England, and they have the men to man them, if they put their heart to it. Maybe just as well we were first in the New World and in Asia. That may be the trouble for the English one day—that there is nothing left for them to discover and to colonize. I tried to talk to my brother about it once, but he couldn't see it. He can't look in all directions at once; it's always one issue at a time with him. Bad chess and bad politics."

The good mood was gone, as always, when he thought of his brother. He fell into silence, and Don Luiz knew his old master far too well to say anything. For a long time Charles V had tried to save the imperial crown for his son, but the German Electors would have none of it. King Philip, to them, was a foreigner and even seemed to wish to be a foreigner. For years and years he had been abroad, yet he steadfastly refused to speak any other languages than Spanish and a somewhat halting Latin. The German princes, of course, spoke no Spanish, and their Latin was all too often not even halting. The result was a stiff, formal atmosphere and a great many misunderstandings, always the best precondition for intrigues.

Almost thirty years ago, when the Electors chose Charles rather than Francis I of France, they laid the foundation for the many terrible wars Charles had to wage against his rival. Now Francis had been dead more than ten years, but the dire consequences of his wars lived on as his will and testament. Why, at some phase he had made an alliance with the Grand Turk himself and the world was to see the spectacle of a Catholic emperor fighting a Catholic king—the former allied with Protestant princes; the latter with a Muslim ruler!

Four years ago, when Charles withdrew to Yuste, he had given the care of the Empire into the hands of his brother, Ferdinand. Three years ago he abdicated as Duke of Burgundy in favor of his son Philip, two years ago as King of Spain.

But only this year had he formally abdicated as emperor, and the blackest day in Yuste was the day when the letter of the German Electors arrived, informing him of the coronation of his brother. He called for his father confessor. "In the future all prayers for the Emperor must mention the name of my brother, Ferdinand. Let those who pray for me, call me Charles and nothing else. For I am no longer anything else." He had all the servants assembled in his room, and the oldest of them had to read the letter aloud. The poor man was crying and could scarcely get the words out. When he had finished, Charles said again: "Yes. Now I am nobody."

From that day on no crest or arms or anything else appertaining to the Empire was tolerated in the "palace" in Yuste. But no one would address him as other than Your Majesty, or Sire.

"Call Padre de Regla", Charles said.

Don Luiz bowed and went to fetch the emperor's father confessor.

When he arrived, the Emperor said: "There will be a Requiem Mass tomorrow for my parents and my wife."

"Yes, Sire."

"Would it not be good, Fray Juan, to have one more Mass said for myself, so that I can see what will be done for me in the near future?"

Padre Juan de Regla tried to get the old man off the subject, but no one could deflect Charles V.

"Padre Juan, don't you think it would be good for my soul?"

"Yes, Sire."

"Very well. Have everything prepared."

They had the coffin placed before the high altar. Everyone was dressed in black. Candles were burning all around the coffin; a candle burned in Charles' left hand, as with his right he turned the pages of an old Book of Hours, ennobled by the shabbiness of much use.

Charles V had prayed for his father, Philip I, Philip the Handsome as they used to call him, who died at the age of thirty; for his mother, Juana, who had loved her husband so much, despite all the humiliations he inflicted on her in their short unhappy marriage, that she became insane when kissing his cold lips on his deathbed and then went on living for almost half a century as a mad woman, disheveled, unwashed, full of insane hatred against all things holy. At Mass she would close her eyes in order not to see the Elevation of the Host, and time and again she tried to commit suicide. He had prayed for Isabel of Portugal, who left him so early; Isabel, who never gave him anything but joy and love. Now Charles was praying for Charles.

This was his coffin. In a very short time this was all the room there would be for the ruler of the world. And they would weep for him, his people, as they were weeping now—he could hear them despite the chanting of the monks.

He could go peacefully. No one envied him, no one—he had seen to that by giving everything away. There was no one who could not do without him, no one who really needed him. So there was no pressure on him to go and none to stay. He would go as a monk goes, unfettered by earthly hatred or earthly love, free in his obedience to God.

He was ready for the voyage, greater than that of Columbus or Cortez. He was ready for the coffin.

On a late September afternoon he was again sitting in the garden, all by himself. Garcilaso de la Vega had come from Flanders and brought welcome messages. Good. Garcilaso was gone. Good again.

Now he could look at the three pictures that he had brought with him. At Isabel, young and fair; she could scarcely be fairer in heaven. At the picture of Christ in Gethsemane, Christ praying. And at a picture of the Last Judgment. The final triumph, the final disaster, the end of all finite things, the end of everything but death, judgment, heaven, and hell.

*Plus ultra* was the motto on his crest. *Still more.* Always more and more and still more. He had lived in accordance with the words. More and still more. Until even the whole world was not enough, and he had to throw it off his shoulders to reach out for God. No. No, no, no, that was not his own thinking; it was the tempter's thinking. God, when he was walking on earth, said: "How is a man the better for it, if he gains the whole world at the cost of losing his own soul?"

It was not an easy thing, to own the world and to renounce it, but he had done it. There was always the tempter whispering that there was no one to replace him, that it was his duty to remain. But that was clearly Satan's voice. For God needed no particular human being to establish his order on earth. He could endow the lowest and the most insignificant and the weakest with his grace and strength, if he so wished. Nothing was so good as to strive for God. And too much love of earthly things, even of a wife or husband, a father or mother, a son or daughter, even of an empire, led away from the one love that mattered most.

*You* taught me that, Mother, when you went insane at Father's death. But I was a child of six then and did not know what happened. So God let you live on for almost half a century—until I had learned my lesson.

And now the Day of Judgment was near. The old man shivered. He raised a small, golden whistle to his lips.

When the servants came hurriedly, he said in a thin, weary voice: "Malo me siento. I do not feel well."

They wheeled him back to the house and called the physician.

The days in Cuacos became hectic now. With the Emperor ill Don Luiz had to stay in Yuste day and night. Messengers had gone in all directions and visitors began to pour in. Princess Juana sent her own physician, Dr. Corneille Baersdorp. Shortly afterward the Archbishop of Toledo, Bartolomé de Carranza, arrived with two Dominican friars. He was received for a few minutes and then went back to Cuacos to have lunch with the Quixadas, a fierce-looking man with long, white hair and a purple cloak over his Dominican habit. Doña Magdalena much admired his beautiful pectoral cross, given to him by Queen Mary Tudor of England. Jerome was more interested in the archbishop's white mule, but that interest passed quickly when he heard from one of the archbishop's servants that the Emperor had received the Last Sacraments.

Everybody knew that afterward a man usually felt better and became better; nevertheless it must be serious.

Jerome went reconnoitering. He found the archbishop together with Tía praying in the tiny chapel Don Luiz had had built. Then he discovered that the groom was saddling the white mule again. The two friars were already waiting in front of the house and with them several other men. He waited. And when the archbishop came out and mounted his mule and everyone started moving in the direction of Yuste, Jerome simply went with them. He had to. And this time he did not care whether his shoes and stockings became dusty from the road.

All the people of Cuacos were on the road, some walking toward Yuste, others standing about and talking in low voices.

Jerome saw a number of his friends among them, the man who had made his new shoes, the man who had cut his new suit, the three sons of the grocer who delivered fresh vegetables every day; but they all seemed to be shadowy people, unreal, like figures in a painting.

At the portal of the monastery church a group of grave-faced monks bowed to the archbishop and at once led him inside, and Jerome followed with the friars and everyone else. The church was full of people praying silently.

The archbishop gave his blessing right and left and walked toward the high altar. As he bowed his knees before the tabernacle, Jerome also knelt, and when the old man turned left toward the glass door, Jerome moved as if he were his shadow. If anyone had asked him what he was doing here, he could not have thought of a reply. But he knew that he had to do what he was doing.

Nobody asked him a question, not even the black-clad servants at the door of the imperial bedroom.

The bedroom was full of people. Jerome had no eyes for anyone except the Emperor, but he could only see heads and ruffs and embroidered coats and a piece of the rug covering the Emperor's legs. It seemed as if only one man was breathing in this room, irregularly, stertorously.

A large figure loomed up suddenly and Jerome stared into the face of Don Luiz. He became frightened. He should not have come here.

Don Luiz took his arm and led him out, past the glass door. "My dear boy", he said softly. "God bless you for this."

Wide-eyed, Jerome saw that the great man was fighting back tears.

"Go home now", Don Luiz whispered. "Go and stay with your aunt." With a strange little smile he added: "Thank you—in the name of His Majesty." Then he went back.

At home in Cuacos everyone was in the chapel.

Jerome joined them and, with Doña Magdalena, stayed on even after the servants filed out when it was time for their supper. Later, she had difficulty in getting him to eat, and he would not go to bed. He refused to undress, and she sat quietly beside him until he fell asleep in an armchair.

He did not know, of course. She knew Don Luiz would never tell him as he had never told her. Was it only the great loyalty the boy felt for the person of his emperor then? Or did he feel in his heart, in some strange, inexplicable way that there was a bond between him and the old man dying in Yuste?

The secret had become a mystery.

She began to say the Rosary. When she had reached the Sorrowful Mysteries for the second time a deep, clanging sound came rolling through the air. The great bell of Yuste. The great bell, not the one striking the hour. The agony bell, the "poor sinner's bell", rung whenever a Christian soul was departing from life on earth so that everyone hearing it would stop whatever he was doing and pray.

Again and again and again came the vibrant call.

Then she saw that the boy was awake. His lips were trembling and there was a great and solemn question in his eyes.

"'De profundis'," said Doña Magdalena. "'Out of the depths I cry to you, O Lord . . .'" Her voice was firm and its loving gravity forbade tears. The boy's voice joined hers, as the great bell went on clanging. From the streets came the noise of running feet, suppressed voices, the sobbing of an old man.

"'For with the Lord is kindness'," the woman and the boy prayed, "'... and with him is plenteous redemption ...'"

Then the great bell stopped.

## CHAPTER 8

ON THREE CONSECUTIVE DAYS Solemn Requiem Masses were said for the dead titan. Each lasted three full hours, and at each Jerome stood next to Don Luiz, both dressed in black habits with black hoods, the boy looking like a miniature replica of his protector.

Don Luiz was master of ceremonies. When a page of the Marquis of Miravel tried to bring a chair into the church, he was promptly ordered to take it out again at once. The page remonstrated that his master was physically not well enough to stand through the long ceremony.

"In that case he may stay outside", Don Luiz replied grimly. "No one is going to sit in the presence of my emperor, be he alive or dead."

The page reported it to his master. "Don Luiz is right", cried Miravel. "And you are a well-meaning fool." He borrowed a walking stick from the Count of Oropesa, hobbled into the church, and stood there stiff as a ramrod, despite his gouty foot.

Almost two months passed before the Quixadas could return to Villagarcía. Don Luiz had to supervise the dissolving of the Imperial household. Inventories had to be made, servants dismissed, bills and debts paid. When at last they crossed the pass again from which Jerome had seen Yuste for the first time, it was snowing.

Life in Villagarcía was just what it had been before—outwardly.

Jerome resumed his lessons with Padre Prieto and his training with Juan Galarza. Now that he was growing stronger the old warrior began to teach him the best tricks of the trade. "You'll never be as big and strong as some I've known—like Don Luiz, for instance—so you'll have to be subtle and quick. Now, when you're dealing with an enemy much stronger and heavier than you are ..."

"Was the Emperor a *very* strong man?"

"You can never hear enough of him, can you?" Galarza grinned sadly. "Well, you're right. The world will never see his like again. It's a rare thing when a great ruler is also a great general and a great general also a great fighter. Before Tunis I've seen him split an Arab's helmet and skull down to the chin." There was no sadness in Galarza's grin now. "The best enemies a man can have, my boy. Arabs, Moors, Turks, Kurds, Persians, everything that yells to Allah."

"The best enemies? How so?"

"Well, there are some who may think differently, but I always feel sorry when I have to split a *Christian* skull. How do I know the fellow doesn't die with a mortal sin on his conscience?"

"He should have made an act of contrition before the battle", Jerome said disapprovingly. "Or better still gone to confession. There are always priests with the army, aren't there?"

"Certainly there are, and many of them as good as any soldier when it comes to courage. Better, maybe, because they wear no armor and as often as not no arms either, not even for defense. And the infidels are always out for them specially. Gets them a dozen steps nearer paradise if they kill a Christian mullah, in their misguided belief. And they do expose themselves, the priests, I mean, because when one of our men is wounded, he usually shouts for them."

Did Spanish soldiers, then, go into battle with their consciences unprepared? It was difficult to believe. They would want to be shriven, of course, when they felt that they might be dying of their wounds.

Galarza was full of stories about fighting, but in Don Luiz' study—rebuilt now and looking just as it had before the fire—Jerome heard more about leadership, planning, and the responsibility for others in the field. "The stomach is at least as important as the arm, Jerome. If your men's stomachs are empty, their fighting won't be worth much. And thirst is ten times more terrible than hunger."

To Don Luiz Jerome did not dare to talk about the Emperor—not for a long time; and the master of Villagarcía also seemed to avoid the subject. Only once—it was a day in early spring and they had just come home from a ride—the boy asked suddenly: "Is the new Emperor never coming to Spain, sir?"

"Certainly not as long as the King is not here", was the reply.

"The poor King", Jerome said compassionately.

"Why do you call him that?"

"He has lost his wife—I mean he lost the Queen not long ago, didn't he?"

"Well, yes ..." Don Luiz admitted. "But it was not a very fortunate marriage. Kings sometimes marry for reasons of state, not the woman they love. Queen Mary Tudor was a very unlucky lady, despite the fact that she married the handsomest prince in Christendom."

"Oh yes", Jerome said surprisingly. "He is wonderfully handsome."

"How do you know?"

"I've seen him", Jerome said proudly.

"You have seen him?" Don Luiz stared at the boy, frowning. "When? Where?"

"Just before I came here, sir. In Valladolid. He rode past the monastery where we had spent the night, Señor Prévost and I. He was riding the most beautiful horse I ever saw."

Don Luiz murmured something unintelligible. After a while he said: "There will be peace with France soon, I believe. Then the King will come back to Spain at last." There was a strange expression on his face, as there had been that day on the mountain pass when he said that the Emperor was an old and weary man. And he said: "Pray for the King, Jerome."

"I do, sir, every night."

Peace with France came and still the King did not return to Spain. Too many other issues had to be settled and there was even a rumor that he would marry Queen Mary Tudor's successor on the throne of England, the young Queen Elizabeth.

Spring passed and the summer was almost gone, when news came that King Philip had landed in Laredo. Six days later he made his entry into Valladolid.

Strangely enough Don Luiz did not go there to meet him. When Doña Magdalena asked him why he did not, he answered curtly: "I have not been called."

She knew better than to go on asking questions. But she felt how restless he was and she could guess the reason. His restlessness increased as the days went by and nothing happened. It was not easy for him to get accustomed to the ways of a monarch as slow as Charles V had been quick.

A full year passed after the Emperor's death.

Suddenly a message arrived, in the King's large, regular handwriting. Don Luiz read it, sighed, read it again, put it carefully away, and went straight to his wife. "I'm afraid we must be prepared to lose Jerome", he said awkwardly.

For a moment she was downright frightened. This could mean anything. "Lose him?"

"Well, yes. I don't know for sure yet. I am supposed to arrange for a hunt in the Torozo Mountains."

She did not know whether to be terrified or to laugh. "I really do not understand. . . ."

"Of course not. I don't understand it myself, but my orders are quite explicit. It will be the day after tomorrow. I—I suppose I can tell you now, the King only wrote that the boy must still not be told. . . ."

"You don't have to", she interposed, smiling. "I have known the secret a long time, without being told by anybody."

He stared at her aghast. "This secret can kill. Since when . . ."

"Since the day you took him to the Emperor."

"You never told me!"

"I had no right to."

He bowed to her. "You are right, my dear, always right. I am grateful."

"But what is the King going to do?" She asked in a low voice.

"The first nobleman of Spain can only want to do what is meet and just", he replied almost vehemently. But she knew that his vehemence was not directed at her. After a while he added: "I don't think he has made a decision yet."

95

The hunting trip started at dawn. Jerome was riding a black horse and Juan Galarza, opening the main gate for the cavalcade, noted with satisfaction that his pupil had learned something from him. He was riding his horse, not merely being carried by it. Elbows correct, shoulders correct, legs where they ought to be, despite the size of the mount.

The one thing Galarza could not understand was what Don Luiz' chief hunter had told him half an hour ago: that he was under orders to follow a false trail at some time during the morning, a trail leading toward the monastery of San Pedro de la Espina.

The chief hunter would not or could not say more. What was Don Luiz up to?

The hunt went well until about ten o'clock. Don Luiz shot a fair-sized stag; Jerome, to his immense joy, was allowed to bag a fox.

But then the chief hunter led them in a new direction, away from what looked like an excellent trail. They crossed a large forest and reached a clearing.

From afar came the call of a hunting horn, and at once Don Luiz raised his hand and listened sharply.

Another call, nearer now.

After a while a stag came racing across the clearing, eagerly pursued by a pack of hounds and a large group of riders.

"Royal hunters", Don Luiz said. "That's the end of our hunt. Come with me, Jerome. All others will return to Villagarcía."

He spurred his horse and the boy followed, somewhat bewildered.

They could see the roof of the monastery and its clock tower beyond a large group of trees. And from that group of trees two riders emerged. One was a soldierly looking gentleman with a grizzled beard; the other, considerably younger, had a pale face and a sandy beard. Both were dressed in black. More riders followed at a distance.

"Beautiful horses", Jerome said.

Don Luiz hid a nervous smile. "Dismount, Jerome", he said and did so himself. As the boy obeyed, the two riders were coming nearer and he could see that the younger of the two had blue eyes. He was very handsome although his underlip seemed to be pouting. Suddenly Jerome knew that he had seen him before and where. . . .

"Kneel down", said Don Luiz, "and kiss His Majesty's hand."

The pale face bent so close above him that he could have touched the silky, sand-colored beard. The blue eyes were strangely intense. The hand Jerome kissed was small and soft, almost like a woman's.

"What is your name?" the King asked.

"Jerome, Your Majesty."

The King smiled. "The name of a great saint, no doubt. But we shall have to change it." He, too, dismounted, Don Luiz holding his stirrup. "Thank you, Quixada. I am pleased. Never have I captured fairer game. You will remain his *ayo*, his tutor, of course. He will need you more than ever." He turned back to the boy. "Tell me," he said, "do you know who your father was?"

Jerome blushed deeply. He said nothing, but he did not hang his head; he raised it so high that his little chin seemed to point at the King's heart.

Again Philip smiled. He gave a nod of satisfaction "I can see that the secret was kept," he said, "but there is no need for that any longer. Emperor Charles the Fifth, my lord and father, was your father, too, and here and now I acknowledge you as my brother."

For a moment Don Luiz thought that the boy was going to faint. But his eyes were shining.

Philip kissed him on both cheeks. His arm still around the boy's shoulders he turned toward Don Luiz again. "I am glad to see you so pleased, too", he said affably. "As my brother's tutor you will have the rank of councillor of state and member of the war council. In addition, you will be made a commander of the Order of Calatrava."

The triple honor made Don Luiz one of the most powerful men in the empire, but a pale hand raised slightly forbade any expression of gratitude.

"My brother's court", went on the King, "will consist of the following persons: Chief of the Household and Tutor: Don Luiz Quixada; Master of Ceremonies: Count Priego; Master of the Horse: Don Luiz de Córdoba; Chief Chamberlain: Don Rodrigo Benavides ..." He hesitated for a moment, drew a paper from the inside of his coat, glanced at it, and continued: "Majordomo *particular*: Don Rodrigo de Mendoza; Chamberlains: Don Juan de Guzmán, Don Pedro Zapata de Córdoba, and Don José Acuña; Secretary: Juan de Quiroga; valets: Juan de Toro and Jorge de Lima; Captain of the Guard: Don Luiz Carillo. Half of the guard will be Spanish, the other half German."

This established the new court according to the Burgundian etiquette, first introduced by the King's grandfather, Philip the Handsome.

"Your Majesty has thought of everything." That was all Don Luiz could say in his amazement. The list was in the King's own handwriting; he could see the large letters. This was the first time he had encountered Philip's love of detail and his irrepressible desire to work out everything himself. First long months of silence, not a sign about his intentions. Then that laconic letter. "You will arrange for a hunt in the Torozo Mountains. You will take the youth in your care with you, dressed simply and uninformed about the purpose of the hunt. You will see to it that your party reaches a spot near the group of oaks south of the monastery of San Pedro de la Espina at noon. I, the King." The arrangement of a "chance meeting"—but he had worked out a complete list of his half brother's household!

The royal retinue was still hovering in the background.

The King gave them the sign to approach. With the help of Quixada he mounted.

Jerome woke from a dream to see Don Luiz hold the stirrup for him, too. In a whisper he asked: "Does Tía know?"

"Everything", Don Luiz whispered back. "Everything, except that we shall stay together. She will be so pleased."

Jerome beamed with delight, and Don Luiz turned away hastily. Mounting his own horse gave him time to regain his composure.

The royal retinue arrived at last and halted, about a dozen noblemen among them. Don Luiz recognized some of those whose names were on the new court list.

The King spoke in his low, even voice; they had to crane their necks to hear him. "Know and honor this youth as the natural son of the late Emperor, and as a brother to the King."

A ragged shout went up. Philip stopped it almost immediately, raising two fingers of his gloved hand. The low voice went on: "His Excellency Don Juan de Austria will receive your felicitations."

Only as the nobles came, one by one, to kiss his hand, did the boy realize that this was his new identity

# BOOK TWO

A.D. 1560–1568

# CHAPTER 9

"GOOD MORNING, UNCLE", said Alexander Farnese cheerfully and he and Juan grinned at each other. They never ceased to be amused at their relationship. Prince Alexander was the son of Ottavio Farnese, who at eighteen became the second husband of Charles V's eldest daughter, Margaret, now Regent of the Netherlands. Alexander was fifteen, two years older than his uncle, six inches taller, and as strong as a bear.

They had met four months ago and instantly became friends.

Both were dressed in the solemn black that had become the fashion at court, relieved only by snowy ruffs around the neck and the jewel-studded gold of sword hilt and scabbard.

"And how is your other nephew today?" Alexander asked casually.

There was no immediate answer. Juan looked around. They were alone in the big, ornate antechamber and all the doors were closed.

A large, beautifully worked and heavily gilded clock on the huge mantlepiece made its noisy journey through time.

From outside came a very different noise, fuzzy and indistinct. The streets of Toledo were full of people today. So were the roofs.

"You don't have to say anything, Juan." Alexander grinned wryly. "One of his bad days again, eh? I might have known. Not a lackey in sight. Has he been out of his rooms at all?"

"Not as long as I've been here", Juan said. "Poor Carlos."

"I'm getting a little tired of hearing that, you know. Poor Carlos, poor Carlos. He's the grandson of an emperor and the son of a king. Why can't he behave in a way that befits his station? I know, I know, you don't have to say it; he is ill sometimes and he has an unfortunate character; we've been through all that often enough. But he doesn't *want* to control himself; he just gives in to those absurd rages. . . ."

"Would you like to change with him?" Juan asked gently.

"*Per Baccho*, no, I wouldn't. But then I've never wanted to be anybody else but myself. Have you?"

"Yes", Juan said. "Many a time."

Alexander Farnese shook his head. "But why? You, too, descend from an emperor; you're a handsome little devil and quite strong for your age. The world's wide open to you—what do you have to complain about?"

"Nothing", Juan replied. "I never had anything to complain about. Not when I was playing 'Moors and Christians' with the other village boys in Leganés and certainly not now."

"Then why did you want to be somebody else? And who did you want to be?"

"Once in an old monastery church an old man was sitting behind me—a friar. He had the happiest face I ever saw—so happy, I thought he looked like God. As a matter of fact, I thought for a moment that he *was* God. I was very small then", Juan added quickly.

"You're not *very* big now", Alexander said, laughing.

"I don't think I shall ever grow to be as big as you, nephew Hercules." Juan grinned. "Anyway, that was the first time I felt I wanted to be somebody else. I wanted to be him—or like him."

"I'd never have thought you would want to be a friar!"

"I don't. I don't think I did then, either. But I thought it must be wonderful to be like that old man. He wasn't

God, but he was very near God, I think. I can't explain it very well. But the very next day I wanted to be somebody else. There was a parade going on, in Valladolid, and there was one man riding all alone, dressed in purple and cloth of gold, on a white charger. He had fair hair and a fair beard, and I knew at once that he must be a prince; he couldn't be anything else, and all the people applauded and shouted their welcome—how I wanted to be him!"

Alexander was amused. "Who was he? Fair hair and a fair beard—you don't mean it was the King, do you?"

"He was the Prince of Asturias then." Juan nodded. "Now he is the King."

Alexander raised his eyebrows. "Does he know that story?"

"No. Why?"

"Never mind. But I wouldn't tell it to him, if I were you—and even less to anyone else."

"I don't understand."

"Uncle, Uncle, you are a baby", Alexander said. "Have you ever heard of a king who liked somebody else's wanting to be in his place?"

"But I didn't want to be in his place", Juan exclaimed. "I wanted to be him instead of being me. Except ..."

"Yes?"

"Except that I like black horses better than white ones."

"Uncle, you are a baby", Alexander repeated. "But a *great* baby. So you wanted to be an old friar and a young prince."

"Yes—and a little later I wanted to be Don Luiz Quixada. I still think it must be marvelous to be Don Luiz. That is all now—except that I once wanted to be a bull...."

"What next! Why a bull, of all things?"

"Oh, it was at a corrida, at Villandrando—that's near Villagarcía, you know—and there was an excellent bull, a black one—but he missed his chance. *I* saw the opening the picador gave him, but he didn't and I thought, I wish I were he. I would have gotten that picador, just like that. And once I wanted to be an eagle. It's a great advantage to be an eagle. You always know exactly where your enemy is; he can never surprise you. Now if I were an eagle—"

"The trouble with you", interrupted Alexander, "is that you have too much imagination."

"If I were an eagle," Juan insisted, "I could spy out what is going on in any enemy camp or fortress, couldn't I?"

"You could", Alexander said dryly. "But you couldn't report it."

Juan nodded eagerly. "Exactly. So I thought, if a very small man could be carried up by an eagle ..."

"Impossible, Uncle. You would have to use a dozen eagles to carry up a man—and they would hardly pull together, would they? When I was a little boy, we used to go hunting in the mountains. There are vultures there, as large or larger than any eagle I ever saw. They could carry up a newborn lamb, but only just. They couldn't carry a man— not even if he were as light as Prince Carlos."

"He weighed himself last week", Juan said. "Seventy-six pounds—at the age of fifteen."

"You wouldn't like to be *him*, I suppose."

"He is a very unhappy person", Juan said, frowning. "And this is a very unhappy day for him. I do wish he would come out now. The trumpets may sound any moment."

"If they do, it only means that the procession has passed the Visagra Gate. A royal progress must be slow—specially when a country gets a new queen, and when that new queen is as lovely as Elizabeth of France."

"Isabella of Spain", Juan said curtly.

Alexander threw back his head and laughed. "You Spaniards! The Queen can't be very Spanish yet, can she? In fact, I very much wonder how Spanish she'll ever be. Don't forget she's been brought up to hate Spain and all it stands for."

"There is peace now", Juan said.

"Yes, now—but the Queen is fourteen years old and all her life, on and off, the two countries have been the bitterest of enemies—to say nothing about the time before she was born. Why, your father allied himself with Protestant princes to fight Francis the First of France."

"And Francis?" Juan asked hotly. "He was even less choosy, wasn't he? He made an alliance with the Sultan! It's unforgivable."

Prince Alexander Farnese dismissed Protestants and Turks with an eloquent Italian shrug. "Anyway, Spain has a French queen now. One can't help wondering how much of a Trojan horse she'll be."

Juan stared at him, aghast. "Trojan horse? What are you talking about?"

"Obvious, isn't it? Or have you forgotten whose daughter she is?"

"King Henry the Second of . . ."

"I don't mean her father, Uncle mine. Don't tell me you know nothing about Catherine de' Medici!"

"A very remarkable lady, and related to all the best families in Italy. Related to the Pope, too—"

"And to me." Alexander nodded. "The most dangerous woman in Europe. Her ears are so good, she can hear the grass grow. Her eyes are so keen she can see what is going on in the boudoir of Elizabeth of England and how much money there is in every single palace in Spain. Her nose is so long, she can sniff the first signs of a scandal across seven frontiers. She makes use of astrologers, magicians, and sorcerers—"

"No!"

"Oh, yes, she does and they include that man Michel Nostradamus, who published a whole book of events to come a few years ago. Now, calm yourself, I don't mean that dear Catherine has sent a few of her pet wizards with her daughter, though I wouldn't put it past her to be sitting in a dark room with some of them at this moment, watching the royal progress in a magic crystal or something like that...."

"Never mind her", Juan said defiantly. "It's the King who has brought about this marriage, and that's a great political victory for him. It's put an end to the stupid war with France, Don Luiz says. And he's right—all morning the people in the streets have been shouting, 'Long live Isabella of the Peace.' "

"I hope he'll be happier with her than he was with the English Queen." Alexander was at his most Italian this morning. He even started humming a little Florentine song.

"Stop it", Juan said. "Carlos might hear you."

"Not through those thick doors. *Il mio cuore* ... anyway, she is supposed to be very pretty, which is more than could be said about María d'Inglaterra. Let's take that as a good omen, shall we? The English marriage wasn't exactly a success.... Oh, come, you don't have to defend the King to me. I know it's not his fault; no one could have made a success of it. What a horrid country it must be, with fog all over it most of the year and people drinking beer instead of wine...."

"Don Luiz says that the last king they had who reigned a long time had a habit of killing his queens when he was through with them", Juan said. "Perhaps that is why God decided to have that country ruled by queens."

Alexander shook his head. "You do think of the most unlikely things. And if I were you I wouldn't try to think about what God wants or doesn't want. Leave it to the Church." He began to laugh. "It's an idea, though. Some strange kind of justice."

"Exactly." Juan was visibly pleased. "There is another thing, too. That man, Henry the Eighth, divorced his first wife because he wanted a son. But he only got one, despite all his wives, and women have ruled his country ever since, except for a few years. Justice, that's what it is. And that's why . . ."

He broke off as the heavy door leading to Prince Carlos' suite was flung open. A lackey in a pale green livery came out, stumbling. Someone banged the door shut behind him so quickly that it hit him full in the back. The man almost fell, but he regained his balance and streaked across the room to disappear through one of the doors on the opposite side.

The two boys looked at each other. They had both seen the deep gash on the man's right cheek. There was a thin trail of blood all across the room.

"Poor Carlos", Alexander said sarcastically. "Lackey hunting again."

The better part of a minute passed before Juan could say anything, and Alexander went on, angrily: "*Mamma mia*, I can well understand that the King was shocked when he saw his precious boy again after all those years in Flanders. He had had reports, of course, but I don't think they dared tell him how bad it was."

"He can be good and generous—you know that."

The Italian shrugged again. "Everybody has his gentler moods, I think. I'm sure Herod and Nero had some. Only last week Carlos would have thrown his tailor out of the window if Don García hadn't stopped him. *Cielo*, Juan, you'd defend anybody. But then, he's always at his best with you; I don't know why."

"I don't know either", Juan admitted. "But I do know that he can't be at his best today. And so do you."

"Then he hasn't gotten over it yet, has he?"

"I doubt if he ever will, Alexander. I doubt if you ever would either, if you were in his place. I mean, if you had his character."

"Royalty", Alexander stated, "has its own set of advantages and troubles. You don't get whipped as a boy; whatever you do, you get the best food, the best horses, and the best teachers. But you must marry an alliance instead of a woman, and you may have to renounce the woman you love or think you love because of some reason of state."

"I know, but perhaps it's harder still to renounce her so that your father can marry her."

"I don't think Carlos knows anything about love, really."

"He's got a portrait of the Queen, the one they sent him when he was engaged to her. I've seen him kissing it madly."

"Did he know that you were looking at him? Ah, well, it's no good going into all this. But I'll bet the whole thing is Queen Catherine's idea."

"What on earth do you mean?"

"It would be just like her—first to foster the engagement of her daughter with Carlos and then when Queen María of England died, to suggest to King Philip that he marry Elizabeth himself. She has her spies everywhere. She knows all about Carlos' character. What better could happen in her opinion than enmity between the King and the royal heir?"

Juan shook his head. It was not the first time that he had heard this kind of thinking—not after four months at court; but he could not take it in. He had learned a great deal lately, and much of it without any effort. But such thoughts were like eels or like snakes, and he was sure that Don Luiz would hate them.

"There—the trumpets", Alexander said. "Hear them? They've passed the Visagra Gate. What are you doing?"

"I am going in there", Juan said. "Carlos *must* get ready now. . . ."

"You can't do that." Alexander was horrified. "You know as well I do that he hates it if one bursts in on him. He'll slash you as he did that wretched lackey."

"Perhaps," Juan said mildly, "but not before I've told him about the trumpets. If he's still in a rage he won't have heard them, but he'll hear me."

He went straight on. But the door opened before he reached it and Prince Carlos came out.

Both Juan and Alexander bowed to the slight, childlike figure.

Carlos, too, was dressed in black. The large white ruff around his neck accentuated the sallowness of his complexion, but hid at least to some extent the curvature of his spine. His eyes, gray and deeply set, were not those of a boy of fifteen; they were old eyes, suspicious and restless. The corners of his absurdly small mouth were pinched.

Instead of walking he seemed to drag himself forward by sheer willpower. His right leg was slightly shorter than the left. He was very nearly a dwarf. And the fashion of the time, with its short doublets and long hose, made his gait appear like the stalking, inexorable march of a black beetle.

"Juan", he said, "and Alexander. You don't seem to have changed." His voice was surprisingly melodious.

"Changed, Your Highness?" Alexander asked.

"Yes. My father has changed, you know. Until now he was my father. Now he is a bridegroom. At the age of thirty-three, too. There are a good many gray hairs in his beard and on his temples. I've seen them. I told him so and he didn't like it."

"The royal progress will arrive at the palace in a few minutes", Juan warned.

"He has hair in his ears and in his nose as well", Carlos went on. "I wonder what the bride will say when she sees it. But then she has changed too. Only a few months ago she was my bride. Now he has taken her from me. The King has given—the King has taken—the name of the King be praised."

"Your Highness, we shall be late", Juan pleaded.

Carlos gave him a twisted smile. "Very well. I will go." He laid his hand on Juan's shoulder. Alexander followed.

"You can do almost everything when you are the King", Carlos whispered. "You can give a promise—any promise—and take it back. You can give a present—and take it back. My father is very good at that. Maybe one day he'll take everything back that he gave me—even my life."

"Your Highness", Juan gasped.

Carlos smiled again. "Even my life", he repeated. "Unless ..."

As they approached the door on the opposite side of the room, it was opened and they passed between two double rows of servants and guards to reach the main staircase.

A few minutes later they reached the outer court and the royal tribune where a visibly relieved master of ceremonies led them to their places.

Everyone was bowing.

Carlos gave a dignified nod. His face was quite without expression. He whispered to Juan, "I know what they think, and I could kill them all." No one else heard it. He had a knack of whispering without moving his lips.

From afar came shouting and the staccato noise of thousands of hands clapping.

The high-ranking officer in charge of the guards rapped out orders.

"Isabella of the Peace", they were shouting outside. "Isabella of the Peace!"

It was long past midnight when Juan was allowed to retire to his own suite in the east wing of the palace. Court ceremonial demanded that two chamberlains go with him to deliver him safely into the hands of his valets, that the valets help him to undress. "Good night, Your Excellency."

"Good night, Pedro. Good night, Diego."

Neither of them would ever have his cheek slashed by a dagger.

There was a large clock in this room too, as in almost every room of the palace, of any palace that Charles V had inhabited in his time. He loved clocks. Fifteen of them had been removed from the six rooms in Yuste. . . .

Juan said his prayers and went to bed. But tired as he was, sleep would not come. Words and images, images and words assailed him on silent wings. "Maybe one day my father will take everything back that he gave me—even my life. Even my life, unless . . ." And that horrible, twisted smile. Unless—unless what?

Hatred. Juan had never encountered hatred before he met Prince Carlos, in whom it was so powerful. But hatred was a small thing—a small, bitter thing, Don Luiz said. "Never let yourself be guided by anything that is small, except that small voice in yourself that is your conscience." What kind of a conscience did Carlos have?

He was ill. He must be ill. Could he really have been in love with the Queen, whom until today he had never seen? Could one fall in love with a portrait?

Nothing here was as it had been at Villagarcía. It was as if Villagarcía was the world as it should be and the royal court the world as it really was.

No one in Villagarcía seemed to envy anybody. Here each one seemed to envy someone else. And the rumors—perhaps they were the worst thing of all. Everybody constantly whispering, murmuring, exchanging meaningful glances. How was one to know what was true and what wasn't?

He tried to think of the lovely face of the young Queen. She was scarcely older than he, but so dignified and gracious; they all had to admit that, even the nastiest old ladies. He had been allowed to kiss the edge of her robe. So had Carlos.

He could see it again with closed eyes: Carlos kneeling before the Queen, who had been his bride, and kissing the edge of her robe; and on her right was the King and on her left the Duke of Alba. And the Duke of Alba was watching Carlos like a hawk, and his hand, that strong hand with the long, sinewy fingers, was resting on his dagger.

They knew.

Later, at the ball, Carlos watched the Queen all the time. He did not dance with her, of course; he never danced. He merely stood there, staring at her as she danced with the King.

Was what the Duchess of Infantado had said to her sister true—he could not help overhearing it—that the King had asked the Queen whether his gray hairs were displeasing to her?

"He has hair in his ears and in his nose as well. I wonder what the bride will say when she sees it."

Was it true that the Cardinal Archbishop of Burgos was in charge of all the ecclesiastical ceremonies because the Archbishop of Toledo had been arrested by the Inquisition? Archbishop Carranza of Toledo—Juan remembered him well, with his straggly white beard and his white mule, that day in Yuste when he went to visit the Emperor.

How strange the world looked when one saw it from the royal palace. A son hating his father. A great nobleman protecting his queen against the son of his king. An archbishop arrested by the Inquisition.

But the Queen was very lovely.

Poor Carlos ...


The very first thing Juan heard in the morning was a rumor. The Queen was supposed to be ill, the valet told him. Half an hour later he knew that it was true. The Queen was in bed with a bad attack of fever. Three doctors were in attendance.

Two more were called in in the afternoon. The fever had mounted and there was talk of an infection.

All celebrations had to be canceled. The enforced idleness doubled and tripled the number of rumors. The enormous palace was seething with them.

Juan joined Don Luiz Quixada and Doña Magdalena in the chapel to pray for the Queen's health. A number of her French ladies were there, red-eyed and pale. They were all sitting in one corner and everyone else seemed to wish to avoid them. Don Luiz saw it, too, and made a point of going up to them to say a few kind words. They appeared absurdly grateful, but also very much afraid.

When Juan remarked on it a little later, Don Luiz nodded gravely.

"They have reason to be afraid, I fear. Her Majesty is probably suffering from smallpox."

Alexander Farnese dropped in on Juan in the afternoon. "It *is* smallpox", he confirmed. "They're all in a turmoil."

Juan sighed. There had been smallpox in Leganés once and for weeks Señora Massy had forced him to stay in the house. "The demon causing it is flying through the streets all the time." When he objected that she herself continued to go out—though rarely and always with a cloth steeped in vinegar held to her face—she replied that the demon had a special liking for young people. Over thirty people caught the disease and more than half of them died. The others . . .

"If she survives, she may become disfigured", Juan said in a low voice.

Alexander nodded. "Such a lovely woman, too", he said. "I wonder whether Carlos wished it on her."

"Alexander!"

"Well, you've seen how he took it, haven't you? Don't you think he's quite capable of it? And wishes are powerful things. If you believe in prayers, you must believe in curses as well."

"Never", Juan said firmly. "Never has Carlos done such a thing. He loves her. He cannot wish her to die or to become ugly. It's not like you to think of such a thing. . . ."

"I am trying to think with his mind", Alexander replied with an eloquent gesture, involving his shoulders, arms, hands, and fingers as well as his eyebrows and lips, and Juan wondered whether there was any part of the body Italians did not use when making an emphatic statement. "Of course it may not be Carlos' work at all, but that of Catherine de' Medici's."

"That lady again!"

"I wouldn't put it past her to send her daughter impregnated with the smallpox poison to Spain. Didn't I tell you the Queen might well be a Trojan horse? Incidentally, Carlos hasn't asked for you today at all, has he? No? I thought so. He has locked himself in his room and wants to see nobody, I hear."

"I am going to the Queen's suite", Juan said.

"They won't let you in, of course."

"I'm going anyway."

"But what is the good of that if . . ."

"I don't know, but I can't go on sitting here."

Shrugging, Alexander followed him. The endless corridors were dotted with small groups of courtiers talking in subdued tones.

At the entrance of the Queen's suite a cluster of doctors seemed to be holding council in a whisper. There was a strong smell of vinegar.

In one corner Don Luiz Quixada was listening politely to the Duke of Infantado, who had been the head of the Queen's escort on her journey from France to Spain. There was a rumor that she had treated him with little courtesy and another that she had to put him in his place when he tried to take himself too seriously as the representative of his royal master.

Somebody mentioned that Prince Carlos was ill as well—oh no, not the smallpox, a fit. "Convulsions—very bad this time."

Someone else murmured: "Of course. He must find it difficult to endure the fact that Her Majesty is getting all the attention."

There was something like a rustle—could it be a ripple of merriment? Don Luiz Quixada gave a stony look in the direction of the group and silence fell at once.

One of the doctors seemed to be holding forth, while the others listened gravely with much rubbing of chins and looking over the rim of spectacles.

Suddenly a hush.

Everybody bowed deeply before the solitary figure in black approaching quietly, steadily.

Always pale, the King now looked like a ghost. He said nothing, but there was something so consistent and decisive about the way he moved that at least one of the doctors guessed what he was about to do and dared to speak before he was addressed.

"Your Majesty is not considering entering, I hope."

"Make room", was the curt answer.

The doctor lifted his hands in horror. "Your Majesty, the diagnosis is now quite certain. This disease is as contagious as the plague itself and almost as deadly."

Before the King could answer, a second doctor, the learned Protomedicus Gutiérrez, said pleadingly: "Your Majesty's life belongs to Spain. If it pleases God, Her Majesty the Queen will recover. But if it does not please him—it is better that Your Majesty should be a widower than that Spain should become a widow."

There was a moment's pause. No one knew and no one would ever know whether the King was weighing the doctor's argument or whether he was just formulating his answer.

Abruptly Philip said: "You have forgotten your place, Doctor Gutiérrez. But I remember mine. It is at the side of my wife."

Such was the general confusion that no one thought of opening the door for him. He struggled for a moment with the handle—he had not opened a door for himself in all his life—but he managed and firmly closed it behind him.

"*Madonna*", Alexander Farnese breathed. "I don't think I would dare ..."

Looking at Don Luiz Quixada, Juan saw in his face the reflection of his own feelings: fear and pride.

"Gone into her room, has he?" Don Carlos' waxen face was twitching as if another fit were imminent. "My dear father is a very, very courageous man."

The hatred in the melodious voice was almost unbearable. Juan said nothing.

"He is also a very foolish man", Carlos went on. "How long did he stay with her?"

"His Majesty is still with the Queen."

"What? All the time?" Carlos began to giggle. "He'll get it", he said. "He can't escape it. How sad it is for Spain. Blotches all over, horrible, horrible pustules." He began to walk up and down the room, limping, dragging his feet, beetlelike.

"She is punished", he said. "Badly, badly punished. Blotches and pustules all over her lovely face. And if she gets through . . . she will have scars, scars for life. No one is ever going to marry her again. Poor Isabella, poor Isabella. She is young. Just my age. She will perhaps survive it. One doesn't have gray hair at fifteen."

Suddenly his mood changed. "I was ill myself", he said bitterly. "I fell. I was unconscious for a long time. My father never bothered to come to see *me*. He doesn't care about me. He never did. For years and years I never saw him. Always there is something or somebody who is so much more important than I am. I'm nothing. When he speaks to me he doesn't even look at me."

When Don Carlos indulged in self-pity his voice lost all its charm and became rasping and shrill. Somehow his self-pity was more difficult to bear than his malice. Why?

Pondering about it Juan came to the conclusion that self-pity more than anything else destroyed the compassion of others; and compassion alone made it possible to bear the company of Carlos.

Again the prince's mood changed. "When my dear father decided to steal my bride he made at least one gracious gesture to me", he said. "He promised to convoke the Cortes of Castile here at Toledo and to let them take the oath of allegiance to me as the royal heir. *Very* gracious, of course, to give me what was my due. Still, it was something.... But now? He only thinks of her. Perhaps he hopes that she'll give him another son, a son as nice-looking as you are, maybe—or as strong as cousin Alexander. Perhaps that's why there is no longer any talk about his promise to me."

He bared his teeth. "I am still the firstborn", he said menacingly. "Nothing can change that—except my death. Do you understand now why I always keep weapons in my room?"

"Your Highness cannot be serious...."

Carlos broke into cackling laughter. "You are a precious little lamb, Juan. And you think that everybody else is as you are. Ah well, stay as you are, stay as you are; it suits me. I can think aloud in your presence—you won't run and tell on me. That's something."

There was a scratching noise at the door, and with a few incredibly swift steps, bounds almost, the prince was behind his desk and grabbed a heavy pistol. "Who is there?" he screamed.

An elderly lackey entered and bowed. "Don García is here, at His Majesty's request, Your Highness."

"It's a lie", Carlos shrilled. "The King is with the Queen."

But Don García came in, Don Carlos' tutor, a tall, dignified old man. "I have never yet lied to Your Highness", he said firmly.

Carlos dropped the pistol. "I never said you had", he replied. "I thought that rogue of a lackey was lying. Where is my father?"

"His Majesty has gone to his study to sign documents of state."

"Really?" Carlos sneered. "And left the Queen alone?"

Don García paid no attention to the taunt. "One of the documents concerns Your Highness," he said, "and I am charged to inform Your Highness that the Cortes of Castile will swear the oath of allegiance on the twenty-third day of February."

"Ah!" Carlos' eyes flashed. He drew himself up. "Very good, Don García. My respects and thanks to His Majesty."

The old man bowed and withdrew.

Juan beamed. "You see, the King has not forgotten you! Despite all his worry . . ."

"You fool." Carlos grinned triumphantly. "He had to do it. Don't you see? He may catch the smallpox. He may die. He *must* have the Cortes sworn. Somebody must rule Spain—and there's no one else."

## CHAPTER 10

"CAREFUL, CAREFUL", cried the fencing master. "Not so violent . . . please, Don Juan. I beg of you, Don Alexander!"

The two young men did not listen. Their thin blades met as if in deadly combat—lunge, parry, lunge, parry, lunge. There was a frown on Alexander's forehead, and his face was flushed. He was the stronger of the two by far, and it irked him that he had not yet been able to pierce Juan's guard. What made it worse still was that the boy was laughing.

"Take this", Alexander snapped, lunging wildly. "And this . . . and this . . ."

Juan warded off the first two lunges. When he saw the third one coming he leapt forward instead of back. A circular blow at just the proper angle and Alexander's sword flew out of his hand, sailed high through the air, and fell into the soft sand of the court, twenty feet away.

Bellowing with rage Alexander raced to retrieve it. But Juan was quicker. Streaking past his herculean nephew he arrived in time to pick up the sword. Bowing he gave it back to its owner.

Alexander glowered. Then he laughed. "That devil's trick again. That fellow taught you well—what was his name?"

"Galarza."

"If ever I meet him, I'll tear out his guts."

"With your sword?" Juan asked innocently. "I don't think I'd advise that."

"You're a dangerous fellow, venerable Uncle." Alexander grinned.

The fencing master came running. "Very nice indeed, Don Juan, but I beg of you, of both of you, not to become so vehement. That second lunge could have cost an eye. If you're not more careful I must ask you to fight with closed helmets again."

Instead of answering they took the sturdy, thick-set man between them and, despite his protestations, marched him back to the armory.

It was four o'clock in the afternoon and the end of both games and learning for the day. They sauntered over to the large terrace, sat down, and stretched their limbs.

"It isn't only tricks", Alexander said. "And it isn't only that man Galarza. You've improved enormously in these two years. When I met you first in Toledo I liked you at once, but I didn't think you had it in you. You were too— how shall I say?—too good. Yes, too much of a dear little boy with an enormous hero worship for Don Luiz Quixada."

"I still think he is . . ."

"Yes, yes, I concede the point. He is everything you think he is plus interest, as the usurers say. But you were so gentle and kind, you always thought the best of everyone. Sometimes I thought you would have made a very nice girl."

"Shall we fence again?" Juan asked lightly.

"No, thank you. I'm only just catching my breath. No need to be offended; I told you you've changed."

"I don't think I have, really", Juan said. "I still think only the best about you."

"I should hope so. Never had an uncle a more devoted nephew. Ah, just what I wanted."

A valet brought wine and cherries, and for the next few minutes conversation ceased.

They drank and ate and watched the squirrels playing in the trees. Building and park belonged to the unfortunate old Archbishop of Toledo, still a prisoner of the Inquisition. There was a rumor that the Pope had asked that he be taken to Rome, but the King would not let him go, Roman justice being notoriously mild.

Behind the clusters of trees rose the many towers of collegiate and conventual buildings, and behind them ran the silvery band of the Henares River. There seemed to be little necessity for the forbidding gray walls around the King's good town of Alcalá. A potential conqueror would have found himself in the possession of a small country place with a very great number of colleges and monasteries. That number had increased year by year. Cardinal Ximénes de Cisneros had founded the University only sixty years ago, and yet today it was a very serious and vigorous rival to world-famous Salamanca.

Alexander put down his goblet. "Have you any idea how long we shall have to go on waxing wise, Uncle?"

"None whatever. Why?"

"Oh, I just wondered. No, that's not true. You deserve a better answer than that. Because, believe it or not, I think I can trust you."

Juan smiled. "You make it sound like a rare thing."

"It *is* a rare thing. I don't think I could name five people in the whole world that I trust."

"Oh come, come. Your father, your mother, your father confessor, the King, the Queen, our much esteemed teacher Honoratus Joannius ... that's six people already, without me."

"Of these six," Alexander said, "I grant you one—without you. My father confessor. And him only because he knows that he's excommunicated ipso facto if he gives away a single word I tell him in the confessional."

"You don't mean it—I mean, about not trusting your own father and mother and ..."

"My father is so full of tricks; he cheats himself at dice! If he told me that the sun was shining, I would ask for a covered carriage. Mother, of course, is quite different—one can trust her implicitly as long as there are no political matters on her mind. Unfortunately they are on her mind all the time. And that goes also for His Majesty and for the Queen. As for the learned Honoratus, why, you innocent virgin, don't you realize that he is keeping a regular dossier about you and me, to say nothing of Prince Carlos? He is probably the most erudite man in the kingdom, positively brilliant, and he was King Philip's teacher before he became ours. And you may remember, or rather you may know, what happened to *your* father's teacher when he had finished teaching your father. . . ."

"No, I don't remember and I don't know, but . . ."

"He became Pope Adrian the Sixth. So maybe our Honoratus Joannius has high hopes. But in any case, how can I trust him when I know he will report everything to the King? You, of course, trust everybody."

"In the circumstances I suppose I ought to be proud that you trust me." Juan grinned a little sheepishly. "Or maybe I should feel ashamed, because it obviously means that you take me for a simpleton. But you haven't told me yet what is on your mind."

"I think we are hostages", Alexander said bluntly. "I think we are being kept under strict supervision. And I hope to God the Queen will soon have a son."

"I don't know about you," Juan said, "but I am not a hostage. Why should I be? I'm no danger to anybody. If I were, they would have left me in Leganés among the villagers."

"It wasn't the King who sent for you there—it was your father, the Emperor."

"Of course. I don't think the King knew of my existence at that time. When he knew, he accepted me as his brother."

"But without the title of prince."

Alexander was subtle enough to register that there was a moment of hesitation before Juan replied evenly: "My mother was a commoner, you know."

"I knew that. What was her name?"

"I have no idea. She was a German lady—that's all I know, and even that the King told me only when he came to visit us here last year. Why do you wish the Queen to have a son—apart from purely patriotic reasons, I mean?"

"For very egotistical reasons", Alexander said. "The more sons the King has, the less my own importance. And yours, incidentally. It's dangerous to be important."

"Are you quite sure you're not emulating your father now—cheating yourself?" Juan asked. "Surely you have ambition . . ."

"I have. But not in the political field. Soldiering—that's what I want."

"That's what I want, too", Juan said, and for a few moments they looked at each other sharply.

"If you're as good at it as you are at fencing," Alexander said thoughtfully, "I'd rather fight on your side than against you. You're doing better than I in military history, too. And it's not much consolation that I am better than Carlos. . . ."

"I haven't seen him all day."

"Of course not. We had mathematics today, remember?"

They both laughed. On days when Padre Dr. Alonzo Díaz came to give them lessons in mathematics and physics Carlos was invariably ill and stayed in bed.

"I don't think he knows much more about anything now than he did two years ago", Alexander said. "That's just it, don't you see? Sooner or later the King will have to decide whether Carlos will be able to reign when his time comes. . . ."

"But he *has* decided! He had the Cortes of Castile sworn. We all swore allegiance to Carlos that day, and solemn enough it was. I never saw so many bishops in one place. The Cardinal Archbishop of Burgos, the archbishops of Sevilla and Granada, the bishops of Ávila and Pamplona . . ."

"And so many grandees! The Admiral of Castile, the dukes of Alba, Najera, and Francavilla, the marquises of Denia, Villena, Cañete, Mondéjar, and Camares, the counts of Benavente and Ureña—do you remember how Alba forgot to kiss Carlos' hand? How furious he was! Alba has made himself an enemy for life, and what's more he knows it."

"It was a magnificent spectacle", Juan said. "A pity the Queen could not be there. She would have seen Spain at its most brilliant."

"She will have many an opportunity to see that, please God", Alexander said. "At least she was out of danger then. I really thought she would die. But the most marvelous thing is that it hasn't impaired her beauty at all. You know, don't you, that Queen Catherine de' Medici—"

"Your eternal bugbear."

"... sent her special creams and lotions, mixed by her pet wizards, to counteract the smallpox poison and to prevent any blemishes. The brothers Ruggieri concocted them. One of the Queen's ladies told me they contained the hearts of tadpoles, dried and pulverized and mixed with honey and the whites of eggs."

"Poor Queen, to have to put such a brew on her lovely face."

"It helped, didn't it? What more do you want? But I wouldn't like to know what incantations they made when they mixed the stuff. The Ruggieri brothers are notorious sorcerers. France is extremely lax about that sort of thing, and that again is probably due to—"

"Don't say it. I know. I think if ever you go to purgatory—"

"I shall be lucky if it's only that."

"... you will probably have to spend a few years in the presence of your bugbear as your only company."

Alexander shuddered. "I didn't know you could be so cruel", he said. "Carlos is punishment enough for me."

"Oh, he could be worse", Juan said a little lamely. "Sometimes he is quite nice and human, really. I've often wondered how I would feel if I had his—difficulties. It cannot be easy, never to enjoy the health and strength of one's own body—to know, always, that people look at one either with compassion or with—"

"... disgust," Alexander helped out.

"With aversion anyway."

"Well, you know what Tiepolo wrote about him. That he was happy only when he could make others unhappy."

"A very nasty phrase", Juan said. "Tiepolo—he's the Venetian ambassador, isn't he?"

"Yes. And Venetians do not mince their words—behind your back. Of all the arrogant, disagreeable, lying, treacherous . . ."

"Now, now, who's not mincing his words behind Venetian backs." Juan laughed. "You in Italy seem to be worse than we are. The enmity between Castilians and Aragonese is bad enough, but it seems like pure Christian charity when one has heard a Florentine talk about Venice or a Venetian about the Genoese—and vice versa. I have yet to learn that Arabs talk like that about Turks or Persians. *They* seem to be united enough."

Alexander shook his head. "Fancy comparing us with infidels!"

" 'If you want to beat an enemy, you must study him', says Honoratus Joannius."

"The infidels look united to us", Alexander said. "But it may be only because they are so far away. I'm sure they also have their dissensions and dislikes."

"Perhaps." Juan looked across the trees to the forest of towers that stretched up to heaven. "But I do wonder sometimes whether the true religion came to Rome with Peter and to Spain with James so early because we needed it most."

"What—more than the Turks and the Arabs? One might think you had a special liking for those circumcised devils."

"I like them as much as you'll like the bellyache you'll get from eating so many cherries, my venerable nephew. But I don't expect them to behave like Christians. And I shudder to think how we would behave if we weren't."

"It's just like you to think of such a strange thing."

"Is it so strange?" Juan rose and stretched his limbs. "I know—or rather I have a fair idea of what I would be like, if—"

"And what would you be like?" asked a melodious voice.

They both turned. Don Carlos was smiling. "I have recovered", he explained nonchalantly.

"There is reasonable hope that you will stay well for at least two days", Alexander said phlegmatically. "Today is Tuesday. The next mathematics lesson is on Friday."

"You are very outspoken for an Italian, dear cousin." Carlos' smile was rather acid. "I do hate mathematics, that is true. Fortunately I shall never need it. Too much knowledge is not good for a ruler anyway, and I shall always have people to do that kind of work for me. Now you go away, cousin, I want to talk to Juan."

Alexander pressed his lips together, rose, turned sharply, and left.

"One must put him in his place from time to time", Carlos said when Alexander was out of earshot. "Besides, I want to talk to you alone. Or rather I want you to come with me for a short walk. No, not that way. Through the park. We have at least half an hour before supper."

It was not easy to keep step with Carlos without making him acutely aware of his physical shortcomings. But he seemed to be in a remarkably good mood, shuffling along and even humming a little song.

They could see the gate now and next to it the gatekeeper's lodge.

"There's a new man in there", Carlos said. "Fellow called Gardetas. And he has a daughter. Mariana. Pretty name, isn't it?"

"Very nice."

"Pedro told me about her", Carlos explained. "My valet. A good man, Pedro. He knew how bored I was. So I went and had a look. What a girl, Juan. What a girl! Hair like flames, flames of . . . heaven. I didn't know one could find girls like that among the simple people. I must say I can't blame my grandfather—your father—for not always being choosy about the rank and station of the ladies who won his favor. *You* know."

Juan frowned, but said nothing. It was not easy.

"So I made her acquaintance, of course", Carlos went on. "She is much more amusing than the ladies at court, you know. Much. Quite astonishing, really, as her father is nothing but a nuisance, always around, and always with a sour face. *She* appreciates the honor, I think. There, she has seen me coming—have you ever seen such hair?"

Juan had. He was just going to tell Carlos that there had been a servant girl at Villagarcía, La Rubia, whom they called that because of red hair just like this, when he suddenly realized with a shock that it was La Rubia. Of course! She came from Alcalá and had returned there. La Rubia, who had set fire to the castle and whom Don Luiz dismissed from service. La Rubia, whom Galarza used to tease so unmercifully because she had freckles.

He saw the flash of recognition cross her pretty face. For a moment it looked as if she were going to run back into the house, but then she seemed to think better of it and stayed where she was.

As she bowed deeply before the young prince, Juan saw that most of her freckles had disappeared.

But before Carlos could say anything a tall, lean man with a graying beard came out of the lodge. He too bowed and inquired somewhat pointedly whether His Highness had any orders.

His Highness gave him a nasty look, hesitated a little, spat out an angry "No", turned away, and began to march back.

After a while he said to Juan: "What an excellent idea it would be if there were such a thing as a childbed for fathers—and if they'd all die in it."

Again Juan said nothing. He knew that any argument would only bring forth further remarks in the same vein.

After a while Carlos said: "She's lovely, isn't she? I must get rid of that old man somehow and I shall. My man Pedro is a sly fellow. He'll get any message to her that I want, father or no father. I want to see her and I want to see her alone."

"But surely . . ."

"Surely what?"

Juan was embarrassed. "I mean—you can't seriously think—you wouldn't consider—marrying a girl like this, would you? After all, the girl you marry would be the future Queen of Spain."

Carlos grinned. "Who said anything about marrying her? Royalty sometimes stoops to pick up very lowly flowers. We don't bother to marry such women. *You* ought to know that better than anyone else."

Juan stopped abruptly. He was as white as marble and his eyes were flashing. Slowly his hand reached for the sword hilt.

Carlos saw. He knew he had gone too far. He was afraid. But even so he could not make himself apologize. He just stood and stared at Juan. He could not even banish his twisted smile.

Juan's fingers pressed the hilt of his sword; it was not the sword Don Luiz had given him when he was a boy. But he was remembering what Don Luiz told him one day, in the armory. "These three you must never strike: a woman, royalty, or a priest. If you strike a woman, you lose your honor;

if you strike royalty, you lose your knighthood; if you strike a priest, you lose your soul."

He drew himself up. "It is true that my mother was not of royal blood. But my father was a greater man than your father."

"I shall tell the King what you said", Carlos threatened.

"Do so. You won't tell him anything he doesn't know."

Juan stalked away. Later, when he met Carlos again at supper, he was icily polite to him. The prince pretended not to notice and showed an almost boisterous good humor.

Three days later his tutor, Don García de Toledo, found out that the prince was secretly leaving the palace by a small door leading from the council room, down a narrow iron staircase to the park; Don García began to make inquiries. Carlos refused to say anything, but Don García was thorough. He interrogated everybody, from the prince's chamberlains down to his personal valets.

The excellent Pedro broke down and talked.

The first result was that Don García had the small door locked and the key removed.

The next was that Don Carlos beat Pedro so severely that the wretched man had to be sent to the infirmary.

For several days the prince was in a terrible mood and rude to everybody, including the venerable Honoratus Joannius.

At the end of the week the prince's mood suddenly changed for the better, so much so that both Juan and Alexander felt he must have found a new solution for his problem. By now Alexander was fully aware of what was going on. Carlos himself had seen to that, talking incessantly about his beautiful redhead and preening himself as the irresistible lover.

At supper, on Sunday, the prince seemed to be in a great hurry to get through the meal. As soon as it was over, he dismissed all the servants, complained about a sudden head-ache, and left, allegedly for his rooms.

"Something's going on", Alexander said. "I wonder what he's up to. Let's see, shall we?"

"We can't go to his rooms—you know how he is."

"Don't I? But I have no intention of going there. Neither, I think, has he. I wonder whether he hasn't got himself a new key to that door. No harm in having a look into the council room, is there?"

"I don't like it", Juan said, frowning.

"Oh, well, then I'll go alone. I must find out whether the irresistible lover is on his way to the most beautiful redhead of all time."

Laughing, Alexander left the room.

Juan never knew what made him follow. It was not curiosity; the very idea of snooping disgusted him. Nor was it the spirit of investigation, so strong in some people and not even remotely related to curiosity. He felt a strange kind of uneasiness and that feeling seemed to increase as he approached the council room. Alexander had half opened the main door and was peering in.

"Come away", Juan said in a sudden gust of anger. Peering through half-opened doors was a business for valets.

Alexander opened the door still wider and entered; and again Juan drifted after him. The council room was huge and forbidding in the semidarkness. On the walls shadowy bishops looked down disapprovingly from within the security of their gilt frames.

Alexander was walking on tiptoe. Then he stopped so suddenly that Juan almost bumped into him.

The small door was open.

As they approached it, they felt a chill. There was a musty smell coming up from the steep little-used iron staircase, and a faint flicker of light.

Alexander began to giggle. "Just as I thought, he's got another key. And a candle. Oh, the enviable redhead. Now if—"

He broke off.

There was a clatter, a crash, and a moment later a long-drawn, terrible scream.

CHAPTER 11

"HOW DID IT HAPPEN?" the King asked.

Honoratus Joannius took a deep breath. They were alone in the council room, fortunately. It would have been con-siderably worse to tell the sordid story in the presence of all the grandees who had arrived, to say nothing of the doc-tors and officials who had invaded his quiet seat of learn-ing. But it was bad enough as it was, with the pale, penetrating eyes of the King staring at him. He tried to evoke the time when Philip had been his pupil, but it was no good. Behind those eyes was an intellect he could no longer fathom, a will he could no longer direct but which, on the contrary, could unmake him in one sudden flash of anger.

Honoratus Joannius bowed his head and began to talk. The prince was at an age when certain physical processes asserted themselves in him and most regrettably. . . .

The King listened stonily. . . . Some wretched servant girl. They had locked the door. They had taken away the key. Carlos had succeeded in having another one made. A nar-row staircase, steep, lit only by the light of a single candle in Carlos' hand. A stumble and a fall and the end of the first independent expedition of the royal heir of Spain. The first and perhaps the last.

"Don Juan and Don Alexander gave the first alarm. They happened to be here in the council room—"

"Why?"

"They told me they had gathered from the prince's attitude that he had some plan of his own and they wanted to find out what he was doing."

"They were not with him when the accident happened?"

"No, Your Majesty."

"You assume that from what they told you?"

"Yes, Your Majesty."

"Has there been a quarrel between the prince and his two relatives?"

"There have been frequent little discords, as is usual between young men of their age."

"When did anything of the sort happen last?"

"To the best of my knowledge a few days ago, Your Majesty."

"With whom did the prince quarrel? Don Alexander or Don Juan?"

"With Don Juan, Your Majesty. I was told about it by the lackey Pedro Sánchez, for whom the prince had a special liking until two days ago when he found out that Pedro Sánchez had admitted to Don Diego García that the prince was using the small door ..."

"The man was present at the quarrel?"

"No, Your Majesty, the prince told him about it. Apparently the prince made a derogatory remark about Don Juan's social standing."

"You will kindly give me the exact words of the quarrel as they were reported to you."

"Yes, Your Majesty. But Your Majesty will remember that I can only repeat what a third person told me about it, a person, moreover, who was not present at the time of the incident. . . ."

"I am aware of that. Proceed."

"The prince told Don Juan he ought to know that royalty did not marry lowly born women and Don Juan made a motion to draw his sword."

"Did he draw it?"

"The valet did not know. But Don Juan is supposed to have replied that his mother may not have been of royal blood . . ."

"Yes. Go on."

". . . but that his father was a greater man than the prince's father."

There was a pause. Then the King said in a low voice: "Don Juan was quite right."

There was a licentiate of the name of Castillo at the university, an elderly man who wore spectacles almost half an inch thick. It was much easier to read the expression in his eyes than in those of the King.

"The prince said he was going to report this to Your Majesty", Honoratus Joannius went on.

"May God permit that the prince will have the opportunity. What were the relations between him and Don Juan in the days to follow?"

"They were somewhat strained, but there was no further quarrel."

"Was there any really serious quarrel between the prince and Don Alexander?"

"No, Your Majesty."

"The friendship between Don Juan and Don Alexander is a close one, is it not?"

"Yes, Your Majesty."

"There has been no quarrel between them?"

"No, Your Majesty."

The King sighed. "The prince has a most unfortunate character. It is perhaps natural that two . . . healthy young men should side against him."

Honoratus Joannius said in a tremulous voice: "I have no evidence for that, Your Majesty."

"Of course not", the King said dryly. Then, in a different tone: "Don Juan and Don Alexander discovered the accident. They gave the alarm. What happened?"

"Don Alexander ran to fetch Don García. Don Juan went down the stairs to see what happened. When Don García came down with Doctor Olivares and two lackeys they found him sitting on the stairs, with the prince's head in his lap."

The King nodded slowly. "Go on."

"The prince had a wound half across his head. There was much bleeding. Doctor Olivares had great difficulty in stopping it. Only when he had succeeded in this did he give orders to carry the prince upstairs and to his bedroom. There he was joined by Doctor Vega and a little later by Licentiate Deza Chacón, the Royal Surgeon. In the meantime Don García despatched Don Diego de Acuña to report to Your Majesty in Madrid."

Again the King nodded. He had sent Acuña back with the protomedicus Dr. Gutiérrez, Dr. Pedro Torres, and the surgeon Dr. Portugués. He himself followed a few hours later.

Carlos was not fully conscious, but all the doctors insisted that there were no disquieting symptoms and that they had no doubt of his recovery.

He did not trust their bland assurances but there was no way of disproving them. He had talked at length with Don García before he sat down with Honoratus Joannius alone.

"We must wait and pray", he said stiffly.

"Assuredly, Your Majesty."

The King rose and walked away to join the doctors again. Once more he received their assurances that there was no need for anxiety, no need whatever. He paid another visit to the patient and spoke to him without receiving an answer. He stayed over the midday meal, talked to Don Alexander and Don Juan, paid a third visit to the prince, who was still not conscious, and left for Madrid.

Eleven days later, on April 30, Don Diego de Acuña came racing to Madrid to report that the prince was very considerably worse. The doctors spoke of complications and feared that the brain was affected.

The King left for Alcalá at once, accompanied by the Duke of Alba, the Prince of Éboli, and Dr. Vesale. A few hours later all other members of the Council of State followed and with them all the grandees who had functions at court. They in turn were followed by their suites and retinues, with the result that the palace in Alcalá became vastly overcrowded.

Carlos' eyelids were swollen to such extent that his eyes were closed. His right leg was immovable.

On May 2 he became so weak that the physicians began to fear the worst. The King ordered that the prince be given the Last Sacraments.

He was conscious now and received the Sacraments reverently. At the end of the ceremony when the priests had retired, he beckoned Don Juan to approach his bed. Juan knelt down beside him.

"You are good", the prince whispered. "You . . . pray for me . . . perhaps . . . the saints . . . will listen."

Juan caressed the inflamed, swollen fingers. "I'll pray all I can, Your Highness."

As he rose he saw the King standing quite close by, at the other side of the bed, looking at him intently.

There was a Franciscan monastery in Alcalá. From then on Juan went there every morning and every evening.

Between April 30 and May 8 the King presided at no less than fourteen conferences of the doctors, with the Duke of Alba on his right and Don García de Toledo on his left.

On May 8 he was told that the prince would not live another day. For the last forty-eight hours he had been lying in a coma.

Philip bowed his head. After a while he asked: "Is there the slightest chance that the prince will regain consciousness before ... the end?"

"None, Your Majesty", declared protomedicus Dr. Gutiérrez.

"Thank you, learned sirs", Philip said dully. "I am sure you have done everything that could be done."

He walked away, and a few minutes later everybody knew that he was returning to Madrid.

The Duke of Alba had to help him enter the carriage. With his face in the shadow the King said: "Please stay until it is all over. I—I do not wish to see his agony."

Alba kissed his hand and remained standing, straight as a ramrod, till the carriage had rolled out of the park. Then, with his stiff, military movements, he went back into the palace.

There he found Don Juan, just back from his evening visit to the Franciscan monastery. The young man was in tears. Don Alexander had told him that the prince's end was near. He could not believe it.

"Even kings and princes are mortals", Alba said tonelessly. Somber, tall, hook-nosed, with bushy eyebrows and a graying beard the great soldier looked like the angel of death himself; and there were many thousands for whom he had been just that. But his voice was gentle as he asked: "Have I Your Excellency's permission to sit down?"

Bar sinister or not, Alba would never have sat down unasked in the presence of one with royal blood in his veins; nor would he remain covered, except in the field.

"I beg of you, my lord."

Alba sat down stiffly beside Juan. Even when he was dressed as he now was, in soft black velvet with a simple, rather old-fashioned ruff, he seemed to wear armor. Ruy Gómez, the Prince of Éboli, used to say: "I know Alba washes every day, which is more than can be said about many grandees I could name. But he always smells of iron and of blood." Somebody reported it to the duke, who coldly replied: "The Prince of Éboli would not know, of course, but that is the only perfume becoming to a man."

"It is good to see that the prince has a friend who weeps for him", Alba said.

There was not the slightest hint of malice in these words, and Juan knew it at once. Alba simply said exactly what he thought. He could be trickier than ten thousand foxes, but only in his own element, in war. He was no statesman, no politician, least of all an intriguer.

"The prince has no friends", Juan replied with equal frankness. "But he has had a most unhappy life. And I think—I think he trusted me. I hoped I would be able to help him."

Charles the Fifth's son, by God, Alba thought. And he hasn't been spoiled yet. He found himself wishing that Juan instead of Carlos were the royal heir, but frowned and banished the thought at once. He never tolerated insubordination, least of all in himself. But the thought was his fault, not Don Juan's. He rose. "I am going to the prince's room", he said. "Will you keep the watch with me?"

"I was going to do so in any case", Juan replied. "Now it will be easier."

Alba's grim mouth twitched. It was his nearest approach to a friendly smile.

They found the prince lying on his back, motionless. His nose had become pinched. His mouth was open. He was breathing stertorously.

Dr. Gutiérrez and Licentiate Deza Chacón were sitting in one corner of the room, and at a sign from Alba kept their places.

After two hours they were replaced by Dr. Torres and Dr. Portugués, and they again by Dr. Olivares and Dr. Vega.

Alba remained standing. Only Don Carlos could have given him leave to sit down, and Don Carlos was unconscious.

Blood and iron, Juan thought in the midst of a stream of prayers.

More than ever the old soldier looked like the angel of death. There was something almost preternatural about his forces of endurance.

For hours and hours there was no sound but the labored breathing of the dying prince.

When dawn came at last, pale and quiet as if the young day respected the end of a young life, Juan rose and walked over to Alba.

"I am going to the Franciscan monastery again", he whispered. "I want to try once more...."

The statue of black marble that was Alba came slowly back to life. Monastery. Franciscan monastery. The King had told him about that monastery, when in his painstakingly exact way he gave him all the detailed instructions for Don Carlos' funeral. The prior and the friars were to accompany the body to Madrid and with them fifty-two torch bearers, the rector of the university, the teaching body, the students; the nobility and the clergy, the guilds.

Philip had enumerated them all in a dry, matter-of-fact way; Carlos was as good as dead; the King had to think ahead, because he was the king. But a little later, when he gave orders to make his carriage ready for his return to Madrid, his voice had broken. And however much he tried to keep his face in the shadow, Alba had seen a sight he had never seen before: tears in Philip's eyes.

The Emperor had often showed his emotions; King Philip never did, and some people at court had begun to imitate his ways, posing as impenetrable, absolutely controlled men.

Philip in tears. It was a shock.

The young prince's death was a defeat, a terrible defeat for the King of Spain, and Alba had been ordered to fight the rearguard action.

"Won't you come with me, my lord?"

Come with him, what for? Ah yes, the monastery. Praying. The only thing left.

Alba nodded. He bowed respectfully to the still-breathing, unconscious body of the Prince and turned and followed Juan.

"Horses!"

How they all jumped when Alba gave an order. The two took only a small retinue with them—most courtiers were still asleep.

Juan showed the way.

Alba had a special liking for monastery churches, just as he preferred the regular clergy to the secular. Monasteries were the strongholds of God on earth, castles with walls and turrets against devil, demon, infidel, and heretic. When they reached the door of the church, he dismounted with the agility of a man half his age.

But Juan beckoned him aside and led him away from the church into the garden and from there to the cemetery. "This is where I have been praying", he explained in a low voice, pointing to a simple tomb. "That's where Fray Diego is buried. You know—the holiest friar they ever had here. They hope he will be canonized. An old man and a little girl from Alcalá have been cured by invoking his help."

Alba crossed himself and began to pray. As he prayed an idea came to him. He forced himself to finish his prayer, crossed himself again, turned, and stalked away, straight up to the rear entrance of the monastery, where he rang the bell. After a short while a friar opened the door.

"Alba", said Alba. "I wish to see the Reverend Prior on business of His Majesty, the King."

Two hours later a long procession approached the palace of Alcalá. First hundreds of people in all walks of life, summoned by the town criers and the incessant tolling of the monastery's great bell, rung only in an emergency. A large number of penitents, dressed in sackcloth, with hoods drawn over their faces. Then four Franciscans, carrying a body on a stretcher.

Just behind the stretcher walked, barefoot and dressed in hood and cowl, Don Juan de Austria and Don Alexander Farnese, Prince of Parma; next came the Duke of Alba, cap in hand; then Honoratus Joannius, the entire teaching body of the university, the students, a group of noblemen, the friars with their prior, the secular clergy, the guilds, and again hundreds of simple people. All was exactly as King Philip had ordered it for the funeral of the prince—all, except one thing: the body on the stretcher was not Carlos' body—it was that of Fray Diego.

The exhumation had taken place in the presence of the Duke of Alba and of Juan. The body was covered with a large sheet, but not the face, paper white and a little shrunken, but otherwise that of a man sleeping calmly rather than that of a corpse. There was not the slightest sign of decomposition.

The procession stopped in front of the palace. Fray Diego's body was carried to the sickroom, followed by Alba, Juan, Alexander, Honoratus Joannius, and the prior.

The stretcher was put beside the prince's bed.

Carlos was utterly unaware. He was still breathing, but his face looked much more like that of a corpse than did Fray Diego's. Dr. Gutiérrez and Dr. Chacón were watching.

The prior went up to the prince, took his right hand, and laid it gently on Fray Diego's chest. Then he stepped back.

Everyone was praying silently. But all prayers stopped when suddenly Carlos began to move. Very slowly he turned to his right side.

A few moments later he took a deep breath and then began to breathe quietly, regularly.

They were all staring at the prince, overawed, wide-eyed, and thus no one saw what no one had ever seen before or would see again: the Duke of Alba was trembling.

A quarter of an hour passed.

Dr. Gutiérrez made a move toward the patient's side. The duke's imperious gesture froze him. A quarter of an hour later he summoned enough courage to whisper: "His Highness is sleeping soundly."

The prior gently removed Carlos' hand from Fray Diego's chest. He gave a nod to the four friars who lifted up the stretcher and carried it out of the room. Only the duke, Juan, and the two doctors remained.

After six hours of sleep Carlos moved again and called out: "Juan."

Juan knelt down beside him. "Here I am, Your Highness." Then he almost cried out in his surprise. The swelling of the eyes had nearly disappeared.

"I can see", Carlos said weakly. "I had such a strange dream, Juan. I met a monk, a friar. He told me . . . I wouldn't die . . . this time."

## CHAPTER 12

THE BALL WAS OVER.

Ruy Gómez turned away from the door where he had been standing for almost an hour, taking leave of his guests and making each of them feel that the event had taken place for his or her sake alone. The art of kings, they called it. Well, they did not speak of him as of "Rey" Gómez for nothing.

He could relax at last. As he sauntered back to the ballroom he let his stomach muscles go slack. Never mind that little bulge now; as for the other one, under his chin, the beard protected it well enough and there was no need to watch it yet, although that, too, would come. He gave himself an appraising glance in one of the huge mirrors. Pretty bad; but it could have been worse, at two o'clock in the morning. Nothing, or not much that a good massage could not put right. And his hair was still black and curly; only the beard showed a few traces of silver. If only he were a little taller. Not as tall as Alba, of course—the King did not like talking *up* to a man—but as tall at least as the King.

The servants had begun to clear the tables, and he walked on. He disliked seeing a room in such a state, like a battlefield, with the scavengers carrying off the loot. Duchesses ate daintily, most of them, but dirty plates were dirty plates and evoked quite unnecessary feelings of disgust and equally unnecessary thoughts about human imperfections.

How few really elegant people there were in the world—elegant inside as well as outside. Like Ana. He must go and see how her headache was—if she really had one.

He sauntered up the stairs, scratched perfunctorily at his wife's bedroom door, and entered.

Ana was sitting in bed, propped up with cushions. She was wearing an ermine-trimmed night-robe and eating an apple. She was smiling.

"A very pretty picture", Ruy Gómez said. "You never had a headache, of course, did you?"

"Heavens no." She was munching away happily. "Sick of the faces. I knew the party was a success, so you didn't need me anymore. It was a success, wasn't it?"

"You arranged it, my dear."

She raised her beautifully drawn eyebrows. "You are becoming more Castilian every day, Ruy. Where will it end? But seriously, I wish you'd tell the King he should stop rushing the court from one place to another. Valladolid, Toledo, Madrid, Valladolid again, and now Segovia. It doesn't become a king to roam around like a gipsy, and you have no idea how difficult it is to give large parties always with a new staff, with different caterers all the time. . . ."

"You did marvelously well", he interposed. "Inez Infantado told me she couldn't understand how you do it."

"That I can well believe", said Ana. "Poor Inez; she has never known how to manage anything, including herself.

Did you see her dress? Apricot-colored silk at her age? And with the King present!"

"There is no law, yet, that we must all wear black. I'm wearing a purple coat myself, as you see."

"Yes, but it's *dark* purple. Besides, you can do almost anything. I don't know why."

"It's my charm, dear. Imported from Portugal. I shall never be Castilian, you know that." He sat down at the foot of the bed. "Not to a Mendoza like you", he went on. "Although the Mendozas came originally from the Vizcaya. And not to a pretty long list of names I could mention. To all of them I shall always remain the Portuguese, with an Italian title to boot."

"Philip made you Duke of Pastrana."

"Which was very gracious of him. He meant very well. So did you when you got him to do it. My dear, of course I knew. He'll do almost anything you ask him to do. I don't know why."

"It's my charm, dear—although I didn't have to import it."

"*Touché*. The trouble is: you are probably quite right. I sometimes wonder ..."

"I'm not going to ask you what about", she said quietly.

"I sometimes wonder whether Philip isn't in love with you."

She began to yawn. "Philip and 'in love'! Why, the only thing he's in love with is his duty. He is not even in love with himself—not really. Only insofar as he is the personification of his duties."

"Well observed", he said, nodding. "And I don't really mind that you let him make me Duke of Pastrana, and do you know why? Because you hardly ever use the title."

"I never disliked being Princess of Éboli", she said, with a shrug. "Especially as I know that it is annoying to many people."

"And because you have never ceased being Ana de Mendoza y de la Cerda", he added.

"Ana the One-eyed", she said, lightly touching the black velvet patch over her right eye.

"Looking at you," he said, "one feels that two-eyed women are vulgar. Such a display of eyes. We have been married six years—you are twenty-five now, aren't you? Your face is too long, your nose is too long, you are too tall, and you are more beautiful than all other women in the world. Dolores de Mondéjar is seventeen, all her features are perfect, she is a raving beauty—and next to you she looks like an absurd little sheep."

"About Philip", she said. "No, I do want to talk about him. The party was stiff and uneasy as long as he was present. Only when he had left did it begin to come alive. It's curious how he always affects people like that. Sometimes I can almost feel sorry for that little beast Carlos. How did he behave tonight?"

"Not too badly. He ate too much and drank too much, and he said a few frightful things to poor Inez Infantado. . . ."

"He will never forget that Infantado was in charge of the Queen's escort, when she came to Spain."

"Whatever his other qualities, His Highness has a very good memory. But I have seen him behave worse than tonight, I will say that for him. He didn't draw his sword, he didn't jump at anybody's throat, he didn't lock himself into the stable to torture and kill horses—"

"Oh, stop it, Ruy. Such a dreary young man. I really don't know why that holy Franciscan bothered to perform a miracle for him that time in Alcalá, when he was so ill—three years ago, was it? What has Carlos done in these three years to justify a miracle on his behalf?"

Ruy Gómez threw back his head and laughed. "Oddly enough I said that to the only man who seems to have a good influence on him. And I added that I could not very well see how this particular miracle could be used as evidence in Fray Diego's canonization process. It's a long time ago that I read it, but I seem to remember that any miracle used as evidence in the canonization of a saint must have done some good. And can one call it good if health is given back to a little monster who uses it to be a plague to many and a nuisance to everybody?"

"How very frank of you! If I had said such a thing you would have called me careless again."

"You are. Leaving a party like tonight's on such a flimsy pretext."

"I told you I was sick of the faces. Something should be done to stir them up. All they can think of is their own little circle, their marriages, their debts, their hunting, and their scandals. Such shabby little scandals too, nothing really outrageous at all."

"I'm afraid that is quite true." Ruy Gómez sighed. "Which means that all the work for Spain is left in the hands of the King and of one or two others."

"Meaning yourself and whom else?"

"Meaning myself and anybody who interferes with me."

"Meaning Alba."

"Meaning Alba."

"Dear Ruy! He will never really be dangerous to you. He isn't versatile enough. But I still think it was careless of you to be so frank about Don Carlos to—to whom, incidentally? Alexander Farnese?"

Ruy Gómez shook his head. "Alexander has no influence on Carlos. I mean his uncle—and Carlos' uncle—Don Juan."

"His Excellency! Dios de mi alma—he's only a boy, eighteen years old. Carlos is twenty. Oh, oh, I know you when you look like that. You think he's important, don't you?"

"My dear Ana, he's the stuff kings are made of—real kings."

"In that case", she said, "he won't live very long."

He made a wry face. "There's no need to be dramatic about it, Ana. Neither for you nor for the King. Philip knows how to keep a man under his thumb. In Don Juan's case it isn't in the least difficult. There's the little matter of his mother. . . ."

"The Emperor didn't marry her secretly, did he?"

"No, he didn't. That's just it, don't you see. The good lady is German by birth, and she's now married to a man called Kegel or something like that. He used to be an officer. Decidedly not a nobleman. The lady is living in Flanders and not behaving too nicely, from all we hear. All that could be arranged differently, of course, but why should it be? Don Juan has been accorded the rank of Excellency. He is not a prince. Old Villanueva addressed him as Your Highness once and was sharply rebuked for it."

"By Don Juan?"

"By the King."

"I see. But why do you attach so much importance to him then?"

He gave an indulgent smile. "Because one must look far ahead in such matters. The boy is extremely gifted. He can rise high—the King can afford to let him rise high, in the circumstances."

"What exactly are Philip's plans for him?"

Ruy Gómez shifted a little. "You have always had the gift of asking questions that one can't answer. I don't know. It's almost the only thing he never discusses with me. But that by itself is rather remarkable, don't you think? One fine day that young man will be a figure of importance in some way, blessed if I know in what."

"My nose may be too long", the Princess of Éboli said, wrinkling it charmingly, "but it cannot compare with yours when it comes to smelling out something like this. It's important, then, that this young man should belong to us and not to Alba."

"Alba seems to have taken some interest in him", Ruy Gómez said casually. "And Juan is having lessons in military history from him. Fairly regularly, I'm told."

"Why didn't you say so in the first place." Ana shrugged her shoulders. "I'll get him for us."

"Alba impresses him, of course", her husband warned.

"We are much more fun for a young man—if we want to be. You horrid old Portuguese intriguer, I believe all you really wanted was to arouse my interest in Don Juan."

"I came to inquire about your headache", he said gravely.

"Well, I am aroused. Don't worry. He is as good as ours."

This time it was he who raised his eyebrows. "What are you going to do?"

"I'm seven years older than he is", she mused. "And of course he may find that my face is too long and that I am too tall . . ."

"Don't you dare." He laughed.

She ruffled his carefully arranged hair. "Don't be silly", she said affectionately. "I never liked *young* men, you know that."

"Meaning that I'm getting old", he said. "And perhaps also reminding me that Philip is about my age."

She frowned. "You shouldn't say that sort of thing, Ruy; it bores me. You shouldn't even think it. It's the sort of game we play with others, not between ourselves."

"What a queen you would be", he said.

"Will you stop it? The Queen is a sweet thing, and I'm not surprised that Philip was so dreary tonight. He misses her. If I were he I wouldn't have allowed her to visit her mother, not even for a few weeks. God knows what old Catherine de' Medici is going to whisper into her ears."

"You're talking like Alexander Farnese."

"No, I am talking sense. I know what you're thinking of, naturally."

"Naturally", he said.

"But that little beast of a Carlos is still very much alive, and he is the firstborn. He may disintegrate, of course, but as things are now there is no real reason to suspect that he won't be king."

"His health is not too good. And miracles do not always happen."

"I grant you that. But the Queen is young and may still have a dozen children. Nevertheless I shall draw Don Juan to our side."

"You still haven't told me how."

"My dear Ruy, there probably isn't a single man in Spain who knows as many secrets as you do, but there is at least one you don't know. You mentioned Dolores de Mondejar as an example of outstanding beauty."

"I said that next to you she looked ..."

"Yes, yes, I know. Dolores is beautiful without doubt. But she's a mere wraith compared to María de Mendoza."

"What? Your little niece? Whom we used to call the Saint?"

"Yes. You haven't been in Pastrana for some time, but I have. She's fifteen now."

"What does she look like, I wonder. I remember her as a pale, little moonshine princess with thin arms and legs and eyes perpetually downcast like a nun's."

"You'll be surprised when you see her again. Now, you let me handle this in my own way. I know what I'm doing."

"Excellent", he said, rising. "I'll retire now, with your permission, my dear. It's very late, and I shall have a heavy day tomorrow. There'll be a sort of extracurricular council meeting at the palace. Just the King, Alba, and I, not the entire war council. Nevertheless the result may well be decisive, as far as the matter in question is concerned."

"Oh? What is it all about?"

"Trouble with the Turks. They're invading Malta."

"What a nuisance for you. Good night."

"Good night, Ana."

## CHAPTER 13

"THE PRINCE OF ÉBOLI has prepared a summary of the intelligence reports up to this date", Philip said. "Let's hear them."

Coldly Alba watched Ruy Gómez unfolding his papers. Intelligence reports were just the right kind of meat for the slippery Portuguese. He knew how to hire spies all over the world, and his shrewdness and cunning made him a master in the art of reading their reports. Secret agents were often as dangerous to their employers as to those whose secrets they were supposed to ferret out. As often as not, they were paid by both sides; and even when they were not, they almost invariably liked to increase their pay by delivering sensational information, and overplaying their own difficulties in obtaining it. Ruy Gómez would check and countercheck, consider the character of the agent, make allowance for natural errors, and piece everything together like a mosaic pattern. But who was going to check up on *him*? He was quite capable of coloring his material, even of suppressing that part of it that did not suit him. He could not go too far, of course. There were always the secret reports of the ambassadors or special envoys, which the King invariably read first, unless he gave them to Gonzalo Pérez. Pérez, the secretary of state, was an old secretary of the Emperor and had no liking for Ruy Gómez. Or so he said. . . .

"Your Majesty will remember", Ruy Gómez said, "that the Sultan's favorite son, Prince Bayazid, revolted against his father and took refuge at the court of the Shah of Persia, in Tabriz. That Shah Tahmasp received Bayazid with royal honors and swore he would be safe in his realm."

Why doesn't he start with Adam and Eve, Alba thought contemptuously. But then the Portuguese always loved the sound of their own voices.

"At the time we had hopes that this would draw the Sultan's interest eastward, at least for some time to come; and this belief seemed justified when we had news of an alliance on the part of Süleyman with the tribes of the Uzbeks around and in Samarkand. But that very alliance had an intimidating influence on the Shah, and when the Sultan offered him war in one hand or four hundred thousand pieces of gold for the surrender of Bayazid in the other, His Persian Majesty chose the gold. Bayazid was seized at the Shah's very banquet table and surrendered to the Turks. He was promptly executed."

But the King knows all that, Alba thought impatiently. By now they should be discussing the details of measures to be taken to counter the attack on Malta. However, let the Portuguese go on making a bore of himself.

"The Sultan is almost seventy years old", Ruy Gómez went on. "I have very reliable reports that he is suffering from dropsy. A Venetian agent saw him dismount before the Süleymaniye mosque; the old man had a spell of dizziness and almost fainted."

"Which agent?" the King asked impassively.

"Donnini, Your Majesty, the secretary of the Venetian *bailo*."

"You may proceed."

"It is now fairly certain—as much as anything Turkish can be called certain—that Prince Selim will be the Sultan's successor, the last surviving son of Roxelana Khanum, whose influence has been so strong over so many years. She has known how to eliminate the sons of other women, including the very gifted Prince Mustapha, the son of Gulbehar Khanum. Of her own three sons, Jahangir, the cripple, has never been seriously considered as a ruler, and his death, three years ago, seems to have been a natural one, which in the circumstances appears to be believable. With Bayazid killed, only Selim remains, and he is not likely to be a strong ruler. And that, I think, is one of the reasons why Süleyman gave the order to attack Malta."

Alba blinked. The sudden swerve from Turkish history to the event that mattered was a surprise. He almost asked why Ruy Gómez came to such a conclusion, but restrained himself in time. It was probably just what the Portuguese wanted him to ask.

The King, behind his heavy desk, remained silent, too, and Ruy Gómez continued: "The Sultan knows that Bayazid was extremely popular. Something must be done to divert the attention of his people, and the best way to do that is to gain one more of those victories that earned him love and admiration in the past. This is one reason. Another is the Princess Mihrmah, daughter of Roxelana Khanum. Reports involving the serail are notoriously unreliable, but

I have a letter from Simonides, who insists that the Princess Mihrmah has taunted the Sultan about being no longer able to give battle to the enemies of Islam. She was very fond of her brother Bayazid and has been wearing mourning clothes ever since his death. Next to her mother, Roxelana, her influence on her father has been supreme. And Roxelana herself is no longer so powerful. Simonides informs me that the Sultan has had the door to her apartments walled up."

Alba cleared his throat, and when the King looked at him he burst out:

"Your Highness' expositions are all very interesting, but we are not dealing here with the intrigues of the harem. The attack on Malta is quite simply the attempt on the part of Süleyman to gain the absolute hegemony in the Mediterranean. I submit that it is our task to stop it."

"Nothing about Turkish affairs could ever be called simple", Ruy Gómez said, smiling a little. "And no one knows better than the Duke of Alba how important it is to be aware of what is going on in the mind of the enemy. The Sultan needs a popular success. Malta, to him, is another Rhodes. He started his collection of military and naval laurels with the conquest of Rhodes. He wants to end it with the conquest of Malta. This is his swan song."

"Amen", Alba said dryly. "If it pleases Your Majesty we shall try to see that it is."

"Malta", Ruy Gómez said equally dryly, "is not Spanish territory."

"It is Christian territory", Alba growled.

Ruy Gómez smiled pleasantly. "Spain would soon be in a sorry way if we interfered in every war involving Christian territory."

"The Sultan", said Alba, "conquered Rhodes because no one interfered. The Venetians had an entire fleet in nearby

Crete but they wouldn't budge. Rhodes, after all, was not Venetian territory. What Your Highness is suggesting is in my humble opinion the policy of death for the Christian cause."

"The Venetians", Ruy Gómez replied, "have been at peace with the Sultan for forty years—and they have waxed rich on that policy of death. I can see no reason why Spain should be more Christian than Venice."

"Maybe Your Highness can't", Alba said. "I can."

"I see I must quote a higher authority than the doge to plead my case." Ruy Gómez was still smiling. "Perhaps my lord Duke remembers what Emperor Charles said when he was told that Rhodes had been taken? No? Then I may be permitted, perhaps, to refresh your memory. The Emperor said: 'Nothing in the world has ever been so well lost as Rhodes.' Surely, my lord Duke, there is no necessity to be more Christian—or more Spanish—than the Emperor?"

Alba's eyes narrowed. "I was the Emperor's humble servant before you were born, Your Highness, and if there is anyone who admires his genius it is I. But even he could make mistakes. And to leave Rhodes without help was one of them. There is no need to imitate the Emperor where he was wrong, when there are so many opportunities to do so where he was right. I cannot follow Your Highness on a speculative journey into the Sultan's mind. . . ."

"It is important, surely, what goes on in Süleyman's mind."

"Perhaps it would be, if we really knew. But speculation, however—brilliant, is not the equivalent of knowledge. Now I am a soldier—"

"All Europe knows that", said Ruy Gómez, bowing.

"And as a soldier I have only two ways of looking at this issue. Strategically it is quite clear that the Sultan wants more than just a cheap victory. Malta is far away from the Turkish coast, a small, rocky island whose conquest means little or nothing to the simple man in Constantinople or Smyrna. It means a great deal, however, to a strategic mind with a plan for making the Mediterranean a Turkish lake. Even now, with Malta still fighting, our ships must hug the coasts, to avoid the Sultan's fast caravels—to say nothing of African pirates. What will it be like once Süleyman is in command of Malta harbor? Even now that accursed man, Dragut, can dare attack His Majesty's towns in Sicily and pillage Naples as he did only last year. Give him Malta and His Majesty will have to double and triple his troops in Sicily, if we are not to lose it within a year or two. And tactically—"

"Please forgive me for interrupting, my lord Duke", Ruy Gómez said. "In matters tactical I must remain silent in the presence of a great soldier. But strategy is closely linked up with politics; and there I would remind you that direct Spanish interference may well mean out and out war with Turkey. And the Sultan can build a hundred ships for every sixty we have. Our last expedition ended in the debacle of Yerba and the loss of fifteen thousand men and of almost all the galleys taking part in it. Besides there is the financial element to be considered. Last year's revenues—"

"Revenues", interposed the King, "are not at present under discussion. I wish to hear the Duke of Alba's opinion about the danger of an out-and-out war with Turkey."

"In my opinion," Alba said at once, "such a war is the more likely, the easier the Sultan finds it to have partial successes. It would be dangerous indeed to think that he will be satisfied with the conquest of Malta. And, may I add, the Prince of Éboli has given us a timely reminder just now: the defeat of Yerba is still unavenged."

"When the Knights of St. John were attacked on Rhodes," Ruy Gómez said, "the Emperor did not interfere. The Sultan took Rhodes, but he did not attack us. When the Knights of St. John lost Tripoli to the Turks, we did interfere and we were beaten. Now these same knights are being attacked on Malta, and the Duke of Alba seems to be determined to have us interfere again."

Impassively the King said: "The Duke of Alba will give us now the military intelligence about the attack on Malta."

"According to the latest reports," Alba began, "the attack started on May eighteenth. The Turkish force consisted of almost two hundred ships. They landed almost five thousand janizaries, over seven thousand spahis, and another five thousand light infantry. The spahis were without their horses. Sixty-five heavy siege guns were landed on the second and third day of the siege. The landing was made outside of the range of the defender's guns; the siege lines were driven forward in the usual Turkish way: zigzag fascines. The siege guns began to fire on the fifth day. The first object of the Turks was the St. Elmo fort. A definite mistake, in my opinion, and not at all like the usual leadership of Pialy Pasha and Dragut. There is some talk that the new seraskier, Mustapha Pasha, is with the expedition. Perhaps the order is due to him. St. Elmo is the strongest point of the fortifications. It will take them a long time to reduce it to rubble."

"Seventeen thousand men in all seems very few", Ruy Gómez interposed.

"Seventeen thousand regular troops", Alba replied. "They have an additional twelve or thirteen thousand men if they bring in the sailors—and they always do when it's necessary. The defenders have about five to six hundred knights, thirteen hundred mercenaries, and no more than four thousand auxiliaries—mostly seamen and natives. Thus the Turks are five to one or thereabouts."

"How long can they hold out?" the King asked.

"Three months, I would say, Your Majesty."

"Five to one—and three months!" Ruy Gómez exclaimed.

"Perhaps even a little longer", Alba said lightly. "But not much longer—without help. Every one of those knights is worth ten men. And I know Jean de la Valette. He is an old man—almost seventy—and a Frenchman. But he is good. Besides, the Turks have still another adversary: Malta itself. All stones and rubble and very hard soil. Digging is difficult, especially as they can only dig at night, once they are within range of the guns."

"*If* I should decide for it," the King said, always in the same cold, even voice, "can we get a sufficient force there in time?"

"Yes, Your Majesty", Alba said firmly. "The tactical side of the issue is fairly clear. I have been working at it all night, and I have brought the plans with me."

Ruy Gómez winced. "What inimitable zeal", he said admiringly.

"Pialy Pasha and Dragut", Alba said grimly, "were in command at the Yerba *incident*; here is the opportunity to square the account with them. If we let them take Malta, the next step will be Sicily; and the one after: regular transports of arms to the Moriscos in Spain proper."

I have lost, Ruy Gómez thought. Very good tactics, to keep his strongest argument to the last. If we win, the Venetians won't have to worry about Cyprus for a long time. How Tiepolo will laugh at us for pulling his chestnuts out of the fire. He said: "I am afraid I have no further arguments, Your Majesty. My liking for the Sultan and all his works is no greater than that of the Duke of Alba. But I knew that he was for war, and somebody had to bring forward whatever arguments could be found against it, to help clarify the issue."

"Everyone knows that the Prince of Éboli always tries to be helpful", said Alba with heavy irony.

Ruy Gómez gave a slight bow.

The King almost smiled.

## CHAPTER 14

JUAN CAME RUSHING into Alexander's quarters like a whirlwind. "Great news!" he shouted happily.

"I have some, too", Alexander replied, beckoning his friend to sit down beside him. "But I don't know how to pass it on."

Juan was much too excited to take any notice. "War is certain", he blurted out. "I thought it would be, you thought it would be, but we didn't know, did we? Well, it's certain now. And I have written to the King. I tried to talk to him, but couldn't get past Gonzalo Pérez, not for a minute. Well, it's understandable; *he* has his hands full. So I've written."

"Who told you first?" Alexander could not help being interested. "You know what rumors are; you've been at court long enough."

"No one has ever been told mere rumors by the Duke of Alba", Juan said. "I couldn't have my lesson in military history today, and he was good enough to tell me why. He's a great man. The fleet is massing at Barcelona. Twenty-five thousand men. Don García de Toledo will be in command. I have written to him, too. I must go and tell Don Luiz—if I can get hold of him, that is. He's a member of the war council, and they have been working day and night. How long do you think it takes to sail from Barcelona to Malta?"

"I have no idea."

Juan told him. He told him about the different types of guns, too, which were mostly of relatively light calibre. "It's not we who have to do siege work; it's the Turks, and *that* will stop when we get there."

He was brimful of facts, figures, and enthusiasm. He pummeled Alexander's desk with his fists. His eyes were flashing, and he could not sit still for a minute.

"The King can't say no, can he? I'm eighteen. Younger men than I are serving in the tercios. Won't you come, too?"

Alexander gave a wan smile. "I'm afraid they won't let me go", he said. "You know how it is—they're responsible for my safety to my mother, that sort of nonsense. As long as mother is lording it over the Netherlands, they'll go on keeping me here. I very much fear they won't let you go either, though for different reasons."

Juan jumped up. "They must let me go. It's the Turks, Alexander, the Turks!"

"I know it's not the Peruvians", Alexander said dryly. "You Spaniards! Say the word 'Turk' or 'Morisco' or 'Arab' and you all begin to foam at the mouth. Well, perhaps it's understandable. They have given you a good deal of trouble for many hundreds of years. Even gentle Honoratus Joannius could not keep his temper when he was teaching us about them."

Juan shook his head. "Is it possible that you don't understand what this issue is really about? This isn't Turkey versus Spain. It is Muhammad against Christ."

"It seems to me", Alexander said, "that many Christians have a greater hatred for other Christians than they have for the infidels. Perhaps there is a good reason for that. After all, a Christian should know better. I had a long letter from my mother—"

"Fort St. Elmo is still resisting, according to the latest news", Juan interrupted. "A tiny ship of the knights slipped through the Turkish fleet on a moonless night and got through to Syracuse. D'you know what the seraskier did? He had the hearts of all fallen knights cut out and nailed on a cross, and he had that cross erected in the trench nearest to the citadel. But the Grand Master of the Knights gave him the answer he deserved. He had the heavy guns loaded with Turkish heads and fired them back at the enemy."

"We ought to be there", Alexander said. "I know it and want it as much as you do. But it can't be done. The only comfort is that it won't be always like this. Malta is only a beginning. There is a great deal of work to be done before we have finished with the Turks, and our time will come. Now, about that letter I had from my mother—"

"I am sorry", Juan said. "I seem to be able to think only of one thing at the moment. What does the princess say?"

"Oh, all kinds of things." Alexander sighed. "I suppose I'd better tell you. It seems that you are destined for a very great honor. Only I don't know whether you'll like it . . ."

"I? An honor? Surely the princess did not bother to write about me?"

"Yes, she did. She seemed to think that you know all about it, but I don't think you do. She is in constant correspondence with the King, as you know, and it seems that the King told her in one of his last letters that he has asked His Holiness for a red hat for Spain."

"Well, we ought to have another Spanish cardinal, don't you think? The French have more than we have. The Prince of Éboli said the other day it might be due to that unfortunate situation in regard to the old Archbishop of Burgos...."

"Maybe so. But the new cardinal is to be Don Juan de Austria."

"What?"

"It is a very great thing, of course, a very great honor for you", Alexander went on, looking past Juan and out of the window. The garden was in full summer glory. "They don't usually have cardinals that young anymore, Mother says. The King must have a very high opinion of you and—"

"Alexander! Alexander! You are not serious. You can't be."

"How did Honoratus Joannius put it? '*Relata refero.*' But that's what Mother said, and *she's* not indulging in rumors. She's as matter of fact as the Duke of Alba any time. I often think she ought to have been a man, though that's a disrespectful thing for a good son to say, I suppose. Come now, Juan, I thought you might not relish the idea, but after all ..."

"Never", Juan said in a strangled voice. "Never."

"Now be reasonable", Alexander pleaded. "It hasn't happened yet. There is no word so far that the Holy Father has agreed. But if he does, you can't very well defy both the King and the Pope, can you? And what's so bad about being a cardinal? You are a good Catholic, a much better one than I am—you are not in love with a girl, as far as I know, in fact you are so ... decent about that sort of thing, it often makes me feel you would be a good priest...."

At long last he looked at Juan and what he saw made him jump up. "Saints above, what is the matter with you? You are as white as the wall...."

"Never", Juan repeated. "Christ knows I want to serve him with every ounce of strength I have and as long as I live. But Christ is God and therefore omniscient, and that means that he also knows full well that this is not the way I can serve him best. I want to be his soldier, not his priest. He needs soldiers, too, doesn't he? This is not the will of my Lord; it is the will of the King, the whim of the King, the fancy of the King."

"Not so loud, Juan." Alexander looked at the door, which was not firmly closed.

"I don't mind anybody hearing what I said", Juan exclaimed. "I shall tell it to the King myself."

"Now I wish I hadn't told you...."

"I'm glad you did. There may be still time to set it right." And he fled before Alexander could say anything.

"Our dear Lord needs soldiers, too", Doña Magdalena affirmed. "It was a Roman officer whose faith he praised as greater than anyone's in Israel. And the first gentile to become a Christian was a Roman officer."

Juan kissed her hands. "You always have the right word for me, Tía, God bless you for it. But what am I to do?"

"You must go and see the King as soon as possible."

"He won't see me, Tía. I know. I tried so hard to see him because I wanted his permission to join the expedition to Malta...."

Doña Magdalena's heart missed a beat. "You *are* a little young for that, my dear."

Juan gave an angry laugh. "A little young for fighting against the Turks, when I've been trained for just that for years! But not too young to become a cardinal, when I know nothing about theology except what every Christian must know. Tía, how could the King think of such a thing? *Why* does he want it?"

She sighed. "My dear, no one knows what is going on in the mind of the King, not even Don Luiz, who always knew what was going on in the mind of your great father. But it is not surprising that the King has not found time for you so far. He is working far too hard as it is, Don Luiz says. He wants to see everything, be told everything, and sign every document himself. His day ought to be a week long. You must have a little patience. Try every day. He will see you in the end."

Juan tried. But Gonzalo Pérez watched over the King like a Cerberus, and Philip had canceled all social obligations where there might have been a chance to talk to him. Neither he nor the Duke of Alba answered Juan's letter.

And all the time galleons, galleasses, galleys, caravels, and frigates were being assembled in Barcelona; huge transports of foodstuff, arms, and ammunition arrived, and detachments of troops departed for the port from many places in Spain.

One such detachment, two hundred men, left from Segovia and Juan saw them marching past his window. Two young noblemen of his retinue were standing behind him, Don Juan de Guzmán and Don José de Acuña.

Suddenly Juan turned around and faced them. His eyes were burning.

"Friends," he said, "tell me: how loyal to me are you?"

Characteristically, the first inquiry about the whereabouts of Juan came from the King himself.

The young man's assumption that the King would not see him because the planned expedition against the Turkish invaders of Malta demanded all his time was far off the mark. True, he read every single list of men and material that the Duke of Alba and Don Jorge de Melito as the naval aide of Don García de Toledo laid in front of him; he read everything very carefully and initialed it. But the

Malta expedition was no longer first and foremost in his mind, in fact it was a thing settled and no longer to be discussed.

But the Duchess of Parma's reports were in about certain signs of unrest in the Netherlands; ulcers were forming there, and sooner or later something would have to be done. The duchess herself was half a man, but half a man might well be not enough for those Flemish squareheads. Detailed secret reports had to be seen to about the activities of Egmont and Hoorn, above all about those of William of Orange. Strange that such a garrulous man, so fond of making speeches, should be called "The Silent".

Reports were in from Paris and from London, where the young Queen seemed to play a strange role: so courteous in her letters to him, so upset about the various acts of piracy committed by what they were pleased to call privateers—and yet at the same time secretly encouraging those selfsame acts. The Flemings and the English—the two nations most difficult to understand. What pains he had taken to be on good terms with the English nobility in those lost years on their foggy island!

All the reports about Elizabeth were contradictory. No use blaming ambassadors and agents for it. The English as a whole were nothing but a mass of contradictions—polite and rude, peaceful and belligerent, stupid and shrewd. Perhaps Ruy Gómez was right when he said that the key to their character was the fact that England was an island.

But what then was the key to the Flemish character—except the fallen nature of man?

Letters from the Queen of the Scots, those dreary people still farther removed from the sun than the English and one of the first nations to succumb to the new teachings that seemed to spring up in the North like dragons' teeth.

The world was crumbling all around him and it was up to him to stop it. No one *really* knew why he was building the Escorial. Five years ago the idea had sprung to his mind; two years ago the work began that, God willing, would endure as the pyramids had endured—the very symbol of his will, square and firm, strong and unassailable, the House of God and yet also the house of the king. Even now he loved it, his child of stone in the Guadarrama Mountains. May the day come soon when he could live there, so near to God and the relics of his saints, with the incessant prayer of the monks warding off every evil thought, every unwise order.

But in the meantime here were Granvella's reports about the situation in the Vatican; Granvella was new at his post, which was not really an official one, but his reports made sense as always. The French influence was still prevalent with Pius IV; it would take a long time to convince him—if he could be convinced at all—that not only the Order of Calatrava but all Spanish Orders had to be cleansed of French superiors inflicted on them time and again. There was the definite danger also that the long quarrel between Spain and France about the precedence of their ambassadors at the papal court might be decided against Spain, and that at a time when Spain was the only country where all attempts to introduce heresy had been nipped in the bud.

In the circumstances it was not surprising that no answer had come as yet to his suggestion that the Pope should make Don Juan of Austria a cardinal. Well, the boy could wait, but Spanish honor could not.

And at that moment Philip's tidy memory sharply reported that Don Juan of Austria had not been present at this morning's Mass.

The King inquired.

He was told that Don Juan would be in the company of His Highness Prince Carlos and of the two young archdukes, Ernest and Rudolph of Austria, whom their parents had sent to the Spanish court to make sure that they were brought up far away from any potential contagion of heresy, now rampant in Austria.

But a messenger sent to Don Carlos' suite came back reporting that Don Juan had not appeared today and was believed to be unwell.

An aide sent to Don Juan's suite found it empty. His own staff did not know his whereabouts.

The King had Don Luiz Quixada summoned. Don Luiz Quixada—his head full of figures and data referring to the Malta expedition, about which he had conferred for several hours with the Duke of Alba—told the King that to the best of his knowledge Don Juan was with Prince Carlos and the archdukes and for the first time the King was seriously annoyed with him.

Aides were rushing about in all directions, but no one seemed to know anything and all that was found out in the course of half a day was that Don Juan de Guzmán and Don José de Acuña had disappeared as well.

In the afternoon the Duke of Medinaceli turned up with the first real news. He had got hold of a postilion of the royal mail who had seen three extremely well dressed young noblemen enter the mail coach in Galapagar, a village a few miles away. From the talk of the three young noblemen he had deduced that they intended to join the fleet in Barcelona.

There were almost half a hundred courtiers with the King when Medinaceli reported. The Duke of Alba's moustachios twitched a little, and the two young archdukes grinned broadly.

But the King remained very serious. "Don Pedro Manuel."

The best and most trusted dispatch rider was found in no more than a couple of minutes; he was commanded to follow the fugitive, catch up with him, and to deliver the message that the King demanded Don Juan's immediate return.

Not content with that, the King had a further dozen couriers sent directly to all Spanish ports on the eastern coast, each one with a written command of the King to return, with letters for the port authorities and special letters for the viceroys and governors of the provinces.

"He left no loophole," Don Luiz told Doña Magdalena later, "and the young rascal should be back in a week, at the latest."

Still smarting from the wound of the King's angry words he paced up and down. "Why didn't he give me a word beforehand", he growled. "At least I would have known."

"It was very foolish of him to want to join that expedition, I suppose", said Doña Magdalena.

"Foolish?" Don Luiz stopped. "Not at all. He's right. He's absolutely right. I would have done the same thing myself in his place. It's exactly what he ought to do. But he should have told me."

Doña Magdalena smiled. "I submit that it was very courteous and considerate of him not to tell you", she said. "If he had told you, you would have felt that you ought to tell the King, and you would have hated telling the King. He spared you that quandary."

"He did, yes. I'm afraid you are quite right. What are you shaking your head about now?"

Her smile broadened. "What a thing for a future cardinal to do", she said.

Mail coaches were first-rate sources of information. Every postilion jumping down from his seat for a stop at this town or that had a story to tell and never had to worry about finding at least a couple of good townsmen who would let him have a few goblets of wine in exchange for news. Now postilions arriving in Segovia, Galapagar, or Sepúlveda, and also at Valladolid, Burgos, Cordova, and Seville, found that there was one new topic of greater interest than all others.

The story of the flight of the King's young brother to join the army and fight the Turks made a lightning journey through Spain and in all directions at once.

The people loved it. Here was a young man—a young man? A boy, a child—who wasn't going to let anybody else do his fighting for him; *he* wasn't going to sit back and have a nice easy life of splendor; he was a chip off the old block.

There was no possibility of keeping the story secret, not with all the servants of the palace of Segovia talking to their relatives, to the caterers and wine merchants, to the jewelers and hosiers and tailors and shoemakers coming and going to satisfy the needs of hundreds of courtiers.

The only regrettable aspect was that it could not possibly last long—the King had sent Don Pedro Manuel to catch young Don Juan, and Don Pedro was the fastest man in Spain. Wagers were ten and even fifteen to one that he could get hold of the boy within three days.

"Has Don Pedro caught him?" was the first question every Spanish postilion was asked when he stopped his coach in front of an inn.

There was no way for three young noblemen to hide themselves for long, even if they chose to disguise themselves. The King's messengers were riding at top speed, twice as fast as a mail coach, and soon Don Juan would be unable to enter a town where the authorities had not been informed of his flight.

Much guessing went on about what would happen then. The mayor of a town or city could not very well arrest the King's brother, could he?

At long last, news came from the town of Frasno, eleven leagues from Zaragoza, that Don Pedro Manuel had succeeded in his mission; he had caught the young fugitive. But a day later there were arguments over wagers paid out too early. According to the latest information, Don Juan had flatly refused to obey!

Don Pedro had tried everything to make him change his mind, he even told Don Juan that the fleet had already left Barcelona and that there would be no ship for him. The only consequence was that Don Juan sent Don José de Acuña posthaste to the port to get hold of a ship; and this did not please Don Pedro, for the fleet was still there; so he rode off to get the help of the Count of Coruña, who had a castle nearby. But the only result of his visit was that young Bernardino de Mendoza, the count's brother, decided to follow Don Juan's example. And he was not the first. Everybody knew that a number of young Spanish noblemen, full of enthusiasm about Don Juan's idea, had left their parents' castles to join the fleet.

The proudest man in the palace of Segovia was Juan Galarza, who told all the servants—the King's, Prince Carlos', and those of the dukes—that it was he who had taught Don Juan the art of war and if only they left him alone he would show the Turks a thing or two.

At night Don Luiz Carillo, oldest son of the Count of Priego, and Don Jerónimo de Padilla left the palace without saying anything to anyone, and soon enough it became clear that they, too, were on the way to Barcelona. It was not long before they were joined by Don Gabriel Manrique, Don Diego de Guzmán, and Don Lorenzo Manuel.

A couple of days later it was reported that the Dukes of Villahermosa and Francavilla had entreated Don Juan to go back to Segovia, each of them brandishing a letter from the King, and that Don Juan had refused again. Now the Archbishop of Zaragoza was mobilized against him and arrived with half a hundred clerics and aides. Don Juan kissed his ring but stated emphatically that he was going to sail for Malta.

So impressed was the archbishop that he wanted to give him a detachment of five hundred soldiers to go with him "as it was not fitting that His Majesty's brother should be without a guard and the Kingdom of Aragón would be proud to supply it". This Don Juan accepted, if the troops would meet him at the quay in Barcelona.

By now Don Francisco Zapata de Cárdenas, Don Pedro de Luxan, Don Juan Bautista Tassis, and Don Gabriel Niño also had fled the palace of Segovia, and there were reports that the same kind of thing was happening all over Spain.

At the street corners and in the inns, in the palaces, castles, and homes, people talked of little else.

Letters arrived from the commanding officers in a hundred different places about volunteers streaming in, and the Duke of Alba was supposed to have said to the King that for the first time in his life he had more soldiers at his disposal than he knew what to do with.

The Viceroy of Catalonia had Don José de Acuña arrested when the young man tried to visit the port of Barcelona. He was detained with great courtesy before he was able to ascertain that the fleet was still in port, though very nearly ready to sail.

The Bishop of Barcelona went to see Don Juan and persuaded him to visit the famous monastery of Monserrat before he left for the war. To this Don Juan agreed, and now urgent messages were sent to the Benedictine abbot to keep his royal guest there as long as he possibly could.

The abbot did his best. He showed Don Juan all there was to see—among other things the sword and the dagger of Don Iñigo de Loyola, which he left in the church as a votive gift to the Queen of Heaven before he set out, in beggar's dress, to become first a holy hermit and then the founder of the Jesuit Order, almost exactly thirty-one years ago. He had died only nine years ago.

To have left immediately after Mass, breakfast, and sight-seeing would have been a grave discourtesy to his Benedictine hosts who proved indefatigable in arousing his interest, until, to their great relief, the viceroy arrived with the Archbishop of Tarragona and the Bishop of Barcelona to take the responsibility off their shoulders. With them came half the nobility of Catalonia who wished to be presented, and after many ceremonies and speeches an enormous procession went slowly back to Barcelona.

There Don Juan found that the fleet had left after all. He did not know that the last sails had disappeared on the horizon no more than an hour before he set foot in the great city. Neither did Don José de Acuña, whom he now met again.

But the whole of Spain was jubilant over Don Juan's reaction. Unperturbed, he declared he would leave for France, to get a ship there.

In despair the viceroy sent a courier speeding to Segovia. But the King had anticipated the situation. His own messenger arrived in Barcelona, and he could not have chosen a better one.

Juan gave a cry of joy when he saw Don Luiz Quixada.

But Don Luiz, haggard and tired from the strenuous ride, bowed ceremoniously and produced a letter with the royal seal affixed to it.

"A letter by His Majesty's own hand", he announced gruffly.

Paling, Juan, too, bowed, took it, broke the seal, unfolded it carefully, and read. The King ordered him to return at once, "under pain of his displeasure".

This was the end. The displeasure of the King meant immediate arrest. Juan knew that now he had the choice of returning voluntarily or of being brought back as a prisoner; that Don Luiz would either ride back with him as his friend and fatherly protector or as his guard. It was the end. The embattled island of Malta, so near to his spirit in the weeks past, now vanished beyond the horizon, became as remote as a star.

Back to Segovia he must go, to life at court, to receptions and a little hunting, to polite talk with jeweled ladies; and soon perhaps there would be an answer from Rome. . . .

Once more he bowed. "His Majesty commands", he said. "I obey."

Don Luiz smiled. The Duke of Francavilla embraced him, much relieved. Everybody was relieved; all faces were wreathed in smiles. They praised his courage, his steadfastness, the strength of his will.

"They have been very kind to me—at least to my face", he said bitterly, when he and Don Luiz were on the road again. "But now they will laugh. All Spain will laugh."

Spain did not laugh. Spain felt quite differently about a young man of eighteen who had resisted the King and all his might for almost a whole month practically singlehanded.

Juan was acclaimed by the people wherever he passed. He could not understand it. Here he was, returning meekly, the fleet sailing without him, and people waved and shouted and threw flowers as if he had come back from a victorious battle.

"We're not going to Segovia", Don Luiz told him. "The court is in Madrid."

When they arrived, they found that the King had left for the frontier to meet the Queen on the way back from her visit to her mother in Bayonne.

But Don Carlos was there, beaming with pleasure. "I never thought you would do a thing like that, Juan. By all the saints, you should have seen the excitement you caused. The palace was like an ant heap that somebody has upset with a stick, and my dear father was the most upset ant of the lot; yes, I know I shouldn't say things like that but that's how it was. I never laughed so much in my life. Here, take this ring. No one shall say that he has given pleasure to Carlos without having a reward. Take it, I say; I shall be furious if you don't."

It was a diamond ring, exquisitely worked by the great Jacome Trezzo. Don Luiz later estimated its worth at no less than eight hundred ducats.

Juan had never seen Don Carlos in such good humor.

"You caused a real fever, Juan, and a most infectious one at that. They all got the itch for this thing in Malta; four of my own chamberlains left overnight. I couldn't stand the sight of any one of them, so that's an added favor to be grateful for. I hope none of them comes back."

At court, too, everybody was full of praise.

Alexander hugged Juan and kissed him on both cheeks. "You're an intolerable person really, you know. One never knows what you'll be up to next."

Doña Magdalena smiled. "I am very proud of you", she said simply, and that was all.

But when, three days later, the return of the King and Queen was announced, Juan began to feel worried. He knew instinctively that all these people praised him because he had done something they had never dared to do: he had opposed the King.

No one could tell him how Philip would react not only to one act of insubordination, but to a whole chain. Don Pedro Manuel, the Count of Coruña, dukes and viceroys, archbishops and bishops—they all had carried the King's authority, and Juan had disobeyed them all, to submit only to an order of the monarch in his own hand, threatening him with the royal displeasure. People had been thrown into dungeons or sent into exile for much less.

Even Don Luiz was worried, much as he tried to hide it.

The royal progress appeared near Madrid on the afternoon of July 30, and many courtiers went out to meet them about three leagues from the city, led by Don Carlos and Don Juan.

"I wonder what he is going to do to you", Carlos murmured as the two cavalcades came in sight of each other, and Don Juan winced. By now he was sure that exile was the very least he must expect. One word from the King and he would disappear behind the walls of a monastery in a faraway province. He clenched his teeth. Perhaps that would be God's answer because he had shown himself so ungrateful when he first heard that the King wanted him to become a cardinal. Now he would be a simple monk instead, in a habit of rough wool, praying, fasting, living in absolute obedience to his superiors.

Well, what if it happened? A soldier could not choose where he was to go, and much of his life was spent in absolute obedience before he became a commander—and even then he had to obey the King—the King whom he, Juan, had disobeyed so flagrantly.

If he had to be a monk, why not be a good one?

And here was the royal couple, descending from the carriage.

Prince Carlos went up to kiss his father's hand and the Queen—the Queen smiled and beckoned.

Juan approached, cap in hand, knelt down, kissed the tiny French hand, and heard just above him the Queen's merry laughter. Looking up he saw the delightfully mischievous expression on her face.

The Queen said: "Well, and how did you find those terrible Turks, Don Juan? Are they brave fighters? How many of them did you kill?"

Very red in the face Juan rose. "Unfortunately, Madame, I was not allowed to meet a Turk", he said bitterly.

Before he knew what happened to him he found himself embraced by the King. Philip's beard, the gold now well mixed with gray, was pressed against his cheek.

"Patience", the King whispered. "Give me a little more time. I know now what your vocation is. I shall soon have to send a fleet against the pirates in the Mediterranean. You will be in command. I promise you. Now keep your face under control. No one must know what I have told you."

When the King released him Juan stood stiff and erect like a soldier on parade. On the way back to Madrid he kept complete control over himself. When Don Carlos asked him eagerly what the King had said to him, he replied: "His Majesty has been most gracious."

But when at long last he was alone with Don Luiz he could contain himself no longer and told him everything. "My brother is the best, the noblest, the most magnanimous king who ever lived. I'll gladly lay down my life for him."

Don Luiz thought of the past few weeks, when swarms of young nobles had had only one idea: to imitate the example of the King's magnificent young brother. They had chosen him as their ideal, and they would one day serve him with that same fervor, that same wild, upsurging enthusiasm which he now had for the King. Almost overnight they had been transformed by this young man's headstrong action. And it had gripped the whole country and had held it in suspense. Juan was now the most popular person in the whole of the realm, and the King knew it.

The King, Don Luiz thought, was a great statesman.


## CHAPTER 15


PRINCE CARLOS DID NOT SEEM to mind his young uncle's new popularity. Up to a point it even amused him. "Now they're imitating your hairstyle", he jeered. "The next thing will be that they'll dye their hair as blond as yours. I shudder to think what they'd do if you had gone and conquered Malta."

But there was no need for that, fortunately. The Turks had broken into the fort of St. Elmo at last, after almost six weeks of siege. They found only a few wounded men, and even they would not give up but fought them, propped up in chairs. The Turks killed them, hacked large crosses in their chests, and threw the bodies into the bay to let them drift to the citadel on the other side.

But the defenders in the citadel were cheered when they found out that Pialy Pasha was wounded; that the terrible Dragut, the Sultan's most daring naval commander, had had his skull shattered by rock splinters and had died soon afterward.

Fierce resistance continued, although week after week passed with no help appearing. The Turks brought no less than seventy pieces of heavy artillery into position against the citadel, including three huge "basilisks". The cannonade went on day and night. They tried to haul galleys overland to launch them in the harbor behind the fortifications and thus make a combined land and sea attack. The knights made a sortie and killed the crews to the last man.

Mining was almost impossible in the rocky earth of the island, but the seraskier insisted on it and it was done. An explosion shattered one of the main bastions, but when the Turks attacked the defenders were ready for them.

Half a dozen attempts to break the enormous chain across the inner basin were warded off by Maltese swimmers.

A mass attack, led by the seraskier himself, failed miserably, and almost cost the life of the last of the three Turkish leaders. With Dragut dead and Pialy Pasha nursing his wound on board his flagship, the fate of the entire expedition depended upon Mustapha Pasha.

He was rearranging his forces for a further assault on the castle of St. Michael when he received the news that a Christian fleet had arrived off the north of the island.

He gave orders to burn all siege engines as well as all ships that could no longer be manned—forty of them. All but twenty-four heavy guns were brought back to the ships.

Victory flags were flying on the towers of St. Michael and St. Angelo.

And still Mustapha had not had enough. He sailed out of sight of the city, turned east, and—made a landing on the eastern shore to try to beat the Spanish troops on their way to the city. The attempt was a failure, with heavy losses for the Turks, and now at last they withdrew for good.

A few hours later Don García de Toledo swept into Malta harbor with seventy ships, flags flying.

And this was the first real defeat of regular Turkish troops and a regular Turkish fleet.

For once old Süleyman had not gotten what he wanted. It remained to be seen what he was going to do next.

"Ah well, we seem to have done quite well without you", was Don Carlos' comment to Juan.

Juan smiled politely and said nothing. He felt immune against the prince's pinpricks, now that he was surrounded by people who showed their respect for him, and some of them in the most flattering way of all: by imitation. It was quite true that the "Austrian hairstyle" was much liked by young Spanish noblemen—a parting on the left and the hair brushed upward. There were some who tried to imitate his way of dressing as well. He loved strong colors and, fortunately, so did the Queen. Her influence first and foremost brought it about that many courtiers again dared to dress in colors other than black.

He did not have to bother too much about Don Carlos. The Prince had made himself very independent lately. Either he went out in the company of a few valets, and no one seemed to know where he went, or he occupied himself with his marriage problem, as he called it. His mysterious excursions caused a good deal of acid comment, but Juan never heard anything definite, and in any case the ladies at court were easily malicious.

Carlos' marriage problem, on the other hand, was rather complicated. Everyone knew that Portugal had sent out feelers about the marriage of the prince with the Infanta Juana. She was beautiful, with her long, golden tresses, and she was kind and devout. But she was also ten years older than the prince—over thirty.

Catherine de' Medici had whispered into the Queen's ear that her second daughter, Margaret, was just the right choice for Carlos.

"Meaning that if the King dies, Spain will still have a French queen", Alexander said. "She knows what she's doing. She'll probably succeed, too, you'll see. I'll bet all her necromancers and soothsayers are working on it this moment."

From France also came the third possibility: the widowed young Queen of Scotland, Mary Stuart. Not a mere princess or duchess, a queen, and with very legitimate aspirations to the throne of England as well. And she was only three years older than Carlos.

The fourth possibility was the Archduchess Anna of Austria.

The houses of Braganza, of Valois and Lorraine and the imperial house of Habsburg. This was not an easy choice to make, and Carlos spent a great deal of time comparing the pictures of the royal and imperial ladies sent by eager ambassadors; pictures painted by the greatest artists of the time and, as each ambassador in turn swore, absolutely life-like and not in the least flattering to the subjects.

Portugal had its lure. His own mother came from there, and there was great wealth in Portuguese India. Mary Stuart meant a personal union between Spain and Scotland, perhaps between Spain and all the British Isles. And the granddaughter of Emperor Maximilian—why, a son from such marriage would be emperor again, surely, as his grandfather had been, before he had given away his throne for a monastery cell. An emperor—not merely a king of Spain.

Carlos knew that his father had never recovered from the fact that the Electors had chosen not him but Ferdinand to be emperor after Charles V. From that came Philip's deep aversion for anything German—including the Flemings, the Netherlanders.

He knew also that some kind of negotiations were already going on with Lisbon, Paris, and Vienna. He said to Juan: "My father is juggling with all my brides. How lucky that he can't marry them all...."

Hobbling up and down his suite of rooms he weighed his chances and divided Europe anew day after day. After a few months he dropped only one of the four ladies: the infanta. Too old.

That day he went down to the stables, ordered everybody out, closed the door, and slowly and painfully killed twenty-two horses.

Not the largest, perhaps not even the richest, but the most delightful house of any in the city was that of Don Ruy Gómez de Silva, Prince of Éboli, not far from the Gate de la Vega and very near the Church of Santa Maria Almudena. Ruy Gómez had houses in almost all important Spanish towns, and those in Valladolid and Burgos were much bigger than this one. But then, Madrid had been the capital for only a few years, and the Ébolis were too busy socially to bother about enlarging their house there. Or so they said.

In fact, the princess had suggested buying a new site and building a house three times bigger, but Ruy Gómez only said one sentence and she gave in. "My dear Ana, when one is living very near the King it is usually better not to display too much splendor; lightning always strikes the highest structures, I'm told."

Juan enjoyed the hospitality of the Ébolis more than any in Madrid. "Ruy Gómez is a great man", he told Alexander. "I think he is the most puissant man after the King."

"Oh, oh." The Prince of Parma grinned. "What about your great friend Alba then?"

Juan began to fiddle with his ruff. "The greatest soldier", he said, "is not necessarily the greatest statesman."

"I can hear Ruy Gómez talking."

"Do you mean I am not capable of having thoughts of my own?"

Alexander pursed his lips. "Didn't Ruy Gómez say that before you said it?" he asked innocently.

"I don't know what you've got against him. He is of course a much more subtle man than the Duke of Alba." Juan's ruff was being maltreated again.

"He must be—as he seems to have taught you the art of being evasive. Come now, admit that you like going there so much because of the princess rather than the prince. And she *is* a very lovely lady, I grant you that."

"She is a very *great* lady", Juan said stiffly. "Both she and her husband have been extremely kind to me."

"You're unsufferable when you're prim", Alexander declared. "Though it's not as often as it used to be. They seem to loosen you up a bit. Maybe it's all to the good. You'll be there tonight again, won't you? I had to excuse myself. Don Carlos wants to play tonight—El Clavo, of course. If he were as good at it as he is keen, he would win millions."

"He usually loses, doesn't he?"

"Yes. And then he goes and borrows money to pay his debts. He borrowed a hundred ducats from his own barber last week."

"From his barber!"

"Horrible little fellow, too; he often accompanies him on his—nightly adventures. Well, give my respects to the Ébolis, and tell them I would have much preferred to be at their hospitable house, rather than trying to lose to Don Carlos."

"Trying to lose, you say?"

"Certainly. He gets so furious when one wins, and I'm not greedy enough to forget that he may be, after all, the King of Spain."

They played El Clavo at the Ébolis too, at least the older people did, after dinner. Don Gaspar de Quiroga, Archbishop of Toledo, was watching the game with some amusement when the princess came up to him, dazzlingly beautiful in a dress of purple silk. The patch over her right eye was purple too, and a large chain of emeralds around her neck encircled her in a ring of green fire.

"Perhaps you would like to join the game?" she asked lightly.

"No, my child. In fact, I must go soon. What an excellent dinner you gave your guests! That game pie will linger on in my memory. Oh, oh, Don Mateo has lost his best chance", he added in a low voice. "He ought to have played the king."

"In any case you don't object to a little game", the princess said, smiling.

"Oh, dear me, no. I object to it when a man plays for stakes higher than he can afford, which includes the man who risks money that he needs for any essential purpose. But otherwise he is entitled to back his skill or his opinion with his money—within limits, of course."

"Limits", Ana repeated. "I often think it is the saddest word in our language—and the most annoying."

"Ah, but you are wrong", the archbishop said cheerfully. "And you forget that I knew you as a child, Ana. I remember a day when you ate fresh plums without imposing any limits on yourself. . . ."

"I confessed that when I was very young. Surely it is wrong to hold it against me when I was given absolution so long ago."

"There you are", the archbishop said, chuckling. "Now you can see what it leads to when punishment is not kept within limits."

"I really should know better than to fence with a theologian on his own ground. But I'll keep in mind what you said about gaming. Though I'm not at all sure you are not letting us poor people indulge in sins in order to make heaven more exclusive."

"Ana, you are incorrigible." The old man rose. "I really must go now. Give my love to Ruy. I don't want to disturb him."

"But I almost forgot what I came for", said the princess, while she passed a long, beautifully manicured finger over her eyepatch. "Here is someone I want to present to you— she arrived only an hour ago from Pastrana."

The finger now beckoned urgently to a slender little figure a few steps away, and the figure moved forward into the light of a huge candelabrum, a very young girl in what might well be her first evening robe, all white and glittering.

"My niece María de Mendoza", the Princess Éboli said, and the girl curtsied and kissed the archbishop's ring.

"Enrique de Mendoza's daughter", the archbishop said wistfully. "How well I remember your father, my dear— and your dear mother. So you are living in Pastrana now?"

"My aunt is very gracious to me", the girl said.

"I'm sure she is. Are you going to stay in Madrid long?"

"I don't know, Your Grace."

"Pastrana is a little too rustic for a girl of her age", Ana said quickly.

"I see." For a moment it looked as if the archbishop were going to comment on that. But when he spoke it was only to add a few friendly words of leave-taking.

Ana's finger indicated dismissal to her niece. The girl saw it, but she did not budge. Instead she looked at the old man entreatingly.

"Yes, my child?"

"I ... would Your Grace give me a blessing?"

As he was lifting his hand he saw the table with the players. He frowned a little and quickly stopped the girl from going down on her knees.

"We had better go outside for that", he said gently and led her away to the hall. Waving to the players, Ana followed slowly.

The hall was empty except for two lackeys who knelt down when they saw María kneeling. Ana remained standing in the door, her hands folded.

The archbishop spoke his blessing, his wide sign of the cross encompassing the servants. Courteously he helped the girl to her feet. As he did, she could hear him murmur: "Keep your heart clean, my dear, and all will be well."

Then only did he seem to see the princess. He bent his curly white head, waved jovially, and departed, his long robes swishing. Outside there were shouts for his carriage.

"He's a wonderful old man", Ana said. "I'm devoted to him. Such a dear. Now come, María; I must introduce you to the other guests. What a shame you arrived so late."

"A wheel was loose and we had to stay for hours at—"

"Yes, yes, you told me. Come now."


"This is Antonio Pérez", said Ruy Gómez, and Juan saw a smiling young man bowing to him, thirtyish, with flashing black eyes and flashing white teeth. "He is His Majesty's new secretary of state."

"Yes, Your Excellency", confirmed Pérez. "This has been my first day in office, and that's why I am so late. To be here is a wonderful way of concluding it. But then, in my life the good and the bad things always seem to come bunched together."

"The seven meagre and the seven fat years", Ruy Gómez said. "Our secretary of state has just been married, too."

Juan congratulated him, and Pérez flashed his eyes and teeth again, bowed, and took his leave.

"A very capable man", Ruy Gómez said warmly. "He's the son of the late Gonzalo Pérez, of course."

"But—but Gonzalo Pérez was a priest", Juan stammered.

"Assuredly, although I would say that he was a better secretary of state than he was a priest. As for friend Antonio, he was born three years before his father was ordained. Gonzalo was not married of course, but the Emperor, *your* dear father, legitimized the child by fiat. He was very fond of Gonzalo as you probably know, and he wanted to clear away all obstacles for Antonio's career. This sort of thing isn't done very often—but it can be done, you know." Ruy Gómez spoke almost casually, but Juan could not help sensing a certain emphasis on the last sentence.

"Even so His Majesty hesitated for some time before giving the son the office of the father", Ruy Gómez went on after a moment. "Friend Antonio is young and good-looking, and he had a great deal of success with the feminine world. It took some time before we could convince the King that this did not exclude very real political talent—one might even say that it demanded just that."

Juan laughed dutifully.

"The best way of convincing the King is by giving him facts", Ruy Gómez added. "Now that Antonio has got himself married—to Doña Juana de Coello Bozmediano, a charming lady and wealthy, too—he has given tangible proof of a change of heart. So all is well. The boy is brilliant, and it would have been a pity if he had been passed by just because of a few little affairs. Ah, here is Ana."

"Not only Ana," said the princess, "but also a lady who has been an admirer of yours for a long time, Don Juan. Permit me to present my youngest niece, Doña María de Mendoza."

Things always happened in this house, and they happened so quickly that one scarcely had time to concentrate on any one of them. The Ébolis were *living*, really living. A new secretary of state—nice-looking man, too. And he was born out of wedlock, but legitimacy was given him by imperial decree. By now Juan knew Ruy Gómez too well not to feel that he had been told that story for a purpose.

Perhaps the King could do for him what his father had done for Gonzalo Pérez—although, of course, in his case it probably involved a good many more issues. He would be a royal prince, not a mere Excellency.

But he had no time to think, because here was a young lady he had to bow to, to be polite to, and it was a bother.

No, it wasn't.

Once in a hundred years God in his goodness created a human being so perfect that the sight made all fallen creatures gasp in wonder. There was no room in such a case for mere admiration, however profound; nor were there means of comparison.

This gleaming, white thing, this elfin apparition, had nothing to do with earthly things. Juan knew that he would never be able to describe her to anybody; one could not call her a girl, for there were other girls; and she had nothing in common with them. The loveliest words he could think of, like fragrance, radiance, melody, and the spirit of spring, were clumsy sacrifices before her altar. At once he understood why the great knights in tales like *Amadis of Gaul* risked their lives ten times over for a smile from Angelica, Melisendra, or Oriana.

When he went to Don Ruy's house he had been quite satisfied with his appearance and his dress of dark green velvet and gold. Now he felt like a beggar in rags and a boor to boot. He was trying to collect himself, to say something, however inadequate. His mind, groping for a straw, fastened in despair on the words of the Princess Éboli, who herself was no more than a background of purple and green for the vision before him.

"An admirer of mine for a long time", he managed to repeat. "Never before have I heard of a seraph in high heaven admiring a mere mortal."

The vision curtsied and gave a shy smile for which Amadis of Gaul would have gladly given his sword arm. "I prayed for you when you were on your journey to Barcelona, Your Excellency."

He felt himself blushing. "I find it hard to believe", he said with an effort. "Surely your prayers should have been heard."

"But they were", the vision said. "I prayed that you would return safe and sound so that you could lead Spain when your time came."

"Bravo, María", said the princess.

Now she is going to say, Spoken like a Mendoza, Ruy Gómez thought.

"Spoken like a Mendoza", the princess said, and Ruy Gómez winced a little. "The orchestra is playing again in the ballroom", he said. "Will you honor my niece by being her partner for her first dance in Madrid?"

"That", Juan replied, "is like asking me whether I want to go to heaven."

"What a pair", Ruy Gómez said when the two young people were out of earshot.

"I didn't coach her", Ana told him. "I know you don't like me to praise my family, but—"

". . . but she is a Mendoza. I know. In any case she seems to be doing very well. Mind you, I don't think all this is necessary. I have been working on him myself and told him a few things. About Pérez, for instance. And about the necessity of having good friends who will remind the King to keep his promise to him—the command of the fleet, you know. I don't know whether there is any need to bring the girl in . . ."

"Perhaps you don't", Ana said. "I do. My dear Ruy, you are by far the most subtle man I know; yet even you are sometimes a child."

CHAPTER 16

"*Habemus papam*", Don Luiz Quixada said, beaming, as he came in.

"At last", Doña Magdalena exclaimed. "At long last, thank God. Who is it, my dear?"

"It has taken the conclave a long time", Don Luiz agreed. "Let me see. We first heard about Pius the Fourth being near death back in December. He fell ill on the fifth and died on the nineteenth, no, the funeral was on the nineteenth just before Requeséns arrived in Rome. The King was in a great hurry to send him, as if Granvella were not able to cope with the situation. The conclave started on the nineteenth, in the evening. And it's taken them until the seventh of January. Nineteen days."

"But who is it? Not Farnese? No? Morone? Orsini? Gonzaga is too young, I suppose, and our Spanish cardinals.... Oh, why are you keeping me on tenterhooks? Who is it?"

Don Luiz drew a miniature portrait from his wide belt. "Here he is", he announced, smiling. "This has just arrived by courier. The King gave it to me for safekeeping. I don't know who painted it, but it's the kind of picture that makes one feel certain it must be lifelike."

Doña Magdalena saw a vision of gleaming white, the apparition of an old, old man as pale as paper, with a long-flowing, silvery beard, a strong, Roman nose, and a forehead like the bastion of a fortress.

"White", she said. "A Dominican! He must be ..."

"Ghislieri", her husband nodded. "Michele Ghislieri. He comes from a poor, simple family in Savoy."

A white pope, she thought. No purple and no scarlet, just white, as if he had just been baptized. The white of the Dominican habit, white for purity. A strong face. A severe face. The face of a man bent on setting his house in order.

"I can imagine some who won't like it much", Don Luiz said. "Ippolito Farnese will be disappointed. And Morone. And not only because they must have had hopes for themselves. There are some who don't like a pope to belong to an Order. And some of the great names may find it a little difficult to bow the knee to a man who in his childhood looked after his father's sheep."

"And why not? That's exactly what he'll go on doing now", she replied.

"Well, yes. You know *I* wouldn't contradict that. But think of the names of the Electors: men like d'Este, Boncampagni, Colonna, Orsini, Sforza, Medici ..."

"But they elected him, didn't they?"

"Yes—and even Farnese was for him, when he saw that he himself had no chance. But the man who seems to have brought about the final decision was Cardinal Borromeo—a very great man, I believe."

"What did the King say?"

Don Luiz gave an almost imperceptible shrug. "He said: 'I must write to the Pope at once.' "

"No other comment?"

"You know Philip as well as I do."

"Which means: very little." She gave a sigh. "I sometimes wonder whether Philip knows Philip well, or whether he does not shield his own heart against his own mind and both against his own will."

"He is not an easy man to understand", Don Luiz agreed. "And thus many little minds feel free to judge him according to their own petty standards. There are moments—and they are getting more frequent lately— when I am heartily tired of life at court. If ever there is an expedition against the Turks again, I'll join it, if I can."

"Forgive me then", she said, with a smile, "if I wish and pray that there won't be another in our lifetime. Do you think there will be?"

"Not yet in any case. From the latest news we have, the Sultan has been greatly affected by the report about Malta. There was no excuse for that failure, no treason, no incompetence. The knights proved to be the better *men*. A difficult thing for the Sultan to swallow—that there could be better fighting men than his Turks."

"You think he is too old to think of revenge?"

"No. If I know anything about Süleyman, he will give in only to death itself, not to old age or to anything or anybody else. He *may* think that it was *kismet*, fate, written in the Book of Life. That's the way the Muslims say that something is the will of God."

Her face lit up. "Then perhaps he won't go to war again after all."

"Perhaps not. Unless . . ."

"Unless?"

"Unless he wishes to test whether or not it is the will of God. But if he does, he won't attack Malta again. He will probably try war on land. The Emperor at present pays him a very large sum of money every year. A 'present of honor' he calls it. The word 'tribute' doesn't come easily to an emperor's lips. Even so—the Sultan will find a reason. A ruler always can, if he looks hard enough."

"Ah well—" Doña Magdalena gave a contented little sigh. "—All in all, it doesn't look as if you would have to go on an expedition, does it?"

"It is not likely. Unless the King gives me leave to fight under the Emperor—if the Sultan attacks him."

"Spain needs you", she said quickly.

He smiled. "If it is the will of God that I should die fighting, I'd much rather die fighting for Spain", he said.

"Don't talk of your death, my dear, I beg of you."

"Now this is not like you", he said, putting his arm around her shoulder. "As Christians we know, surely, that everyone of us owes God one death. Would you rather have me die of a long-drawn, painful illness like poor old Pablo Vejar? However, I just proved to you, didn't I, that there is little likelihood of war in our part of the world. Also I'm not particularly keen on joining the Emperor's forces in case of war, unless Juan does—and I don't think he will, not after having been promised the command of the Mediterranean fleet. Where is he, by the way?"

"At the house of the Ébolis, as usual."

He looked up. "You do not approve of that?"

"I don't know."

There was a pause.

"We agreed before", he said thoughtfully, "that Ruy Gómez has too much influence on the King in some ways. But also that it is not really a bad influence. The Duke of Alba is all too rigid and Ruy Gómez all too elastic— perhaps the King needs them both to keep his own mind in balance. Juan can profit from a friendship with Ruy Gómez."

"And vice versa", she replied dryly. "Besides, I wasn't so much thinking of *him*."

"She is a great lady. The Mendozas ..."

"She would be a great lady if she were less volatile and capricious. You never know what she will do next, and I could swear she doesn't know herself. I think she is quite capable of dropping a very great matter for a very small one that has suddenly taken her fancy. It is a pity, really. The woman could be great, but for that. As it is, she will never be great—and she may not even always be a lady."

He shook his head. "We haven't been at her house very often ..."

"Of course not, my dear; we are much too stodgy for her."

"Maybe we are. But Juan is young. They give parties for him and he's enjoying himself."

"He is also there when they are not having parties."

"You mean they want to draw him into their camp politically?"

"They have done so. He is under their influence, and it hasn't done him much good, I fear."

He smiled good-naturedly. "You're not by any chance a little jealous of the princess, are you? The boy is the apple of your eye . . ."

"Don Luiz," she said energetically, "I'll have you know that you did not marry a fool. I'm not jealous of anybody. I'm jealous *for* Juan—for his well-being, his career, and most of all for his character and soul. I don't think the atmosphere at the palace Éboli is good for him. They flatter him there, and God knows he's vain enough as it is. Now why do they flatter him? What do they want of him?"

"Surely," he said, "Juan is too young to be of much help to them. If there is one man who need not worry about his position at court it is Ruy Gómez. May I have that miniature back, my dear? I must give it to Don Cristóbal to put it away."

"Let me have one more look. A pope in white—what a wonderful thing. I wish they would always wear white."

"We can't have only popes who are Dominicans", he said, chuckling.

"No, of course not. But it would be such a beautiful innovation all the same. I scarcely know anything about him, but it's a strong face. They should have chosen him on the first day and not after three weeks. I'm talking nonsense, I suppose. I only wish . . ."

". . . that all popes would wear white."

"No, that's not what I meant now. I wish *he* would exert an influence on Juan."

## CHAPTER 17

GLIMPSES WERE ALL Juan could get of María de Mendoza whenever he went to the house of the Ébolis—and that was the only place where he could get that much. The princess had no intention of presenting her at court as yet. "It is a little early for that", she told him.

Thus María would not visit any of the other great houses of Madrid, except those of close relatives, so there was no chance of meeting her anywhere else.

Even so Juan felt that the princess was right. The more precious the jewel, the more thorough the custody. Within six months he managed to see her three times, and never alone, of course. If the princess herself was not with her, then Doña Pilar, her dueña, a plump little lady in her fifties, talkative and giggly. "Dueñas are all like that", Alexander Farnese once told Juan. "They are part of man's punishment for the fall in Eden."

Alexander was right. He might have added that they could tempt a man to murder them. Juan was far too much in love to be aware of an inconsistency here, and in fact there was none from his point of view. He did want his jewel to be guarded, but not against him.

There was no chance of telling her that he loved her. There was no chance of telling her anything but a few well thought-out compliments. He rehearsed them twenty times and promptly forgot all about them when he saw her.

She was no longer just a vision, as she had been when he first met her; he had been able to make the princess talk a little about her, to tell him little stories of her childhood, and he knew now that she had always been extraordinarily serious for her age and so devout that at one time the family really thought of letting her become a nun. But such a decision should not be made too early either, the princess said, and she was right again, of course. There was no doubt that the princess was the most intelligent woman he had ever met. No wonder everyone adored her. He told her so, and she curtsied to him, not quite seriously and yet not mockingly either. "I am above all your devoted friend, Don Juan", she said. "You may believe me when I say that you have no more devoted friends in the world than my husband and myself."

"I know you read me like a book", he said. "Perhaps one day you will consent to tell me what you have read. To myself I am quite incomprehensible."

"I will interpret you for yourself one day, I think", she replied. "But let me first read a few more chapters."

"Which is your charming way of telling me that I am still too young for anything", Juan said.

"But you are making great progress", she said, smiling. "A few months ago you wouldn't have guessed that."

That day he was allowed to see María for a moment, and he used it to ask her for her permission to regard her as his lady.

She bowed most charmingly and said that she was honored, which was the correct answer according to the code of chivalry.

He was now entitled to ask for her colors and for some small object belonging to her, and she gave him a tiny handkerchief that seemed to consist of embroidery only, and two small pieces of ribbon, green and red.

Doña Pilar was watching it all, giggling and fanning herself.

All this was in the best tradition of Amadis of Gaul; it meant very little, except that he had taken upon himself to lay at María de Mendoza's feet whatever brave deeds he would do and that it was his duty to defend her name and honor against any who might offend or insult her. And as he knew only too well that he would not be allowed to do any brave deeds in the near future and that it was extremely unlikely anybody would be so foolish as to insult the name and honor of a member of the Mendoza family, he could console himself only with the thought that his day would come, whether in a year or in five years.

He said something of the sort to Alexander Farnese, who nodded with a kind of grave amusement. "You are a realistic romantic, Juan, or a romantic realist, whatever you like better. I really believe you mean every word you say."

"I'd fight anybody who doubts my word", Juan said vehemently.

"Well, you won't fight me." Alexander grinned. "If I hadn't already told you that I believe you, I'd do so now and quickly. You're far too good a swordsman. And as I'm not in love with any girl at the moment—not seriously, I mean—I am quite willing to concede that there is no more lovely lady in the world than yours. Now are you satisfied?"

Juan stared at him. Then he burst out laughing. "You know, I was quite ready to fight you. It is astonishing how stupid one becomes when one is in love."

"I know, I know." Alexander nodded. "It's happened to me many a time."

"Impossible", Juan said.

"What do you mean, impossible? No, don't tell me. I'll tell you. You mean you will never love another woman, not if you live to be ninety. I thought so too, twice—and I am quite ready to think so again. No, don't be angry with me, Juan. I know it's stupid of me to talk sense to you when you're in love. It's exactly like talking about colors to a man born blind. Even so I think I must talk to you. You will get over this one day, you know."

"You don't know me, Alexander", Juan said simply.

The young prince sighed. "So much the worse for you if that is so, Juan. For you'll never ..." He broke off.

"I shall marry her", Juan said. "Or I shall never marry."

"Exactly", Alexander said. "You never will, then."

"But why?" Juan was bewildered. "I have to ask three people for permission, I know. The King. Ruy Gómez. And María. Of course, I don't know what she'll say, but—"

"You must first ask the King", Alexander interrupted. "And you'll never get any further than that."

"But—but why shouldn't he ..."

"Look, Juan. Imagine, if you can, that you have fallen in love with the Infanta Juana."

"I can't imagine that. She is sweet and lovely, but ..."

"All right, but let's assume that you have fallen in love with her and you go to the King and ask him for permission to marry her. What do you think he would say?"

"I—I don't know. It has nothing to do with—"

"Yes, it has. She is a royal princess. She has a right to marry the ruler of a country."

"But María is not a royal princess!"

"She is the niece of Don Ruy Gómez de Silva, Prince of Éboli, the second most powerful man in Spain. He isn't called *Rey* Gomez for nothing. And she is a Mendoza, and the Mendozas are one of the most powerful families in Spain. Try and think for one moment with the King's brain, Juan. Is he likely to let you, his brother, be backed by such an accumulation of power? *Spanish* power, Juan! And you, like him, the son of Charles the Fifth?"

Juan was pale now. "The King can't think such thoughts", he said angrily.

"Oh, can't he? Think of the history lessons we had—you, Carlos, and I—under good old Honoratus Joannius in Alcalá. Egyptian history, Greek history, Roman history—any history you want. And then think of the role that brothers played in it—royal brothers. But I mustn't say more. I've said too much already."

"I don't believe it", Juan declared. "History is not always the same. And the King is above such petty thoughts."

"I was only trying to prepare you for an inevitable disappointment", Alexander said, with his Italian shrug. "I know it was assinine of me, but I happen to be fond of you, which also may turn out to be assinine of me, though I don't think it will."

"There has never been a girl like María ..."

"Of course not."

"Do you know what was the very first thing she said to me? The very first thing? She said, 'I prayed for you when you were on your journey to Barcelona—I prayed that you would return safe and sound so that you could lead Spain when your time came.'"

Alexander raised his eyebrows. "Did she say that? Then don't tell it to anybody else. It does sound rather ambitious, you know."

Juan stamped his foot. "You're trying to poison everything", he cried, then he wheeled around and left.

# CHAPTER 18

ONCE MORE IT PROVED to be impossible to have a word with the King. To the natural egoism of a lover it seemed as if the world were in a conspiracy against him.

The Turks were on the march again and had invaded Hungary. The old Sultan himself was leading them. And the Emperor had sent courier after courier, embassy after embassy to the King to ask for support and help: soldiers, equipment, and money.

Philip was hesitating, as usual. Apparently he did not want an open break with the Sultan at this moment. Besides he was worried about the Queen, who was pregnant, and for that reason he had gone with her to the castle of Valsain in the Segovia forest. "There are three physicians for every statesman in Valsain", they said at court. The child was born in August. It was a girl, and Don Carlos grinned happily while he penned a letter of congratulation to his father. "I don't mind my father having daughters", he told Juan and Alexander, who both remained in Madrid with him. "Let him have five or ten or fifty—as many as the Sultan. Do you think he is disappointed? I am sure he is. But he will never have another son. You'll see. Never. And why should he?"

The Queen fell ill, and for some time there was anxiety about her recovery. And when she had recovered the most dreadful news came from the Netherlands.

Incited by fanatical Calvinist preachers the mob had invaded Catholic churches in Ypres, Dunquerque, and Armentières, burned the "idolatrous" pictures, smashed the tabernacles, and desecrated the consecrated Hosts. Soon the same thing was happening all over Flanders and in Seeland, Holland, and Friesland. Unique masterpieces were destroyed; priests, monks, and nuns were beaten. Books and manuscripts were burned by the thousand, priceless stained glass windows smashed. In some places the destroyers sat down to a meal in the church they had "purified" in this fashion. And this time William of Orange really remained silent. But as soon as he had left Antwerp for Brussels, the mob rose in Antwerp as well. Not a single church, chapel or monastery, not even the hospitals, escaped destruction. After little more than two weeks over four hundred churches and monasteries had been reduced to rubble.

The new Pope, Pius V, much better informed than the King, had warned as early as February that in his opinion Philip's personal presence was required in the Netherlands, if an open outbreak of hostilities was to be avoided. He repeated his warning in March and in May. He went so far as to say that any further vacillation would have grave consequences for the Catholic Faith.

Philip's answers spoke of the preparations necessary for a voyage of the sovereign, of lack of funds and many other difficulties. However, he promised to go as soon as he possibly could. But he could not go without an army and that army had to be assembled and equipped. The Pope answered that the presence of the King was far more important than that of an army and that even the strongest army would be of little avail without him. This was Philip's personal responsibility. As the king he would have to account for every soul endangered by his vacillation.

This was a new language. The pale, worried man on the throne was not accustomed to it.

"I don't understand my father", Don Carlos said. "Why, everyone knows how much he loves traveling. I have made a little list of his journeys in the last years. Look ..." He carefully unlocked his desk and produced some sheets of paper. "'The great voyages of King Philip the Second'", he read, smiling. "'From Madrid to El Pardo—from El Pardo to El Escorial—from El Escorial to Aranjuez—from Aranjuez to Toledo—from Toledo to Valladolid—from Valladolid to Burgos—from Burgos to Madrid—from Madrid to El Pardo—from El Pardo to El Escorial—from El Escorial to Madrid.' I could go on for quite a while. What are the conquistadores compared to him?"

Juan and Alexander remained silent. The prince's list was not only *lèse majesté*; it was also childish. And yet, for the first time they both felt that Carlos was seeing his father's faults with the sharp eyes of his hatred. The King strongly disliked the idea of leaving Spain.

"He should send *me*", Carlos said bitterly. "I'd put things right soon enough. But just as he can't see things from afar, he can't see those right under his nose. Blind, blind, blind."

Only at the house of the Ébolis did everything go on as before. Ruy Gómez seemed to be quite unruffled; the princess was as witty and charming as ever; and once Juan was lucky enough to have a few minutes with his lady again, and that on a day when memorable news had come from the Turkish war.

He spoke to her about it; he could not help it. "Such a story," he said, "such a sad, wonderful, terrible and magnificent story."

She did not know what had happened. Of course not. They were still treating her as if she were a child. "Sziget has fallen", he told her.

"S-siget? What is it?"

"Sziget is a fortress. It was a fortress. Now it no longer exists. A small Hungarian castle, ringed by water—yet it held up the entire Turkish army for a month. Count Nicholas Zrinyi defended it."

"Another Malta", María de Mendoza said, and he beamed at her; she had understood him at once, yes, another Malta, only much smaller and the besieging army much bigger. And perhaps that was why the Sultan insisted on the siege; perhaps to him it was like making good the failure at Malta. He could have bypassed the little fortress so easily—his rear was in no danger from such a tiny garrison. But he insisted on its conquest.

For four weeks the Hungarian flag and Zrinyi's own flag with the crest of his family still flew from the citadel, and the Sultan still waited for victory in his huge tent of green silk.

At long last the Turks succeeded in digging a mine shaft under the moat; the citadel went up in one gigantic explosion—with Zrinyi and the rest of the garrison. But the Sultan was not able to enjoy this victory. Three days earlier he had died.

Mehmed Sokolli, Grand Vizier and seraskier, tried to conceal the death. He had the Sultan's body put into a litter, as if he were still alive, and pretended to have the Sultan's orders for an immediate withdrawal.

Zrinyi and his handful of men had stemmed the tide.

"It can be done", Juan said. "Malta has proved it and now Sziget."

"Perhaps it will be up to you to prove it the next time", María de Mendoza said, and there was such unbounded confidence in her tone that he needed all his self-control not to take her in his arms, despite Doña Pilar's presence.

"That word of yours", he said hoarsely, "has made me richer than if I had been given all the gold of the Indies."

Doña Pilar, somewhat alarmed, ended the conversation by mixing in it, and a moment later the princess came in, looking for an earring she had lost. She was always losing jewelery and seemed to enjoy the general upheaval it caused, with everybody looking under tables and chairs.

Later Ruy Gómez took Juan to his study, leaving the princess in charge of the treasure hunters, as he put it.

"I thought you would be pleased to hear that I have given orders to build a flagship for you in Barcelona."

"A flagship—for me?"

"Certainly. I told you before; I am doing everything in my power to secure that command for you. Even the best of monarchs can be forgetful, but friends should not. And even the worst of monarchs does not dislike it when a faithful subject anticipates their wishes. Especially when the official funds are a little low." Ruy Gómez smiled cheerfully. "Here is the model", he said, pointing to a three-foot galley, beautifully carved. "It is made of the same kind of wood as the real one—larch, Catalonian larch, the best there is. Venetian style, as you see. Bergamesco made the plans for the poop. The galley will be eighty-two feet long, with a keel length of sixty-eight feet, a breadth of twenty-two and a depth of twelve. . . ."

Nothing was missing, from the galleon's figurehead—Hercules, leaning on his club—to the large, bronze lantern, heavily gilt, the mark of the flagship, astern.

"She is beautiful", Juan said breathlessly. "I don't know how to thank you. But when . . . when . . ."

"I do not know when you will receive the official decree", Don Ruy said. "But on the day you receive it, your ship will be ready for you. I promise you that."

Later Juan asked himself why he had not talked to his benefactor and friend about Sziget. His heart had been so full of it. Could it be that he did not expect him to be interested? Surely that was nonsense. How could he not be!

The death of the Sultan was bound to be a matter of the first order politically. It was stupid not to have asked for his opinion, his views about the consequences.

He had thought of it, too—twice. And each time he could not make himself speak up. Ruy Gómez was a great man, in his own way. A wise man. The King might well be glad to have such an adviser. He was the most generous man too. To build a ship like this meant vast expense—and it was done solely to please him, Juan. And the King, of course. Ruy Gómez had said so himself. And yet one could not talk to him about Sziget and Zrinyi. He ... he might have made some ironical remark, some witty aphorism about simple-minded soldiers perhaps, the way he liked to talk about the Duke of Alba, for instance—and that would have been like a profanation, a desecration. A deed like Zrinyi's was a holy thing. But not—perhaps—to Ruy Gómez. The princess also would not understand it, although she would make a far more elegant comment than anybody else. They knew so much, these two—but there were things that they did not know, because these things were too simple for them.

María, of course, understood at once, and even went a step further than he himself had done in his conscious thoughts. Malta—Sziget—perhaps it would be up to him to stem the tide the next time. He had not dared to think that far. He had felt the urge, that was all. She had put it into words. She believed in him.

He knew now that such belief was the foundation of love.

"Well, did he like his little ship?" the princess asked.

"Oh, yes." Ruy Gómez helped himself to a goblet of his favorite wine. Portuguese wine, of course; poor fellow, he could never indulge in it when he had guests, Ana thought.

French wines were the fashion, though there were houses where drinking them was still regarded as unpatriotic. How stupid people were. But Ruy had been drinking a little too much; there was that flush on his face again—just as well they had no more guests tonight. When Ruy drank too much, there was something on his mind that he could not cope with. Not yet cope with. She tried to think of what it could be.

"He was extremely pleased", he went on. "And he asked me a number of quite pertinent questions, more than I could answer. I think he has read a number of books on ships, seamanship, all that kind of thing. I'm afraid I started him off by giving him the ship's exact measurements. But how am I to know how gunpowder is stored on a galley as compared to the way it is stored on a galleon? Or what chance a galleass has trying to fight four frigates at such and such a distance under this or that circumstance—I forgot what."

"My poor Ruy."

"I tell you, this boy won't be content with playing the admiral—he wants to *be* one, and he may well succeed. Do you know, I think I had better tell Sánchez and Il Bergamesco to go ahead and actually build that ship."

"You haven't done so yet?"

"Well, no. But now I will. I don't want to be caught unawares. It's no risk, really. The King always needs ships, and I can always find a way to raise money. If only—" He broke off.

"I'll have a goblet of that atrocious wine of yours", Ana said. "Thank you. What *is* worrying you?"

"Oh, very much the usual things and the usual people. We have a new Grand Turk, you know, and it's my business to know all about him."

"Even little María knows about the old Sultan's death", the princess said, smiling. "Don Juan told her today. He was full of some heroic stand made by some Hungarian with an unpronounceable name, at some place that sounds exactly like a hiss."

"Sziget, you mean. I've forgotten the man's name, but he ought to be richly rewarded by the Emperor. That siege has saved Vienna a great deal of trouble. On second thought, I think the man's no longer alive. If old Süleyman had gone on, he might have taken Vienna. The Emperor's army was a very disorganized affair. Above all, most of the soldiers were in a nasty mood—hadn't got their pay. Many a time I've told the King that an emperor without money is no emperor at all. He understood, too. What are you laughing about?"

"Fancy Don Juan talking to María about things like that. He is still half a boy."

"He always will be, I think." Ruy Gómez poured himself another goblet of wine. "But hero worship is natural, at his age. I'm sure he saw himself defending Sziget to the last. By the way, dear Maximilian has decided to go on paying his 'present of honor' to the new Sultan. Alba will find it disgraceful, of course."

"Well, it is, in a way, isn't it?"

"It is good policy, Ana dear. Gives the new Sultan no pretext to win laurels against him. Not that Selim seems to be particularly bellicose, but he has his troubles, too, with his janizaries clamoring for war all the time, because that's the only way *they* can get their pay. Few people understand the importance of money, Ana. Sometimes I think I'm the only man in Spain who does."

"You've proved it, haven't you? You're as rich as Croesus."

"That's not what I mean, Ana. And I wish you would leave my hair in peace."

"It's very nice hair, for a man of your age. I know it's not what you meant. *I* mean it. And I'd distrust a poor man posing as an expert on financial matters just as much as I distrust Inez Infantado on matters of taste or one or two prelates I could name when they talk about sanctity."

"You are wrong there, Ana. I grant you poor Inez, but not the prelates. They didn't invent what they're passing on, and the truth remains true even when a liar utters it. Even in everyday life no liar will always lie, no murderer always kill. The great art is to sense when the liar is speaking the truth and when he isn't. You can't identify a man with one of his attributes. On second thought, I cannot even grant you Inez Infantado. She told you last week that your dress was lovely. Now where are you with your philosophy? If you're consistent you must now think: Inez Infantado tells me my dress is lovely. Inez Infantado has no taste. Therefore my dress must be horrible."

"To be quite frank, I've had my suspicions about that dress ever since", Ana admitted dryly. "And Inez wouldn't praise it, unless she felt that it might do me harm in some quarters. It *is* a trifle too—never mind. You still haven't told me what is worrying you. Except the Grand Turk."

"What's worrying me is that it's becoming more and more difficult to get things done. Every time I suggest something, Alba tramples on it with his big, mailed feet. And the King listens to him more often than not. . . ."

"Which of course is exactly what Alba is saying about you. Go on."

"The King is playing us against one another, of course. Pérez says that's his way of clearing his mind. He'll learn better. It's no more than a very welcome excuse for Philip to do what he likes to do most: to vacillate. D'you know what Requeséns wrote to me the other day? 'If Death came from Spain, we'd all live to be a hundred.'"

"Requeséns is an old dodderer anyway. But surely you have more enemies than just Alba. There's Aguilar, there's Zayas. . . ."

"Aguilar is old and Zayas is lazy and no match for Pérez. I could add to the list considerably, of course—but none of them and not even all of them together are dangerous to me, except through Alba; they are his fingers, his carriers, his gatherers of news. Without him they are nothing. And I can't get rid of him. Now this new Pope of ours is constantly writing to the King about the situation in the Netherlands. He wants the King to go there in person, and he says so in extremely strong terms. And Alba is all for it, simply because he is devout. . . ."

Ana began to laugh. "Ten years ago he fought against the Pope; didn't he? He's just got a bad conscience. . . ."

"He didn't fight against the Pope; he fought against the Duke of Guise, the Pope's ally, I grant you that. He won, too—and then begged the Pope's pardon on his bended knees. Paul the Fourth that was, and he didn't like Spaniards much. Anyway, bad conscience or not, Alba is all for the journey to the Netherlands. That means that he and I are going, too, of course—everybody is going. And all my plans here must remain in abeyance. We shall have to travel about in those dreary northern provinces, make a great show of royal power, comfort abbots and priors whose churches have been destroyed, win over beefy nobles— and all the time I have Alba at my side, looking over my shoulder. . . ."

"I see", Ana said thoughtfully. "And the King—has he decided to do as the Pope tells him?"

"I'm afraid he'll do it. He hasn't said so in so many words, but there are signs of preparation. He doesn't really like it, of course. He's not fond of leaving Spain."

"He won't be a success with the Flemings either", Ana said. "They're merry people; a little coarse, they like eating and drinking and trading; they won't like Philip much."

"And he can't stand them. To him they're Germans, and you know he's never forgiven the Germans for electing the late Emperor Ferdinand instead of him. You're right; the whole thing will probably be an abysmal failure."

"Then why do it?"

"I told you, my dear, the Pope and Alba ..."

"If Alba is so keen, let him go alone. Wait! I have an idea ..."

"Heaven preserve us."

"Now don't be rude, Ruy. Just wait—I've got it. The word is: conspiracy."

Ruy Gómez groaned. "What ever next. With whom am I to conspire and about what?"

"With the King, of course."

"Good. That means I won't be beheaded when the conspiracy is discovered. Go on. Ana! What are you doing?"

She took the goblet from him and put it down. "You've had all the wine you need, Ruy dear. Listen. Tell the King to go on with his preparations for the journey. Tell him to write to the Pope that he is going to the Netherlands in great style. That sort of thing takes time, of course. You can't go unprotected—therefore Alba must raise and equip an army. And when all is ready, the King must change his mind, quite suddenly, you understand—and tell Alba to go alone."

He stared at her. "I'm not sure whether there isn't a spark of genius in that, Ana. Of course, if Alba goes there alone, it will be war. He knows nothing else and his hand is hard."

The princess shrugged her shoulders. "From what you told me about the situation there it'll be either failure or war. If Alba goes, he'll win, at least. He always does, give the devil his due. It'll be another feather in his cap, too. But, Ruy dear, it will take some time. And during that time he'll be away from Spain and you can get your plans through."

"So I can, by God. He'll need six or seven months at the very least, and when he's at war, he has no mind for anything else. I can't put this plan of yours to the King just like that, naturally. He'd never agree. But I can plant the idea in such a way; he'll believe that it was he who thought of it first."

"Excellent."

He rose. "It's a great plan, Ana." Suddenly he began to laugh. "I'm thinking of Alba", he said. "That's the most amusing thing about it all—he'll love it. He'll think it is a great military ruse, making the Netherlanders believe that the King is coming to visit them in state and then he comes instead with an army. It'll make his work much easier."

"Spoken like a general", the princess said with curling lip. "I didn't know you had military genius as well." She walked to the door. "I'm going to bed now."

"Good night, Ana. I can't come yet. This must be thought over very thoroughly."

"You don't need me for that. Once an idea is born and set into motion, it no longer interests me much." She gave him a quizzical look. "About that Hungarian", she said.

"What Hungarian?"

"The one who defended that little fortress against the whole Turkish army and wouldn't give up. He must have known that it was hopeless, surely."

"Oh, yes. Why? What makes you think of him?"

"I just wondered what you would have done in his place."

Ruy Gómez laughed. "My dear, I would never have permitted myself to get into such a position."

She nodded. "Of course not. Good night."

As the door closed behind her he shook his head. What on earth made her ask such a question? But then, a man who thought he could understand an ordinary woman was a fool—so what of a man who tried to understand Ana? Just as well she was a woman, and his wife. Had she been a man, she would have been far more dangerous than Alba.


## CHAPTER 19


"I LOVE HER, TÍA. I shall never be happy in my life unless I marry her."

Doña Magdalena took a little time to assort her thoughts. Then she said, still a little stiffly: "I am told that the young lady is very beautiful."

She listened patiently to the stream of praise that followed. When it ceased she asked: "Have you told the young lady?"

"Oh no—of course no."

"Have you mentioned anything about it to Don Ruy? To the princess?"

"Not one word."

"And they—they've never said anything about such a possibility? Perhaps not in so many words—they are very—elegant and subtle people and such people often talk in allusions or innuendos."

"They've never mentioned it in any way. I don't think they have the slightest idea. But why ..."

"Forgive me, dear Juan, if I go on asking a few questions. Who knows about this, apart from you and me?"

"Only Alexander Farnese."

"Oh. And what did the Prince of Parma say?"

Juan told her, fidgeting with his ruff. "Isn't it absurd? I didn't speak to him for a week. But he didn't say those things to hurt me, he really believed in his nonsense. He was frank and sincere and I have forgiven him. I told him so."

"In that case", Doña Magdalena said, "I hope you will forgive me too."

"Tía! You don't think he's right! You can't."

"I don't know whether he is right or not in everything he said. But I very much fear he is right in most of it. He is a good friend of yours and I don't think he'll talk. At least I hope not. He may write to his mother about it, though—and she is in constant correspondence with His Majesty."

"I don't think I'd mind that", Juan said bitterly. "It would be one way to let the King know. I've been trying to see him for I don't know how long, but he's as unapproachable as heaven is to an unrepentant sinner. And I couldn't very well talk to his new secretary of state about it...."

"Indeed, no. I am glad you left Señor Pérez out of it. Almost as glad as I am that you have honored me with your confidence. I was beginning to fear that I had lost it."

"Oh, Tía. How could you think such a thing?"

"I have seen very little of you lately. But now I understand the reason for that. But never mind me. The Prince of Parma was right in many of the points he made, I think. But there are others that he didn't touch at all. May I speak as frankly as I always used to?"

"But, Tía, dear Tía, nothing has changed between us, has it? Why, you have tears in your eyes!"

Doña Magdalena stamped her foot. "Of course I have. Don't you think I'd love to be happy, jubilantly, absurdly happy with you about your being in love with a beautiful young girl of one of the finest families in Spain? Oh, I'd be jealous all right, stupid old woman that I am, but happy all the same. Do you think I enjoy sitting here with a sour face, as if you had given me bad news?" She produced a sensible handkerchief and dabbed at her eyes furiously. "I am not particularly fond of the Princess of Éboli", she went on. "Don Luiz disagrees with me. I suppose I'm too stodgy for her, but then I like being stodgy, perhaps only because I couldn't be anything else. There I go again, talking about myself. I don't matter. There is one who does matter, however, and that is His Majesty."

"Exactly. That's why I have to see him and tell him about it."

"And if you get a flat no—what are you going to do then?"

"That's what Alexander said. Why should the King be against it?"

She sighed. "My dear Juan, you are not just an ordinary nobleman, asking his king for permission to marry. You are the King's brother. He is bound to have plans for your future. He may want you to marry some foreign princess ..."

"But, Tía dear, I am not a royal prince." Juan's lips twitched. "The King has made that quite clear. He is very much displeased when anyone addresses me as Prince. Why should I regard myself as anything but an ordinary nobleman?"

She looked at him sharply. "For the first time in all these years I must ask you whether you are quite sincere, Juan. Whether you have resigned yourself to remain an 'ordinary nobleman' all your life? No, perhaps it will be better if you do not answer that question. You may not be clear about it in your own mind. You probably aren't. Neither, I think, is the King. In any case you must leave it to him."

"I am quite willing to leave it to him", Juan said slowly.

"It's all nonsense about the ordinary nobleman anyway", Doña Magdalena said testily. "You have royal blood in your veins. Your career hasn't even started yet. An early marriage could endanger it. The King is bound to feel that."

Juan gave a bitter laugh. "Alexander pointed out to me that he wouldn't like me to marry into the Mendoza family because they are so powerful. Now you seem to tell me that they aren't good enough for me. What am I to think?"

She said nothing. After a while he went on: "I am sorry, Tía. I am harsh and bitter and you are only being good to me. But I love María. I can't calculate about what chances I may or may not have in life. Please help me, Tía. Help me to find a way to tell the King."

She gave another sigh. "Do I have your permission to tell Don Luiz about it? He may be able to say something to His Majesty—and what is more he will choose a favorable moment."

Juan took a step forward. "Do I have your permission to embrace you?" he asked happily.

When she had disengaged herself, she said gruffly: "Save your kisses for somebody more suitable. I wish I knew how to say 'No' to you. I'm being very foolish about this. But I'll try my best."

Waiting was the worst thing on earth. Even hope was pain when one was waiting, because it never came alone but always in the company of doubt and fear. Weeks passed and nothing happened, except that it now seemed certain that the King and half the court would go to the Netherlands after all.

Don Carlos was giving instructions about everything he wanted to take with him, and he told Juan and Alexander to do the same.

"Looks as if we shall be away for years", Alexander grinned.

Juan nodded sadly. In other circumstances he would have enjoyed the expedition as at least a change, and there was always the chance that there might be some fighting. But it meant that he would not see María again for a long time; and those brief moments at the palace Éboli were—life. He could no longer imagine the time when he had not known María. And he felt certain—although she had never said so, of course—that it was the same with her.

There was peace again between him and Alexander. The young Italian was not the kind of man one could be angry with for long.

A few days later on Carlos made another announcement to them, very solemnly and stiffly. He had decided to marry the Archduchess Anne of Austria. "The issue has never really been in doubt", he declared. "But it was my duty to consider all the potentialities—political and otherwise. I have done so and I have notified my father. He has promised me to speed up the negotiations with the Emperor." Abruptly he told the Prince of Parma that he wished to talk to Juan alone.

Alexander, quite unruffled, bowed and left. He was quite accustomed to the prince's eccentricities.

"Has he shut the door?" Carlos asked suspiciously. "You'd better go and have a look. Closed, is it? Good. He needn't hear what I have to tell you. Reasons of state, my dear boy. Yes, yes, reasons of state. You'll soon see what I mean." He came up quite close and laid his hand on Juan's arm. "I love her", he whispered. "I have loved her ever since I saw her portrait. Here, look—the future queen of Spain. And more, much more."

The portrait, in a frame of ebony and silver, showed a fairly good-looking girl, dressed in blue and silver brocade. Her nose was rather long, and she had the typical Habsburg underlip, which made her look a little sullen.

"All the others are pale shadows compared to my fiancée", Carlos stated. "And there is real power connected with this union. Those young monkeys, the archdukes Ernest and Rudolph, will be surprised by the name of the next emperor, I think. Do you understand? Do you understand? Now this is a deadly secret, Juan. No one knows about it, except us two—you won't tell anybody, will you? If my father knew what I'm aiming at, he would be furious—and he would be furious out of jealousy. He lost the imperial crown because he didn't know how to deal with those Germans. Very well—I shall know how to deal with them."

Juan felicitated the prince on his choice as warmly as he could. The whole court knew that the King was already negotiating with Vienna about this marriage. Carlos probably liked to pretend not only to others but also to himself that it was he and not the King who had made the choice. Besides, he had the gift of falling in love with a portrait. He had proved it before. There was no doubt that the King had also considered the possibility of regaining the imperial crown in consequence of such a union. This was no deadly secret—the idea was obvious. Obvious also—and at the same time touching and frightening—was the tremendous ambition of the poor young cripple, who could not control himself and yet longed to control the world.

"This journey of ours is the first step", Carlos resumed. "The Duchess of Parma has shown that she cannot cope with the situation in the Netherlands. She will have to resign. And the new governor will be—Carlos." He laughed. "I thought that would astonish you", he said. "It will astonish many people—not excluding friend Alexander, who thinks his mother is the most astute statesman in Europe. Now you understand why I didn't want him to listen at the door."

Juan was going to say with some heat that Alexander was not the man to listen at doors like a servant, but stopped himself in time. Only a few weeks ago Prince Carlos was found listening at the door of the small council room where the King was discussing political issues with several of his ministers. The chamberlain, Don Diego de Acuña, reproached him for it and tried to make him leave. The prince promptly boxed his ears. Don Diego went straight to the King and offered his resignation, but Philip very courteously apologized for the prince's behavior and gave the grandee a position in his own household.

"This was entirely my own idea", Carlos went on. "But I told my father and for once he quite agrees with me. Just imagine! We shall all go there. But after a while my father will return to Spain and I shall stay on, the governor of the States-General—and no longer just one more dressed-up nothing at my father's court. I shall give the orders, with no one to interfere. If there's anything my father doesn't like, he will have to write to me, and I shall write back. Paper is the most abject of slaves. Juan, I am beginning to live—at last I am beginning to live. And you—you'll stay with me. I shall ask the King to let you. You'll be my right hand."

Juan came out of the prince's study with his head awhirl. If Carlos had his way—and it was just barely possible that he would—it really meant staying in the Netherlands for years on end. Then what about his Mediterranean command? And when would he see María again?

Apparently the King had time to discuss his son's projects at length—but not his brother's. If Carlos spoke the truth—and if he did not misjudge his father's attitude—he was going to get everything he wanted, with Juan of Austria thrown in as a kind of aide-de-camp. He would not see María, he would lose his command, and he might lose even his friendship with Alexander, whom he could not tell about the plan to make his mother abdicate her governorship in Carlos' favor. And the prince was quite capable of mentioning it to Alexander just when it suited him and to add that this had so far been a well-kept secret between him and Don Juan of Austria. . . .

To say nothing of the doubtful honor of having to carry out whatever mad plans Carlos thought up for the Netherlands, once his father had left for Madrid.

Juan groaned. He thought of going to Don Luiz—he must be in the palace somewhere—and telling him everything. But if he did, the only effect might well be the reverse of what he hoped for. Don Luiz might well refuse, after this, to speak of Juan to the King at all.

Then for one wild moment Juan seriously thought of crashing into the King's private rooms, throwing himself at his feet and forcing a decision then and there.

But at once he knew that this was madness, that it was the sort of thing Philip hated most. No one in the world could do that with even the faintest hope of success.

He had an all-powerful longing to see María again, today, at once.

He needed her more than ever. He needed strength. If he could see her for just a few moments, for one moment only, he would be able to bear everything, this whole world of intrigue and scheming, of vacillation and mad ambition.

He must see her.

Only when he was already on his way to the palace Éboli did the idea strike him that he might be able to talk to Ruy Gómez. Of course—that was the solution. And if the most intelligent and the subtlest man in Spain did not know a way out, then there was none.

Marquez, the butler, told him that His Highness had left this morning for his estates, and he asked if he should announce His Excellency to Her Highness. Juan was still trying to recover from this latest blow when the princess herself entered the hall and welcomed him very affectionately. Such a nice surprise. A pity Ruy was not here, but he had to go to Pastrana; in fact his going there was long overdue. It didn't do any good at all to leave a large estate without personal supervision, administrators being what they were, rascals, all of them, and would he come into the Yellow Room; María was there, too.

María was there, too.

The Yellow Room was part of the princess' private suite and took its name from the yellow silk covering the walls and the golden yellow carpet of unusual design woven in faraway Cathay.

María, wearing a honey-colored dress, looked like the very spirit of the room, and Juan told her so.

"Well observed", the princess said. "But then, a future admiral must be a good observer."

This was his chance to mention that, from what he had heard from Prince Carlos, he was more likely to become the prince's aide-de-camp than an admiral. He could not make use of it. Not before María.

222

"Her dress suits her", the princess went on. "There aren't many girls who can wear that color. You must admit that I am a heroic woman, though."

"I will admit anything you want me to", Juan replied with a bow. "But why heroic?"

"My dear Don Juan, a woman of my age, allowing herself to be seen in the company of a girl like María is either heroic or a fool, and I do hope you don't take me for the latter."

He tried to think of a suitable reply and could not. How boring a witty woman could be, always bantering and at the same time angling for compliments. "It is a very lovely dress", he said. "But then I feel that if Doña María were dressed in rags they would be changed by her touch into the robes of a queen."

"I take it all back", the princess said, laughing. "You're not an admiral; you're a courtier."

"Don Juan is only mocking a poor girl", María said. "What am I next to Tía. Everybody knows she is the most beautiful lady in Spain."

"How nice of you." The princess began to fan herself. "Unfortunately the one little word 'tía' spoils it all. I'm no longer a woman; I'm an aunt."

Juan made an effort to fall in with her mood. "If I am not grossly deceived," he said, "it is impossible to be an aunt, unless one happens to be a woman." He turned to María: "Mocking you would be a deadly sport for anyone who tried it in my presence. As for myself . . ."

"Good, good, you've made your point." The princess laughed. She rang a silver bell and gave her servants orders to bring in wine and fruit.

Old Marquez himself brought oranges, dates, and figs, both fresh and dried, almonds, nuts, and small, red-cheeked apples. The wine was a heavy, brown Xeres.

The princess went on chatting and bantering. For the first time Juan almost hated her; even Doña Pilar would have been better, despite her giggling. There simply was no way of exchanging a word of sense with María.

Suddenly the princess jumped to her feet. "Dios de mi alma! I have forgotten the letters." She passed a weary hand over her eyepatch—silver today, to match her robe of silvery gray and violet. "Such a nuisance", she said. "Ruy left early this morning, and all his mail arrived here after he had gone. I promised him I would sort it out and send him only the important ones. If I don't do it now the courier won't be able to reach him today, and he must have those letters. Will you forgive me, Don Juan? It will only take me half an hour, perhaps a *little* more."

In the door she turned. "I ought to send Doña Pilar in, of course", she said smiling. "But the silly woman has a stomachache, and I told her to go to bed and drink hot water. What a hostess I am—one breach of etiquette after another. Ah, well, you will excuse me, won't you?"

Outside she found Marquez. "Where is Doña Pilar?"

"In the patio, Your Highness."

She nodded and went to the patio, where she found the dueña busying herself with the rose bushes. Doña Pilar was very found of plants and herbs. Abruptly, the princess sent her to her room. "Stay there until I have you called."

The dueña goggled at her. "Have I had the misfortune to displease Your Highness?" she stammered.

"You will have that misfortune unless you do as I tell you."

"Yes, Your Highness. I'm going. I'm going at once."

In the Yellow Room the door had scarcely closed behind the princess when Juan said: "Doña María, I have had grave news this morning. I shall have to leave Madrid with Don Carlos. We are going to the Netherlands—and I don't know when I shall be able to return. I—I don't know when I shall see you again."

In a trembling voice the girl said: "I knew this had to come. You must rise. You will rise high. I—I am glad."

He stared at her. "Doña María," he whispered, "you are crying. You are crying for me."

"N-no—oh no." She tried hard to make her voice sound firm, but firmness was far away and could not be regained. "I am crying for myself", she said faintly. "It's very—wrong of me; I am so stupid. So selfish. Oh, I shouldn't have said that . . ."

He was trembling from head to foot. "Then I, too, will say what I should not say, my lady, my sweet lady. . . . I have asked my fatherly friend, Don Luiz Quixada, to approach the King and to ask him in my name for his permission to marry you—if of your gracious kindness you should think me worthy of such good fortune."

"Worthy?" she repeated incredulously. "Oh, but I'm nothing—except for one thing only—that I love you."

At once he was at her feet. "I did not know there was such happiness in the world", he said in a breathless voice. "Now I can defy them all. If the King does not give me permission, I will leave Spain with you. If the whole world is against us, we will still conquer. There is no greater force than love. And I have loved you from the first moment I saw you."

He covered her hands with kisses. Then he felt the soft touch of her lips on his hair, and looking up, he saw her face bent over him, more beautiful than ever in the radiance of her love, the very fruit of paradise.

"You are mine", he said vehemently. "Mine. Mine."

# CHAPTER 20

Several weeks later Ruy Gómez returned from Pastrana to Madrid and went straight to the royal palace, "to get the feel of things", as he liked to put it. He came back to his house in sparkling good humor.

"Your plan is working beautifully, Ana", he told the princess.

"Did you see the King?"

"Oh, yes, he even interrupted an audience to welcome me back. I believe it was old Hernández—he'll be furious, of course, but that doesn't matter. The King sticks to his plan—your plan—and what is more, he's kept the secret beautifully."

"How do you know?"

Ruy Gómez laughed. "I know because no less than four people in high positions asked me whether I had come back to bid the King farewell or whether it was to supervise the packing of my luggage. This means they weren't sure whether I had not fallen from favor and would have to remain here instead of going on the royal journey; and also that this journey is very much 'on', officially."

"But the King told you he won't go."

"Exactly. And the best of all is that the King now quite seriously believes it was his idea. I'm very glad about that because of Castagna."

"The papal nuncio? Well, of course, it's a defeat for him."

"A very grave one. This new Pope of ours is tenacious, you know. Time and again Castagna has come with new exhortations and reasons why the King should hasten his journey. It no longer occurs to him that the King may not go at all. I'd hate to write the kind of letter he will have to write to his master. And I don't particularly care to have Castagna as an enemy. He's extremely intelligent—you know I don't say that easily—and he may go far yet."

"A future Pope, you mean?"

"It's not impossible. So, in the circumstances, I'm rather glad it's the King's own idea and not mine. Yours, I mean of course."

"You unscrupulous old rogue." Ana began to fan herself. "What else is new at court?"

"Oh, one or two things. The King has applied to the Pope for a red hat again."

"Not for Don Juan, I hope?"

"No. For Espinosa. There's a career for you: head of the royal council, head of the state council, Bishop of Siguenza. And he may well become Grand Inquisitor as well. Oh, well, he has my blessings. I hope he'll get the hat—despite the disappointment we shall cause His Holiness over the Netherlands affair. As a matter of fact this new application makes it certain that Don Juan won't ever be a cardinal. The Vatican is not exactly generous with red hats. Very wise, too, but a little irksome to His Majesty, at times."

"So the King has other plans for Don Juan."

"No doubt he has. But they are not connected with little María, I'm afraid."

Ana put down her fan. Her face became intent. "What do you mean, Ruy? Dios, I wish I could cure you of that unsufferable habit of keeping the most important thing back to the last and then serving it up as if it were just one more bit of gossip or rumor. What do you mean? Has the King chosen someone else for the boy? Who? Why don't you say something?"

"Because I didn't want to interrupt you", he explained patiently. "No, I don't think he has any particular marriage planned for Don Juan yet. But he won't hear of his marrying María."

"Why not? How do you know?"

"Pérez told me. You see, the Queen is pregnant again and—"

"Never mind the Queen. How do you know the King is against Juan's marriage to María?"

"The Queen is pregnant again", Ruy Gómez repeated quietly. "And Don Luiz Quixada, when he heard about it from Pérez, decided that was the moment to approach the King and to suggest that Don Juan be given an audience so that he could ask for permission to marry."

"So it was Pérez who told you. What happened?"

"The King flatly refused the audience. He gave no reasons. And he did not inquire about the name of the lady Don Juan wished to marry. But later he told Pérez: 'That young man must wait. I may have plans for him at some later stage.' That is all I know. I am sorry if this upsets your scheme, my dear, but you can't expect the King to carry out *everything* you think up in that beautiful little head of yours, you know."

"This is terrible", the princess said between her teeth. "Terrible. It is also a trifle late in the day."

He looked up. "Late in the day?"

She began to play with her fan. "Certainly", she said. "They are in love with each other, you know."

"How can they be? They have only seen each other a few times and for a few moments."

The princess rose and began to pace up and down. "They have seen quite a bit of each other, I'm afraid", she said. "I—went out of my way to see to that. I *want* those two to marry."

Ruy Gómez shook his head. "I hope you have not broken the rules", he said, frowning. "That's just what they are for—to prevent disappointments and trouble."

She stamped her foot. "You're unbearable when you are more Spanish than the Spaniards", she said. "And I won't give up either. This is not the end. It can't be. Maybe there's a way to force Philip's hand ..."

"I wouldn't do that. I wouldn't even think of trying. Besides, how could you?"

"All went so well", she exclaimed angrily. "And now this—this debacle. What am I to do now? Quixada is a clumsy ox. I should have tackled that angle myself, too. But how could I expect this absurd attitude on Philip's part?" She stopped in front of him. "I won't have it", she said vehemently. "I'll think up something."

"You can't", he said firmly. "What's more, Don Juan mustn't see the girl again. Send her back to Pastrana. I'm sorry for her, if she's in love with him, but there's nothing you or I can do. This kind of thing has happened before, when royalty is involved, you know."

She gave an odd smile. "I suppose it has", she said. "But then I had nothing to do with it. This time it's different. I won't send María back to Pastrana. And I won't give up."

Again he shook his head. "I didn't know this idea meant so much to you. But it's hopeless now. Don Juan is an important person—I have done everything I could to win him for us and so have you. Well, we have won him and we don't want to lose him. Therefore María must go—or else he won't come to our house after this."

She flared up. "María is a Mendoza. The Mendozas are my business, not yours. I don't want her to go and I have my reasons for it." She added quickly: "She won't meet him—that I can arrange easily. And we can always *say* that she has left for Pastrana."

Ruy Gómez shrugged his shoulders. "Sometimes I don't understand you, Ana. That way the poor girl will have to live here virtually like a prisoner. Why do you want that? What is it you want?"

The princess drew herself up. "I don't know what I want—yet", she said. "But this I am sure of: I don't want to be thwarted."

## CHAPTER 21

"I DON'T BELIEVE IT", Alexander said as he came in. "It isn't possible."

"Anything is possible." Juan did not even turn his head. He sat staring out of the window.

"This isn't. I've just heard the journey is canceled."

"Is it really?" Still Juan made no move.

"Diego de Acuña told me in confidence—you know he's with the King now. And he's not the man to say things lightly, and I don't think he's made a joke in the last fifty years. He was fifty last month."

"Maybe it's true", Juan said. "I'm past caring."

Alexander gave him a compassionate look. Three months, almost four, had passed since that day when Don Luiz had to tell him that the King would not hear of his brother's marriage "to anybody", and yet the boy had not recovered from the blow. The first towering, terrible storm had passed when Juan quite seriously wanted to collect a number of young nobles loyal to him, to storm the palace Éboli, "save" his lady and flee with her. Young Guzmán had sense enough to blurt it all out, and Don Luiz stepped in just in time to stop the absurd enterprise that would have ruined him as well as everyone else taking part in it. Even so Juan would not give in but went alone to the Ébolis—only to be told very politely that the girl had gone back to Pastrana. . . .

They all talked to him in turn, after that—Alexander, Don Luiz, and Doña Magdalena. Her argument that he was ruining the girl's reputation by such behavior won the day, and he promised to abstain from any act of violence.

But since then he had completely changed. The cheerful, laughing, radiant leader of youth no longer existed. He was unnaturally quiet and seemed to take no interest in anything.

When Doña Magdalena told him that the Queen was expecting another child in October he said: "Perhaps María will come up from Pastrana for the baptism." There was such pain, such longing in his voice and expression, that Doña Magdalena burst into tears. But he went on, bitterly: "I won't be here then, of course. I shall be in the Netherlands."

But week after week went by and still they did not leave, and now it seemed that they would not go at all.

"It's probably very foolish of me to say it," Alexander remarked, "but if we really stay here, you may have a chance of seeing you know who, if she comes up for the baptism of the Queen's child."

At last Juan turned around. He looked pale and haggard.

"They will find ways and means to stop me from seeing her", he said. "I just might get a glimpse of her in the cathedral, if I'm lucky. But if I do—no, no, I won't do anything foolish. Not in the House of God. Besides, I have been thinking . . ."

"Far too much, I fear."

"It's all that is left to me—thinking. But it's added pain. She ought to have found a way to send me a message, oughtn't she? Not a line, Alexander, not a word. Yet they always say that a man is quicker to forget than a woman. Not one word! And surely ..."

The door burst open and a young noble tumbled in, white as a sheet. "Your Excellency—please, come quick!"

"Why, what is the matter?" Alexander asked.

"The prince—Don Carlos—he is killing the Duke of Alba!"

Juan jumped up. "You must be mad", he cried.

"You—or the prince", Alexander said. "Where?"

The young man was already on the way, and they hastened after him.

They did not have far to go. When they reached the anteroom of the private council chamber, they saw what none of them would ever forget. The Duke of Alba, tall and erect, was holding Don Carlos by his wrists, trying hard to keep him at arm's length. Powerful as he was, he needed every ounce of his strength. For Carlos at this moment was a madman, twisting and turning his grotesque body, throwing himself backward and forward and shrieking insults at the duke. The sword in his right hand seemed to have a life of its own, feebly trying to pierce the duke's body wherever it could find it.

Half a dozen servants stood around, either paralyzed by horror or simply afraid to interfere.

Both Juan and Alexander rushed in. They succeeded in separating the two, which was easy, as Alba at once let go of the prince's wrists and stepped back; but they could not get hold of the prince's sword. Carlos was lunging out with it in all directions and then tried once more to run up to Alba.

The duke stood immobile and coldly quiet, his sword untouched in its scabbard.

But now a whole swarm of high officials and courtiers had arrived and formed a kind of barrier between the two. Carlos tried to throw his sword at the duke and Alexander tore it out of his hand as he lifted it.

He and Juan took the prince by his arms and frog-marched him back to his suite. Carlos did not seem even to recognize them. His eyes were rolling and saliva was dribbling from his mouth in great, frothy blobs.

"I'll kill him", he screamed. "He won't go to the Netherlands! I'll kill him. Where is he?"

Then he went limp and they had to carry him into his bedroom. A few moments later the physicians arrived and busied themselves about him, and Juan and Alexander left, white-faced and shaken, to find out what happened.

They found the anteroom empty except for a few lackeys making their report to a youngish chamberlain, obviously very ill at ease.

Alexander beckoned him aside. "How did all this happen?" he asked in a low voice.

The man threw up his hands. "His Grace had made his farewell visit to His Majesty and was leaving, when suddenly His Highness turned up in a state of ... of great excitement and ... ahem ... forbade His Grace to leave. His Highness said it was he whose business it was to go to the Netherlands and not that of His Grace. His Grace said quite respectfully that His Highness' life was much too precious to be exposed to danger and that he, His Grace, I mean, was only going to the Netherlands to establish order and security so that His Highness could then go there without risk. Unfortunately His Highness then saw fit to draw his sword and to attack His Grace—"

"I understand", Alexander interrupted. "We saw much of what happened then. The duke was not wounded, I take it?"

"No, Your Highness, not a scratch, Your Highness, and if I may say so, it's the nearest thing to a miracle, with His Highness going for His Grace absolutely like a—absolutely vehemently."

They thanked the man and walked on.

"If I know anything about the King," Alexander said, "Carlos will never set foot in the Netherlands after this, if he lives to be a hundred. And our journey is off, too, definitely. *Per Baccho*, but the King will be angry. It was a great disappointment for Carlos, of course. Mother wrote to me about that. She had a letter from Carlos in which he told her point-blank that he was coming to supersede her in government...."

"So that was how Carlos kept his own 'deadly secret'." Juan gave an angry laugh.

"Do you realize what all this means?" Alexander asked. "It's a terrible surprise for the Netherlanders. They're expecting the King and the court; they are sure to have prepared long lists of demands for the negotiations with him— and then Alba turns up instead. And no one can negotiate with Alba—not even Don Carlos, as we've just seen. What I wonder about is when the King decided to send him, instead of going himself. Perhaps he never intended to go? Perhaps all our preparations were so much eyewash for the Netherlanders, the most gigantic hoax! If so, the King's a genius. What do you think?"

"He'll be here now when the child is born", Juan said. "And everybody will be here for the baptism. Perhaps— perhaps I shall see her again after all."

## CHAPTER 22

MADRID WAS ABLAZE with joy. On October 9 the Queen had given birth to another girl; she was well, the child was well, and today it was to be baptized at the Church of San Gil, served by the Discalced Franciscans. Madrid did not mind in the least that it was only a girl. Here was a perfectly good reason for feasting. Besides, one had to show oneself worthy of being the capital, not only of Spain but of an empire. If it was true, as the learned men maintained, that the earth was round, then it was true also that at all times the sun was shining over some part of Spanish territory. Somebody had coined the phrase "In the Spanish Empire the sun never sets", and the Madrilenians were fond of repeating it. They were intensely loyal to a king who had chosen their city—neither the largest nor the most beautiful in Spain—to be his capital.

And nothing, not even the most magnificent parade entering the cuadrilla gate for the Big Circle could compare with the solemn procession passing from the palace through a covered way into San Gil's. True, not many ordinary Madrilenians were able to see the baptism, as the church was packed with members of the finest families in Spain, many of whom had traveled to Madrid from faraway estates, cities, and towns of the kingdom. But after the ceremony they would stream out, one long stream of the bluest blood.

"Grandees are six for a maravedí in there", somebody joked.

When the first little infanta had been born, fourteen months ago, the court was in Valsain and she was baptized there, in the chapel of the castle. Isabella Clara Eugenia she was. But this time they were doing things in style and just as well, too. There was a great deal of guessing about the name of the new infanta. María? Manuela? "Ridiculous; her mother is French, and the mother matters most. She'll have a French name."

"Man, you're ridiculous yourself. Wasn't the first infanta named after the Queen? They can't both be called Isabella, can they?"

"Who said they will be, onion-head? Besides, the first infanta was called Isabella not after her mother but after the great Isabella, the Spanish Isabella."

"Are you insulting the Queen, you father of cockroaches and brother of bedbugs? I'll show you. . . ."

A guard in red and yellow, with a gleaming cuirass, had to separate the two irate citizens.

The long double line of officers of the household, officers of state, and bodyguards filed through the middle aisle. They were followed by four archers, four heralds, and the masters of ceremonies of the Queen and of the Infanta Juana. Then four more heralds in heavily embroidered dalmatics and behind them the dukes of Gandía and of Nájera, the Prior Don Antonio de Toledo, the Marquis of Aguilar, Count Alba de Liste, Count de Chinchón, Don Francisco Enriquez de Ribera, and the royal majordomos.

Next were six grandees: the Duke of Arcos, chief of the house of Ponce de Léon, carrying the white baptismal hood, the capillo; the Duke of Medina de Rioseco, carrying the taper; the Duke of Sesa with the maçapan; the Duke of Béjar with the salt cellar; the Duke of Orsuna with the aguamanil, the basin, and a napkin; and finally the Count of Benavente with the fuente, the ewer, and a second napkin.

There was a quick exchange of glances in the packed rows when Don Juan de Austria followed, resplendent in a dress of cloth of silver and a furred crimson mantle, carrying the royal baby, wrapped in a mantle of crimson velvet edged with gold lace, the cañutillo.

This should have been Prince Carlos' office. Was it true, then, that Don Carlos was ill again? Some of the initiated whispered that he was well enough, but that the King had forbidden him to be present because he feared another scandalous act on his part, especially as the entire procession had to pass Archbishop Espinosa with four bishops behind him and everybody knew that Don Carlos hated Espinosa for some mysterious reason.

At Don Juan's right hand walked the papal nuncio, Giovanni Battista Castagna, at his left, the Emperor's ambassador. Behind them marched the ambassadors of France and of Portugal. Then came the godfather, Archduke Rudolph of Austria, and the godmother, the Infanta Juana, Princess of Brazil. Thirteen years ago Juan had climbed the wall of the Franciscan monastery in Valladolid to see the procession of Prince Philip returning from a visit he made to her before setting out for England. . . .

The masters of ceremonies followed, Don Juan Manrique de Lara and Count Lemus, then the Mistress of Ceremonies Doña Isabella de Quiñones, Doña María Chacon, the Dueña Guardamayor Doña Isabella de Castilla, the honorary dueñas of the Queen and of the infanta, the ladies-in-waiting, and the pages.

Present were also the various councillors of state, among them Don Luiz Quixada, now head of the council of the Indies.

Gleaming beneath an enormous canopy the ancient silver font was waiting, at which St. Dominic had been baptized almost four hundred years ago.

The organ was playing.

Slowly walking on, the tiny girl in his arms, Juan looked sharply toward the corner reserved for the Ébolis and the

Mendoza family. He saw the Princess of Éboli, magnificent in a robe of cloth of gold. He did not see María.

That evening there was a large party going on in the suite of rooms belonging to the Infanta Juana, but it was not going too well. Perhaps this was due to the presence of Don Carlos, who seemed to be determined to spoil everybody's good humor by an attitude of chilly silence, interrupted by an occasional yawn.

The younger men became restive.

Finally the prince rose abruptly and hobbled up to the infanta. He obviously intended to leave, and she knew only too well what he intended to do. Everybody was talking about his strange almost nightly adventures in the worst quarters of the town—armed, disguised, and in the company of that horrible barber of his and of a few lackeys.

Just before he reached her, she clapped her hands to attract attention and suggested an encamisada.

There was a general outburst of enthusiasm, and some of the young men began shouting for cloaks, wraps, and torches.

Carlos gave a contemptuous smile. "I have no time for that kind of childish nonsense", he said. "If you will excuse me now ..."

"Oh, but what a pity", the princess said, hiding her annoyance as well as she could. "I hoped you would lead it, Carlos dear."

"Some other leader will be found easily—for *that*", the prince replied coldly. "Anybody will do. I must thank you for a delightful evening." His tone belied his words so obviously that the poor princess came close to bursting into tears. Few people ever grew accustomed to the prince's manners. He hobbled away without bothering to answer the respectful greeting given to his rank by all those he passed.

But he was right about one thing: another leader was found and chosen almost before the prince left the room. The princess did not have to make any suggestions. Thirty, forty young men were already clustering around Don Juan, and many more were joining them.

At first he did not seem to welcome the idea either; but suddenly he jumped up. "Very well, I will lead you." They promptly cheered him; they had seen little of him lately, they had missed him, and they said so as they dressed up in the strange outfits usual for the ancient custom: fantastic turbans improvised from wraps and shawls of all kinds, berets adorned with long, flowing ribbons or feathers. More ribbons, in the colors of "their" ladies, were worn on the right arm, and now indulgently smiling servants arrived with the torches.

The whole swarm of them, grouped around their leader, took solemn leave of the princess and of all the ladies present and then streamed down the broad staircase toward the stables, where horses were being held in readiness for them.

Juan chose a black horse as he always did. He mounted. A stable boy lit the torch in his left hand.

He was sporting a green and a red ribbon around his right arm, María's colors. "Now", he shouted. "Follow me."

The cavalcade clattered off, with capes flying and the torches cascading sparks. A dozen trumpeters and drummers on horseback joined them at the gate.

Up and down the streets and plazas of the town they paraded, and wherever they passed, the Madrilenians yelled and stamped and clapped their hands. Everybody loved an encamisada.

Every young noble they met on the way joined the procession.

They passed the Plaza de Santiago, where Don Luiz and Doña Magdalena came to the balcony of their house to wave at them, and from there to the royal palace where all torches were lowered to give a loyal salute to the King. Many windows lit up and many hands waved at them, as they wheeled and swung in some of the more difficult figures of the equestrian dance. Then with a last swing of the torches they clattered away again, following their leader to the palace of the Ébolis.

On the plaza in front of it they spread out. "What's the matter here?" young de Soto asked. "Have they all gone to sleep so early?"

All the windows of the palace were closed and none was lit. It was strange.

"Don't worry"; Juan said, "we'll wake them up. Hey, there, music!"

The drums rolled and the trumpets blew, and at once the great dance began, the dance on horseback, poetic outcome of centuries of battles against Saracens and Moors. The music, too, was inspired by the turbaned world of the East, soaring up and down in fierce cadenzas, triumphant and mourning at once.

And still the windows remained unlit. Still no one appeared on the balconies.

"This is very wrong", young de Soto said angrily.

Not to take any notice of an encamisada given in one's honor was a grave offense.

Juan ordered a "Viva" to the house of Éboli, to the prince, to the princess, to all the ladies of the house. Everywhere in the vicinity the windows were lit now, but the palace remained as dark as before.

"Somebody must be ill", the Count of Rojas remarked. "Ill or dying or dead—otherwise it would be intolerable." Then he vanished in the exercise of the next movement.

Ill. Dying. Dead. The house looked dangerous, threatening. She was not in it—she could not be. She could not be in a house that looked like this.

Juan stared at it. Suddenly he saw a hand touching the saddlebow just in front of him, a large, hairy hand, and he instinctively pulled the reins sharply. The horse reared and the hand lost its grip.

Juan could see the man now, a large Negro, the white of his eyes gleaming in the torchlight; no, it was not a Negro—he was wearing a black mask; he was brandishing something; it was not a weapon, but he might have a dagger in the other hand.

Juan drew his sword and drove his horse so close to the man that it touched his body.

"A message, Your Excellency . . ." The man was trembling.

Transferring the torch to his sword hand Juan took the message, a folded note, and at once the man turned and fled across the plaza, adroitly dodging the groups of riders wheeling by. He disappeared in the shadow of the Church of Santa María Almudena.

The note was not sealed, simply loosely folded—Juan could open it easily with his one free hand. The torch illumined two lines of shaky handwriting. He read and felt the whole plaza, riders, and all turn around him in giddy circles. The paper in his hand was shaking violently.

"An apology, I suppose." The Count of Rojas was back. "Somebody ill, Your Excellency?"

Juan stared at him, but he did not see him.

"Let's go to the Plaza Armeria", Rojas suggested.

Before Juan could say anything the call was taken up by ten, twenty, forty voices. "To the Plaza Armeria."

The cavalcade reformed around their leader and swept on. Juan did not resist. He could not think yet, but that strange and mysterious mechanism that takes over when conscious thinking forsakes a man raised no objection. The others were downright relieved. Away, away from the place whose silence protested against joy and merriment.

On the Plaza Armeria the triumphant end of the encamisada was performed, the cuadrillas, and here all windows were lit and hundreds of people shouted and clapped and yelled themselves hoarse.

Reason returned on silent, gray wings. It was better like this, much better—get them all away; if only this madness would end, riding in circles, swinging torches, left turn, right turn, and all the devils of hell shouting with enthusiasm, well done, beautifully done. Hell on horseback it was, senseless and giddy, and he could not escape because he could not tell them why.

At last the cuadrillas, too, came to an end.

"We disperse here", Juan ordered. He even managed to thank the riders for their performance. They all wanted to accompany him home, but he shook his head. "Forgive me, compañeros, but I must be alone for a while." They forgave him merrily. There were beautiful women in Madrid and the night was young, some thought; others that their young leader was a poet and needed solitude, perhaps for a rousing poem inspired by the encamisada. Something of that kind often happened. There was no one, not even the simplest and roughest, whom it would not rouse in some way.

They left, and as they were leaving the windows became dark and all noise gradually ceased.

Juan turned his horse and rode off, back to the palace of the Ébolis. He dismounted in front of the entrance and knocked. When no one came he knocked again, violently this time.

After a while the heavy door was opened and old Marquez bowed to him. He was sorry but the prince and the princess were out.

How much did he know? He was the oldest servant of the Ébolis, here in Madrid.

"I must speak to Dona María de Mendoza", Juan said hoarsely.

"Dona María is not here", Marquez said.

Juan began to shout. "I must speak to her at once."

"Dona María is not here", Marquez repeated. The entrance was not very well lighted, but Juan could see that he was sweating.

"You're lying", he said. "I know she's here. I had a message", and he made a move to enter. Old Marquez stepped into his way. Juan's hand flew to his sword hilt.

Marquez made the sign of the cross. He did not budge.

Juan dropped his hand. "How is she, Marquez?" he murmured.

The old man stared past him. "Dona María is not here", he said for the third time.

Juan nodded. His eyes were burning. "Forgive me, Marquez", he said. "You're a good servant. God bless you." He wheeled around, went back to his horse, mounted, and rode off without looking back.

## CHAPTER 23

"Of course you couldn't do anything else", Doña Magdalena said energetically. "Except that you should have come to me straightaway, instead of trying to storm the palace Éboli singlehanded. I know, I know, you don't have to tell me that you *had* to go there."

"I'm going back in the morning", Juan said wildly. "And then no one is going to stop me. . . ."

"You should stop behaving like a little boy now", she told him severely. "Besides you'd better lower your voice, or Don Luiz will wake up. And I don't want him to wake up. Be quiet and let me think."

"I never felt so helpless in my life", he murmured, burying his face in his hands. "God, I didn't know there was such pain. When I think . . ."

"You will have much time to think about it—a lifetime", she told him grimly. "Now *I* must think."

It took her only a few minutes. Then she said, "You stay here. Don't move from this room. I'll be back in a few hours."

"But, Tía . . ." Juan rose awkwardly. "I came to you for advice—God knows I need it badly—but not because I wanted you to *do* anything. Surely I myself must do what is to be done."

"My dear boy, you may one day be a match for the King's enemies; but you're no match for the Princess Éboli. This is a woman's business. Sit down and wait for me."

"I am utterly ashamed. . . ."

"So you ought to be." She swept past him and closed the door behind her. In the anteroom a sleepy footman rose at her approach. "Go and wake Juan Galarza", she ordered. "I want him as an escort, I also want my litter, at once. When I've gone, you may go to sleep. Adelante."

She went into her dressing room and changed with great speed. She rammed a large comb into her hair and fixed her veil. When she returned to the anteroom Galarza was waiting for her, armored and armed.

She gave him a short nod and marched on. Outside the litter was ready.

A quarter of an hour later Galarza's mailed fist knocked at the door of the palace Éboli.

Doña Magdalena remained sitting in her litter.

Once more old Marquez opened.

Galarza said gruffly: "Announce to Her Highness: Her Excellency Doña Magdalena Ulloa de Quixada—*on the King's service.*"

Marquez, who had already opened his mouth, closed it again. He seemed to waver.

"What are you waiting for, hombre?" Galarza barked at him. "Do you want to obstruct His Majesty's service?"

Marquez fled. Galarza, a mailed foot in the door, turned his head and nodded.

Doña Magdalena descended from the litter and walked in. The huge anteroom was empty. After a while she could hear hurried steps.

The princess appeared, impeccable as always, in a simple black house gown and followed by two dueñas.

The two ladies bowed to each other, murmuring the prescribed greetings and courtesies.

"How stupid of Marquez not to have led Your Excellency into the Yellow Room immediately", the princess said, showing her guest the way. "He must have lost his head completely. I apologize most humbly for his outrageous behavior."

"Not at all, Your Highness. Even the best of servants cannot be prepared for a visit at such an unseemly hour."

Entering the Yellow Room they waited until the dueñas had lit a number of candelabra. Doña Magdalena accepted a chair, but sat down only when the princess did so. Two fingers of the hostess dismissed the dueñas.

After a suitable pause the princess said: "This house is *at the King's service* at any hour, Your Excellency."

"I would never dare to doubt it for a moment." There was a shade of dryness in Doña Magdalena's voice. "And that encourages me to break ordinary etiquette for a second time tonight and to come to the point of my visit at once. I beg to be allowed to see Doña María de Mendoza."

Ana raised her brows. "On the King's service?" she asked.

"The King's Majesty", Doña Magdalena said quietly, "is sometimes best served by those who do not inform him of what they are doing."

"In other words, the King does not know you are here", Ana said between her teeth.

"Not yet", was the reply. "And perhaps he will never know."

After a while the princess said: "My niece is ill."

"Naturally", Doña Magdalena answered sweetly.

Ana stared at her, frowning. Was the Quixada woman trying to find out or did she know? Most probably she knew; and so did Don Juan. That was the reason for the visit he attempted two hours ago. But how could they know? The girl must have managed to send out a message. Every woman was a cheat, and those sweet little creatures who looked as if butter would not melt in their mouths were sometimes the worst.

What pains one had taken to keep her isolated, all these months, making her stay here in Madrid despite all inconvenience, instead of sending her back to Pastrana or to any other family estate where neighbors, friends, and servants were bound to find out something. But she had to send her lover a note, the goose. Whom did she bribe— the Pilar woman? The physician? One of the two maids in charge?

"I feel quite sure", Doña Magdalena said, "that Your Highness will not do anything to antagonize the King."

The insolence of the woman! Sailing into the house under the pretext of being sent by the King—of being on the King's service anyway—and then threatening her with the King's disfavor, when Ruy was the man Philip leaned on.

"The King has not spoken yet", Ana said, controlling herself with an effort.

Doña Magdalena raised her brows. "Your Highness will forgive me if I contradict you. His Majesty strictly refused the wish of a certain highly placed personage to marry. But perhaps Your Highness was not aware of that."

"Perhaps I wasn't", Ana said blandly. Her brain was working furiously. This woman was dangerous. Quixada was no mean enemy for anyone, even Ruy. And Ruy was upset by what had happened. They had had one or two very disagreeable scenes, and now it looked as if he had been right all along. But then who could have thought that the fool of a girl would get in touch with the world outside? What had Ruy said? "You always think you are doing the right thing, Ana, because it's you who are doing it." But she was not going to give in so easily.

"That was a beautiful sight, at San Gil's, this afternoon", she said, with a charming smile. "Don Juan carrying the King's daughter to her baptism. He looked as magnificent as the godfather. An unforgettable sight."

Doña Magdalena nodded. "Assuredly. But it is always a grave risk to forget God in any human relationship."

"No doubt. No doubt." Ana went on smiling. "But once a risk has been taken, no one can undo what he has done, not even a highly placed personage."

"But the thing not to do", Doña Magdalena replied gravely, "is take further and still greater risks. A mortal cannot force the hand of God. And only at his own grave peril should he try to force the hand of the King."

This time Ana could no longer control herself. She jumped to her feet. Crossing over to the opposite wall she looked up to a picture of St. John on Patmos, as if she were praying.

She has guessed everything, she thought. She has guessed more than Ruy did. The ultimate plan—if one could call it a plan. The web, the trap, the ambush not even laid yet—to be laid only when the moment for it was propitious, when the King for some reason felt weak, when a scandal must be avoided at all costs. Even then it might not have succeeded, Philip being Philip. Now that the Quixadas knew about it, it was hopeless. She could have cried. Instead she turned around, smiling.

"What do you intend to do, Your Excellency?"

"To see Doña María de Mendoza."

"And then?"

Doña Magdalena told her.

"And if María does not agree?" Ana asked slowly. "After all, it is up to her. . . ."

"Yes", Doña Magdalena said heavily. "It is up to her. Shall we go and see her now?"

Suddenly the princess relaxed. "Oh very well", she said, with a shrug. "Let us go."

Galarza had been waiting for about two hours when Doña Magdalena came out again. She was carrying a bundle closely wrapped in a dark cloth, and she shook her head vehemently when he made a movement to take it. She mounted the litter with great caution.

Whatever his mistress had been after, she seemed to have got it. Contented, Galarza mounted his horse.

"Home", Doña Magdalena said in a tired voice.

When at long last she entered the room where Juan was waiting she was pale and her eyes seemed to be preternaturally large.

He sprang to his feet. "Tía . . ."

"I wrestled with a devil and with an angel", she said. "But I won in both cases." She dropped into the nearest chair and began to undo her veil.

He was in no state to solve riddles. "Did you see her?"

"Of course I saw her."

"How is she?" he gasped. "Is she very ill? Is it dangerous? What . . ."

"She is ill, yes. I don't think it is dangerous, but it'll take some time before she is well again."

"I must see her. I must . . ."

"Indeed you won't. Put that out of your mind at once. It was hard enough for her without your adding to it."

"But . . ."

"Anyway, *she* won't see *you*." Doña Magdalena said wearily. "She is much wiser and better than you are."

"I always knew that", he said humbly. "But I beg of you, Tía, tell me more. Tell me all you know."

"She was weak, of course", Doña Magdalena said. "She was pale and thin and penitent and proud. I don't like her family, I never did, and of all her family I like the princess least. But Doña María—at least you have shown good taste. Not because of her beauty. There is little of that now, though no doubt it will return. But she is a great lady and she is Spanish, and next to calling a woman a good Christian these are the highest compliments I know. She has charged me to tell you that you must not try to see her again."

"But why, Tía . . ."

"Because she loves you."

He passed a trembling hand over his forehead. "I don't understand", he murmured.

Doña Magdalena said severely: "If you are your father's son you must understand."

"I have done what he did", Juan said tonelessly. "I have no longer any right ..." His voice became inaudible.

"Right", she repeated. "We love talking about our rights. But are we ready to concede their rights to others? Who gave you your rank and wealth? Who acknowledged you before the world as his brother? Who has a claim, next to God, on your loyalty?"

Juan hung his head. "I know what I owe to the King."

"I'm not sure you do", she said. "If you did, you would obey his command. Royalty and nobility have many privileges. But these privileges would be hateful and absurd without a way to merit them. If we forget our duty, the poorest beggar in the street has a perfect right to spit at us when we pass by. We do not own ourselves or anything we are or have. We are stewards of God and stewards of the King. I thought we taught you that in Villagarcía, Don Luiz and I."

After a while he said, "I wish I could contradict you. But even now I would give my right arm for a glimpse of María."

"Your right arm is not yours to give", Doña Magdalena said evenly. "It belongs to the King."

"You are right again." He looked up. Pain had drawn sharp little lines around the corners of his eyes and mouth. "There is another thing I must ask you—how is ... did you see ..."

"Your daughter, you mean?" Doña Magdalena asked in a matter-of-fact voice. "She is here."

"She is ... *what* did you say?"

"She is here. She is very well, and Inez and Luisa are looking after her until I get back to the nursery—which used to be my dressing room." Despite her weariness Doña Magdalena could not help smiling a little. "She was born three days ago, and they baptized her at once: Ana Juana. I think I shall call her just Juana."

"María ... gave her to you?" he asked incredulously.

"She did—when she knew that I was seeing her in your name. She trusts you, poor child. And I shall take little Juana with me to Villagarcía and do my best for her, as I once before tried to do my best for her father. Do you also trust me with her, Juan?"

He could not speak.

"Strange", she went on wistfully. "It seems only yesterday that a little boy was brought to me in Villagarcía ..."

He knelt before her as if he were at the altar rails. "You are a saint", he sobbed.

"Rubbish and nonsense", she said. "I'm a practical woman, that's all. This means that I have a fair notion of what matters and what doesn't. And what matters as far as you are concerned is that you now do your duty." She stroked his hair gently. "You should go to Del Abrojo, you know", she said in a whisper. "All I could do for you was to clear your way in the world. But that will be of little help to you unless you set things right with God. If you value my advice at all, go to Del Abrojo for at least a month."

"Del Abrojo", he repeated. "It's a long time since I heard that name. A monastery —somewhere near Valladolid ..."

"A Franciscan monastery, yes. You will meet Fray Juan de Calahorra there. I think he is a saint. And whether you know it or not—you need him. Now you had better go home and get some sleep. It will be dawn in a few hours.

And don't worry. I shall bring up little Juana well—for you, for María, and for God."

When Juan reached home, a sleepy valet told him that an aide-de-camp had been here and left a letter. "I have put it on Your Excellency's desk."

More news from María? She would hardly be able to dispatch an aide-de-camp to him, but then, nothing was impossible. He raced to his desk. There was the letter. He recognized the seal and blanched. The King's seal. He broke open the envelope and read. It was a dry order to appear in the small council room at ten o'clock in the morning.

An audience. Now that all was over—an audience. But— was it over? Perhaps the Princess Éboli had been in touch with the King. Or she had told her creature, Pérez? If so, tomorrow morning's audience could mean anything, anything. Exile, for instance. Or a monastery—not for a retreat of one month, but for the rest of his life.

He gritted his teeth. This may be God's answer, he thought. One month is not enough. Only a lifetime can expiate what you have done.

The valet came to help him undress. He waved him aside. He could not go to bed now. Much better to sit and think till dawn came. Better still—to kneel and pray.

Secretary of State Antonio Pérez flashed him a generous smile, when he passed through his room, as he had to, and he could not help wondering whether this was the last time he would receive a smile at court.

A moment later an aide announced his title and name and he marched into the small council room.

The King, pale and dressed in black as usual, was sitting behind his desk, writing. Looking up for a moment, he said in a low voice: "You will have to be patient for a few minutes, till I have signed these decrees."

Juan bowed deeply and stood still as if on parade.

Philip's tone had been affable enough, but that did not mean anything; he took pride in the fact that no one could gather from his tone or from his expression what he was really thinking or feeling.

Some courtiers tried to imitate the royal impassivity—others were in constant fear of it. "The King's smile is akin to a stab."

The only sound in the room was the scratching of the King's pen.

What if that document in front of him concerned ... María? The thought was hot, agonizing pain. What if it was María who was being banished? Fool that he was, he had thought of the Princess Éboli getting in touch with the King or with Pérez—but not of another possibility, so much more likely: that the King had spies in the household of Ruy Gómez, and that he had read everything that had been going on in the palace Éboli in a number of cold, unfeeling, policelike reports. The mere thought of it was enough to make a man wish to jump out of the window. . . .

The King stopped writing, put the pen down, and rang a bell. Out of the corner of his eye Juan saw that the man who came in was not an officer, but a simple lackey.

"Sand", the King said.

The lackey took a small vessel and carefully sprinkled the document with sand. Then he walked away.

"This", Philip said, tapping the document with a long, thin finger, "concerns you very much."

There it was. Juan stood immobile, determined to show the King a face as impassive as his own.

"It makes you the commander of my fleet in the Med-iterranean", the King said amiably. "Your official rank is that of Captain General of the Sea. I have recalled my ambas-sador in Rome, Don Luiz Requeséns y Zúñiga, the Grand Commander of Castile. He will serve as vice admiral of the fleet. His skill and his great experience will be of much help to you. Your two personal secretaries will be Juan de Quiroga and Antonio de Prado. They are both gifted men, especially de Prado."

Juan felt as if a gigantic hand had taken him up and put him down on the summit of a mountain.

"You are still very young for a position of such impor-tance," Philip went on, "and we must see to it that your subordinates will not appear to be superior to you in other honors. You will therefore be invested with the insignia of the Order of the Golden Fleece."

Once more the hand had lifted him up, this time to starry heights, where only royalty could breathe.

"I shall write to you at length about many matters in connection with your appointment", the King continued. "At present only a few words about some of the most impor-tant necessities. You will carry out your duties as a good Christian and in your life and habits give an example to everybody under you. You will be devout, not only pri-vately but also in appearance. Be distrustful of flattery. Acquire a reputation for truthfulness and above all for absolute reli-ability. Avoid swearing and cursing and do not tolerate any such thing on the part of your officers or men. . . ."

The King's voice droned on for the better part of an hour. Virtue after virtue was demanded of the new com-mander of the Mediterranean fleet—moderation and tem-perance; justice and decency; calmness and dignity; simplicity in dress, food, and service; and suitable warnings were uttered against the vices both general and special to those whose life was spent for long periods on the high seas.

"Your commission takes effect from today", Philip concluded. "And it is my wish that you should start work immediately. Your secretaries will report to you as soon as you have returned to your rooms here in the palace. Your staff is awaiting your arrival in Cartagena, where you will proceed immediately for an inspection of the fleet, the arsenal, and the port. I shall expect your personal report in two months."

Don Luiz Quixada came home early that day, so delighted over the good news that he did not have his return announced to his wife, but went himself to find her.

She was not in her favorite room. Of course not. This was the time when she took her afternoon siesta.

He went to her bedroom. She would not mind being waked for news like this.

But she was not in her bedroom either, only good, fat Luisa, watering the flowers.

"Where is my wife?" he asked.

Luisa turned as red as a peony and began to stammer incoherently.

The door of the dressing room opened and Doña Magdalena appeared.

"Back so early, my dear?" she asked. "I had no idea. Stop this nonsense, Luisa, and go back into the . . . into the dressing room."

The fat girl fled and Doña Magdalena closed the door behind her.

"I have the most magnificent news", Don Luiz began. He told her about Juan's appointment, now known all over court. "He had to go at once", he concluded. "I had only just time to wish him Godspeed, and he told me to give you his love, 'for what it is worth', as he put it. His first great appointment, my dear, and what an appointment!" He was beaming. "It is a little absurd," he said, "but I'm as proud of him as if I were his father."

"There was a time when I thought you were", Doña Magdalena said, smiling. "But how wonderful. And just in time. The King couldn't have done better."

"What do you mean, just in time?" Don Luiz inquired. "Well, of course, there was a longish period of waiting, but at his age . . ."

A thin wail came from the direction of the dressing room, and he stiffened. "What on earth was that?"

Doña Magdalena laid a hand on his arm. "Only a very small girl", she said. She went on, in a strangely solemn tone: "In the name of my love for you and yours for me I beg of you let me take care of her and to give her my motherly protection. She is the daughter of one of my best friends whose name I am not permitted to reveal . . ."

"What are you talking about?" He stared at her, round-eyed.

Smiling, she went on: ". . . but whose nobility and renown is beyond questioning. She must receive the education due to the daughter of a caballero."

"By the heavens above, I wrote that to you once", he said, still completely baffled. "But what . . . who . . ."

The thin wail could be heard again.

Doña Magdalena's mouth twitched in suppressed amusement. "I didn't ask *you* any questions then, did I?"

"A child," he said, "a girl. The daughter of . . . Dios de mi alma!"

"Will you be good enough to ask the King's permission for me to return to Villagarcía?" Doña Magdalena inquired innocently. "The estate needs looking after very urgently."

# BOOK THREE

A.D. 1568–1570

# CHAPTER 24

"READY?" PRINCE CARLOS ASKED.

"Quite ready, Your Highness." The dumpy, little French engineer beamed. "If Your Highness will be good enough to observe: the door is so thickly armored that not even a musket shot will pierce it. As for mere pistol shots, they will not even leave an impression."

"Good. If it's true, that is."

Engineer Foix raised his hand. "I guarantee, Your Highness; I swear. But this is only a small part of the door's secret. I have built in certain springs—they are my own invention, if I may mention that—and these springs are controlled by a thin red cord—Your Highness will observe how it runs down here—and passes under the carpet here—and comes out the other side—here, behind Your Highness' bed. Now when Your Highness pulls the cord—so—the door is hermetically closed. No one can get in, no one can get out—so! Another pull—and it is open again. If Your Highness wishes to try . . ."

His Highness did wish to try. His Highness tried half a dozen times and it worked beautifully. "Excellent, Foix. This means that no one can enter my bedroom—or leave it—unless I permit him to do so. You haven't told the secret to anyone, I hope?"

"Of course not, Your Highness. I guarantee, I swear— Your Highness and I alone know the secret of the little red cord."

"Here", Carlos said. "Take this."

Deftly the engineer caught the fairly heavy purse the prince threw at him. He broke into a stream of gratitude and began to bow his way toward the door. When he reached it, it closed with a click. The prince had pulled the little red cord. There was a shattering crash and Foix jumped back with a howl, as the bullet whizzed past his ear and buried itself in the wall beyond.

Carlos, the smoking pistol in his hand, grinned cheerfully. "Not much of a dent. You didn't lie to me. Lucky for you. You may go now." He pulled the cord; the door opened and Foix bowed himself out, rather green in the face. He was promptly seized by two of the prince's chamberlains who had heard the shot in the anteroom.

"Let the man go, you apes", Carlos cried, still grinning. "Send de la Cuadra in, and Osorio—and keep out."

De la Cuadra came in first, a large, fleshy valet, smiling all over his cunning face.

"How much?" the prince asked quickly.

"Another twenty thousand from Burgos, Your Highness."

The prince thrust his underlip forward. "Very little", he muttered. "Thirty from Toledo; ten from Medina del Campo. Satan take them for the disloyal, distrustful bunch of usurers they are and now a measly twenty. Still, it's better than nothing. Where is that two-legged animal, Osorio? Did you get it in gold, de la Cuadra? I want only gold. I hate those letters of credit; you never know whether the rascals will honor them."

"They are all in good, solid ducats, Your Highness."

Osorio entered, the prince's chief valet. "Your Highness will excuse the little delay—"

"I excuse nothing. Have you got news from Sevilla at last? You've been back ten days; they should have sent what they promised."

"They did, Your Highness." The valet's sallow face was creased in smiles. "Another hundred and eighty thousand."

De la Cuadra bit his underlip.

Carlos beamed. "Now that is something." He began to make a few hasty notes on a piece of paper. "How much is one hundred and eighty and two hundred and seventy, Osorio?"

"Four hundred and fifty, Your Highness. And I just heard that Don Juan de Austria has returned from Cartagena to report to His Majesty."

Carlos jumped up. "Where is he? Here at the palace?"

"Yes, Your Highness. He did not know that His Majesty had gone to El Escorial for the feast days."

"I want him", Carlos spluttered. "I want him immediately. Go and get him. Run, man, run—you too, de la Cuadra. See to it that he doesn't leave the palace before I've seen him."

The valets obeyed. Carlos walked over to his audience room and sat down. Four hundred and fifty, he thought. And the sixty-five that I had before—makes five hundred and something. More than half a million ducats. Good enough for a beginning.

Perhaps even the King himself did not have such a sum at his disposal. Money was scarce in Spain; the King was always wailing for money, as if he could not raise any amount he wanted simply by taxation. No need for the King to pay twelve percent monthly to usurers. He could tax it out of them, couldn't he? Ah well, those people in Sevilla, Burgos, Medina del Campo, and Toledo would be surprised when they came for their interest. More than half a million good, solid ducats. And they only paid thirty pieces of silver for Christ. How many Christs—no, he mustn't think that. Confession would be troublesome enough as it was.

He couldn't go to Father Chávez, not this time. Much too clear what *he* would say about the *idea*. But the idea was more important than Father Chávez. If he only knew ...

Here was the half-baked captain general of the sea, looking brown and damnably healthy, damnably healthy. "My dear Juan, I am delighted to see you again. It is up to me to welcome you in Madrid; my father has gone to El Escorial for some time. The place seems to grow on him even before it is finished; I can't think why—it's all a mass of mortar and wood and Jeromite monks and a lot of sweaty laborers. How is Cartagena? How is the fleet? I was very happy to hear about your appointment; for once I wholeheartedly agreed with my father. Now sit down—no, I insist—I have a great deal to tell you. . . ."

Juan obeyed, somewhat bewildered. He knew that the prince had in his own way a kind of liking for him, but such effusiveness was not normal. Antonio Pérez had already told him that the King was at El Escorial, also that Don Ruy Gómez and the princess were well. Juan did not dare to ask about anyone else, but he had hoped to pay a quick visit to the Éboli palace before setting out for the Escorial. He hoped very much that the prince would not keep him long.

"Tell me," Carlos said, "absolutely between ourselves, what has the King promised you for the future?"

"For the future? I don't understand, Your Highness. I have only just begun ..."

"Yes, yes, I know, a fine appointment; I told you how much I agreed with it, and you're a knight of the Golden Fleece, too, that's all very well. But what are the King's plans for you, his real plans, I mean. You can't be in charge of the fleet for the rest of your life, like a professional sailor. What is it that the King has in store for you?"

Juan shook his head. "He has never said anything . . ."

"Just as I thought", Carlos sneered. "And your official title is still Your Excellency, I suppose. Nothing more than that. In other words he is intelligent enough to see that you can give him good service, and mean enough to keep you from attaining any kind of position that he could not take away from you any time he likes."

"But surely, Your Highness, the King can always . . ."

"The King cannot change *my* rank, can he? Neither could he change yours, if he once granted you the title Highness."

Juan bit his lip. The prince had a knack of putting his finger where it hurt.

Smiling, Carlos said: "Fortunately there is somebody who can and will grant you what you have a right to expect. Someone who soon now will be in a position to do even more than that for you. Tell me, Juan, which would you prefer: the dukedom of Milan or the kingdom of Naples?"

Juan frowned. "If this is a jest, Your Highness, I would much rather . . ."

"A jest?" Carlos jumped up. "My dear Juan, this is the most serious hour of your life." Some of the old shrillness was back in his tone. "It is the hour of decision, Juan. Now you will have to prove your mettle. Are you a born subject, just one more of those bended backs of which there are so many at this court—or are you more? This is the first honor that I grant you: to think that you are more. You are of the blood. You should be more. Juan, I want something of you, just one small thing. Give it to me—and I will give you everything you want—the fulfillment of your dreams."

"If there is anything I can do for you, I will do it without asking for anything in exchange", Juan said gently.

Carlos gave a short laugh. "You don't understand", he said. "You think you're still dealing with the Carlos of Alcalá. You don't believe that I have power. I must show you a few things. You know, perhaps, that my father has kept me short of money. There have been times when I've had to borrow money—small sums here and there. Well, at present I have more than half a million ducats at my disposal, of which the King knows nothing. Borrowed, too, certainly. But from a number of men who have put their confidence in me—men in various cities and towns of Spain."

What on earth was he driving at? Juan opened his mouth to say that he was in no need of money, but then thought it better to let the prince go on. Half a million ducats was an enormous sum. What did he want it for?

"I never cared much about money", Carlos said with a contemptuous gesture. "I'm told my father speaks of little else lately. He ought to have been born the son of a merchant, sitting on a merchant's stool and adding and writing. But just now I need money, so I procured it for myself. What I need next is—a ship. And you have all the ships in the Mediterranean at your disposal. One galley is all I want—for the moment."

In a sudden flash Juan understood. "Your Highness, you cannot seriously think of—"

"One galley", Carlos interrupted him. "To take me to an Italian port that I shall name to you. All I want from you is a letter to the fleet authorities, ordering them to put that galley at my disposal. Has anyone ever been offered a better bargain: a duchy, a kingdom for one miserable galley? But I'm not going to talk to you as if you were a dirty shipowner. You and I, we are of the same blood; we understand each other. I am leaving Spain—but not for long. Everything is well prepared. I have written letters to a

264

number of the most powerful men in the realm and told them I would leave and wanted them to come with me. The dukes of Sesa and Medina de Ríoseco have accepted; so has the Marquis of Pescara and many others."

"But do they know what your intentions are, Your Highness?"

Carlos smiled. "Perhaps they do and perhaps they don't. In any case they're coming with me. And when I tell them what it is all about, they won't be able to change their minds. And indeed why should they? They have sworn allegiance to me as the heir apparent—you were present that day, Juan, and you swore allegiance yourself. Besides, they also will have their reward. I'm giving them back their rights of private taxation, which my father took away from them because he wants to be in control of all taxes. For the good of the country, of course, everything my father does he does for the good of the country."

Juan waited till the prince's laughter subsided. Then he said: "Have you thought of the consequences this—act of yours will create in the Netherlands, where . . ."

". . . where Alba is now viceroy when it was promised to me?" Carlos shrilled.

"Your Highness, I beg of you to consider what it must mean to all the peoples and nations of the realm, when the King's only son rises against his father!" Juan had overcome his first numbness. "Why, they will all feel that they can claim their own freedom of action with equal rights at least. The Moriscos in the south . . ."

"Don't mention that scum. Of course there will be some upheavals at first, there always are. There were when Caesar crossed the Rubicon, weren't there?"

Carlos hobbled up and down the room. As always he seemed to drag himself forward by sheer willpower. As always his gait was like the stalking, inexorable march of a black beetle. "You have no idea," he said grimly, "no idea, my poor Juan, how far my plans have progressed. Everything is ready—except that letter of yours. Here in this desk are the letters to the Pope, to Queen Catherine, to all the princes of Christian countries, to the grandees, the great chancelleries, the courts and cities of the kingdom, giving them the reasons for my flight from Spain. . . ."

"But what are they, Your Highness?" Juan asked miserably. "Why should you give up voluntarily what will be yours in God's own time! When I last saw you, you told me you had decided to marry Archduchess—"

"Don't mention her name", Carlos shrieked. After a pause he said tonelessly: "That's just one more of my father's crimes. He stole my first fiancée. Now for some time his envoys in Vienna have done everything to *avoid* progress. Avoiding progress! My father has brought that to a fine art. He wants to cheat me out of that marriage as well. He hates me, Juan; don't you realize it? But I will no longer live under his tyranny. In a few days time I shall be free."

"You must have drawn many people into this scheme of yours", Juan said. "Aren't you afraid there might be at least one among them who will give the secret away?"

Carlos stopped in front of him. "That danger always exists when a *coup d'état* is planned", he said slowly. "But those who know about it also have the misfortune of knowing my father. This means they know that he is not the man to reward them for telling him what must hurt his mountainous pride." He smiled again. "You for instance, Juan dear, could not find a quicker way to lose your present command than by telling the King that his son intends to leave the country and to rise against him in force. Even if he should believe you—and his hatred against me might lead him to believe it—there is one thing he will never believe: that you told him for any other reason than that you intend to take my place as his successor."

Now Juan, too, jumped up. "Your Highness!"

Carlos grinned. "Calm yourself, Juan dear. Noble indignation has never impressed me much. But perhaps you will see now that I have thought of everything. You have underrated me. I forgive you for that. Everyone else has, so why shouldn't you? And now I want your decision. Are you going to give me that letter or not?"

Juan shook his head. "This is too grave an issue to be decided on the spur of the moment, Your Highness. I must have time to think. Are you sure that you yourself won't change your mind?"

"I have been waiting for this for years", Carlos said. "And I have been planning it for many months. Change my mind? I might as well try to return into my dead mother's womb."

"You have been planning it for many months", Juan said. "It is only fair to give me twenty-four hours to think it over."

"I don't like it." Carlos resumed his walk. "You really ought to know now what you intend to do. But very well—stay here at the palace and think it over."

"Impossible", Juan said firmly. "Many people have seen me since I came to the palace, including Secretary of State Pérez, who told me that the King is waiting for my report on the fleet. If I do not go to the Escorial, it will arouse suspicion."

"To the Escorial?" Carlos' eyes were glittering dangerously. But suddenly he laughed again. "You needn't have told me that. And you wouldn't have, if you intended to give me away. Go and make your precious report. But remember: in twenty-four hours I must have your decision.

Remember also that all I want is one short letter. I'm not asking you to put the fleet at my disposal—yet. Think over what I told you about Milan and Naples, too. Perhaps there is something else that attracts you more. If so, just let me know. The choice for you is between Philip, who wants to keep you down, and Carlos, who wants to raise you up. Between remaining forever a subject, to be deprived of rank, title, and position at any time—and a throne in your own right, with a queen of your own choice. Think, Juan— think whether that is not worth the risk!"

Juan was riding across the bleak, arid plain. Somewhere at the end of the long road, still hidden to the eye, were the Guadarrama Mountains and El Escorial.

He was alone, and yet he was not. No aide was riding with the captain general of the Mediterranean fleet—no staff, not even a valet. But thoughts kept him company, and the faces, minds, and souls of many people.

A throne in your own right, with a queen of your own choice. A duchy or a kingdom. With a queen of your own choice; a queen of your own choice, yes, if all existing order is upset a man only half royal may well become a king, and a king might choose his queen with no one to gainsay him. And the devil led him up on to a high mountain and showed him all the kingdoms of the world in a moment of time. I will give thee command over all these, the devil said, and the glory that belongs to them. And the Lord had the answer to it; he always had.

A queen of your own choice, that was it. How did he know, the devil, that this last word of his would stick, this parting shot come true as nothing that he had said before? Perhaps he knew—not only the King; Carlos also might have his spies.

The plan was mad, quite mad. But mad plans had succeeded in the past. Human history was full of mad plans that failed and others that succeeded, and failure or success alone decided what men would call them: mad or daring, absurd or a stroke of genius.

Carlos was mad. But madmen too sometimes succeeded, and no one called them madmen any longer then. Carlos was mad, but he was also shrewd and cunning, and most of his answers today had shown not only an iron will but also that his scheme included much more than he had chosen to divulge. Could it be that all his absurd behavior, all the pranks and nightly adventures and revolting cruelties, were only a mask, hiding the real Carlos and his real aim, making him appear as one utterly incapable of a really deep-laid plot?

María and the throne of Naples—for one short letter, putting a ship at the disposal of the King's son.

But then you see, devil, that is not the whole of the story. Not only because the plot might not succeed, and then: imprisonment for life and perhaps even the executioner's sword; but because of something far worse. The contempt of those who happened to believe in loyalty. Doña Magdalena and Don Luiz—to mention only two. Try to argue them away, if you can. And the king who won his throne by treason—how could he ever trust anyone? And what is life, if a man cannot trust anyone?

And why should María accept a crown from a traitor?

The foundation of love is faith. What faith could she have in a man who conspired against his king?

Traitor. A nasty word. But he could not escape it now, whatever he did. The King or Prince Carlos—one of them he would have to betray. And even silence was betrayal, now that he knew about the conspiracy. . . .

Fray Diego, Fray Diego, why did you have to hear my prayers for a dying prince! What good has it done him, me, anybody, that he went on living because of your intercession?

Then he saw the Guadarrama Mountains rising into the setting sun, and not long afterward, quadrangular and forbidding, the slowly growing humanmade mountain that was El Escorial.

No one could live there yet. A house and chapel had been built for the first of the Jeromite monks, whose home it would become one day. The chapel was small, the house primitive. There was a camp of tents for the laborers, hundreds of them. Still more of them were living at the village nearby. There was one other new building—a hospital the King had built for the workers. "Where men are crowded together, disease loves to appear", he said. "And where men are erecting a building, there will be cuts and broken bones."

Almost all the materials had to be carried here from afar. Pine wood from the forests of Valsain and Cuenca, jasper from Burgos de Osmar, white marble from the mountains of Filabres, marbles brown or green and veined with red from Granada, from Aracena, and even from Portugal, all transported by fleets of carts, each dragged by ten, twelve, twenty oxen.

Later the more delicate objects would follow—the wrought-iron grilles, the bronze lamps, the candelabra and censers, the ornaments of silver and gold, the cloth for the altars, the sacred vestments, cut and sewn and embroidered by the patient hands of nuns. Great artists in Florence and Milan were working to have the statues ready by the appointed time; great artists in Flanders and Holland were painting the pictures, while the mob was destroying their work in the churches of their own country.

The King supervised everything, saw everything, and gave all the directions. This was his world.

Juan inquired at the village where the King was. They did not know. He left his horse with a blacksmith, as one shoe had come loose, and walked on toward the towering structure, where hundreds of men were at work. He asked again. "I couldn't tell you, Your Grace", a worker said. "He was here an hour ago; that's all I know." An overseer grinned. "He's all over the place, Your Mercy, you never know where he's going to turn up next."

And there were no officials in sight, no chamberlains, no guards, nothing to indicate the presence of a monarch. This was another Philip.

It is always difficult to try and approach him, Juan thought, but usually for very different reasons. There was only one thing to do: to go to the house where the monks had their quarters and inquire there whether they knew his whereabouts.

On his way to the house he passed the chapel. He stopped, turned, and entered it. It was more than primitive. A small, wooden crucifix on the simplest of altars. A couple of benches. On the first, three men were sitting; on the second, five.

Juan went up to the first bench, genuflected, and sat down. He prayed for a while, and there was one single thought he wrapped in the folds of his Our Father: Lord, let me do the right thing in the right way.

The man next to him on the bench had a smudge of mortar on his coat. The coat was of fine material.

The man next to him on the bench was the King.

## CHAPTER 25

THREE DAYS LATER Don Carlos went by carriage to the monastery of the Jeromite monks near Madrid in order to make his confession. He refused to see his usual confessor, Fray Diego de Chávez, and asked for "just anyone else". Fray Pablo de Servaz was put at his disposal.

In the confessional Carlos said briskly: "My most important sin is one I have not yet committed, but shall commit within a few days. I intend to kill a man."

After a moment the priest asked calmly, "Why?"

"Because I hate him."

"This is not a confession, Your Highness", the priest said. "It is a threat. It is impossible to give absolution for a sin you intend to commit. Your very intention shows that you are not penitent."

"I must have absolution. I have to appear at High Mass tomorrow, and if I do not receive Holy Communion, it will cause talk. Make up your mind, Father—and quickly."

"I regret, Your Highness, but I cannot absolve you."

Carlos rose from his knees. "I do not accept what you say. I wish to consult theologians about the matter. Send for the Dominican fathers at Atocha. You may use my carriage."

Fray Pablo de Servaz complied. The first two Dominicans arrived soon enough, but now the prince insisted on having all the most learned fathers present. Neither the Jeromites nor the Dominicans had a carriage of their own, and the prince's could only hold two men at a time. For the next two hours it went back and forth till no less than fourteen theologians from Atocha were present, including the prior; and still the prince was not satisfied. He sent to Madrid for the erudite Augustinian Alvarado and an equally learned Trinitarian.

They tried hard not only to give the prince all the arguments that made his absolution impossible in the circumstances, but also to make him give up his terrible intention.

Carlos, quite unmoved, insisted on having his own way.

"He is mad", the Trinitarian whispered to Alvarado.

"Perhaps he is." The Augustinian sighed. "But now I begin to understand why Satan cannot repent. His own will-power stands in the way."

"But for every man there is sufficient grace for the asking—"

He broke off, for at that moment the Prior of Atocha said: "Your Highness has not told us yet of what position and rank the man is whom you hate so much."

Now why does he ask that, Alvarado wondered.

"He is of the highest rank", Carlos replied at once.

"In that case," the prior said, "he is likely to be one of Your Highness' relatives, is he not?"

"He's my father", Carlos said.

In the sudden hush the prior asked calmly, "Have you enlisted the help of anyone else in this venture?"

Carlos smiled. He said, "We must come to an end of this. Will one of you hear my confession and give me absolution or not?"

The silence was icy.

"It is a great pity", Carlos said, rising. "I'm afraid there will be very substantial changes under my reign." He sauntered away.

On the next day he appeared in state at High Mass. He did not partake of Holy Communion. It was the twenty-eighth of December, the Feast of the Holy Innocents.

On the same day the King and Juan attended Mass at the rickety little chapel in El Escorial. Twice during the service the King cried softly.

In the afternoon they went together to inspect a new provisional church, only a little less primitive than the chapel, but with a much greater seating capacity.

The King had made it clear that there was to be no change of program, and life went on exactly as he planned it when he came here.

There was no alarm, no hasty return to Madrid, nothing that seemed to point to an emergency of any kind.

It seemed quite consistent with the way in which Philip reacted when he first received the news, on the evening of Juan's arrival. He listened without interrupting, without asking a single question. In the end he still remained silent for a while; his eyes were half closed; his lips moved a little, but there was no sound. Impossible to say whether he was praying or just talking to himself. Then he said in a low, dry voice: "Thank you, brother." And that was all. All, except that a little later he gave Juan the order to remain with him for the time being.

Juan dared to remind him that Prince Carlos was expecting an answer from him within twenty-four hours and suggested that he write a few lines, saying that the matter would have to wait until his return. The King replied that there must be no communication whatever.

Juan did not know that during the same night four couriers were speeding to Madrid with sealed orders, nor that in the following nights a number of highly placed personages arrived at El Escorial to depart again before the break of dawn. They included several members of the council of state and the Prior of Atocha.

On January 6 the provisional church was consecrated.

On January 11 the King and Juan were present at the solemn profession of a Jeromite monk. On the same day the King sent a circular to the abbots and priors of all the monasteries of Madrid and its environment, asking for special prayers to be said for the finding of the best and the wisest solution of a problem of great importance to the realm.

On January the fifteenth the King and Juan left the Escorial for El Pardo. One of the King's guests was the Prior of Atocha, Don Antonio de Toledo.

In the afternoon a messenger arrived with a letter for Juan. The prince asked Juan to meet him the same night at eleven o'clock at the rear entrance of the park. There was a postscript: "Bring the Prior of Atocha with you."

Juan took the letter at once to the King.

Philip read and said: "Go; listen and delay."

At ten-thirty Juan and the prior walked to the gardener's lodge near the rear entrance and waited there. Shortly after eleven the prince came, with five riders. Juan and the prior went out to meet him.

The prince asked the prior whether the King had heard about the fact that he had not received Holy Communion on the Feast of the Holy Innocents.

The prior replied that His Majesty had been much displeased.

Carlos turned his back on him, took Juan by the arm, and walked a dozen yards away with him. "I know you couldn't write to me at El Escorial", he murmured. "But time is running short. I must have that letter. And I must have a second document in which you swear by your honor that you will come as soon as I call you."

"I can't do that here", Juan answered. "When do you intend to leave?"

"On the morning of the eighteenth."

"I shall be in Madrid on the seventeenth", Juan said. "There it will be easier."

Carlos nodded. "Let's go back now", he said. "I don't want the prior to become suspicious."

A minute later he and his five companions had vanished into the darkness, and Juan asked himself for the hundredth time whether the wretched man was mad or supremely cunning. The way in which he had arranged this meeting was downright childish; the idea that a man of the prior's intelligence would not find it suspicious from the start was too naïve for a half-grown boy. On the other hand he had correctly guessed—or known—that Juan could not communicate with him while he was at El Escorial; and he had known that the Prior of Atocha was at El Pardo, although the prior's visit was secret.

Both Carlos' and the King's behavior were utterly incomprehensible; it was as if they were engaged in some deadly game, a cat-and-mouse game in which each claimed for himself the role of the cat.

Together with the prior Juan returned to the King and reported.

"I very much fear the story of the journey is a feint", the prior said. "A feint, to cover the other plan."

Juan did not know what he meant.

The King frowned a little. He said nothing.

If the story of the journey was a trick, it was carried through consistently. The very next day the prince gave orders to the master of the Royal Mail, Raymond de Taxis, to keep eight horses in readiness for the eighteenth at five o'clock in the morning.

On the morning of the seventeenth Taxis hurried to El Pardo and reported to the King.

At noon Philip and Juan returned to Madrid, leisurely and with no more than the usual escort. Philip went straight to the suite of the Queen, as always when he returned from a journey.

With the Queen were the two little princesses with their *aya*, Doña María Chacón, and the Infanta Juana.

The infanta took the tiny Princess Catherine from her *aya*'s arms and showed her to Philip triumphantly. "A tooth", she said. "A tooth, when she is only three months old, would you believe it? It came through three days ago, and ever since I've been dying to show it to you; look, here . . ."

"It is a very beautiful tooth", the King said.

"I have never seen a finer one", the infanta cried. "But then she is the most beautiful little girl, an absolute angel, isn't she, Isabella? Isn't she, Doña María?" She began to coo to the child.

The Queen, laughing, led the firstborn princess to her father, who took her in his arms and lifted her up high. "She looks well", he said. "I have a lovely wife and two lovely daughters. I must thank God for making me so rich." His voice faltered a little.

The Infanta Juana went on cooing and did not rest until Juan emerged from the background to admire the miracle of the tooth also.

The Queen was amused. "Dear Juana is at her most Portuguese again this morning, isn't she, Philip?"

The King sat down, the older of the little princesses in his lap, and began talking to her softly. Only when he heard hobbling, dragging steps approaching did he look up, without changing his position.

Prince Carlos came up to him, bowed low, and gently disengaging his father's hand kissed it respectfully. "Welcome back to Madrid, Father", he said. "We have been widowed and orphaned much too long."

"You are right", Philip said in a low voice. "It was time for me to come back." He remained sitting, but he was holding the little princess too tightly now and she began to cry. At once Doña María Chacón removed her from his lap.

Carlos very courteously inquired about his father's health and the King answered equally courteously.

Father and son were smiling at each other.

"Oh, but I almost forgot", the Infanta Juana exclaimed. "Today is the seventeenth, isn't it? That means that the day after tomorrow is the nineteenth."

"An admirable calculation", the Queen said gravely.

"I am giving a large party on the nineteenth, as you know." The good infanta was quite unruffled. "All young people. And Don Carlos will be the king of it. There'll be fireworks and we shall all wear masks; won't that be wonderful? You'll come, Carlos dear, won't you?"

"Most certainly I will", Carlos said. "Thank you very much, my dear."

"And you, too, Juan?"

"Yes, Your Highness." Juan had some difficulty with his voice.

They all left the Queen's suite at the same time. Outside more than a dozen high officials were waiting for the King to welcome him back and Carlos took Juan's arm. "Come with me."

They walked through half the palace to the prince's rooms. Carlos chased chamberlains and valets away in his gruff, impatient manner and closed the door. "At last", he said. "Now give me that document, Juan."

Juan took a deep breath. "Your Highness promised me time to think it over . . ."

"I gave you twenty-four hours. You've had more than three weeks."

"Your Highness, please believe me: it will be much better to renounce this plan of yours."

"Never. Give me that document."

"Your Highness, I beg of you—the plan cannot succeed. The very best thing you can do is to go and see the King immediately, tell him everything, and assure him that you have given up your plan for the sake of Spain. . . ."

"You're mad", Carlos said. "You're either mad or a traitor."

"Do it now, Your Highness", Juan urged. "I don't know what the King intends to do, but this is the moment; this is perhaps the last moment when you can still set things right. Nothing has happened yet. But you must confess to him. Swear an oath of allegiance to him as a sign of your repentance; swear it on the cross of your sword, on a holy relic, invoke the name of God. I wish that I could talk with angels' tongues—"

"Judas cannot change into an angel", Carlos said. His voice was strangely calm. "You have given me away, haven't you? *You* confess, if you're not too much of a coward."

"I am not at liberty to tell you about that", Juan said. "But this much I will tell you: I owe allegiance to the King."

"You swore allegiance to *me*", Carlos snapped. "But perhaps you've conveniently forgotten that."

"I swore allegiance to you as the son of your father and the heir apparent of the throne of Spain", Juan said hotly. "Your father must be my first consideration. And it is one of the terrible wrongs of your plan that you are violating the conscience of a friend—of many friends, I daresay."

"Listen to the traitor, preaching to me about loyalty and conscience!"

"Call it preaching, if you wish, Your Highness. But remember, if you please, that the first disloyal act was yours. If you can act disloyally to the King, how can you expect others to be loyal to you?"

"Juan", Carlos said softly. "My dear Juan, will you give me that document?"

Bad smile. Very bad smile.

"I can't", Juan said.

"Then, my dear, sweet Juan, you must die—now!"

"Your Highness!" Juan exclaimed. "Stay where you are!"

But Carlos rushed at him, his sword in his right hand, a dagger in his left.

Juan pushed a chair in his way and drew his own sword. "Stop this nonsense", he cried, parrying the first thrust. Carlos lunged out again and again, and Juan had some difficulty in warding off the thrusts without hurting the prince. At the fourth lunge he made half a step forward. A slight twist of his wrist and Carlos' sword flew out of his hand. Suddenly the room was swarming with people, officials, valets. Carlos shrieked insults at them as they hemmed him in; the door was open and Juan slipped out.

He went straight to the King's suite, was allowed to the presence, and reported, as was his duty, that he had been forced to draw his sword against the prince.

Philip nodded. He asked no questions. Instead he ordered him to stay the night at the palace, but not in his usual rooms. Don Diego de Acuña would see to it that he received suitable accommodation. Despite his excitement Juan observed that instead of the usual two guards at the entrance of the King's suite there were eight, and two more at every door.

Carlos needed only a few minutes to get rid of his attendants. Alone he walked through all his rooms, aimlessly, softly whistling to himself. As so often before he was playing with thoughts, hugging them and then throwing them away. Juan was a traitor. So, possibly, was the Prior of Atocha.

Or the Jeromite monks. But Taxis was a reliable man because he was stupid. The horses would be there in the morning. Of course, if he could persuade Osorio or de la Cuadra to try and—no, valets weren't any good at that kind of thing; they'd only mess it up and it would endanger the other plan. A great party, Juana dear; with fireworks and masks. And I shall be the king. Pity about the document, but one could always brandish some kind of paper before their noses, down there in Cartagena, and see to it that they didn't scrutinize it too carefully. They couldn't refuse a galley to the King's only son, could they?

Suddenly he stopped. Juan would report to the King. He had to. And then, maybe the King would send for him and there would be a scene. No good having a scene just now.

He hobbled to his bedroom, rang the bell for the valet on duty, and complained that he didn't feel well. The valet helped him to undress and he slipped into bed.

He giggled into his pillows when, half an hour later, one of the King's chamberlains was announced. "Show him in."

When the chamberlain entered, he found the prince in a state of great suffering, born with fortitude. The chamberlain nevertheless delivered himself of his mission. "His Majesty commands His Highness to come and see him immediately in the small council room."

Carlos gave a heart-rending groan. "You can see the state I am in, Don Jorge. Please give my apology to His Majesty and my filial respects. No doubt I shall be better tomorrow and then I will not fail to—oh, my poor head. You know what to say, Don Jorge, forgive me. . . ."

The chamberlain bowed and withdrew.

Carlos stayed in bed till about six o'clock. Then he rang the bell and ordered a boiled capon, a gamepie, and a pitcher of wine for his supper. He had a fire lit in the fireplace, sat down close to it in his night clothes, and consumed the entire capon and most of the pie. There was nothing very unusual about that. He invariably ate either nothing or too much. Besides, this was his last day before the great journey, and he simply took in food to give himself strength.

He gave Osorio the order to remove the plates and to wake him at four o'clock in the morning without fail.

When the valet had gone Carlos closed the armored door, using the thin red cord. He grinned. He was safe now, absolutely safe. That damned Frenchman had worked well. No one could come through the window either . . . at least not without making a great deal of noise, breaking the lead frame. He was safe. Safer, certainly, than he would be for many weeks to come, sleeping in out-of-the-way inns, with the King's agents looking for him everywhere. He would never be safe anywhere so long as the King was alive. That was what the monks couldn't understand. But kings weren't killed easily, not without time and preparation.

He had thought of everything. If Taxis should prove to be a traitor too, there were still his own horses in the stables, riding horses, of course, and he did not like riding such long distances, but in that case it could not be helped. Let's see, Taxis. Maybe we shall have to add your name to the list of enemies, a pretty long list as it was, and headed by the King. Strong characters always had many enemies, even old—what was his name?—old Honoratus Joannius had said so. In any case we shall have to add Uncle Juan's name, in due course.

He looked around. The last night in this cursed room, so full of horrible memories. A few hopes, a few moments of triumph—all putrefying now like that big, green beetle that he once crushed against the wall, the stinking thing. Only the thwartings, the disappointments, the humiliations were still alive. To whom would they give this room when he had gone? Whoever he was, he would have no pleasant dreams. This room was part of hell. They could not understand that, those monks, that he had to get away from hell, from the crushing, laming, deadening proximity of the King. One way or the other.

But tonight he was safe. Even so ... he would still take the same precautions as before. They could not possibly break through that door. But it made one feel better.

He took the musket out of his cupboard and looked it over carefully. It was in good order and there was no need to replace the charge. He leaned it against the chair beside his bed. He drew his sword and put it, naked, next to the musket. He drew his dagger and slipped it under his pillow. "Safe", he said contentedly. "Safe." And he went to bed.

It was now nine-thirty.

At ten o'clock Juan, lying on the bed of a room assigned to him by Don Diego de Acuña, was interrupted in his thoughts by the heavy tread of armored feet outside. He rose, went to the door, and opened it.

At once the pikes of two guards crossed before him and a gruff voice said: "King's orders."

In the corridor six guards under an officer were just turning the corner.

Juan withdrew and closed the door. He was a prisoner. Was it for his own protection against the vengeance of a madman? Had the King become suspicious of him as well?

Anything was possible. The night hung heavy about him, so full of suspicions and hatred that poor reason could no longer find its way.

Shortly after eleven a number of shadowy figures appeared at the entrance of the royal suite. They arrived singly, gave a password, and were allowed to enter.

The first to arrive was the Prince of Éboli. Then came the Duke of Feria, the Prior of Atocha, and Don Luiz Quixada, and finally the two chamberlains, Don Pedro Manuel and Don Diego de Acuña. They were all in a state of deep emotion. The King presided at a conference lasting for almost one hour. No memorandum was made of it, but according to one participant the King spoke "as no man ever spoke before".

At midnight they all left together. First the Duke of Feria, with a small lantern; then the King, wearing armor under his cloak, a naked sword in his hand; then the others.

At the entrance of the suite twelve guards were waiting under the command of an officer; here also stood two valets, Santoya and Bernal, and between them the engineer Foix, who was shaking like a leaf.

They all walked on, first along a number of corridors, then down a small staircase. More corridors. One of the guards stumbled in the darkness, and the officer cursed him under his breath.

At the door of the prince's anteroom they met the two chamberlains on duty, Don Rodrigo de Mendoza and Count Lerma.

The King ordered them to stand back, to close the door of the anteroom behind them, and to let no one else enter. Six guards were left with them.

In the anteroom the King looked at engineer Foix and nodded.

The Frenchman drew a strangely formed key from his pocket, approached the armored door, and opened a tiny aperture fairly low down on the right side. The Duke of Feria, holding his lantern close, saw what seemed to be a number of iron hooks, which the engineer manipulated. After a few moments Foix closed the aperture again, stepped back, and bowed low to the King.

Feria, very cautiously, pressed the door handle. The door opened at once.

Again the King nodded. Feria and Ruy Gómez, on tip-toe, entered the prince's bedroom.

Carlos was fast asleep. They discovered the musket and the sword and removed them. They made only a very faint noise, but Carlos woke up.

"Who is there?" he asked in a voice heavy with sleep.

"The council of state", the Prince of Éboli replied.

Carlos jumped up. The dagger slipped from under his pillow and fell to the floor. Swift as lightning Ruy Gómez bent and picked it up.

The prince saw that his musket and sword were missing. He turned back, snarling with rage, and by the light of the lantern he saw the King entering the room, pale as death, the naked sword in his hand.

The prince recoiled, step by step, until the wall stopped him. "Has Your Majesty come to kill me?" he quavered.

"Set your mind at rest", Philip said heavily. "You will suffer no harm. Santoya—Bernal—light the candelabra."

Ruy Gómez gave the prince's arms to one of the guards who carried them outside.

"Remove all other weapons you find", Feria told two others. "Look into every cupboard. Take the pokers of the fireplace too."

The room was fully lighted now.

"Santoya—Bernal", came the King's voice. "Nail up the windows."

Ruy Gómez was already removing the papers from the prince's desk.

"An arrest", Carlos stammered. "No. No. Not that." He rushed at the King and was stopped by Don Luiz Quixada's hard, sinewy body. "Kill me," he howled, "kill me, but don't have me arrested. If you do, I'll kill myself."

"Only a madman would do that", the King said.

Carlos broke free. He rushed toward the fireplace and would have thrown himself headlong into the fire, if the Prior of Atocha had not caught him just in time. The prior and Feria then drew him back to his bed, where he lay, cursing and slobbering.

The Duke of Feria suggested that a physician should be called.

At once Carlos sat up. "I'm not ill", he shouted. "And I'm not mad either—only desperate because my father is treating me like this."

"Henceforth," the King said stonily, "I am going to treat you not as a father but as a king."

Santoya and Bernal began to hammer away at the window shutters.

The King turned around and left.

For several days all the roads leading away from Madrid were blocked by troops against everyone but the King's couriers. No mail was allowed to leave.

When at last the troops were withdrawn the King could be certain that the official version of the detainment of Prince Carlos would be known, both within and without the realm, before gossip and rumor had had a chance to interfere with it.

A small number of arrests were made, among them the valets Osorio and de la Cuadra and a few merchants in various towns.

Ruy Gómez carefully studied every scrap of paper that he had removed from the prince's desk. Most of the letters that Carlos had intended to send off—to the Pope, the princes of other countries, to chancelleries and courts, in short to all those who now were receiving the King's official version—were grossly insulting to the King and his advisers. Nothing was found, however, that seemed to point to a secret understanding between the prince and the rebels in the Netherlands.

After a week the prisoner was given a different room—the smallest room in his suite, forming part of a tower. It had one door and one window. The window was barred so that light entered only at the top and the fireplace was covered with an iron cage. A hole was pierced into an adjoining chamber, which was transformed into a chapel. Mass was said there every morning by Fray Diego de Chávez, and the prisoner could thus hear it in a way not entirely dissimilar to that of the cloistered nuns of an Order of strict observance.

All the household of the prince was dismissed, with the exception of Count Lerma. Five new chamberlains were appointed.

The King himself drew up the most exact instructions for the custody of the prisoner. The prince was to be treated with all the respect due his rank. His orders in all things referring to his personal service were to be obeyed, unless his wishes were opposed to the King's commands. No other orders were to be carried out. The prisoner was not allowed to communicate with the outer world by letter or message. The utmost care had to be taken to prevent him from committing suicide. No one was allowed to enter his room armed. The prisoner was not to have a knife for his meals. His meat had to be cut up for him in the kitchen.

The door of the room must be kept ajar at all times, day and night. Two chamberlains were to remain on watch in the anteroom, and one was to sleep in the prisoner's room.

The prisoner was allowed a missal and books of devotion, but no other reading. If he tried to talk to an attendant about his arrest, he was not to be answered.

Apart from his six attendants only one other person was allowed to enter the prisoner's room: the man who was personally responsible to the King for the royal prisoner. During the first week it was the Duke of Feria. From then on it was Don Ruy Gómez, Prince of Éboli.

At the King's request, Don Ruy and the princess installed themselves in the suite previously used by Prince Carlos.

At about the same time Don Juan de Austria received orders to return to Cartagena. His first official act would be to welcome the fleet returning from the Indies and to safeguard it against the African pirates. After that he was commanded to make an extensive cruise with the object of clearing the coast of the western Mediterranean of pirate ships.

CHAPTER 26

"GOOD EVENING, JAILER", said Princess Éboli.

Ruy Gómez winced. "That's not a kind reception, my dear. I've had a tiring time with His Majesty. . . ."

"As usual. But I thought you'd be interested to know what we are being called by everybody here in the palace. The jailer and the jailer's wife. Flattering, isn't it?"

He sat down beside her. A valet appeared with his favorite wine, and conversation ceased until the man had gone. Ruy Gómez emptied a goblet, gave a deep sigh, and said sullenly, "You know perfectly well that I'm enjoying this as little as you are."

"I wonder how Feria got himself out of it", Ana said. "Very adroit of him. I always thought he was rather stupid."

"He is. And he didn't get himself out of it. The King simply called him off. He wants me here." He poured himself another goblet. "I suppose I really ought to feel flattered. What a nuisance Carlos is. He's never been anything else and he manages to be one even now, when he has less liberty than an ordinary inmate of one of His Majesty's prisons. It's bad enough for us, but it's worse for the King, you know."

"Oh, is it? *He* doesn't have to live in the same suite with that little abomination, does he? He doesn't have to receive daily, almost hourly reports about His Highness' humors and personal wishes and temperature and idiotic outbursts. . . ."

"You're wrong, my dear. I have to report all that to the King every day. And ever since we had a formal complaint about the prince's arrest from the Constable of Castile, damn the man, to say nothing about the Aragonese seriously thinking of sending a deputation to Madrid, we have been doing a fearful amount of legal work in the matter. It looks as if we shall have to convoke the Cortes or else institute a process before the council of state. . . ."

"Either of which would be a farce, of course."

He shook his head. "My dear Ana, sometimes I think that I, the Portuguese, know your compatriots better than you do. . . ."

"Are you calling the Aragonese my compatriots?" she jeered.

"Well, at least they are Spaniards. . . ."

"They are that . . . of a sort, I suppose."

"Well, anyway, you know that the King, in a weak moment, made us all swear an oath of allegiance to Carlos. He is still the legal successor of the King. And if something, God forbid, should happen to His Majesty . . ."

". . . The little animal would be out and about, they'd crown him and his first act as King would be to have our throats cut. A charming prospect . . ."

"So you understand that we must do all we can to strip Carlos of his right of succession, and it's not an easy thing, within the existing laws of the constitution. A number of brilliant legal experts are working on it, and a mass of testimony is being taken every day in regard to the prince's sanity or otherwise."

"As if there could be any doubt! Why, last week he tried to strangle poor Lerma again . . ."

"He always hated him."

". . . And on one day he refuses all food and the next he eats almost as much as his own weight. He asks for huge pitchers of ice, empties them on his bed, and rolls on it, shrieking and cursing. If he's not insane, who is? He's as mad as his great-grandmother."

"You don't have to convince *me*", Ruy Gómez said, with a shrug. "But all this may sound less convincing to those who wish to uphold Carlos' sanity for some purpose of their own. And we don't want a secret Prince's Party to be raised in the realm, especially as I can think of some foreign princes who would be only too glad to assist it. This kind of thing can lead to a civil war."

"Oh, no!" Her eyes narrowed. "Does the King think as you do?"

"I think he does, but you never know with Philip, do you? Now less than ever. Much may depend upon the Queen, of course."

"You mean, if the next child happens to be a son?"

"Exactly. And it's due in November. She has been most upset about what happened to Carlos. . . ."

"Yet it's the only chance for her own son—if she has one—to become the heir apparent."

"That's not her way of thinking, Ana. You know that."

"True enough", Ana admitted. After a while she said almost wistfully, "It must be nice to be such a good, simple soul. Sometimes I almost wish . . . bah, we must all be as we are."

"She wanted to visit Don Carlos, but the King wouldn't permit it."

"He was right. It wouldn't have done her any good."

"It might have done him some good, though."

"Nothing can do him any good", Ana said coldly. "He's mad."

"He confessed at Easter", Ruy Gómez said uneasily. "And he received Holy Communion devoutly."

"Madmen have their clear moments, I suppose."

"They're talking of nothing else at all the courts of Europe", Ruy Gómez resumed. "Even the Emperor can never hear enough about it. We know that he has told the Venetian ambassador all the gossip he has got from Madrid. . . ."

"Well, that's at least a change from his usual theme—his own dyspeptic symptoms and the pernicious qualities of prawns and salad."

Ruy Gómez laughed. "You're amazingly well informed about dear old Maximilian's habits. Mind you, he's not just fond of gossip for gossip's sake. He's seriously worried."

"About the match between Carlos and his daughter?"

"Yes. And I hear he's dispatched Archduke Charles to try and negotiate here in Madrid. . . ."

Ana began to laugh. "Does he want his daughter to share the tower room, the peculiar diet of nothing today, and half an oxen tomorrow, the rolling about on ice—Ye saints, what a father!"

"The archduke is supposed to try to bring about a reconciliation."

"What? And let the madman out again, with a deadly hatred against you and me? What does the King say to this? Do you think the archduke can succeed? When will he be here?"

Ruy Gómez smiled. "Archdukes are slow travelers, as a rule", he said. "Especially when they are not particularly keen on their mission. I don't think he's left Vienna yet."

"I hope he breaks his neck before he arrives here", Ana said irritably. "We have troubles enough without him. If anybody had told me that one day I'd have the custody of a lunatic and that my husband would be called the jailer—"

"I know of a man whom that cap fits much better", he interrupted dryly. "And he's not only a jailer but also an executioner."

"Alba, you mean."

"It's simple enough for him", Ruy Gómez said bitterly. "He doesn't have to bother about constitutional difficulties. D'you know what they call his Emergency Court? The Council of Blood. Egmont is dead and Hoorn, and thousands of others...."

"Well, that's what he was sent to the Netherlands for, wasn't it? And he hasn't got hold of William of Orange ..."

"... or of Louis of Nassau, true enough. He'll get them, though. He's in his element. And so is our little friend, Don Juan, it seems."

Ana pursed her lips. "Captain general of the sea at the age of twenty-one", she jeered. "Well, I suppose anybody could do it, with old Requeséns looking over his shoulder all the time."

"You're wrong, my dear."

"How do you know? How do you know anything about what he's up to? He's on the high seas, isn't he?"

"The Mediterranean", Ruy Gómez said patiently, "is full of ports. And in most of them I have my agents—the King has, I mean, of course."

"Of course."

"So we get our reports long before he sends his own. He's doing extremely well, Ana. He's managed to acquire the confidence of both officers and men, which by itself is a rare thing. It's usually one or the other or neither, but not both. Even the rowers like him. . . ."

"The scum of the earth . . . But I know he's a charmer, though I don't quite know how he does it. Women fall for his looks, of course, but . . ."

"He is that rare specimen, a man who is loved by every-body", Ruy Gómez said thoughtfully. "When he took over the command, we had the exact repetition of what happened when he staged that mad escapade to join the expedition to Malta. The young men of our finest families are streaming to join the fleet just so they can serve under him—the two Padillas, Luiz de Córdoba, Quizmán, Portocarrero, Benavides, Ledesma, Gamboa, Zapata de Calatayud, Zanguera. . . ."

"All right, all right, I loathe statistics. But he hasn't *done* anything yet, has he? It's all his charm, his looks, his enthusiasm, if you wish. . . ."

"He's been at sea only five weeks so far", Ruy Gómez said. "With thirty-three galleys. He's been looking for pirates near the Río de Oro, went back to Puerto Santa María, where he reviewed his troops, inspected the naval stores, the cannon foundry and the fortifications. Then he launched a surprise attack against the Moorish fort of Fagazas; he took in water at Peñón de Vélez, where he beat off a Moorish attack. He freed a merchantman from two Moorish galliots and then engaged two Moorish cruisers, maneuvering so well that one of them ran ashore. Despite covering fire from Moorish towers he launched a landing party and captured the cruiser. The last news I have is that he is underway to Oran. . . ."

"And how much of all this is thanks to his merit? After all, Requeséns—"

"Requeséns seems to give him a free hand. He is amazed by the boy's knowledge, and even more so by what he calls his natural instinct in naval matters. There's nothing sensational about this first enterprise of his, but it's promising, to say the least. I'm glad I got his ship ready for him in time."

She nodded pensively. "He's forgotten all about María, of course", she said. "I wish she had forgotten him."

"You think she hasn't, then?"

"She refused to marry young Guzmán, didn't she? A perfectly good match for her. In the circumstances . . ."

"I don't think Juan has forgotten her either, Ana. I know he didn't mention her name when he came to say goodbye to us before he left for Cartagena, but I also know he made careful inquiries about where she was and how she was."

"So that's why he didn't ask any questions. He has learned prudence."

"He didn't learn anything else, though—about María's whereabouts, I mean", Ruy Gómez said with a little frown. "And this time there must be no nonsense, Ana. We can't afford to antagonize the King."

"I don't care about María and I don't care about Don Juan", she said bitterly. "All I want is to get out of this jail.

Yes, jail, Ruy. The jailer is just as much in prison as the prisoner."

"We are living at the royal palace in Madrid", Ruy Gómez said stiffly.

"We're living in rooms full of hatred", she murmured. "It's *live* hatred, Ruy. I can feel it. I can almost grasp it with my fingers. It's seeping through the walls and creeping about. . . ."

"Ana, Ana! You mustn't let yourself go like this."

She was staring at him from the corner of her one eye. "Have you ever asked yourself whether madness can be infectious, Ruy? It hovers over these rooms like a thin mist. I am going mad here, Ruy. Another three months and I'll be mad like that gibbering, cursing, foul little wreck of a human being whose watchdogs we are."

"Ana!"

She clutched his arm. "Tell me, Ruy, why has the King done this to us? Why to us?"

"Don Carlos", Ruy Gómez said, "is the King's son. He is blood royal. His . . . custodian must be a man of high rank. Don Carlos is also the most dangerous prisoner in the realm. His custodian must be a man whom the King can trust. He doesn't trust many people, you know that."

She let go of his arm. "Is that all?" she asked. "Do you really think that is all? Any well-born captain of the guards would fulfill these conditions. But you are to be the man, you, the best brain at his disposal and his closest friend. Surely there is a reason for that."

"I do not understand you", he said bravely. "And if I do, I don't want to."

"He wants you to use your brain", she said breathlessly. "He wants you to guess what is really on his mind and what is really good for him—and for Spain. And he wants you to do that."

"For the love of God, Ana", Ruy Gómez said in a very low voice. "Be quiet."

The news of Prince Carlos' death reached Don Juan in September, when he landed in Barcelona.

He was received by the Viceroy of Catalonia, the Duke of Francavilla, who only a few years earlier had done his utmost to stop him from joining the Malta expedition. When the duke welcomed him, Don Juan answered with a smile: "It's good to be received so warmly. Last time we met, you were certainly glad to get rid of me." And the duke replied in the same spirit: "On the contrary, Your Excellency. I tried hard to keep you in Barcelona and Your Excellency thought of nothing but leaving for Malta."

They drove to the palace together, and there the duke managed to get his guest away from everybody else and into his private study, where he stiffly offered his sympathies "on the occasion of the tragic death of His Excellency's nephew, His Highness Prince Carlos".

Juan's face became rigid. Twice he tried to speak, but his voice would not obey.

"It happened almost two months ago", Francavilla said. "I knew from Your Excellency's first words that you had no knowledge of it."

"I was at sea", Juan managed to say.

"Quite so."

"But—but how did it happen? I hope to God he didn't— How did it happen?"

The duke rubbed his chin. "The poor prince seems to have had or to have acquired some rather ... immoderate habits of eating. He fell ill about the middle of July, and he refused to take any of the medicines offered to him by his physicians. On the nineteenth his case was regarded as hopeless. He still had the strength and the clarity of mind to dictate his will, to make his confession, and to receive the Last Sacraments. He died a Christian death on the Vigil of the Feast of St. James, at one o'clock in the morning."

Suddenly and unexpectedly Juan burst into tears.

The fleet had to sail back to Cartagena. From there Juan traveled to Madrid. He found the city deathly quiet, with most of the windows closed and the few people in the streets hurrying by as if they had no right to be seen. At the palace everybody went about on tiptoe. The Queen had had a miscarriage. The Queen was dying.

In the night of October 4 the body of the Queen lay in state in the chapel of the palace, surrounded by a forest of tapers.

At one side of the head of the bier stood Don Juan of Austria; at the other, Don Ruy Gómez, Prince of Éboli.

The Queen was a young girl who smiled in her sleep.

Prince Carlos had died a Christian death.

The great bell of Yuste was ringing again in Juan's ears, the agony bell, the "poor sinners' bell". For with the Lord is kindness, and with him is plentiful redemption.

An old emperor, tired of his almost superhuman power, renounced it, to die in a monastery among monks.

A young prince, so thirsty for power that he tried to usurp his father's throne, came to die as his father's prisoner.

A young queen, twenty-four years old, died in the attempt to give an heir to Spain, a country she had been brought up to hate and to fear. She had dreaded the Spanish husband. From her journey across the Pyrenees she sent a little poem to her mother. Alexander Farnese had heard it from somebody who came from France—and he once recited it. Juan only remembered two lines: "*Tantost je sens mon oeil plorer puis ryre / Mais la fin est toujours d'estre martyre.*" Was she right, the young Queen—a few tears and a little laughter, but the end would always be martyrdom? Her mother never answered her poem, but her sister-in-law did, another young queen, as beautiful, perhaps even more beautiful than she—María Stuart, once Queen of France, in her own right Queen of Scotland and now a prisoner of Elizabeth of England, to whom she had fled for asylum. Catherine de' Medici must have sent the poem to Scotland when María Stuart was still wrestling for her throne there. And she answered: "*Les pleurs font mal au coeur joyeux et sain / Mais au dolent ils servent quasi de pain.* Tears hurt a joyful, healthy heart—but to those in pain they serve as bread." Alexander shrugged his shoulders as he recited the answer from across the sea. "Only a woman is allowed to feel like that." Perhaps he was right. But power seemed to be a strange thing. . . .

A man must stand quite still when he has the watch in the presence of dead royalty; he is the guardian of the threshold, the living link between life and death, the symbol of those companions of ancient kings, who killed themselves or were killed to accompany the kings on their last and most perilous voyage to the other world. He must neither speak nor move. But his thoughts could not help moving—unless he was a man like the Duke of Alba, who seemed to be able to transform himself into a statue altogether, as he had when he was watching in the room of a prince who was supposed to be dying, though the prince was saved by a miracle, only to be a tyrant and tormentor to his friends and servants and a danger to his king and to his country. A madman, perhaps—all his plans were mad, as if they had been conceived by the mind of a malicious and cruel child never fully aware of the consequences of his acts. And tears to him had never been relief—only the signs of impotent hatred or self-pity. And yet, and yet . . .

I am sorry for Carlos, Juan thought. I am perhaps even more sorry for Carlos than for the Queen. She was lovely and loved. She had soon lost her fear of her husband and of Spain. She had learned to love him—perhaps when he insisted on sitting beside her, daily, when she had the small-pox? Or when she saw his delight over her firstborn daughter. Her death came quickly, and while she still was as lovely as ever. And no one could say that she had lived in vain.

But Carlos, unlovely and unloved, had he ever known a moment of real joy? Not the unholy joy of his mad escapades, when he killed animals senselessly or wounded or hurt men—but the real joys? Yet Juan knew that this was not why he felt sorry for Carlos. It is not given to man to pity those who constantly are feeling sorry for themselves. With them it was as with those of whom Christ spoke somewhere in the Gospels—the ones who prayed in public, to be seen and admired, and who that way already had their reward.

But throughout his life Carlos had carried a heavy burden—the royal heir; the only son of the King was ugly and deformed in mind and body. And Juan, too, carried a burden, the burden of his birth. He had what Carlos had not—and Carlos had what he had not. It was this that related them to each other beyond the bonds of blood. Perhaps it also accounted for the liking the prince had had for him—at times.

He could not carry his burden, Juan thought. Am I going to learn to carry mine? And, in a corner of his heart: By feeling sorry for him, am I feeling sorry for myself?

Up to that moment in Barcelona, when the Duke of Francavilla told him that Carlos was dead, he had been radiantly happy. Then he was cast down into the abyss. His first command—and he had made a success of it. He knew it, not by what the others said, even by Requeséns, who was too old to indulge in flattery. He knew by the feel of it. The fleet was like a body and he was the mind. He had to learn to move this new body around—it was like learning to walk and sit down and get up and run and stop, with a new body extending over so and so many miles, capable of such and such speed. He must know whether to shift his weight to the right or to the left foot, whether to rush forward or to sidestep or dodge, and every one of these movements had its own timing and only when the timing was perfectly clear in his mind could he say that he could really use his new body.

And after almost four months of constant exercise he knew that he was one with this new body of his, that he could use it as he could use that of his horse when he was riding or even his own body when he was fencing. Most of what Galarza had taught him, what Don Luiz had taught him, applied here too. It was, in a way, like growing.

Of course there were a thousand other things in which his knowledge was still very scanty, particularly in those where experience was almost the only possible teacher. For such matters—navigation, the skillful use of sails and rudder, the study of tides and currents, knowledge of many special types of work—he still had to rely on his officers, not those who had joined the fleet for the honor of serving with him and under him, however great their names, but on the old sea dogs, with twenty and thirty years' experience in their fingertips, their stomachs and their noses. They also had the "feel" of it, each within his own limited realm. There wasn't a man in the entire fleet who knew as much about sails as Enrique Martínez, for instance. García de Soto only had to look at a man to know at once what branch of service he was fit for, and whether he was reliable or not. As for Requeséns, he was a treasure, but his experience of battle was far inferior to that of Abrantes, Quiñónez, Carrero, or Molina. Quiñónez was the born leader of light ships, and that was particularly valuable, because the Moors had mostly light ships and even the Turks made more use of them than of heavy galleasses. Brigs, brigantines, and frigates were Quiñónez' element; Molina had been serving on galleasses, Abrantes and Carrero on galleys. And they all seriously believed that their own type of ship was the only one that really mattered.

Surely that was not the way to train men who might have to lead a fleet? Or was it deliberate, was it a system to keep the leadership of the whole reserved for a few chosen men who had the King's confidence and trust? Men who had the knack of grasping quickly what mattered most and whose brains were unfettered by those thousand details of routine, which only too often made a naval officer incapable of seeing anything beyond his little circle of specialized activities?

He asked Requeséns that question, and the old man gave him a look of surprise and said he had never thought of it, but perhaps that was the idea and then proceeded to tell him about the magnificent reception he had given Emperor Charles twenty-two years before when he came to review his cavalry regiment in Bavaria, at some place with an entirely unpronounceable name. Requeséns was the type of man who was good at almost anything—soldiering, diplomatic service, or war at sea. He could be very stern, but he had a sense of humor and he loved telling stories. Time and again Juan had to lead him back gently to what he wanted to know: the personalities of Turkish commanders, for instance, Turkish tactics, and strategy in naval warfare....

From the Church of San Gil came the deep, booming sound of a bell, and Juan's thoughts broke off. The high seas were far away and he was in the presence of death. In San Gil's they were praying incessantly for the poor Queen's soul, and here he was, thinking of nothing but his naval command and feeling very self-satisfied about it, too, when he really had nothing much to report to the King.

The King—each time Juan came to report to him, something else happened that demanded the King's entire attention.

How proudly he had come back from his first mission of inspecting the fleet—only to be drawn into poor Carlos' frightful plot, ending with the prince's arrest. And now, coming back with a carefully considered report about his labors from June to October, another tragedy, a double tragedy, made it all appear so insignificant, so puny—it just made no difference at all.

Was tragedy the only thing that made a difference in human affairs?

Was it God's way of showing him that nothing really mattered, except the ultimate end?

What was a man to do?

He tried to pray for the Queen. But surely she was in heaven, sweet, innocent creature that she had been. His prayer fell lamely to the ground. He prayed for Carlos instead. But that, too, was no more than a leaden recital of words. Judas, Carlos had called him. He was no Judas. He had only done his duty. But ... but ... had he done it entirely without thinking of himself? Was there a hypocrite in him, subtly disguised as an upright, loyal subject of the King?

He could not pray. Was it that God would not accept his prayer, as he had refused the sacrifice of Cain? Surely that was absurd. Cain had killed his brother, and he had not killed Carlos.

O God, he could not think clearly in this terrible room of flickering tapers. Flickering, yes. There was a gentle wind blowing through the room; it came from the large door at the other end—it was opening. Something black and formless was drifting into the chapel, a black cloud, a cloud of black-clad men, all hovering in the background. All but one, who approached slowly, his hair and beard glistening white in the candlelight, an old man.

The Emperor, Juan thought, shaken to the core. Was he dreaming? The great bell of Yuste . . . the Emperor . . .

It was the King. Slowly he approached till he reached the foot of the bier. Slowly, painfully, he knelt down and folded his hands in prayer.

The King was an old man.

## CHAPTER 27

PASSING THE HEAVY GATE of Del Abrojo monastery was a little like dying, Juan felt. The world vanished behind him, and he entered a kind of in-between state or phase or place, no longer entirely earthly and not yet really anything else. So strong was the feeling that when the gate clanged shut behind him he stopped in his tracks and looked back with instinctive apprehension. There was something irrevocable about that metallic sound.

Next to the bearded brother doorkeeper a chubby little friar was standing, grinning at him. He had a round face, eyes like merry black cherries, and a tuft of gray hair in the middle of his forehead.

"Welcome, Your Excellency", he said, waddling up to him on his short, stubby legs. "And may your leaving be happier than your coming. Your luggage arrived this morning with your valets. The valets have departed, but the luggage is in your room, unpacked and in good order."

Juan nodded. He wanted to spend his time here alone, without the constant, nurselike activities of personal valets to which one was subjected at court. He had cut that kind of thing down to a minimum when he was on board ship and found the result to his taste. There would be no need for elaborate dressing in Del Abrojo. But where were the prior and his good fathers? He looked around. From afar he could see a few friars walking in the garden, whose bleakness was softened by evergreen shrubs. They were reading.

"Our prior", the little friar said, "hopes Your Excellency will hold him excused. He is quite well, really, but he finds the stairs a trifle difficult lately." He gave an apologetic little shrug. "He was ninety-three on the last Feast of the Annunciation, so perhaps it is only natural."

"Oh", Juan said. "Yes. Of course."

"The steps up aren't as difficult for him as the steps down", the friar explained. "This may be just the right thing, morally, when I come to think of it." He positively beamed. "You know what Del Abrojo's real name is, don't you, Your Excellency? Scala Coeli. Could easily be regarded as a little presumptuous, don't you think? Staircase to Heaven? Everybody calls it Del Abrojo anyhow, from the forest all around. This way, please. . . ."

They entered the great, gray building with its turrets and pinnacles, a fortress rather than a monastery, through a narrow door that Juan had not even noticed.

"It's a shortcut", the friar explained. "If we had entered by the main door we would have gone up a staircase and down another. Sometimes it's better not to insist on the grand entrance. Here all we have to climb is six steps—there—the next door is your room." He opened it and they entered.

Juan saw a fairly large room with a bed that did not look too uncomfortable, a desk, two chairs, and a fireplace, with a fire burning in it lustily. A few nicely painted flower pots with some green plants were on a shelf. There was a large crucifix hanging on the wall.

"Your chests are all under the bed", the friar explained. "Mass is said from five o'clock on up to half-past seven. Meals are at eight, noon, and half-past six. And I am at your disposal whenever you want me."

"That's very good of you", Juan said indulgently. After all, it wasn't the little man's fault that he had not been received in accordance with his rank. If the prior was too old to receive him, he ought to have sent the subprior or someone else in charge. He could not deny himself a little hint of his displeasure. "I suppose the subprior is also ninety-three?" he asked with a quizzical smile.

The little friar shook his head. "He's only fifty-six", he said. "And no good at his work at all. Strongly dislikes figures. Saint Augustine loved them, had quite a theory about them, too, but then he had a theory about almost everything. What a brain! But the subprior still dislikes figures, and all the rest of the administrative work. He should never have been made subprior."

"Are you sure that is the right way of talking about a superior?" Juan asked, frowning.

"It is definitely the wrong way", the friar said cheerfully. "But in the present case it's only self-cognition."

Juan stared at him. "You mean . . . you are . . ."

The friar bowed courteously. "The subprior, at Your Excellency's service."

"I do beg your pardon, Reverend Father", Juan said in confusion. "I had no idea . . . I should have known, of course. The very fact that it was you who received me at the gate . . ."

"I should have introduced myself, I suppose", the friar said, shaking his head. "It just shows how right I was—I'm no good at this work at all."

"I shall not be much of a burden to you, though", Juan said kindly. "Doña Magdalena Ulloa de Quixada has asked me to convey her most respectful greetings to one of the friars here whom she seems to hold in high esteem—Fray Juan de Calahorra. May I have the pleasure of meeting him? I would be grateful if I could have him as my spiritual director for the period of my retreat."

The little friar bowed again. "Fray Juan de Calahorra, at Your Excellency's service", he said dejectedly. "And quite unworthy of the great lady's high esteem."

He made such a woebegone face that Juan could not help laughing. It helped in hiding his disappointment. This was the man Doña Magdalena had once mentioned to him as a saint. . . .

"We have the same Christian name anyway", he said politely.

The little friar's face lit up. "Ah, yes, so we have. But the apostle must have looked much more like you than like me. The real San Juan, I mean, not the one one finds in so many paintings. Perfectly good paintings, but so often with a tendency to make him look weak, almost like a young woman. San Juan wasn't like that at all."

"How do you know?" Juan asked, surprised.

"From our Lord directly", the friar replied. "He used to call him Son of Thunder. You don't give a weak, girlish young man that kind of nickname, do you? He must have been a magnificent orator and an explosive one. Very impulsive. And of course, at least on one occasion he was a bit too ambitious."

"Was he? How is that? I didn't think a saint could have such a fault."

"No one is born a saint", Calahorra said, smiling. "I don't think any of the apostles could be called a saint—before Pentecost. We can't be saints before the Holy Spirit descends on us, can we? Most of us aren't even after that. It takes some collaboration. Ah, well—the occasion when San Juan was too ambitious was when he—and his brother, too—wanted our Lord to assure them that they would have the places at his right and left. Remember, how he asked them whether they could drink from the cup he was drinking from and they said yes they could?"

"I remember", Juan said.

"Well, San Juan at least had the opportunity to see what his wish implied, when he stood at the foot of the Cross and saw who was hanging on our Lord's right and left. Must have made him think—later. Quite all right. Main thing is not to think only when it is too late. It rarely is, though. Certainly isn't in your case." The little friar pursed his lips. "It all depends on what we mean by 'ambition'", he went on, taking no notice of Juan's surprise. "If we mean self-aggrandizement, we are in for a shock sooner or later. If we mean ambition for the Kingdom of God, we may still be in for a shock, even for a whole series of shocks, but they won't be able to harm us; because we are not disappointed. We can't be. We only wanted God's glory and no defeat can darken that, can it? Only it's not always easy, at first, to separate our personal ambition from the real one. Right?"

A thin bell began to ring.

"Suppertime", the little friar said. "I'll show you the way to the refectory." In the door he turned, smiling. "Don't forget—San Juan was our Lord's most beloved disciple—before he became a saint."

A firm little nod and Calahorra marched on, on his stubby little legs.

Juan followed, wondering what Calahorra knew about him.

There were some thirty-odd friars in the refectory, all standing when they came in. Calahorra moved toward the prior's chair, so the old man seemed to be too weak even to preside at meal. Juan's place was at the subprior's right. Grace was said and the serving brothers came in with steaming dishes. The meal was simple but good. As usual there was no conversation. One of the friars read first from the Gospel and then a passage from some book of devotion that Juan did not know. He read in Latin, and after a few halfhearted attempts Juan gave up listening. Plates and cups were pewter, rough but spotlessly clean. He studied the faces of the friars. Almost all of them looked far more saintly than Fray Juan de Calahorra. He seemed to have a good brain, though. Again he asked himself what Calahorra knew about him. Probably as much as Doña Magdalena had told him, which could mean everything or nothing. The story of the Apostle's ambition was of course a kind of indirect attack. Could it be that the chubby little man was a fighter?

Everybody was rising for grace again. Then they marched out in single file, praying as they went. They would assemble in church for the *Salva Regina*. All this had happened before ... a long, long time ago. When he was still a child.

In Valladolid, not very far from here. He had gone after them, that time, and listened to their singing. And there was that old man, sitting behind him in church, the old man who looked like God. Tía had told Juan about him later on, he was a very great and saintly man, Pedro d'Alcántara. Juan did not feel like going into the church. He was just a little angry, something in him was a little angry. He went back to his room and lay down on the bed.

He was not going to stay here long. Certainly not two or three months as Tía suggested when he paid her a visit in Villagarcía, her and the child.

The child had María's eyes. Did Tía know where María was? Once or twice he had had the feeling that she did, but she would not talk about her.

They were singing in the church; he could hear it faintly. Every day they sang, and prayed and instructed and studied and said Mass—and they were happy. Their faces were happy, even the most austere and ascetic ones. They were whole, made out of one piece. Probably none of them was ambitious.

That chubby friar was shrewd. He seemed to have courage, too.

But Juan was not going to stay here long. Perhaps he should not have come at all. He was restless and irritated and not at all ready for an atmosphere of joyful tranquility.

The trouble was really that he had nowhere to go. María was somewhere far away and beyond approach. And he could not stay long in Villagarcía, where the child looked at him with María's eyes.

The fleet was in port. At such a time everything went according to a fixed schedule, and the presence of the captain general of the sea was only a disturbance.

The court was in deep mourning. The King was working every day with Pérez, and the members of the various councils and apart from that would see no one. He, too, had lost the woman he loved—and he had lost her irrevocably. No wonder he had become an old man. How would it feel to know for sure that one would never see María again? Poor Philip. But there was no way one could comfort him. Perhaps that was what had started Carlos' terrible enmity against him—that Philip was always the King first and a father or brother afterward.

Alexander was in Italy. Now that his mother had ceased to be governor-general of the Netherlands he was no longer "confined to court", as he liked to call it.

Life was asleep. He had tried to wake it up, but his attempts had been childishly ineffective. He was unimportant. Perhaps he always would be. Each time he tried to do something about it, life seemed to laugh in his face and showed him that he did not matter at all. Lately it seemed trying to convince him that nothing really mattered at all. What had been the sense of Carlos' life? Why did the young Queen have to die before giving birth to a male child who might have become what Carlos could never have been? Wait, little friar, we'll ask you a question or two in the morning. . . .

They had stopped singing.

"According to your judgment," the little friar said, "it was God's duty to see to it that the Queen, God rest her, did not die before she had given birth to a male heir."

"I wouldn't quite put it that way", Juan said, frowning. "But there doesn't seem much sense to her death. I could understand God calling Carlos, who probably would have made a bad king—though there again I cannot understand why he worked a miracle through one of his saints first to keep him alive, knowing, as he must know in his omniscience that

Carlos would use his new lease on life only for more mischief. And—"

"Just a moment", Calahorra interrupted. "Neither of us being God we must consider one thing at a time. Now if the Queen had given birth to a son, how do you know he would have made a better king than Prince Carlos? Let's assume the child had lived and had become king and as such he had made, say in his twenty-first year, a decision that plunged the entire country into a catastrophe. You, by then forty-two years of age, would promptly censure God for *that*."

"Then you think God made the Queen die because her child would have become a bad king?"

"I have no idea", Calahorra said cheerfully. "But I have enough confidence in him to believe that he knows what he is doing. I just mentioned one hypothesis out of many possible ones. Can you stand a shock? No, that's a stupid question of mine. You are the leader of the King's navy, you must be able to stand a shock. Well then: how do you know whether God wants the present dynasty ruling Spain to continue?"

Juan stared at the little friar, aghast. "But surely . . ."

"There was a time", Calahorra said calmly, "when God allowed our country to be ruled by Moors. A very long time, as you know. Many centuries. Moors. Muslims. During the first centuries of that time the present dynasty did not exist at all, either here or elsewhere. And history goes on. How can you be sure that it won't repeat itself? And if it does, you will have to censure God again for letting it happen. But God has not to my knowledge given any country guarantees about its frontiers or its rulers. What he has guaranteed is our individual and personal salvation, if we believe and keep his commandments." He slid off his chair, knelt, and began to stoke the fire.

The warm light on his face made it look like that of an elderly cherub.

"Now about Prince Carlos", he went on, rising to his feet. "Fray Diego interceded for him, didn't he? And you prayed to him for intercession, didn't you? Mark you, this time you are censuring God for the reverse of what caused your dissatisfaction in the previous problem. He should have let the Queen live. But he should have let Prince Carlos die."

Steel met steel. "You have just told me that God knew better than I what kind of king the son of the Queen would have made", Juan said sharply. "By the same argument God knew what Carlos would do with the time after his recovery. You are not going to tell me that God wanted the prince to rebel against his father, to become a prisoner and to die wretchedly—or are you?"

"Praying for something or somebody", Calahorra said slowly, "is a very, very dangerous thing to do. One is always heard. And one never really knows what one is asking for. I'd never ask God for anything without adding, 'if such is thy holy will' or 'if such is good for me'. Of course, sometimes God says no to our prayers . . . seemingly. But when he does, his no in one issue will be transformed into a stream of grace in another, often in many others. There is no such thing as a prayer not heard. In the case you mentioned your prayer was heard and answered directly. The prince was healed. Do you remember how our Lord met the man who was born blind? His disciples asked him whether the man was punished with blindness because he was guilty of sin, or because his parents were guilty of sin. And Jesus answered: 'Neither he nor his parents were guilty; he was born blind so that God's action might declare itself in him.' And then he healed him. We are not told whether the man from then on lived an exemplary life or not, are we?"

"N-no, but—"

"You prayed for the prince", Calahorra interrupted firmly. "He was cured. And you received a stream of grace solidifying your own faith for the hours when you would most need it. For at least that once you were allowed to see God in action."

"You mean—Carlos was cured for *my* sake?"

"Certainly. But not only for your sake, although that would have been quite enough. Other people were present, among them a number of learned physicians. Well, one of them, never mind which, came here soon afterward for the first retreat he ever made in his life. He had been besieged by heavy doubts. To him who knew that medically speaking the prince had been as good as dead, the shock of the cure was an eye opener."

"I never knew . . ."

"Of course not. In this particular matter it so happens that I was allowed to see some of the reasons why. And the grace given to you and the grace given to Doña Magdalena brought about your coming to see me and asking me that question; me, who could answer it from knowledge as well as from faith. It is not often that we are allowed to see a larger piece of the pattern of God's work on earth, and that has its good reasons without doubt. After all, a little faith and hope and love is all we can contribute to the building of the Kingdom and faith would be unnecessary if we knew all things. Thank God, we don't. This life of ours here would be immeasurably poorer for it. It's a wonderful thing to be able to trust a man or a woman, isn't it? To say with the inner certainty that is faith, this man is honest, this woman is faithful. If we knew it from knowledge alone, it would be like stating that stone is hard or water liquid. Of course, human beings can deceive us and thus we meet with disappointments and have to fall back on the faith in God, who never deceives—and who never is deceived."

After a while Juan said: "It seems a terrible thing that the man had to be born blind for the sake of the moment when God would show his power. . . ."

"I don't agree", Calahorra said cheerfully. "If it were not for God, he wouldn't exist at all. And he had countless joys of other kinds before our Lord gave him his eyesight on top of it all. What right have we to claim from God that we should all have the same assets? I might as well demand of King Philip to make me captain general of the sea—or of God to make me a king as powerful as King Philip. God has a perfect right to distribute his gifts as he thinks fit. Besides, when a man has had more than his usual load of difficulties in this life, God will make it up a hundred and a thousandfold in the next."

He leaned back in the rickety old chair. "You and I, we are Christians", he said. "That means among other things that we believe in this life only as the preparation for the next. Our Lord mentioned that again and again, starting with the Sermon on the Mount. But so often when good Christian people try to judge this or that situation in life, they seem to forget about life after death altogether. They are like children who think that the sweetmeat they dropped into the mud is an irretrievable loss for all eternity. They are quite desperate about their sweetmeat—whatever it may be, a girl, a dignity, a rank, a house, a privilege, a new dress, or the victory of a bull on which they placed a bet. Anything. And they proceed to blame God for the grave injustice he has done to them by taking their sweetmeat away from them. Phhhha! And do you know what that proves? Do you, Your Excellency?"

He did not wait for a reply. "It means that the action of our Lord did not concern that one blind beggar in Jerusalem only. It concerns us all at some stage. You too are a blind beggar, Your Excellency, unless our Lord opens your eyes."

Juan's stare met a cherubic smile.

"Obviously," Calahorra said, "we shall find it difficult to be happy as long as we are spiritually blind."

Juan rose. "I think that's about as much as I can take in for the present."

The little friar did not seem to be surprised. He too got up, elastic as a cat. "As you wish", he said pleasantly. "But do remember that our Lord can still work miracles—when we ask him."

Doña Magdalena came a few days later for a visit. She had to meet Juan in the special visitors' room, as all others were forbidden to women. The child was well, she told him. Don Luiz had written from Madrid; the King was working too hard, mainly because he wanted to do everything personally—and he sent his love to Juan and to Fray Juan de Calahorra.

"I shall not fail to pass it on to him, Tía."

"What is your impression of him?" she asked innocently.

"I don't know whether he is a saint," Juan said smiling, "but I do know that he can be pretty rude. The one, of course, does not necessarily exclude the other. Saint Jerome was very rude sometimes, if I remember rightly what I learned in Leganés."

She laughed. "Perhaps you have been at court too long, my dear. However, if you want to leave and keep me company at Villagarcía ..."

"Not just yet, Tía", he said. "There still are one or two things I want to ask him about."

"That's what I thought you'd say."

"The blind beggar wants to ask some questions", Juan said.

The little friar chuckled. He said nothing. They were walking through the bleak, wintry garden—Juan gloved and dressed in a warm cloak, the friar in the same brown habit he always wore, but with his arms crossed and his hands tucked away in his sleeves.

"You know my story, Fray Juan. Do you think I was separated from María because of my father's sin or my mother's sin?"

"I don't think so."

"Or for the sake of my own sin?"

"Possibly. You confessed and received absolution a long time ago. But pardon does not mean exemption from punishment. But here again: I don't think that it is only a question of cause and effect."

"I don't understand you."

"I mean, there is more to it than you seem to see at the moment. I mean that God most probably has other plans for you—and not only the King."

"I thought so myself, once", Juan said bitterly. "And I ran away to join the expedition sailing for the relief of Malta. It was childish, I suppose."

"Do you really think so?" The little friar's voice was very soft. "I wonder whether it wasn't the finest and the most generous thing you have done so far."

"It certainly wasn't successful. . . ."

"As if *that* mattered. But why did you do it? I know what Don Luiz taught you. I know the books you read about knights errant and great deeds and so on. And you wanted to fight; you wanted adventure and glory. Also you didn't want to be a cardinal. I don't blame you. Neither would I. All very well. But was that all?"

Juan gave an embarrassed little laugh. "Strange you should ask that", he said. "The defenders of Malta were the Knights of San Juan. I—I felt that I belonged there. I never told that to anybody before."

"Juan", the friar said slowly. "The King gave you that name, didn't he?"

"Yes. Why?"

"And the King is your only close relative on earth . . ."

". . . except for my mother, whom I have never seen and probably never shall see", Juan said tonelessly.

"The King is your brother . . ."

"My half brother", Juan corrected. "That's it, don't you see? My birth will always block my way. Always. I know it. I felt it in every sneering look from Don Carlos. And even the King . . ."

"The blind beggar bewailing his fate", Calahorra said.

"What do you mean?"

The friar stopped. "The first day we met, we discovered that we had the same Christian name, you and I. Now I will tell you about still another Juan, a friar like myself, but from what little I know of him, much nearer to God than I can ever hope to be. His name in religion is Fray Juan de la Cruz. He is a saint. He also is a poet. I shall now give you two lines, only two lines, of a poem he wrote. But when you understand them, you will have the recipe for happiness and all the rest is prayer. This is what he wrote: 'When you want to be everything—you must go where you are nothing. / When you want to have everything— you must go where you have nothing.'"

Juan shook his head.

"Namely, to God", Calahorra went on. "God is every-thing, and to him belongs the universe. Unite with him and you are everything and everything is yours. Can't you see that? And have you forgotten that the crown of the King of Kings, infinitely more precious than all the crowns in the world, is one of thorns? When our Lord walked on earth, what was he to the learned Jews? To the priests of the great temple? A wandering rabbi, making false claims. What was he to the Romans? A provincial subject of the great emperor and a man charged with crimes. He himself has warned us that the servant cannot expect better treatment than his Master, hasn't he? Your Excellency, Don Juan of Austria, don't you recognize Christ as your Master, that you expect to be great and honored and allow yourself to be bitter when all greatness and all honor is not given to you because of your birth? What about your Lord's most sacred birth? Can you claim it as your right to be born in a palace, when he was born in a stable?"

"If ever I meet the infidel in battle," Juan said, "I hope he won't be as strong as you are."

"And he won't be", Calahorra exclaimed. "For he cannot talk to you as I do, in the Name of Christ Crucified."

## CHAPTER 28

DECEMBER WAS EXCEPTIONALLY COLD, and a sharp wind was blowing from the north. They had to give up their daily walks and sat instead in Juan's room. A log fire was burning noisily.

Calahorra was warming his short, stubby fingers.

"A man I knew", Juan said, smiling, "once said to me that the best thing to do was to treat God like one treats fire. One mustn't go too far away from him, or one freezes— nor too near, or one gets burned."

Calahorra nodded. "If you ever see him again, tell him that our Lord has said: Not those who are too hot and not those who are too cold—it is the tepid ones that God has spat out of His mouth."

Juan blinked. "There goes a very witty man—pierced through the heart."

"He is witty because he formulated this thought in an amusing manner", the friar said. "And a hundred and more unthinking people will repeat the witty saying and use its wit as a shield for their cowardice. The devil knows his game well. He can use everything for his purpose, even the human sense of humor, one of God's most wonderful gifts. Oh, it's almost bound to be a popular saying. But live it and what happens? Exactly what is happening all around us now. Pay your respects to God by all means, they say, but don't run any risks. Don't say, above all don't do, anything that isn't politic. Stay neutral. What is it to you if the Turk is attacking this country or that? He hasn't attacked you, has he? So don't be too cold; send the attacked prince a nice message, perhaps even a few promises; but don't get too near the fire either. Stay neutral—benevolently so. How many so-called Christian princes do you think acted like this in the very recent past? The Venetians did not lift a finger when the Sultan attacked Rhodes. Volunteers, real Christians, assembled in Italy, thousands of them. But no one would give them ships. And Rhodes fell, one of the bastions of Christianity against the flood of Islam." He stared into the fire. "Habit", he said grimly. "Habit is one of mankind's worst enemies. Sometimes it looks as if we had become accustomed to our heritage. We take it for granted, as if we could not lose it tomorrow. We aren't even aware that the spirit has gone out of us."

"Yet Spain does not lack courageous men", Juan said reproachfully.

"No, and Spain never will, please God. But most of those who have the spirit of adventure combine it with the spirit of acquisition. They go to faraway countries not so much to plant the Faith there as to rob them of their gold. These men want their courage to serve them, not to serve God. You don't have to be a Christian for that! Every pagan can do the same. Where is the man who still has the pure spirit of the crusades? The man who wants to fulfill a task not because he wants it, but because God wants it? *Deus lo vult*—I haven't heard that cry in all my life! Let things go on the way they do, and future generations won't even understand that such a cry was ever uttered! They will translate it in their own mercenary minds as some strange kind of hypocrisy or, God forbid, as a superstition."

"Surely there will always be good priests who will go on teaching us what is right...."

"Yes, there will be. The gates of hell will not prevail, we know that. But each of us must live as if that promise of Christ depended upon him alone. And priests and nuns are not enough. Christ needs the layman, too. He may need the layman more and more as time goes on."

Juan shook his head. "I have never heard anybody say that before."

"Priests, monks, friars, and nuns are set aside for their own specific purpose", Calahorra said. "But their work will be brought to nought, perhaps not only in single cases, but in whole countries, unless God will give us apostles who are laymen, yes and laywomen."

"It's a new thought", Juan said.

"Not so long ago ecclesiastics were the only people who could read and write", Calahorra went on. "Not because the seats of learning were closed to all others, but because the people did not take the trouble to learn. That's what priests and monks were for, reading and writing. And thus one day they will say, 'That's what priests and monks are for, praying and preaching', and, like learning, piety also will shrink, and coagulate in the monasteries. Let that go on long enough and a priest will be the only one to remember the Our Father."

"I cannot believe that."

"Since that German fellow invented a new way of writing with that printing machine of his, we are in for a different kind of trouble as well. What is it they are going to print on those sheets which generate so quickly you can cover cities and towns with manifestos and pamphlets? Princes and teachers are going to make use of it to spread their commands and their knowledge. What commands and what knowledge? The power of the layman increases and will go on increasing. That by itself is all to the good. It will make for more modesty and humility among ecclesiastics; and it will increase the layman's responsibility. But now all depends upon what use he makes of it. Whether he will use his new power for his own aggrandizement, or in the service of our Lord." He rose and put more logs on the fire. "Don't think that's a new thought", he said. "Christ himself had it before—as usual. Didn't he speak of the scarcity of laborers in the vineyard? And he sent out his apostles not to teach a few select people only, but all the nations. Laymen, laymen! Here's a new crusade. *Deus lo vult.*" One last log went into the fire.

The friar pointed to it. "If God is like fire, let me be burned by it. If God is like water, let me drown in it. If he is like air, let me fly into it. If he is like earth, let me burrow my way into it until I reach its very center."

It was from that time that Juan came to assist the little friar at Mass every morning at five o'clock. The winter

321

night hung heavily over Del Abrojo, and the church was full of shadows and the whispering voices of other friars saying their Masses at other altars.

Calahorra's Mass was a revelation. He did not hurry and slur over the hallowed texts, nor did he make long sentimental pauses like some of the priests Juan knew. He spoke clearly. He was neither quick nor slow. He was ploughing his way across his Master's field, conscientiously and lovingly, and the Lord was safe in his hands.

But if such was the way he served God, there was also something that God did for him. His strong, coarse features were ennobled almost beyond recognition and every gesture, every movement was royal. From a chubby little man, chubbier still in the thick robes of his office, he was transformed into a being of such dignity, such majesty, that he seemed to reach the far limit of mere humanity.

Here, at the altar, was the source of his power; from here he drew his strength as Antaeus once did from touching his mother, the Earth.

Juan found himself able to think of things he had never thought of before. Antaeus, the titan of the Greek legend, was invincible as long as his body touched the body of his mother. The Christian was invincible as long as he kept in union with Christ, with the Word that had become Flesh; with God, who had become Man, and of whose living Body he partook in the Host. As so often the pagans had had the first whisperings, the first, primitive ideas of things to come.

The Muslim, however, tried to cut the newfound bridge between God and man. Christ, no longer the God-Man, became a mere, minor prophet who had to bow to Muhammad. And Muhammad, too, was a prophet only. Once more the bond between God and mankind was to be severed, the closest and most loving union broken.

Once more God would become remote, no longer the Father of men but only the King, the terrible, awesome Lord of olden times.

Islam was . . . regress. And inasmuch as it tried to nullify Christ's supreme sacrifice, it was worse than that and therefore it had to be fought and fought again.

That was what mattered. That alone mattered, to uphold and spread a realm on earth over which God would rule not only as a King but also as a Father; where men were allowed to partake in the divinity of him who had not disdained to share man's humanity. This was what God wanted when he spoke as Christ did: "Go and teach ye all the nations. . . ."

What a man was called, whether prince or excellency or nothing at all, did not matter; what he ate or drank or wore or whether he sat on a throne or on the lowliest footstool did not matter.

Even whether or not he found happiness in the arms of a wife was of no account in comparison to the greatest of all tasks. For man did not belong to himself but to God.

That was why the knights of past ages left their wives and their castles for the sake of the Cross. *Deus lo vult!*

That was why Don Luiz jumped into the fire to rescue the crucifix the Moors were trying to burn. Why hadn't he thought of that before? Here was another who was not afraid of getting too near to God in the fire—he had jumped into it.

For many years now that crucifix had hung over his bed, and he had said his prayers before it, prayers that he would find María, prayers that the King would grant him royal rank, prayers again and again concerned only with his own dignity and happiness in this form or that. Asking, asking all the time.

Until now, when he would still have to ask for one more thing, but for that one thing only: Lord, let me *serve* you!

Christmas at Del Abrojo was unforgettable. It was as if Christ had been born here that very day and all the friars were trying to make up for the fact that fifteen odd centuries ago there had been no room at the inn. They vied with each other to show that there was room for him at Del Abrojo. Every altar was covered with flowers—Juan wondered where they got them at this time of the year. The very walls no longer looked forbidding, the turrets no longer grim.

A child was born—but Psalm 109 [110] spoke with the voice of God the Father: "With thee is principality in the day of thy strength; in the brightness of the saints, from the womb before the daystar I begot thee." And King David sang: "The Lord said to my Lord: Sit thou at my right hand, until I make thy enemies thy footstool."

The entire monastery seemed to rock and vibrate with strength.

Two days later Doña Magdalena came again, full of news from Madrid.

"The revolution in the Netherlands is over", she told him. "Alba has won, though I sometimes wish he had not been so terribly severe. It's difficult to believe that it is over, isn't it? It seemed to go on forever. But it must be so or the Queen of England wouldn't have sent her congratulations to the King."

"Elizabeth? Congratulating the King on *that*?" Juan shook his head. "The rebels were of her own faith, weren't they?"

"I suppose she is a queen first and a Protestant afterward. There is news from Granada, too; rather disquieting, I'm afraid."

"From Granada? Not the Moriscos?"

"They have rebelled, yes."

"But the Viceroy? Mondéjar? Surely he can deal with a few rebels?"

"He is asking for reinforcements and he seems to be rather worried. I don't know more, and I only heard it myself from your secretary."

"Quiroga? I must talk to him at once. Is he ..."

"I thought you'd want to, so I brought him with me. He's outside."

"Tía, you're a wonder. May I call him in?" He was bubbling over with excitement, and she nodded and let him go. He was different this time, and not only because of the news. Something had happened to him. She could feel it.

Calahorra has happened to him, she thought. Or rather: he has made it happen.

Juan came back with Quiroga, bombarding him with questions. The secretary gave quick, clipped answers and Doña Magdalena listened carefully. He really had not told her much so far; most of the time he had raved about how wonderful his master was and how everybody in the navy almost venerated him.

"... in the Alpuxarra Mountains, hundreds of villages."

"What's Mondéjar done so far?"

"Punitive expeditions in some cases, attempts at reconciliation in others. He thinks there are many loyal Moriscos."

"He should know; he's been there long enough. Yet he wants reinforcements?"

"Yes, Your Excellency."

"How did the King take it?"

"There have been four meetings of the council so far, and the fifth was starting when I left Madrid."

"How many ... I do apologize, Tía, but you see ..."

"Of course you must know all about it. If I disturb you . . ."

"Not at all, the very idea. How many Moriscos are supposed to be in arms, Quiroga?"

"According to the last reports nearly twenty thousand, although of course . . ."

"Mondéjar may believe that because then he can ask for reinforcements. Who's their leader?"

"They have chosen a king—Muhammad Aben Humeya."

"Who is he?"

"The richest Morisco in the Alpuxarras, and a sherif, a direct descendant from Muhammad. He is related to Abd-er-Rahman."

"Their old royal family. Now I know it's serious. Anybody can rise and play war for a while in the Alpuxarras, all rocks and crags and glens; you can hold a mountain pass with five men against five hundred. But if they have dug out what they'll call the rightful successor of their kings . . . one question, just one more, Quiroga. Is there any sign of Turkish help?"

"There is the suspicion of it; there have been a few prisoners dressed like Turks, but they turned out to be subjects of the King of Algiers."

"Do you know how it all started?"

"Yes, Your Excellency. The first . . ."

"Leave it. You'll tell me on the way to Madrid. I must go at once."

Quiroga smiled broadly. "I thought you might wish to, Your Excellency. I've brought Fuentes and de Lima with me and six horses."

"Excellent. Then let's . . ." he stopped. His face became void of expression. After a while he said: "No. Wait. I must first go and find Fray Juan. Will you excuse me, Tía? I'll be back soon."

326

The friar was in church, but there was no service at this time. Juan found him sitting all by himself. He seemed to be asleep; his eyes were closed, and he looked as if he were made out of tree roots.

Juan sat down in the row behind him. His excitement drifted away, and in a short while his thoughts followed it, and thus he became ready. The tree roots before him began to stir a little; the large head turned toward him and the eyes opened. Juan could hear a whisper:

"It has come sooner than you thought."

He nodded without surprise.

Calahorra rose, genuflected before the tabernacle, turned, and walked out. Juan followed. In the door he knelt to receive his teacher's blessing.

Then they shook hands.

"You know what has happened?"

"Yes. Doña Magdalena met me before she met you."

"You approve of my going?"

"You must go."

"I shall volunteer. If only the King will let me go. . . ."

"He will", Calahorra said. "And you will conquer, and your conquest will make your name known all over Europe."

CHAPTER 29

ON APRIL 13, 1569, His Excellency Don Juan of Austria, Knight of the Golden Fleece, commander in chief of the Spanish forces for the suppression of the rebellion, proceeded from the little town of Hiznaleuz to Granada, five miles away, to make his official entry.

Every single detail of that entry, including the number of persons attached to the supreme court and of the chapter who were to attend, was fixed by the King.

The vanguard consisted of two hundred picked men, heavily armored, under the command of Count Tendilla, eldest son of the Marquis of Mondéjar.

Then came Don Juan himself on horseback, in silver armor, with high boots of white chamois leather and golden spurs. Instead of a helmet he wore a velvet hat. On his left sleeve a large red cockade proclaimed him as the supreme leader.

Don Luiz Quixada was at his right side, the Count of Miranda at his left. Fifty great nobles were riding in their wake, and behind them came the staff and a long quadruple line of troops with full equipment.

At the Elvira Gate Don Pedro Deza, president of the Supreme Court, was waiting with four auditors and all the judges, the archbishop with four canons, and the dignitaries of the chapter and the town judge with four councillors and four vice councillors.

The Beyro plain was almost filled with Mondéjar's soldiers, a little over ten thousand of them.

The one thing the King had not specifically ordered, but which no one could have stopped, was the presence of half the town of Granada, the nobility, the citizens, and thousands of Moriscos, all dressed in the Spanish way to proclaim their loyalty and howling their "Vivas" even more enthusiastically than anybody else.

Don Juan jumped off his horse to embrace President Deza and to kiss the archbishop's ring. He shook hands with the town judge, with auditors, judges, canons, councillors, and vice councillors, introduced one by one by their superiors.

Two beautifully caparisoned mules were held in readiness for Deza and the archbishop. They mounted, and Juan made them take the places of Don Luiz Quixada and the Count of Miranda at his side.

When the cavalcade began to move again, all the church bells of Granada began to ring. Drums were beating and all the detachments of infantry fired salvos.

But Don Juan had only just passed the Elvira Gate when he was stopped.

Hundreds of women, disheveled and dressed in black rags, rushed up to him. At least fifty of them threw themselves before the hooves of his horse, others surrounded him—the president, the archbishop, and the cavaliers—and a tall, old lady with flowing white hair raised both arms and shouted, "Justice, sir—justice for the widows and orphans of your country!" Then she broke into a stream of complaints. The Moriscos had murdered their husbands, their fathers and brothers and sons; they had burned their houses and stolen their property—yet nothing was done to bring the criminals to justice and now they were told that there would be an amnesty. . . .

Juan listened. But as he did, he saw the Marquis of Mondéjar, now only a few yards away, biting his lip; and a little to his left Don Pedro Deza seemed to find it difficult to suppress a triumphant smile.

Juan knew about the rift between the two. The incident was organized to embarrass Mondéjar and to win the sentiments of the new supreme commander. But this did not mean that these poor women had no grounds for complaint. Mondéjar himself had had to report some of the atrocities done by the Moriscos—men, women, and children butchered in the most bestial way, burned alive within their churches and with them, priests tortured to death. To prevent them from invoking the name of Jesus or of the Blessed Virgin, their mouths were filled with gunpowder;

the powder then was touched off by a linstock. According to Mondéjar's own reports more than three hundred churches had been destroyed, looted, and profaned and more than four thousand Christians killed. The main instigator of these actions was not so much "King" Muhammad Aben Humeya as his righthand man or constable, Aben Farax.

Juan said a few words of sympathy and comfort to the women and promised that justice would be done and done speedily, and much to the relief of Mondéjar, who after all was responsible for the city; they allowed him and the procession to go on.

And now the picture changed entirely. Streets, windows, and housetops were crammed full with people, hailing him as their liberator; showers of flowers poured down on him and the cavaliers and troops all the way past the tower of St. Andrew, the long wall of the Capuchin monastery, the Church of St. Peter and St. Paul, and across the Plaza Nueva to the massive portals of the palace of the audience, where he dismounted and took leave of the dignitaries. "A triumphal entry", he said to Don Pedro Deza. "Now let us do something to earn it."

He had only just been led into the apartments reserved for him when a deputation of Moorish citizens arrived. "I will see them at once", he said, taking no notice of Deza's rather obvious disapproval. "And I want Quiroga here at my side."

The Moorish deputation consisted of four well-to-do men who gave the appearance of the most perfect adaptation to Spanish ways, habits, and customs that the government could hope for. Their names were Spanish, their dress was Spanish, and their leader, a fat gentleman with shrewd eyes, proclaimed with much eloquence that their loyalty was Spanish as well. They were all loyal citizens, and they represented the great mass of loyal Moorish citizens who had been brought into sorry disrepute by a few bands of brigands claiming to be Moorish and consisting partly of ruffians and cutthroats of the kind that could be found anywhere and partly of subjects of the kings of Algeria and Tunis.

Don Juan listened politely.

"We have been suffering greatly because of these miscreants", the speaker went on. "Our houses have been invaded by soldiers, and, alas, they did not content themselves with looking for rebels and arms, none of which were found, but they took with them whatever they could lay their hands on. The damage done to the possessions and indeed the honor of the King's most loyal subjects is very high and very grave, and we are happy to see that His Majesty, doubtless well informed, has thought fit to send so high and mighty a prince as Don Juan of Austria to reestablish normal life and normal relations and to protect the lives, the honor, and the possessions of his subjects of Moorish descent."

Don Pedro Deza was seething with rage, but Juan calmly said that loyal citizens were worthy of reward and not punishment and that everybody loyal or otherwise would be dealt with justly. "Send in a petition with exact and specified information about your damages and I shall order a very thorough investigation", he concluded. "But see to it that your petition contains nothing that is not true. For if you lie or exaggerate you will damage your cause rather than further it."

"The audience is over", Don Pedro Deza exploded.

As the deputation withdrew, smiling and bowing, Juan gave Quiroga a sign to accompany them to the palace door.

When the door had closed behind him, Deza let fly. "Your Excellency does not, perhaps, realize that these dogs are liars from birth and have been most carefully trained to become archliars. If it were not for rich merchants of their ilk, the Moriscos would never have been able to arm themselves."

Juan smiled and Deza continued, trembling and sputtering with rage: "We'll get a list of damages as long as the road from here to Madrid and every item of it will be sworn to by fifty witnesses who would swear that the prophet Muhammad himself was a Christian if somebody paid them a maravedí for it. A few bands of ruffians—and a match for both the Marquis of Mondéjar and the Marquis de los Vélez—two of His Majesty's viceroys! But I should be glad Your Excellency listened so carefully. It made them feel secure, and they thought they could say almost anything. That's one thing about the Moor: he never knows where to stop lying; I should know them by now."

Quiroga came back and Juan said: "Speak up."

"They said wonderful things about you in Spanish, Your Excellency", Quiroga said. "They called you the Sun of Justice and the Ray of Mercy and some more such names, but alas, it was only for my benefit. For the fellow who made the speech to you muttered in Arabic, 'He's dangerous, I think', and one of the others replied, 'The son of a dog did not believe a word you said.'"

"Thank you, Quiroga", Juan said. Then he turned to Deza: "I was not allowed to leave Madrid before His Majesty had settled a great number of things, but I have not been entirely idle. Neither as you can see was my secretary, whom I had study Arabic several hours a day for four months."

Deza beamed. "Who could expect the eagle to know all the tricks of the fox", he exclaimed. "Now you know that I was right. They stand convicted out of their own mouths."

"Nevertheless," Juan continued gently, "I want an alcayde of the royal audience to study their petition very seriously.

And every case must be judged according to its merits. Quiroga, I want a council of war assembled here at three o'clock this afternoon. . . ."

The first man to speak before the war council was the Marquis of Mondéjar, Viceroy of Granada.

Juan knew the marquis' views from his countless reports to Madrid; he had had ample time to study them, and they showed not only a picture of the country and its situation but also that of the writer, a man of honor without doubt, a good man for certain, but the kind of character who would deal with a desperate situation simply by refusing to admit that it was desperate.

Mondéjar was bound to regard the arrival of the King's brother as a slight. But he had known of that arrival four months in advance, time enough to reestablish order, if he was the man to do so. He was not. And he had to look around for a scapegoat. He found two. . . .

"A few months ago," the marquis said, "I could have dealt with the entire issue easily."

A huge man, no longer young, but looking like the god of war himself, gave a short laugh, and Juan frowned a little. The giant was the Marquis de los Vélez, Viceroy of Murcia, and Juan knew his character and his views too. Mondéjar was water, de los Vélez fire, and they loved each other accordingly.

"Easily", Mondéjar repeated sharply. "I know this country and I know the Moriscos. At the beginning the percentage of rebels was small—the overwhelming majority of the Morisco population was not willing to join them; they would not even have anything to do with them. Why, the first attempt of Aben Farax to start a revolt in Granada was made with no more than a hundred and eighty followers, all of them brigands of the worst kind, and the Moriscos of Granada closed their doors to them. He had to leave town."

"Quite right", President Deza said dryly. "But why was it that he did not find any support? Not because your precious Moriscos were loyal. Because Farax had promised the arrival of eight thousand men under his command, and he could not keep his promise. The Moriscos of Granada certainly had no wish to risk their lives and possessions by making common cause with such a small band. Even now, when there are twenty thousand men in the field against us, they are very careful not to show their true face—not with the city full of Spanish soldiers and the nearest Moorish army many miles away."

"The rebels hoped for an alliance with the kings of Algiers and Tunis", Mondéjar went on as if Deza had not said anything. "All they received were promises and a few hundred volunteers to support their cause. I could not stop them from landing because I had not enough ships at my disposal, and my repeated dispatches, asking for naval support, did not find a gracious reception by His Majesty's ministers in Madrid. It was winter. There was no possibility of deploying big forces in the Alpuxarras Mountains, quite apart from the fact that I did not have big forces at my command. Nevertheless a number of minor encounters took place, showing that we were in earnest. And at the same time I did my best to seize the so-called king of the Moriscos *and* his vizier...."

"And you lost six hundred and forty men of the seven hundred who took part in that remarkable expedition", de los Vélez sneered.

Mondéjar nodded. "That is so. And why? Because the troops are completely undisciplined and out only to get booty. The King and his vizier escaped because the soldiers were more interested in the Moorish women they captured. They are not regulars. They're auxiliaries of the most doubtful value in the field, and I venture to say that His Excellency is going to have very similar experiences with them."

"Everybody knows that your soldiers are a bunch of ruffians and a dishonor to the fair name of Spain", de los Vélez said. "But the reason why that expedition failed was that Aben Humeya and Farax knew about it two days in advance. And they knew about it because some soft-spoken, gentle, loyal citizen of Granada told them."

"You have no proof . . ."

"I have proof enough to fill a room in the palace of justice with the papers. We have Moriscos in Murcia too— and I have ways and means to make them talk. Your Excellency! The suburb of Albaycín in this beautiful city is as full of Moors as the head of a Moorish beggar is full of lice; and there isn't a single soul among them who would not be ready to do a bit of spying for that new kingling of theirs. And why not? If we win, we don't know about it and the man still remains a loyal citizen. And if we lose, he can claim a reward from His Majesty King Muhammad Aben Humeya; may his soul rot in hell."

"Albaycín", Deza said, "is the ulcer of Granada. I very much fear we shall have to lance it."

"Many patients", Mondéjar said, "have died under the physician's knife."

"There will be no mass killing of noncombatants", Juan said quietly, and Mondéjar gave him a grateful smile.

"I did not suggest such a thing, Your Excellency", Deza protested.

"I did not say you did", Juan replied. "Let us hear the Marquis of Mondéjar to the end."

"I have since tried to seal off the rebels in their mountain strongholds", Mondéjar continued. "But the Spanish population, embittered by the death of this or that relative, committed a great number of acts of vengeance, each of which made more Moriscos join the rebels and at the same time the Viceroy of Murcia thought fit to indulge in a little warfare of his own, in which however he was as little successful as I was. . . ."

De los Vélez jumped up and began to bellow.

Mondéjar said cuttingly: "You certainly show that you merit the name the Moriscos of *your* province have given you: the iron-headed devil."

"When dealing with that brood of vipers I'd rather be that than soft-headed", de los Vélez jeered.

Mondéjar's hand flew to his sword hilt and Juan said coldly: "I will have none of this kind of thing, my lords. Indeed I have come to put an end to it. Private feuds will have to wait until the war is ended. I now want the Marquis of Mondéjar to make practical suggestions about what, in his opinion, has to be done in the present situation—never mind how that situation came to exist."

"I suggest encouraging the submission of the villages in the Alpuxarras by every means. At present these people are overawed by the power of the rebels. We must convince them that their safety lies in remaining loyal. Secondly, I suggest garrisoning important places in the mountains for that purpose. And, thirdly, I suggest reinforcing my troops at Órgiba and letting them ravage the countryside, destroying the food, so that the rebels will be forced to surrender."

Juan looked at Deza.

"I am not a military man", the president said. "But I think that not a single effective military measure can be taken as long as we have thousands of Moorish spies in our very midst here in Granada. The suburb of Albaycín must be combed and all suspects evacuated. Also an example should be made at least of one Moorish village to show that we do not acquiesce in the crimes committed against Spanish men, women, and children."

Juan thought of the Moorish delegation. "We shall have a vote of the entire council about the suggestions of the Marquis of Mondéjar", he said. "But as far as Albaycín is concerned I must go one step further than the suggestion of Don Pedro Deza. By order of His Majesty the suburb of Albaycín will be evacuated altogether and the inhabitants sent to camps in Castile and Andalusia until the end of the war."

Don Luiz Quixada nodded gravely. Deza and de los Vélez beamed.

"I am afraid I do not share the Marquis of Mondéjar's view that little or no help will be forthcoming from North Africa and possibly even from a far more dangerous enemy", Juan went on. "We've had reports about possible Turkish landings on the east coast. The day I left Madrid I gave orders to my vice admiral, Don Luiz de Requeséns, to cruise along that coast with twenty-five galleys, as soon as he can get there. He must be at sea now. Special orders of His Majesty have gone to Admiral Giovanni Andrea Doria to keep the most careful watch for Turkish fleets off the east coast of Sicily. We don't want any surprises, if we can avoid them."

There was a pause.

Don Luiz Quixada stared fixedly at some point above Deza's head, trying hard to remain grimly serious. He knew only too well what was going on in the minds of the local rulers. They had expected to meet an inexperienced young prince, a mere figurehead, who would have to depend upon the knowledge and skill of the men on the spot; and each of the two factions, Mondéjar on one side, Deza and Vélez on the other, hoped to be able to draw him into its camp without too much difficulty. What they found now was something different. . . .

Mondéjar was the first to recover. "I am certainly happy to see that the entire issue is being given the importance it deserves—"

". . . and which the Marquis of Mondéjar refused to acknowledge for a long time, treating it as if it were the mutiny of a few villages." De los Vélez could not keep his peace.

"There will be no further discussion of previous measures", Juan said firmly, before Mondéjar could reply in like coin.

But when it came to the vote about Mondéjar's three points, the Viceroy of Granada found that his was the only yes. Pale and trembling he announced his intention to tender his resignation to the King, but Juan declined to pass it on. "I shall certainly need your experience to help me in the many tasks ahead." He then ordered Deza to draw up plans for the evacuation of Albaycín and declared the council adjourned.

Only Don Luiz Quixada stayed on. "Nicely done", he said warmly. "The only thing that had me worried was that vote you suggested. Mondéjar's three points were so hopelessly inadequate."

"I know", Juan said. "But there was no need to increase his enmity against me by pointing that out to him. I knew they would all vote against him, so there was no risk involved. What worries me is something quite different."

"Albaycín?"

"Yes. Old people. Women and children. If only I could be sure that they will be well looked after. What misery this order will cause—the first order I have given in this war! I tried hard in Madrid to find a different solution, but the King wouldn't hear of it. He insisted on total evacuation."

"The King was right", Don Luiz said. "They won't be well looked after, but not badly either. And they'll be considerably better off than if they stay here. Let them go and go quickly, or we shall have a massacre. And we haven't got enough troops to stop it *and* fight the enemy. Worse still, the troops most likely would join in. They're the scum of the earth, Mondéjar is right there, at least. How I wish we had a few regular regiments here. But the tercios can't be everywhere and the Duke of Alba needs every man he has got to keep those Netherlanders down. What do you think of Vélez?"

"He'll be more trouble than three Mondéjars", Juan said. "He believes only in himself, and he is not accustomed to obey."

Don Luiz nodded. "Bad soldiers and bad commanders, a mutinous population and a fierce enemy in strong positions in the mountains. I wish the King had given you an easier task."


## CHAPTER 30


WHAT FOLLOWED WAS one long nightmare.

The first bit of news Don Luiz had for Juan was that Count Tendilla, Mondéjar's eldest son, had left overnight for Madrid.

"The first complaints about us", Don Luiz said, smiling bitterly.

Juan nodded. "It could have been worse", he said. "Tendilla is not a very intelligent young man, and his record in this war has not been too impressive either. . . ."

"I should say not", Don Luiz growled. "All he did was to have a defenseless village sacked, and to have his troops trounced by the Moors on the way back."

"Mondéjar himself would have been far more dangerous, but *he* can't slip away like a minor commander and I shall not give him leave—at least not for the time being."

A few days later the evacuation started. Half of the troops had to stand by to prevent a last-minute revolt by thousands of Moriscos, half crazy with rage and desperation; strong contingents had to escort them; and the rest of the army formed at all strategic points lest the "king" or one of his captains made an attempt to strike at the capital. Juan organized flying squads to supervise the behavior of both Moriscos and troops, with the result that there were relatively few incidents of bloodshed. A physician and a priest went with every batch of five hundred people. Even so it was a heartrending spectacle, going on for days.

There were daily sessions of the war council, but although the Marquis de los Vélez returned to his province, the atmosphere did not improve much, especially as the news arrived that Requeséns' fleet had run into a terrible storm. Four galleys sunk, many others badly damaged, and all that were still afloat driven off their course to Sardinia.

"Now the Turks will land on our flank", Mondéjar said, horrified. "There is nothing to stop them—or the Algerians and Tunisians."

"The gap will be closed", Juan announced tersely. "I have ordered Don Álvaro de Bazán to cross over from Sardinia and recommended to Madrid that Admiral Doria send us some of his galleys from Naples. According to my calculations the serious danger will last only about a week, but of course in that week at least the Algerians may try landings."

Boats were sent out to give smoke signals by day and fire signals by night, if they saw Moorish ships approaching, and troops were held in readiness at many points.

Even so, a number of light galleys from Algeria managed to land by night, with several hundred volunteers and cargoes of arms, ammunition, and food for the rebels, some of them at Murcia.

"Even an iron-headed devil sleeps at night", the Marquis of Mondéjar jeered.

By now the war council was larger. The Duke of Sesa had arrived, and Mondéjar insisted on the presence of two high-born personages, de Muñatones and Diego Hurtado de Mendoza, related not only to him but also to the Prince of Éboli.

Both Diego Hurtado de Mendoza and Don Luiz Quixada soon developed the habit of writing to Ruy Gómez what they did not want to write directly to the King. Mendoza's reports were veritable models of caustic brevity: "Most Noble Lord: nothing new in Granada. Don Juan listens, the Duke of Sesa is excited, the Marquis of Mondéjar goes on complaining, Luiz Quixada growls, Muñatones conciliates, and my nephew Tendilla is with you in Madrid. We don't exactly miss him."

Don Luiz Quixada's letters were irascible explosions. The climate of Granada did not agree with him; he was ailing, and he said so. "It prevents me from getting as busy on those damned soldiers of ours as I would like to. Never have I seen such rascals. There is nothing soldierlike about them except their uniforms, and *they* are in bad condition. It is not surprising as they have never been soldiers before. They have neither guts nor manners. All they want is to enrich themselves at the expense of God, the King, and their neighbors. They will have to be kicked into battle, and then what will happen? If only we could get a few tercios here, but what hope is there for that, now that Requeséns has suffered his misfortune? There will be more landings from Algeria, according to our intelligence reports, and once these dogs have enough arms and ammunition, the rebellion is going to grow by leaps and bounds. The captains and subaltern officers are not much better than their soldiers either. The only good troops we have is the cavalry, and of those we have too few. Don Juan is working himself to death, trying to get these devils of ours into some sort of shape, and he will not tolerate their crimes, God bless him for it; they are robbing people right and left and swindling everybody as much as they can, which is a lot. Our auditors and judges are having the busiest time of their lives. . . ."

Strangely enough, Juan's popularity with both officers and troops grew despite his severity. Part of that was due to methods that caused not only consternation, but downright horror among the nobles. He would share the food of his soldiers, talk to the ordinary man as well as to his officer, and even take part in their training, as if he intended to carry a musket himself in the campaign to come.

"By God and his saints", the Duke of Sesa swore. "I've seen the King's brother giving a fencing lesson to a simple soldier! And all around him a couple of hundred of those devils, yelling their heads off as if they were at a bullfight."

But what seemed to please the men most was that their young commander in chief was always cheerful and courteous. They were rabble, and they were accustomed to being treated as rabble by swearing subalterns and icy commanders. Here was a noble of nobles, the very brother of the King, and he treated them as if they were caballeros—as long as they did not do anything that was really wrong.

"He'll still be polite", musketeer Vicente Díaz told a man from another regiment. "He won't say, 'You misbegotten son and grandson of apes, you piece of dung, you'll rot in jail for a week for this.' He'll say: 'I am sorry you behaved so badly. You will go to prison for a month.' He's severe all right. Last week he had three men sent to the galleys, and what for? Just because they hit an old woman over the head who didn't want to part with a bracelet. They couldn't know that the old hag had a skull as thin as a wafer, could they? But the way he sent them to the galleys, you should have heard him—as if he was suggesting a nice pleasurable leave for them. Ai, compadre, he's a one!"

Every day young nobles arrived to serve under Juan. He sifted them carefully and gave them special tasks.

By June he began to feel that his efforts had not been in vain.

Don Luiz Quixada had recovered, and Juan took him along on a general inspection tour. The old soldier was delighted. "When we came here and I saw the beggars we were supposed to beat the Moriscos with, I knew we didn't have a chance. Now we might be able to do something. I don't know how you've done it."

"Another four weeks or so," Juan said, "and we can march. I think there is a good chance that we can force Aben Humeya into giving a decisive battle. Let's look once more at the maps, shall we?"

They were still studying them when news came that the Marquis de los Vélez had attacked on his own and won a great victory. A few hours later two of Juan's agents in Murcia came to report that the "victory" was no more than a fierce encounter with heavy losses on both sides and that de los Vélez had withdrawn. A third report added that Requeséns had landed in Murcia and that de los Vélez had used the naval commander's men for his raid.

Don Luiz was beside himself. "I know what he was up to—trying to collect laurels at our expense, that's all."

"It is much worse than that." Juan was pointing at the map. "Look here, Don Luiz—now that the marquis has withdrawn, Aben Humeya can strike into the Almanzora valley. How strong are our garrisons?"

"Güéjar: two hundred and fifty men; Galera: three hundred odd. Serón should have four hundred, but I very much doubt if any of these figures is correct. The plague on all provincial governors."

Juan sent a terse note to de los Vélez, reprimanding him for his action and ordering him to keep all his troops in readiness for a general offensive next month.

A week later he found his worst expectations confirmed. A young officer came galloping through the streets of Granada. Two hundred yards from the palace door his horse collapsed. The officer had to be helped to his feet and led to the palace. His head and his left arm were bandaged, and he was covered with grime, but he insisted on being taken before Don Juan at once and he was.

"I am Fernando Olmedo, Your Excellency, serving under Don Diego de Mirones, commander of His Majesty's fortress of Serón; Don Diego reports that since last Friday Serón has been under siege by at least five thousand Moriscos under a chief named Ali Mecebe."

Serón! Right in the Almanzora valley.

"How strong is Don Diego?" Juan asked.

"All in all, one hundred and thirty men", the officer replied. "And we have two priests and eighty women in the citadel who have managed to take refuge from the village of Úbeda. Úbeda is burning—or was when I left."

Don Luiz Quixada growled. "Anything else?"

"No, sir."

Juan gave orders to have the young officer's wounds attended to and to provide him with everything else he needed. Alone with Don Luiz he said: "How many men shall I need to lift the siege in your opinion, Don Luiz?"

"Two thousand foot under a good commander", Don Luiz answered, "Or three thousand under a mediocre one. And for every cavalryman you send, you can leave three to four infantrymen at home."

"I will not change the date of the general offensive", Juan said. "I'd like to but I won't. They may want me to attack in strength at Serón."

"And so they may", Quixada said, studying the map again. "You would have Güéjar and Galera behind you, of course, but for all we know they also may be under siege by now. I think you're right. Reconnaissance in strength is what we need."

"Fifteen hundred foot", Juan said. "Hundred and fifty horse. And Alonzo de Carvajal as commander. Ye saints, how I wish I could go myself."

"Impossible", Don Luiz said. "The general offensive ..."

"I know. It's hard all the same." Juan rang the bell for his aide.

Within six hours the expedition was on its way to Serón.

Carvajal, an excellent soldier with just the right character for this kind of raid—bold and yet cautious—had promised to do his utmost.

Now all that could be done was to wait, and Juan found it far more difficult than anything else. "I should be accustomed to it by now", he said bitterly. "God alone knows how difficult it has been to appear cheerful and happy. When everything in me has wanted to give battle to the Moor, all I could do was to try and make soldiers out of brigands in uniform and to settle their stupidities and crimes—no, I forgot my most frequent activity: to write reports to Madrid. This reminds me that I must write another one now. Paper, paper; I never knew that the main work in war is fighting on paper."

"His Majesty is indeed very fond of detailed knowledge", Don Luiz said a little stiffly.

In the morning the courier from Madrid arrived with dispatches.

Juan read them and had Don Luiz summoned at once. "This is rather tiresome", he said, with a nervous smile. "The King has presided at a special session of the grand council of war, and they have made a number of decisions. They foresaw just as we did that the Moriscos might use de los Vélez' withdrawal for an attack against the Almanzora valley and they decided that in such a case de los Vélez should counterattack ... and not we! In fact we are strictly forbidden to do so. It's just as well Carvajal is already on the march, or else ..."

"Carvajal must return at once", Don Luiz said sadly.

"What?"

"If we send off the order by a man on a fast horse, Carvajal will have it long before he gets anywhere near Serón."

"Don Luiz! We can't leave Serón in the lurch. How do I know what de los Vélez is doing? Surely we have every excuse ..."

"None, Your Excellency. You cannot disobey the King. And not to change an order already given when there is still time to do so is disobedience and will be regarded as such in Madrid."

Juan knew only too well what it meant for Quixada to address him by his official rank, although no one else was present. He was indicating that he was speaking as a king's officer and member of the war council. It was an official protest as well as a personal warning.

"The matter should be brought to the attention of *our* war council, of course", Don Luiz went on. "If ever I have given advice to you—don't act on your own in any way, not in this case. Even if Carvajal wins through and relieves Serón, they'll regard that as far less important than a case of direct disobedience to a royal command. They will inquire about the exact time when the message from Serón arrived, when Carvajal left, and when you received the courier's dispatch—the rest is a simple enough calculation. They'll know in a few minutes that you could have reached Carvajal, if you had wanted it."

"Serón, Serón . . ." Juan said between clenched teeth.

"The war council should be convoked at once", Don Luiz said gravely.

Two hours later the war council decided that Don Alonzo de Carvajal had to be recalled at once. The decision was unanimous—except for one member who abstained from voting.

The news became worse every day. The whole of the Almanzora valley, thickly populated by Moriscos, declared for Aben Humeya.

De los Vélez, instead of marching on Serón, ordered his brother-in-law at Baza to do so. His brother-in-law, who was ill, sent all available troops under the command of his brother—five hundred foot and seventy horses. They got within three leagues of Serón when they were attacked so fiercely that they had to withdraw with the loss of two hundred men.

For a while the communications between Murcia and Granada were interrupted, and when they were again opened after much difficulty, it was too late for Don Juan and too late also for Serón.

The fortress capitulated on the condition that the lives of the defenders and the civilians would be spared. As soon as the Moriscos took over, they butchered them all in cold blood, except for the women, who were distributed as slaves among the conquerors.

For twenty-four hours Juan refused to see anyone.

His secretary, Quiroga, warded off all visitors, however exalted their rank. Only the royal courier was allowed to deliver his dispatches, and even after that hours passed before Juan emerged, haggard, pale, and looking so ill that Quiroga asked in a quavering voice whether he should summon a physician.

"Don Luiz Quixada", Juan said tonelessly and returned to his study.

Quixada was called for. He found Juan slumped in his chair, his eyes closed and swollen.

"It is all over, Don Luiz", Juan said in a leaden voice. "There will be no offensive. The King has forbidden it. We are not strong enough. As for me, he gravely reproaches me for taking too active a part in everything. I am to give directions only from the palace. And in no circumstances am I to lead the troops in person."

Quixada was speechless.

"You know what this means, don't you, Don Luiz? It means that I am not a general, but a functionary, passing on the orders of the Supreme War Council in Madrid to the minor war council in Granada. All the fighting will be done by others. It means that I am a figurehead, a dressed-up doll; that any fool could fulfill my mission as well as I can. Where would I have got, if I had acted like that from the start? The way Madrid sees it, all my work should have been done by subalterns."

"In which case you wouldn't have an army. You have done wonders with the soldiers", Quixada said.

"The King doesn't seem to think so, Don Luiz. And what are the soldiers going to think when they have to go into battle, and I stay behind, safely tucked away in a comfortable palace?"

"The King has no son", Don Luiz said in a low voice. "And he has only one brother."

"Much better to lose that brother, than to have him regarded as a coward by the army", Juan burst out. "And much better to command one single galley, the smallest of the whole fleet, on the high seas, where no one can interfere with my command, than to be in charge of an army and to have to ask permission before I send out a patrol. Surely it was not like that with my father's battles!"

"No", Quixada admitted. "It wasn't. This is a new age."

"You fought beside my father at Tunis and at Muehlberg . . ."

"I did. And the day will come, please God, when I'll fight at your side, too." Quixada gave a slow smile. "I hope it won't be on board a galley, though. I am a bad sailor and would do you little honor."

Despite his misery Juan was sensitive enough to perceive that the old soldier was trying to cheer him up. He seized his hands and pressed them warmly. "I know what it really is", he whispered. "They have no confidence in me yet in Madrid—and indeed, why should they have? I have done nothing so far to gain it. But how can I ever gain it, if they forbid me to move?"

"It's a pity about the offensive", Quixada said. "But there is at least one thing I liked about what you told me. They say we're not strong enough. That means they're thinking of sending us reinforcements, and God knows we can do with them. One regiment of regulars and we could really give body to our attack. Well, I suppose I'd better get the war council together again to inform them about the new situation. . . ."

Alone, Juan buried his face in his hands. He thought of Del Abrojo and Fray Juan de Calahorra. "You will conquer, and your conquest will make your name known all over Europe."

How can I conquer, Fray Juan? Neither Godfrey of Bouillon, nor the saintly Louis of France could have conquered with their hands tied behind them . . . the King won't allow me to fight. . . . He keeps me here at my desk, and all I can do is to write orders and letters. They give me a pen, Fray Juan, a pen instead of a sword. . . .

From far away the cheerful, cherubic face of the friar smiled at him.

Juan sat up. He was to write? Very well, he would write.

He took the pen and began to write to the King.

## CHAPTER 31

MEHMED SOKOLLI, first vizier and seraskier of the late Sultan Süleyman, first vizier and seraskier of the present ruler, Selim II, knelt and, bowing, touched with his forehead the labyrinthine design of a priceless carpet from Tabriz.

A hoarse voice said: "Rise, and be brief."

Mehmed Sokolli rose easily, despite his age. As always, he kept his eyes down. "Lord of the Two Worlds," he began, "Ruler of the Faithful, may Allah give you a thousand years." Having been asked to be brief, he omitted the rest of the formula, honoring the Sultan as Lord of the Black Sea and the White Sea, as the Kanuni, the Law Giver, and the Ghazi or Conqueror and went straight into his report.

"Word has come to us again from the headquarters of the faithful in Spain. They have shaken off and killed Muley Muhammad Aben Humeya, whom they elected as their king at the outbreak of the war; and they say this was done because of his intention to do away with his allies from Algiers whom he accused of trying to win all power for their own king."

"This is true or not true?"

"It is not true, Ruler of the Faithful, for according to our very accurate reports no more than five thousand volunteers have crossed over from Africa to Spain within almost a year of war, a number quite insufficient to make a bid for power. True are two things: that Aben Humeya had taken away the flower of another man's harem, one El Guazil; and that he was too cautious and hesitant for many of the leaders. El Guazil laid a trap and won over Aben Aboo. Together they killed Aben Humeya, and now Aben Aboo has been proclaimed as his successor and was accepted by all the caids and chieftains and will now be known as Muley Abdallah Aben Aboo and has chosen as the inscription on his banner the words: 'I cannot wish for more and I will not be content with less.' He intensified the war and has shown more skill and bravery than Aben Humeya, spreading his power and yet at the same time increasing his army."

The hoarse voice said: "Briefer."

"Lord, you know that I have long advocated strong measures in that part of the world. There is only one God, and there should be only one Lord of the Faithful. These Moors are Muslims. Therefore they are your subjects and not those of anyone else, be he Aben Aboo or the King of Spain. All we needed was the right moment to say so and act accordingly, though action should precede speech in this case."

"Lala Mustapha and Pialy Pasha do not agree with you."

For the first time Mehmed Sokolli looked up to the golden throne. There, seven steps higher than the world, was not Süleyman but Selim. Not the familiar, lean figure with the long neck, the pallid face, and piercing eyes, but a squat, obese man, yet so terrible to look at that even most of the shameless and impudent ambassadors of the West preferred to keep their eyes on the carpet when they were permitted to the presence.

Under the enormous turban of white silk the bloated face was painted the color of blood, and the eyebrows, the moustachios, and beard jet black.

They whispered in the serai that the Sultan had taken a fancy to this strange makeup after having killed one of his women, cutting her throat with his scimitar so that her blood splashed into her master's face, and that story could well be true. But it was also true that the Sultan's skin was blotchy and reddish from wine and this was his way of hiding it. More than once his father, Süleyman, had warned him against wine, "that mad red thing", but Selim would never give it up, not with that accursed Jahudi, Jussuf Nassi, procuring for him the choicest vintages from the Christian countries. Some fools even thought that this and only this accounted for Jussuf Nassi's influence on him and for the fact that the Sultan had made him lord of the isle of Naxos and other isles, with the hereditary title of duke.

Mehmed Sokolli knew better than that. Not even Selim would make his wine merchant a duke. Nassi was much more than a procurer of illicit pleasures. For a while Mehmed Sokolli had thought he was a creature of Pialy Pasha, but probably he was more than that. A Marrano from Spain—a "new Christian", one of those who allowed themselves to be baptized because that was the only way to escape exile under the Spanish law; yet later he left Spain and went into exile anyway; nobody knew why—perhaps the Inquisition had got wind of the insincerity of the man's conversion and he had had to get out quickly. He went to Holland first, where lately bloody battles were again raging, involving the Spanish King's best general. And from Holland he came to the Dardanelles. He had cast off Christianity as soon as he could and reverted to the faith of his fathers, and he had changed his original name of José Miquez to Jussuf Nassi.

It was astonishing, really, how seriously all those infidels took their errors and heresies ... almost as if it mattered to them whether they landed in the fourth instead of the seventh hell.

Anyway, Nassi set up business in Constantinople, married a rich Jewess, and made money. So far there was nothing extraordinary about his career. But somehow he managed to get into Prince Selim's favor, so much so that the prince made him Duke of Naxos almost immediately after his accession to the throne. Allah knew how he did it, and the Sheitan, ruler of the seven hells, probably knew it too. There was some sort of a tie between him and Lala Mustapha—could it be money? Nassi could smell a ducat at a mile's distance. And he knew Pialy Pasha. But his main influence on the Sultan was a direct one, that was certain. There was talk that he was led into the serai by one of the thousand back doors to confer with the Sultan for hours, with no one else present.

That was Jussuf Nassi, Lord of Naxos, Lord of the Cyclades, and just because his comings and goings were secret and he had no official status at court, his influence was difficult to combat.

"Ruler of the Faithful," Mehmed Sokolli said firmly, "your servant is well aware that Lala Mustapha and Pialy Pasha are against this venture. But why are they against it? Because they favor another one, the conquest of Cyprus. The reason why I asked my lord for this audience is this: the time has come to make a decision. At first glance it would seem that Cyprus is obviously our next objective, as it is so near to our shores. But the nearest is not always the best. Cyprus belongs to Venice. We have had an unbroken peace of almost forty years with the Serene Republic. They kept the peace even when your great father was besieging Rhodes. Why upset, before the right time, the established equilibrium of the Mediterranean? On our list of conquests, the Venetians should come last. Now it so happens that this is the opportunity of a hundred years and more to deal a deathblow to the oldest enemy of the Faith. Spain is facing a serious rebellion in many of its provinces, so serious that the King's troops have not been able to break it in the course of ten months—on the contrary, it is stronger than ever. Emissaries of the faithful in Spain are asking for our help. This is a greater thing than the conquest of an island, however rich and fertile. One word from the lips of the Lord of the Two Worlds, and the Mediterranean will be a Turkish lake. We shall be able to seal it off at the narrows still called after the great Tarek who first planted the banner of the prophet on the summit of the big rock there."

"Perhaps I shall speak the word", the Sultan said. "We shall see."

"Cyprus is no more than a tactical advantage", Mehmed Sokolli dared to add. "Spain gives us the possibility of taking the whole of Europe between our pincers. The Christian princes are fighting each other; there is no danger that they might use Cyprus as a basis of attack against our shores. Allah has smitten them with blindness, and none of them sees the danger that threatens them."

"We shall see", the Sultan repeated, sharply. "Go now."

Mehmed Sokolli knelt, touched the carpet once more with his forehead, rose, and left the presence. He had no idea whether he had won or lost. One never had with Selim. Many things were different now. But if the Sultan's first vizier was worried, the Sultan's seraskier was not. What mattered ultimately was the army and the fleet, and they had never been better. The realm was safe in the East, thanks to Süleyman's policy. If Europe was to be conquered, now was the time to attack.

The squat, obese little man with the face of the color of blood was sitting on a low couch in a small room whose walls were covered with tortoise shell, and he was sipping wine from the goblet his guest had just given him as a present. It was of gold, but that was of little account. The Sultan emptied it slowly and then held it at arms' length to admire the exquisite workmanship. "By the glory of Allah," he said, "I have seen the finest art from Persia and India, but never have I seen anything like this."

"The artist's name", said the guest, "is Benvenuto Cellini, and there is no one in the world who can match his work." He was a man of medium height, pale, with large, dark eyes, and a strong, curved nose.

"The wine is good, too", the Sultan said. "Not as sweet as the one you brought me last week from Samos, but more fiery. Where does it come from this time?"

"From Hungary, Lord of All the World. And it would have gone to the Emperor's caves, if my agent hadn't been quicker."

"I should demand fifty loads of such wine every year from the Emperor", Selim said. "He'd give it to me, too, if it were the last wine he had in the country. Everything, as long as he doesn't have to face my little janizaries. Pity I can't do it."

"I'll get you the fifty loads, Lord of All the World", his guest said at once. "Never let it be said that the greatest monarch on earth had to ask for so little a thing."

Selim grinned. "Never let it be said that an Osmanli asked for wine, you mean. You are a subtle man, Jussuf."

Jussuf Nassi bowed. "What subtlety I have is at my lord's disposal like the rest. If my lord wishes to put me to test . . ."

"I will, too. Mehmed Sokolli came to plead a cause today."

"About Spain."

"Of course. He wants a decision. I shall give it to him. But what will it be?"

"No one may dare to guess what is in the mind of the Lord of All the World."

"Loyally spoken", the Sultan said ironically. "But not subtly. And I trust your subtlety, not your loyalty. No, do not say anything; you might make things worse. You want Cyprus as a present from me, don't you? It's a kingdom and there hasn't been a Jewish king for a long time—not since they nailed the last one to a Cross."

Nassi knew that perhaps everything depended upon the right answer. They were alone in the small room, but behind the door the Sultan's mutes were waiting, huge, black slaves, as docile as dogs. There was a large assembly of people, both men and women, at the bottom of the Bosporus, who had died because two black slaves twisted a bow string around their necks and pulled for a minute or two. The Sultan had seen through him. Protestations, justifications, were of no avail whatever.

"Lord of All the World," he said boldly, "God forbid that I should say anything to you that is not true. Yes, Cyprus is the deepest wish of my heart—except for one other thing: vengeance against Spain. Not only for the wrong I suffered, but for all the wrongs that accursed country has done to the people of my race."

Selim was watching him closely. "Go on", he said.

"Perhaps one day the war with Spain will come", Nassi said. "But first things first. My shirt is nearer to my body than my coat. Cyprus is the shirt. The first vizier may have pointed out that this is the moment to attack Spain. But a still better moment will come when Cyprus is Turkish and can be used as an assembly place for the huge fleet necessary for such a conquest. First the Venetian fleet. Then Spain. Such were my calculations and that is the reason why I was so glad when I heard the news about the arsenal."

"The arsenal?"

Nassi raised his dark brows. "It is not conceivable that the first vizier has not told the Lord of All the World about the arsenal of Venice. But yes, perhaps it is. My agent only arrived this morning. On the thirteenth of September the arsenal of the Serene Republic went up in one huge explosion. The fleet has lost all its reserves of ammunitions, all reserve artillery, and even all the cannon castings." Nassi smiled significantly. "There was much talk of deliberate action on the part of an enemy unknown," he added softly, "so my agent left very quickly."

The Sultan lifted his finger. "By the all merciful and compassionate Allah," he said, "this is your work, Jussuf."

Nassi was still smiling. "It is, if the Lord of All the World says so", he answered.

Two weeks later Jussuf Nassi, Duke of Naxos, landed on the beautiful island over which he ruled "as a faithful lord, vassal and prince" of Selim II. He enjoyed every moment of it—the salvos of salute, the hoisting of his own flag, the honor guard of native soldiers under their plumed and armored captain, the ragged cheers of the people. Dressed in resplendent clothes in the Turkish style he mounted a white mule to ride up to his castle. An old official, riding beside him, was carrying a large leather bag filled with silver coins. From time to time the duke would take out a fistful and throw it to his cheering subjects. What a pity his parents had not lived to see their son now. What a pity his wife had died in Constantinople before she could enjoy her position. Now there was only Grazia. . . .

She was waiting for him at the entrance of the long, rambling building that was the palace, attended by two ladies; twelve soldiers and forty-two servants were standing in formation in the courtyard.

Suppressing his emotion he formally kissed his daughter's forehead, cool and of the color of old ivory.

Grazia was beautiful. He was watching her with pride when after the formal meal of welcome he asked her to come into his study. More beautiful even than her mother had been. She was tall and slim—almost too slim—with fine wrists and ankles, tapering fingers, and a long, aristocratic neck, bearing her head as proudly as a king his crown. But then there was no aristocracy half as ancient as the Jewish, and his family went back in a straight line to Prince Ephraim himself, ruler of the tribe of that name and member of the Sanhedrin, of whom it was said that he walked out of the session in which the fate of Rabbi Yeshua bar Joseph was to be decided—because he would have no part in injustice.

Rabbi Yeshua bar Joseph, to whom Sultan Selim had referred as the last Jewish king . . .

Yes, Grazia was beautiful. Her finely chiseled profile would look well on a coin. This was a favor the Sultan would have to grant him—to coin his own money.

"Sit beside me, my little dove, I have much to tell you." She obeyed.

"The present I let you choose has pleased the Sultan", he told her. "But he was even more pleased with the news that the arsenal of Venice has been destroyed in an explosion." Nassi smiled. "I was the first to tell him about it—and now he thinks I engineered it."

"And did you?" she asked gravely.

"No, but I did not exactly deny it. Selim is a fox and respects nothing so much as a good brain. Mehmed Sokolli is too slow for him and makes him impatient. I think we shall have war soon—no, do not be worried, not in this part of the world."

But her fear was not abated. "Father ... You didn't—I know how greatly the Sultan values your judgment and wisdom—you didn't advise him to go to war, did you?"

He frowned. "His mind is set on war in any case. The only issue to be decided is where the attack should take place. There I may have influenced him."

"But why, Father, why? The Sultan has land enough, peoples enough, greater riches than any other ruler. . . . Why should he want still more?"

"You know the Muslim religion, don't you? They must spread it—just as the Christians must."

"But surely that needn't be done by war?"

"I don't know. They think so, apparently. So let's see what advantage can be gained from their behavior. That is all we can do. Now, my little dove, I needn't tell you that you must keep that secret in your pretty little head, need I? The

Sultan is going to send an ambassador to Venice with an ultimatum. . . ."

"Venice . . . I thought they were friends, almost allies. . . ."

"The Venetians are merchants, ready to pay much for peace because peace means profits. They may accept the Sultan's conditions, in which case we shall gain Cyprus without a shot. A great island, my little dove, worth the lives of many men—much bigger and richer and more fertile than Naxos."

"Naxos has grown in my heart, Father. And I also have news, and I need your permission and signature for a number of things."

He smiled indulgently. "You do, do you? Well, what is it this time?"

"Old Sotros should have a pension, Father. He is too proud to accept alms."

"He's an impudent old rascal. I had to swallow my pride many a time, so why shouldn't he? Ah well, you know I can't say no to you. What else, God forbid?"

"Thank you for Sotros, Father. I want to build a hospital for the poor people on the north coast, and Iskander has discovered a marvelous site for it, just where the river . . ."

"That's the second hospital you want of me. And a home for the old and infirm, and another one for old Jews . . ."

"And I want torture to be abolished in all legal matters."

"Now that", he said angrily, "is really childish. You'll never get the truth out of any criminal without it."

"And only lies out of fear of the wheel and the screws as long as those horrible things are used."

"Who told you so?"

"I talked to everybody—Judge Simonis, the lawyers— one of them has studied in Salamanca, isn't that strange? And to some of the prisoners too. . . ."

"What? You went into the prison?" He was pale with anger now. "How dare you do such a thing? You demean yourself, your rank ..."

"I have been going there regularly, once a week", Grazia said courageously. "Father, you don't want me to bear this high rank only for show, do you? If I am to be what they call me, I must look after them when they are in trouble."

"Child, you don't know the world; you don't know people. They'll always cheat you—flatter you to your face and curse you behind your back. He who wants to rule must have a heavy hand."

She smiled at him. "I get along quite well with a little love, Father."

"Love", he repeated wryly. "That's what the Christians always talk about. Talk is cheap." An idea crossed his mind. "They haven't been trying to get at you, have they? The Christians? You talked to the jailbirds—perhaps you talked to a Christian priest as well?"

"To two of them", she said cheerfully. "And to at least five mullahs and imams as well as to the rabbis. They're all very nice, but none of them has been trying to 'get at me'."

"We are Jews", he said fiercely. "Jews."

"Is there anything in the Torah", Grazia asked, "that says that Jews must not be loved?"

He said nothing.

"I want them to love us", she said simply.

"You are a dialectician", he said. "Worse than if I had sent you to the rabbinical school." But he grinned. "Go now. I'll sign your papers afterward. No doubt you'll ruin me with your plans and I shall have to find new ways and means to bleed the Sultan."

"You are a wonderful father", she said.

Looking after her a strange thought floated down on him from nowhere—the thought that he might be forgiven much for her sake. He was angry with himself for it. It was the kind of thought Father Núñez could have had, old Father Núñez who once taught him the Christian catechism in Valladolid.

Go away, Father; I'm a Jew again and so is my child and so will her children be, for ever and ever.

Cyprus. The Venetians wouldn't accept the ultimatum; they couldn't. Cyprus meant too much to them. A jewel of an island. They would fight. But who would come to their aid? No one. On the contrary, the rulers of other Christian countries would commiserate officially, but smile inwardly. The King of Spain because Venice was a republic; the Genoese because of ancient rivalry. The French had troubles enough of their own and the German princes even more, with that new schism splitting them into two warring camps. The Emperor was glad to buy off the Sultan every year at the rate of thirty thousand ducats. Much cheaper than a war. Only the Pope wouldn't smile. But the Pope was weak.

Nothing better could happen to the Sultan than a Europe divided by religious as well as political hatred, Christian fighting Christian.

The Venetians would have to fight it out alone—and that would be the end of the Serene Republic.

Cyprus, and Sicily next, all stepping-stones to the last and greatest of all ventures, the conquest of Europe. Once the Venetian fleet—what was left of it—was incorporated in the Turkish naval forces, the Mediterranean could be swept clean of everything else, and at any given moment an armada of unheard-of size could land on the coasts of Italy, France, and Spain.

The Turkish soldier could live on almost nothing. The masses of men at the Sultan's command were overwhelming. And the Turkish fleet had never been beaten.

But first: Cyprus.

Jussuf Nassi, Duke of Naxos, took a piece of paper and a pen. Carefully, diligently, he began to draw a figure, a crest, topped by a large crown. Underneath it he wrote in bold, sprawling letters: "Joseph, King of Cyprus."

## CHAPTER 32

THE LONG, GRAY COLUMN was crawling up the hill, half hidden by the morning mist.

The cavalry had dismounted. The men were leading their horses up the steep mountain path. Mules were dragging up the cannon with much clattering, and from time to time there were shouts and oaths.

Don Juan had vanished again—it was the fifth time this morning—but Don Luiz Quixada was getting accustomed to that. It would have been easier to try to guard a bagful of fleas than the commander in chief.

Ever since that permission to attack had arrived from Madrid he had been a different man, to put it mildly. It was a transformation to take one's breath away—and it certainly took his officers' breath away. He seemed to be at a dozen places at once and one never knew where he was going to be next.

"He's erupting like a volcano", as Don Diego Hurtado de Mendoza put it.

The yes had come from Madrid after months and months of waiting; it was a somewhat sullen and reluctant yes and of course it came at the worst possible time of the year. The enemy had had all summer and all autumn to expand his strength and he had done so in all directions, taking Purchena, Tahali, Xurgal, Cantoria, and Galera and even invading Murcia. This new "king" of theirs, Aben Aboo, was a far more active fighter than the late and little-lamented Aben Humeya, whom he had helped to assassinate. The entire mountain tract between the Almanzora and the Ebro became a new danger zone, and they had pushed on almost to the gates of Granada, taking Güéjar, only four leagues away.

And all the time Juan had been sitting at his desk in the house of justice in the capital—forbidden to fight, forbidden any kind of major action. Yet after that first great outburst of despair he had been astonishingly calm—as if he were sure that he would get his way in the end.

He had written letter after letter to the King, to be sure, and so had Don Luiz. But Madrid's silence never seemed to discourage him again. Such calm was unnatural in one so young. Don Luiz himself exploded a few times, especially when another of those nice, courteous letters from Ruy Gómez arrived, inquiring about Don Juan's and his health and mentioning the King's many burdens, but never containing any definite news, as if the Supreme War Council in Madrid regarded the mere presence of a Spanish army in Granada as all that was required to stem the Moorish flood.

It was particularly galling that the King permitted the Marquis de los Vélez to attack several times, which that worthy did, but without much success.

And then the sudden yes at the end of December—it arrived on December 21; two days later the army was on the move and Don Juan retook Güéjar as easily as a knife cuts through cheese, and then immediately moved on toward Baza and Guescar. Baza meant a march of four days, and most of the time Juan would not ride, but marched now with this detachment of infantry now with that, talking to the soldiers, helping to get the guns across a bridge. And now that things were really moving, the noble Marquis de los Vélez thought fit to feel the burden of his years and to withdraw. Not quite quickly enough, though; they had caught up with him at Guescar and Juan had had a talk with him, the two alone, with the result that de los Vélez went home with only a small escort, leaving his troops at the disposal of the commander in chief!

How the boy did it was a mystery. He wouldn't talk about it, trying to save the marquis' feelings, of course.

I'll have to find out, nevertheless, Don Luiz thought. He was riding a mule. Juan Galarza was leading Quixada's horse as well as his own. A man in his mid-sixties and heavily armored found it a trifle disagreeable to ascend a steep mountain on foot. Don Luiz Requeséns, the Grand Commander of Castile, whom they had found in de los Vélez' headquarters, was doing likewise, and Quixada caught up with him at a turning.

"Don Juan is up there on the pass", Requeséns said, pointing.

"This means that he can see Galera almost at his feet", Quixada said. "How strong a fortress is it, my lord?"

The question was not wholly devoid of malice. Requeséns and de los Vélez had laid siege to Galera for weeks without success.

"Unconquerable, I'm afraid", Requeséns answered, with a shrug. "Unless Don Juan can slip through a keyhole there is little hope that we shall see its gates from the inside.

Santísima, how the good marquis swore each time we were repulsed. One could fill a book with the curses he knows."

"They don't seem to have been very effective", Quixada remarked dryly. "As for the keyhole, we shall see about that. I only wish His Majesty had permitted *us* to attack before this cold set in."

"His Majesty", Requeséns said, "has a great many troubles. The financial position of Spain is one; the Netherlands another—the last news from there is bad, despite Alba's victories. The devil take this mule of mine—it always insists on walking along the very edge of the abyss."

"Mules", Quixada said, "have many human qualities. You are more accustomed to the sea than to the mountains, my lord, so perhaps you will not take it amiss if I suggest a remedy used by many muleteros: to close the eye next to the abyss and to look straight ahead with the other one."

"I'll try that, thank you. Can't see anything degrading about it, considering that the Princess of Éboli has been doing it for years. Amazing lady. Have you heard from her husband lately?"

"Fairly recently", Quixada said cautiously.

"Some people seem to think that he is the King's left hand, just as Alba is the right one." Requeséns grinned. "If that is so, His Majesty certainly follows Holy Scripture to the letter by not letting his right hand know what the left one is doing."

But Quixada would not be drawn into a discussion that a week later would be repeated in Madrid. "We heard that a large transport of arms and money destined for the duke's army was sunk on the way. Is it true that the English did it?"

"Indeed it is, my lord. One of Queen Elizabeth's captains attacked it—a man called Dragon or Draco or some such thing; I have never been able to memorize English names. As for pronouncing them one must be either the devil or an Englishman. We protested, of course. The Queen will probably express her deepest horror and promise to punish her captain for acting against her orders and to pay damages and that will be all we shall ever see or hear about it."

Quixada was not listening. He was thinking of something else. "There is one thing I can't understand", he said. "We captured five Turks when we took Güéjar. Five! And from all the reports there are no more than a few hundred in the Moorish camp, plus a few thousand Algerians and Tunisians."

"Turkish engineers have fortified Galera", Requeséns growled. "Done far too good work for my liking. Glad there aren't more of them."

"So am I. But why aren't there more of them? The war has gone on long enough—by now the Sultan could have sent a hundred sails and thirty thousand volunteers to come to the aid of his co-believers."

"Not being the Sultan, I can't tell you", Requeséns said testily. "Mind you, there's some rumor about an impending war with Venice—most unlikely, I think. The Porte and the Serene Republic have always been as thick as thieves. I'd give something to see those two fall out, smash each other's fleets. Spanish galleys would lord it everywhere then. Here's the pass now. And His Excellency."

His Excellency was standing on the rocky plateau with a dozen of his young nobles, looking down at the hill, far below between the two small rivers, the Huéscar and the Orce. Hearing the clattering of the mules' hooves he turned and beckoned. "Please join me, my lords", he said cheerfully. "I've been studying the place and I think I know what's to be done."

The two old commanders dismounted and approached.

Galera had its name from the shape of the hill on which it was built, which roughly resembled that of a galley. The higher part of the rock with the castle on it was the stern; the prow descended into the plain, near the place where Huéscar and Orce met.

"The ridge over there, east of the rock," Juan said, "seems a good site for our main encampment. We'll have one battery there, you see, where that pointed crag is—and another on the north. The position of the third I don't know yet— we'd better have a closer inspection of the enemy's fortification on the south. Padilla with his infantry will occupy the sector covered by the Huéscar on the left."

Quixada nodded. He did not want to say in front of Requeséns that the battery of light guns on the north had not much chance of being effective against massive rock formations. He would tell that to the young general later.

But Requeséns said it for him. "Your guns won't even tickle them from there, Your Excellency. These rock are solid."

"I'm not going to use them as siege guns", Juan replied almost impatiently. "They'll only join in when I have shot a hole through the wall with Inez and Dolores."

"With ... whom?" Requeséns asked.

"Inez and Dolores", Quixada explained, "are very heavy pieces of artillery. But ..."

"Surely you know them, my lord", Juan chimed in. "You sent them to us from Cartagena. Ships' guns. I wish we had a few more like them."

"Santísima", Requeséns exclaimed. "You can't bring ships' guns of heavy calibre up on roads like these; they'd never get here. You must have seen what the bridges are like."

"Of course", Juan said casually. "That's why I ordered Vásquez to build a couple of new ones just for our two heavy ladies. Vásquez de Acuña—you know him, don't you?

He's never so happy as when he can perform a little miracle of calculation *and* put it into practice. He built both bridges in one night, and the guns will be here about five hours from now. Not up the pass here, of course, but on the road down there. I gave Vásquez two hundred men as an escort, apart from the mule train."

Quixada cleared his throat noisily. This was news to him too, but he wasn't going to let Requeséns see it.

"The light battery", Juan went on, "will serve to cover the assault, when Inez and Dolores have done their work. Sánchez! Tell Captain Pacheco to lead the descent of those men straight to the main encampment site. Wait! My lord Requeséns, you were present at the first siege of Galera: What is the heaviest type of gun they have?"

Requeséns told him and Juan made a few quick calculations.

"Sánchez, tell Captain Pacheco to lead them along this line—no nearer to the fortress than these shrubs."

Sánchez ran.

"We don't want unnecessary casualties", Juan said to no one in particular. "Here's Zapata coming up with his cavalry. My lords, what about examining the defenses on the other side?"

"Over my dead body", Quixada said sternly. "Not before we have *all* the cavalry here."

Juan made a wry face. "That means another two hours at least. We might as well have breakfast then."

"Now that", Quixada said, "is a very good idea. Mind you, Your Excellency, I don't know whether even your two big ladies will be strong enough to make a sizable hole in those rocks."

"No harm in trying", Juan answered. "If they don't, I must get hold of Molina. There's no one like him for laying a mine. There, I think, under the castle itself. I'd better tell him as soon as he comes up. He's with number two battery. And Fernan! I want a zigzag trench built from the main encampment toward the castle. Tell Captain García to have his men start digging as soon as they've had their meal." He grinned up at Quixada. "Remember how you taught me never to make men work before they had a meal?"

"You haven't forgotten much of what I once taught you", Quixada muttered. "And you seem to have learned a few more things since."

"Don Luiz Quixada, Don Luiz Requeséns, and the Duke of Alba", Juan said. "No man ever had three better teachers than I had. Francisco! Follow Pacheco's men; don't get nearer to the fortress than they do, if you please. Cristóbal! Tell Don Pedro Martínez to deploy his men along the Orce river bend; they'll be out of range there, too."

"Your Excellency is most kind", Don Luiz Requeséns said.

Quixada said nothing. He was thinking of a little boy, fair-haired and blue-eyed, who once gave him on a cushion the keys of Villagarcía. For some reason the thought made him clear his throat again.

A deputation of young nobles came to Juan, asking for the honor of being allowed to form the spearhead of the first assault column.

There were over two hundred of them, each with his own retinue, unpaid volunteers of course. Juan knew every one of them personally, some from Madrid or Valladolid—he had dined and wined with them, gone hunting with them—others had served under him during his cruise with the fleet; and all of them had been tugging at the leash for months, and this was their first real opportunity, for Güéjar,

Baza, and Guescar had been conquered practically by the arrival of the Spanish army.

Juan knew that he could not very well refuse them, although he would have much preferred to have them with him when he himself was going into action. But that he could not tell them now, with Don Luiz Quixada standing beside him. "The general does not fight; he directs the battle—" Quixada had told him that a dozen times, and the King wrote in letter after letter that he must not expose his own life "unnecessarily" as this might well give the Moriscos the chance for a triumph, the news of which would serve their cause in all Muslim countries as well as hardening their resistance. Juan had his own ideas about it, but this was not the moment to air them.

Reluctantly he gave his permission, and they cheered him and ran to pass on the good news.

Don Luiz had tears in his eyes. He could see himself as he was almost half a century ago, behaving exactly as these young men did now—he and two of his brothers who later fell on active service, one in Tunisia, the other in Germany. And his general at the time was the present general's father. . . .

Requeséns was silent. But after a while he pointed to the tower of the castle. "I hope they'll avenge him", he said grimly.

Juan saw a long pole with what seemed to be a small ball at the end.

"It's the head of Don León de Robles", Requeséns said. "Son of a cousin of the Marquis de los Vélez. I knew him well."

Juan said nothing. They went to inspect the forest of tents growing at the main encampment and the building of the zigzag trenches, snaking up to the foot of Galera hill.

"Tedious work", Juan said aloud. "A song would help, I think. Where are the musicians?"

The men grinned, but soon enough a band of musicians marched up and began to play popular songs. By then Juan had joined the men fetching brushwood from the nearby mountain slopes, and he carried two dozen loads himself to the trenches, although he was in full armor.

Requeséns was disgusted and even Quixada growled, but the men were all singing now and as much amused by the obvious disapproval of the two old commanders as by their young general's flagrant breach of etiquette. And the zigzag trenches wriggled forward with double speed.

When Juan emerged, perspiring profusely, he went up to Quixada: "I've had an idea", he said. "Why not go on digging at night as well? They'll fire as soon as we get into closer range, but we can mislead them with lanterns—small ones—so that they can't see that we're elsewhere—and in the morning all will be ready for the assault."

"You're in a hurry, aren't you, Your Excellency?" Requeséns said dryly. "They'll probably fire all night, and we won't get an hour's sleep."

"Neither will they", Juan replied. "And I *am* in a hurry. I have to catch up with ten months of doing nothing. Now, if you please, my lords, we'll go and inspect the defenses on the other side."

They did, with three hundred horsemen and fifteen hundred infantry, and soon afterward battery number three followed them and went into position. A short council of war followed in which Requeséns informed them about de los Vélez' unsuccessful attacks. A young captain entered the tent to announce, beaming, that Inez and Dolores had arrived and Quixada suggested a feint attack by the troops they had left on the south side.

"But that's why I left them there", Juan said, a little surprised. "I thought you knew."

"But you told Don Alonzo to refrain from any attack."

"I did, too. He's a hothead and I want him to wait for my signal."

Quixada smiled. Later, when they had dined and rose to retire, the old man said in a low voice: "You are doing well . . . son. I don't think you'll need me much longer."

"I'm beginning to get the feel of it", Juan said. "It was the same some time ago, when I had to learn how to use ships, many ships, a fleet. It's like acquiring a new body. The batteries are like fists. Tomorrow I shall push in the gate of Galera. But I still have much to learn, and I thank God that you are with me in my first battle. Good night . . . Father."

Quixada pressed his hand and walked away, with short, tired steps.

It was dark now, and campfires were burning like a ring with widely spaced rubies around the besieged fortress.

Against all expectations the Moriscos did not open fire at night against the trenches.

In the morning the cannonade started. Inez opened a breach with the fifth shot, and an assault column spearheaded by the young nobles under Padilla, de la Favara, and de Luzón penetrated it, followed almost immediately by Don Juan Pacheco and his men.

But the counterattack threw them back, with heavy losses, and shortly afterward a giant Morisco threw Pacheco's body over the wall—in four pieces. They had quartered him, because, as a Knight of Santiago, he was wearing the large, red cross of his Order on his breast.

"Mines", Juan ordered. They were laid, right under the castle itself. When all was ready, four thousand men filled the trenches, waiting for the explosion.

It came with a roar that deafened both armies, blowing up half a thousand defenders, wrecking the outer wall and bursting open a small hole in the inner.

The trenches erupted soldiers who began to climb up the bare crags, like goats.

Meanwhile the light batteries had opened fire, too.

"They're rallying", Quixada roared, pointing to the east end of the town, where small guns blazed away in increasing numbers, all directed against the assailants from the trenches.

A young ensign, Don Pedro de Zapata, was the first to reach the breach, waving the banner of his unit. Half a dozen Moriscos jumped at him, and he fought them singlehanded in every sense of the word, for he would not let go of his banner. He killed two, but the other four threw him back, wounded in face and shoulder, and he fell headlong into brushwood smoldering from the explosion.

"Save that man", Juan shouted.

"Not a chance in a thousand", Requeséns said, shrugging and turning away not to show his emotion.

But Quixada dispatched a handful of men to get Zapata out of the brushwood. "Save his body at least", he said. Turning back to Don Juan he found his place empty.

"Santísima," Requeséns cried, "there he is, with Cabral's men; they're storming the other end. He'll get himself killed! All the demons in hell take that cursed town. Look here ..."

The rest Quixada no longer heard. Spurring his horse he crashed through a unit of harquebusiers and rode after Juan, whose black charger he could see, dimly, in the midst of an upheaval of helmets, bucklers, and swords. Somebody was riding just behind him. He knew it was Galarza, but he had no time to really register the thought.

374

The Moriscos were quiet. Holding their fire, of course, and the young fool would be picked off like a sitting pheasant . . . dear God, don't let it happen . . . what will I tell the King, if . . . there was the salvo. He stared about wildly—the boy was gone; they had killed him; no, there he was—he had dismounted and was climbing up the damned rock with Cabral's men; they were falling like flies. The whole thing was utter madness, but if God wanted him to die at his age while climbing like a silly goat, he would do it. . . .

Another salvo, just as he dismounted. Again they had not hit Juan, by sheer miracle, but now there were only fifty men left around him, and even he could see that he could not storm a fortress with them. He turned back, thank God, taking cover behind rocks, too, and sliding down, and there they were holding his horse for him and there he mounted, and if only Requeséns would have the good sense to give the signal for general retreat now—stupid old man, should have stuck to his ships, that was all *he* was good for. . . .

The signal came and a minute later Juan passed by without seeing him, and what a face, by God and Santiago, what a face; not a drop of blood in it and the eyes like burning coals, but not a scratch, thank God in high heaven, not a scratch. . . .

Quixada rode back slowly to Requeséns. "Thank you for the signal, my lord", he said. "It was about time."

"Somebody had to keep his head, my lord", Requeséns replied, and he was right, too, damn him.

Everywhere Spanish soldiers were streaming back.

Three hours later all commanders were ordered to appear in the general's tent.

"I told you Galera is unconquerable", Requeséns said when he met Quixada at the entrance. "Now our young master and friend will be a little more amenable to the advice of experience, I think. And I most certainly shall vote for giving up the siege."

Quixada thought of Juan's face as he had seen it last. He said nothing.

To their astonishment they found about sixty senior officers in the tent. Only the war council could be asked to vote, and this looked more like a briefing.

It was.

Juan came in, looking just as Quixada remembered him. "My lords, friends, and officers," he said, "the setback we have received has shown me the way to victory. Our obstacle is a castle wall. The castle wall will go. The plans for that are ready. On the tenth day of February Galera will fall, and only God can prevent it if such is his wish."

The officers cheered.

Quixada carefully avoided looking at Requeséns.

"This is not all", Juan went on. "An answer must be given to the rebels for what they did to Don León de Robles and Don Juan de Pacheco. I will have Galera razed to the ground and the site sown with salt. All Moriscos and Turks inside will be put to the sword."

The officers left, still cheering.

Juan turned to Quixada: "My lord, please see to it that no mail is forwarded from the camp till February eleventh. I want the news of our success to reach the King at the same time as that of today's misfortune. And now you must excuse me—I must see how Zapata is doing. He is still alive, you know."

He strode out of the tent.

Quixada turned to Requeséns: "My lord," he said solemnly, "if you so desire I shall put it on record that you

would have voted for the raising of the siege of Galera ...
if there had been a vote."

"Nonsense, my lord", Requeséns sputtered. "Nonsense.
Don Juan is quite right. Raze the place to the ground, sow
salt, give no quarter. I quite agree. Glad he said so, despite
the setback. Very glad."

"Somebody had to keep his head, my lord", Quixada
said innocently.

Unexpectedly, Requeséns cackled with laughter.

Juan found Zapata fully conscious. The young ensign even
wanted to sit up when his commander came in. Juan stopped
him gently. "All Spain will be proud of you, Don Pedro",
he said. "I shall mention your name and action in my special report to the King. And I want you at my side in every
future campaign on land or sea. Get well quickly, Don
Pedro."

The ensign's handsome face was radiant. "Your Excellency ... has given me ... the best medicine there is", he
whispered.

Every day for several hours Juan went to see the
wounded—there were more than five hundred of them.
And every day he conferred with Francisco de Molina,
the expert on mines, and watched the tunnels—one east
and one west—biting deeper and deeper into the rock.
Molina laid a great number of small mines to blast his
way for the large ones, and the defenders jeered at the
amount of powder the Spaniards wasted.

On February 10 the two large mines went off together
and Padilla's infantry stormed up the smoke-veiled rocks
into the flaming, shrieking hell that was Galera.

Detachments of cavalry, carefully posted, butchered all
fugitives.

Two thousand four hundred Moriscos and fifty-four Turkish engineers died that day, and there was enough booty of all kinds to satisfy every officer and man.

Juan put Quixada in charge of selecting the King's Fifth and del Marmol of fulfilling his vow to raze the town to the ground and sow salt on the soil.

The next day he gave order to break tents.

"Cúllar first", he said, "then headquarters at Caniles."

Quixada and Requeséns looked at each other. Both these places were villages and could not be defended. The real objective was clear to them at once. Very near Caniles was the fortress whose capture by the Moriscos had caused Don Juan such pain, that fateful day in July: the fortress of Serón.

## CHAPTER 33

THE RECONNAISSANCE PARTY consisted of two thousand infantry and two hundred horses, and Juan took both Quixada and Requeséns with him, leaving the camp at Caniles in charge of Padilla. One of the two old commanders ought to have stayed there, but neither of them could be induced to do so. Quixada insisted that he was personally responsible for Don Juan's life, and Requeséns countered that as vice admiral of the fleet he was in exactly the same position and had a letter from the King to prove it. They started quarreling like boys, until Juan cut them short with the courteous remark that he would be loth to be without the counsel of either of them.

To their surprise they found Serón very badly defended. A few hundred Moriscos tried to intercept them, but their fire was sporadic and they were soon in full retreat behind the walls, hotly pursued by Tello González de Aguilar, who was in command of the cavalry.

"They hate cavalry", Quixada said. "Their own used to be very good, but now they are no longer accustomed to riding, it seems."

A young officer came up in full gallop. "Your Excellency, the respects of Don Tello, and he is in possession of the main gate. The enemy had dispersed."

"This is too good to be true", Quixada said. "We should send scouts into the streets, though. It may be a trap."

Juan nodded. "I'll send out scouts", he said. "But five hundred of them." He gave the orders, and twenty minutes later a second messenger arrived.

"Don Tello reports there is very little fighting. We have taken the main stores."

Juan turned in the saddle. "My lords, it looks as if we had taken them by surprise. If we use this opportunity we may shorten the whole campaign by a week." He drew his sword and pointed forward.

The troops cheered and advanced.

"Serón taken by a reconnaissance party." Requeséns chuckled, spurring his horse. "This will look well in a report to Madrid."

But Quixada shook his head. "We are supposed to give him the wisdom and counsel of age. Instead he is making us young and foolish."

"Our men seem to be getting out of hand in there", Requeséns said. "They're burning houses."

"Either that or the enemy is giving smoke signals", Quixada replied. "In either case I don't like it." He tried to tell the commander in chief, but Juan was shouting something to the soldiers, and he could not make himself heard. Then a swarm of soldiers rushed between them, obviously eager to get their share of the looting. In vain their officers tried to establish some sort of military formation.

"Fine men you have there, my lord", Requeséns shouted angrily. "If I couldn't keep better discipline on my ships, I would . . ."

Quixada heard no more, for now another herd of soldiers separated them, roaring and laughing, and that was too much for the rest. The entire force began to run toward the main gate, jamming it and piling out on the other side as best they could.

Somewhere in their midst was Juan. Roaring, Quixada rode into the thick mass of men, hitting out right and left with the flat side of his sword, and a couple of dozen lengths behind him Requeséns and a few other officers did the same.

Emerging on the other side Quixada saw Don Tello with two aides and rode up to him. "Where's His Excellency?"

"I saw him ride up the main street to the citadel a moment ago", the young cavalry leader replied.

"Where the devil are your men?" Quixada snapped.

"I kept them here as long as I could", Don Tello was visibly embarrassed. "But now they're looting like everybody else. The town is ours", he added as a kind of afterthought.

Quixada glared at him. "Get twenty of them together at once—at once, do you hear? And keep a lookout at the main gate. If there are any Moors left in the vicinity, we shall be trapped like so many rats. At the first sign of the enemy, send me a messenger. I shall be somewhere near the citadel. I make you personally responsible for the main gate."

He rode on. The noise all around him was familiar to every old soldier. The crash of breaking doors, the rumble of furniture upturned, curses, and the screeching of women, all mingling with ragged shooting—the sound of a conquered town in the first hours.

A number of houses were burning, but when he turned a corner and saw the citadel, he found the red flag of the new Moorish "king" still flying and a column of fat, black smoke rising up—a signal, of course.

And here was Juan, trying to get a few hundred men together and berating them at the top of his voice.

Quixada, relieved, looked up to the citadel again. Just as well that its guns were in fixed positions and could not be trained on the plaza, or everything here would be a shambles in five minutes.

"You stupid idiots," he thundered at the nearest men, "fall in and behave like soldiers. No one will be allowed to keep the loot he has got—it will all be divided fairly later on. Fall in, I say!"

But it took the better part of two hours to get as much as six hundred men together.

"They're all in the houses, of course", Quixada told Juan.

"I'll get them out, if I have to set the town on fire", Juan raged. "They're rabble, not soldiers."

Requeséns came with another hundred men he had collected. Some of them were wounded; one had had his ear bitten off by a Moorish woman whose jewels he had torn off *her* ears and neck.

"How many do you think are up there?" Juan asked Quixada, pointing to the citadel. But before he could get an answer, Don Tello came clattering across the plaza with thirty men on horseback, and Quixada paled. Don Tello was no coward. If he dared to leave the main gate despite explicit orders, it meant the worst.

"Moriscos by the thousand", Don Tello reported breathlessly. "A whole army of them; they're filling the valley. They'll be here in ten minutes."

Juan bit his lip. For a moment he seriously thought of making a desperate assault on the citadel. If it succeeded, he could hold it, until Padilla came to relieve them. But up there were probably more Moriscos than he had soldiers, and in a quarter of an hour he would be between two fires. The whole thing was madness. "What's the enemy's objective?" he asked curtly. "Are there several columns or one?"

"Several", Don Tello replied. "But all converging against the main gate, as far as I could see. I've got another fifty of my men together, and they're holding a small gate near the church over there."

"That's where we get out", Juan decided. "Trumpets! Drums! The general alarm!"

"If that won't wake them up, the enemy soon will", Requeséns said grimly.

Shame-faced officers tried to lead the men off in an orderly way, but soldiers came hastily from all sides and the withdrawal soon became a streaming mass of men, many of them packed with loot they would not let go, some of them even dragging women behind them.

From afar came a new kind of noise: a shrill, high-pitched, long-drawn howl, answered by a similar howl from the citadel.

The houses were spouting Spanish soldiers now.

"Old man Serón is combing the lice out of his beard", Don Tello said. "I hope I have done right, leaving the main gate in the circumstances, my lord?"

"Perhaps you did", Quixada said gruffly. "Without cavalry we'll never get out of this alive."

Don Tello's thirty men had swollen to forty-two by now, and there were another fifty or so at that minor gate. Better than nothing. A man on horseback was worth not three or four but thirty on foot, in this war.

If only those riders at the gate were still there—yes, they were; Quixada could see them now, and what was more there were at least seventy of them.

It was not easy to get the men out, as at least some of them were panicky and no more than two-thirds had passed the gate when the Moriscos appeared, howling like wolves.

"Turn and fight", Juan ordered. It was the only way to ward off complete disaster. The retreat had to be covered.

To his utter dismay he saw himself disobeyed. They were thinking only of themselves and of their loot.

"Let me take over", Quixada begged. "The major part of the men are outside, and you as the general...."

But Juan rode into the panting, roaring mass of men. "Fight", he shouted. "Are you Spaniards or not?" He reined his horse across their path.

"To his side, Don Tello", Quixada said hastily. "And guard him better than the main gate. A dozen of your men—form a ring."

He could hear only a few words of what Juan was shouting: "... men, not old women ... honor ..." He was laying about with the flat side of his sword, too, and after a while, with Don Tello's help, he had a front of sorts together and they fired away at the Moriscos, who were as hemmed in as they were and packed so tightly that every shot told.

Quixada arranged a contingent of harquebusiers to cover two more streets leading up to the gate and made frantic signs to Don Tello to get the commander in chief away with his riders.

"Time to go, Your Excellency", Don Tello urged. "You've dubbed more of these rascals knights than His Majesty ever did in his life." A bullet whined past them and a volley of stones crashed into the group around them, killing three men and wounding a dozen others.

"They've got their slingshots up", Don Tello said. "Time to go."

Another volley.

"I want Don Luiz Quixada out first", Juan said.

From the other side came a ragged salvo.

Horrified, Juan saw Don Luiz slump in the saddle and slowly slide off his horse.

The men around the old commander were still screaming with rage when Juan landed in their midst. He saw Galarza's scarface looking up to him and heard him say: "Musket shot through the shoulder, sir. Don't get off your horse, sir; they're coming." He saw Quixada smiling at him—the old man was lying with his head on the lap of a harquebusier, and his cuirass was spattered with blood. And he saw the Moors coming, a fat, white cloud of them, howling with glee.

"Harquebusiers!" he roared. "Get ready . . . fire!"

The volley told. Death and confusion reigned within the white cloud.

"Fire!"

Again death sailed through the air. But this was nothing. Juan looked about wildly. He saw Don Tello and his horsemen. "Follow me!"

He rode toward the cloud without even looking back to see if his order was obeyed. He was entirely past caring.

"Santiago!" Don Tello screamed, waving his sword, and the horsemen repeated the cry. A fraction of a minute later a thundering mass of well over a hundred horses broke into the cloud of Moors.

A slingshooter's stone crashed against Juan's helmet and almost knocked him out of the saddle. Through a red mist he saw a dark face, bearded and screaming, and stabbed it through the mouth. A naked arm was raising a lance, and he thrust under it into an armpit.

Another stone, ricocheting, hit his buckler, and out of sheer fury he smashed the buckler into the nearest dark face.

Four arms were grasping his reins and saddle. He let his horse rear, and they disappeared, except for one which he slit its full length.

The next brown thing in front of him was a back, naked and glistening. He opened it with a deep thrust and it disappeared. Here was another. . . .

Backs? *Backs?*

By God and all the saints, they were fleeing. Don Tello's face appeared from nowhere, grinning like a devil's, and reason came back and cleared the mist before Juan's eyes.

"Back", he shouted. "Back to the gate, Spaniards." He reined his horse. Foot soldiers, put to flight by a cavalry attack, did not rally quickly. Somebody had taught him that— ah, yes, Alba, back in the maproom of the palace. Except, the old soldier had said, when the flight is a feint, to lead the cavalry into a prepared trap.

He had no time to find out. What mattered was to get all the troops out of Serón and back to Caniles . . . if possible. All the troops that were left. For the looting rascals who missed the general alarm there was no hope left.

At the gate he found the situation easier. Requeséns had taken things in hand; most of the troops were out, and the rest were following in an orderly manner. Galarza had managed to improvise some kind of a hammock for his wounded master and to get hold of two mules to carry it.

"Ninety-six of us back, including seven wounded, sir", Don Tello reported, still grinning. The fellow seemed to be enjoying himself.

"Very good", Juan said. "A dozen of them will escort Don Luiz Quixada back as quickly as possible. Pick the best men you have, Don Tello. And you'd better command them yourself. Galarza here will come with you; he can ride one of the two mules."

"Begging your pardon, sir, but Don Luiz charged me to guard *you*", Don Tello said anxiously.

"My master told me to stay with you, Your Excellency", Galarza joined in. "He'll bite my head off."

"You heard my order", Juan snapped. "Off with you, and quickly." He turned away to hide his emotion.

With the remaining eighty-odd horsemen Juan himself covered the retreat of the troops and then followed them.

"We have lost over three hundred men", Requeséns told him, when they met on a small hill half a league's distance from the town. "And from the reports I have, there are five thousand brown devils in Serón now. Unless they're the worst cowards in the world, we shall have them all here in a quarter of an hour—and it won't be dark for some time yet."

Juan nodded. "You're right, my lord." He pointed to the gate, still visible at a distance. "Here they come now."

Quixada was unconscious most of the time during the journey back to Caniles. When he woke up, he was back in his quarters there and a surgeon was holding a tumbler to his lips. "Drink this, my lord."

"Where is Don Juan?" Quixada murmured.

"We have no news yet, my lord. Please drink this ... it will make you drowsy. We must operate on you, my lord. The bullet is still in your body."

But Quixada turned his head away. "Reinforcements", he whispered. "Padilla must send ... reinforcements."

"They're on the way, my lord."

"How ... how many? How many ... cavalry?"

This the surgeon did not know.

"Send for ... Padilla", Quixada ordered. His body hurt as if it had been hit not once but a dozen times, but he knew he would not die yet, not within the next few hours anyway. First he must know Juan was safe and report to the King. No news yet ...

"What time is it?"

But the surgeon had gone to send for Padilla.

Padilla arrived a few minutes later with a young officer. At the sight of him Quixada's eyes lighted. He was Juan de Soto, one of Don Juan's aides.

"De Soto just arrived", Padilla said. "I thought you'd like to hear his report yourself."

"His Excellency is safe and well", de Soto said, "despite a slight arm wound."

Quixada's face shone.

"He beat off two attacks in the vicinity of Serón," de Soto went on, "and then it became darker. The Moors nevertheless prepared a third attack with all their strength—almost six thousand men; but Don García de Manrique, who is on his home ground here, knew a footpath that enabled us to withdraw in time. We lost about six hundred men, all told...."

"No need to go on", Padilla said. "Don Luiz has lost consciousness."

Doña Magdalena arrived in Caniles five days after receiving Juan's letter. She had traveled to Granada in a litter, accompanied by a few friends of the family and a dozen armed servants, and from there to Caniles on muleback.

Juan, his left arm in a sling, helped her to dismount. He would not allow anybody else to touch her. He had done everything in his power to smooth her journey. His first messenger to her was his own valet, Jorge de Lima, who brought her a map, drawn by the commander in chief of the army himself and indicating the safest route. Relays of horses were ready for her at all the places where she stopped to spend the night. Each time a new bulletin was awaiting her, too. In Granada she was given an additional escort of fifty men.

There was no need for explanations. All she asked, as she was entering the wretched, ramshackle house on Juan's arm, was: "Is he conscious?"

"He wasn't quite, this morning", Juan said. "But he is now. I told him about your arrival, too, an hour ago. Here is the door, Tía."

As she entered, her love performed the miracle of a warm, happy smile. Juan saw it and its reflection on Don Luiz' waxen face. He closed the creaky door behind her and broke into tears.

A few hours later he was told that Don Luiz was calling for him. He found him relaxed and calm, fully conscious.

"I want to thank you", the old soldier said, "for all the care and goodness you have shown to my wife. You'll look after her, won't you, when I have gone? Ah, well, I needn't have asked. Have you got news from His Majesty about reinforcements?" His voice was low, but he spoke quite easily.

"Yes, Don Luiz. Two thousand men are underway— regular soldiers."

"Good. You can do with them. Who is the commander?"

"Don Francisco de Córdoba."

Don Luiz nodded. "He's not as good as I am, but he's good. And he knows the Moors and their warfare. The King . . . has chosen well. You'll stamp out this rebellion . . . son. I know . . . none better."

"Enough now, my dearest", Doña Magdalena said.

Don Luiz smiled at her. "One would think—you are—the commander."

He had a good night. The next day he asked for the army auditor and made his will, making Doña Magdalena the sole beneficiary for her life. After her death, everything was to go to the poor. Silos for grain; schools were to be built in the four communities, Villagarcía, Villanueva de los Camalleros, Satofimia, and Villamayor; hospitals to be endowed. "And if Doña Magdalena should find it more practicable to combine her possessions with mine and to found monasteries or convents—except convents for barefoot nuns, because they could not live in my part of the country, it being too cold—I hereby empower her and the executors to do so, for our wish has always been that we should make a permanent foundation and be buried in its grounds, so that we should remain reunited in death in the same harmony in which we have lived together."

Then he asked for a father confessor. Juan introduced Friar Cristóbal de Molina to him. He was an ugly little man, but it was he who had led the Spanish forces across the chasm of Tablate, over a "bridge" consisting of a single beam of wood. The most courageous soldiers hesitated. The beam had the breadth of a man's hand and the abyss a depth of several hundred feet. Friar Cristóbal walked over it, a sword in one hand and his crucifix in the other, with Morisco slingshooters shooting at him from the other side; his example made the others follow him. The very audacity of it so discouraged the Moriscos that they fled—and thus the Spaniards were able to come to the aid of the hard-pressed town of Órgiba. All this had happened before Juan's arrival.

Don Luiz could not help shaking his head, when he saw the wizened little man who looked as if he could not harm a fly. But he said: "Reverend Father, you can lead soldiers across an abyss—lead me across mine."

Later in the day he received the Viaticum and the Last Sacraments and, as is so often the case, regained strength. For one more full day he seemed to be almost well again. Then he sank back into weakness and unconsciousness. The bullet was still in his body. . . .

During the evening of February 25 the end was coming.

Juan had put the candle in his hand and supported it. Doña Magdalena was holding the crucifix to his lips. At the foot of the bed Friar Cristóbal de Molina was reading the most majestic and most moving of all prayers: the prayers for the dying.

When all was over, Juan embraced Doña Magdalena, until she had ceased sobbing. Together they closed Don Luiz' eyes. Doña Magdalena gently pressed his lids down, and Juan closed them with a few drops of the death candle, as was usual.

The next day the entire army marched past the bier on which the body of the great commander lay in full armor, hands folded over the cross of his sword hilt.

All muskets were carried with the muzzle downward; all lances, pikes, and flags were dragged in the dust; all drums draped in black.

The only flag carried upright was the standard of the captain general.

In the afternoon the coffin with the body was interred in the cemetery of a nearby Jeromite monastery, until it could safely be transported to Villagarcía. Doña Magdalena stayed on for three more days. Then she left in a black litter, with a strong escort, to retire for a while to a convent near Madrid. Juan accompanied her for several miles.

He returned to preside over an assembly of all senior officers.

With a face of stone he looked at one after the other.

His address consisted only of one sentence: "My lords and captains: the fortress of Serón is doomed."

The fortress of Serón fell in the first days of March.

The fortress of Tíjola fell after a siege of eleven days.

Purchena was taken, Cantoria conquered, Tahali occupied. Then Don Francisco de Córdoba arrived with his two thousand regulars and Terque and Los Padules de Andarax were taken. On April 17 the commander in chief entered Santa Fé.

The entire Almanzora valley was reconquered and the Duke of Sesa was smoking out one Moorish nest after the other in the Alpuxarras.

On May 24, one day before the Feast of Corpus Christi, the Moors capitulated. The two main leaders after Aben Aboo himself, El Granadino and El Habaqui, made a token surrender with three hundred of their men and Aben Aboo's flag was laid at Don Juan's feet.

In the days that followed, the Moriscos surrendered by the thousand.

Aben Aboo, suddenly changing his mind, tried to resume hostilities, and one of his first actions was to have El Habaqui murdered. But the spirit of war had gone out of his followers. Word had gone around that the young, fair-haired captain general of the Spaniards was invincible; that nothing was more dangerous than to win a temporary advantage over him: but that he was surprisingly mild and gracious to those who submitted to his power voluntarily.

Aben Aboo was led into a trap by his own men—and murdered. His body was delivered to President Deza in Granada.

The Morisco rebellion was over.

# BOOK FOUR

A.D. 1570–1571

THE CONFERENCE GOING ON in one of the smaller rooms of the Vatican on November 7 was if anything even more list-less than those preceding it.

Five days ago, when the news came that the Turks had conquered Nicosia, the capital of Cyprus, and butchered twenty thousand Christians, the two Venetian ambassadors, Suriano and Surenzi, had withdrawn, pale and trembling, and for forty-eight hours it looked as if the fate of the Holy League were sealed once and for all.

The Pope had spent those two days fasting and praying; he refused to see anybody.

On November 4 the Signoria ordered her ambassadors to resume negotiations, but everybody was still so much affected by the terrible blow that very little progress was made.

The Spaniards were embarrassed and suspicious; the Vene-tians reproachful and suspicious. The Pope alone, presiding as usual, seemed to have regained his vigor, although he was the oldest of all the participants.

"His Holiness seems to thrive on fasting", Cardinal Granvella murmured into the ear of the Spanish ambassador.

Zúñiga gave an almost imperceptible nod. "I wish I had his energy", he whispered. "Anyone else would have given up long ago."

"He'll never give up. The league is his child. . . ."

"There isn't much life in it. In fact it may be stillborn."

"Then he'll breathe his own life into it. Besides, we are getting on with it; most of the figures are fixed. . . ."

"You know as well as I do that everything can dissolve again into nothing at any given minute. These Venetians—" He broke off as he saw that the Pope was looking in his direction.

"Two hundred galleys", said the fierce old man in the white habit, "and one hundred transport ships. Fifty thousand infantry, four thousand five hundred cavalry—but no commander in chief. Still, after all this wrangling no commander in chief."

"Because their eminences from Spain will not agree to our suggestion", Suriano fell in. "Yet there is no man who could be compared with Admiral Sebastiano Veniero, when it comes to seamanship, experience, and—other qualities very much needed for this command."

Cardinal Pacheco gave an eloquent shrug. "It is not a question of *our* agreeing to it, Your Excellency. King Philip . . ."

"King Philip has not lost Nicosia and Limasol and almost all the rest of Cyprus", Surenzi interjected hotly. "We have. And why? Because the powerful allied fleet sent to Cyprus dallied and dallied until it was too late to save Nicosia. And who was in command of it?"

"Admiral Marc Antonio Colonna", Cardinal Zúñiga answered quickly, avoiding the Pope's reproachful glance. "And he's no Spaniard."

"From all we have heard Admiral Colonna has never been much more than a figurehead." Surenzi paid no heed to the warning cough of his colleague. "And the real commander *was* a Spaniard—a vassal of Spain: Admiral Giovanni Andrea Doria. Let there be no mistake about it: as long as I am ambassador, the Serene Republic will never allow her ships to be commanded by that man again."

"Not only the Serene Republic has lost Nicosia", the Pope said. "But all Christendom and above all our Lord

396

himself. While we are speaking here—still secure at least for some time—churches on Cyprus are being destroyed or turned into mosques. We cannot afford to harbor suspicions and enmities between us even at the best of times. It is not Christian. But at a time like this . . ."

"Not Doria, Your Holiness", Surenzi persisted.

"I find myself in agreement with His Excellency, Holy Father", Cardinal Morone interposed. "Admiral Doria is the actual owner of the ships under his command. They are Spanish only because he puts them at His Catholic Majesty's disposal. And the man who owns ships is not the man to take risks with them."

Cardinal Granvella protested energetically. "Surely no one can say that King Philip is inclined to trust anybody too easily!"

On another occasion this might have provoked a smile. But smiles were rare at these conferences. Surenzi shrugged his shoulders. "It is not for me to say what motives the King of Spain has or had. I can only state that Admiral Doria, even when he is not commander in chief nominally, is utterly unacceptable to us."

"To a Venetian", Granvella said sharply, "apparently only a Venetian is acceptable. Only yesterday we heard that Admiral Colonna was not in the Serene Republic's favor either, although Spain, the most powerful nation of Europe, was willing to forego supreme command in his favor to please the Holy Father. . . ."

"His Eminence Cardinal Granvella is a master of diplomacy", Suriano said icily. "That indeed is why he is here, and there is no doubt whatever that his royal master trusts him implicitly, and for good reasons. His suggestion to give the supreme command to Colonna was made only because it was clear that Venice would have to veto it. And Venice has to do so because Spain would promptly send us Admiral

Doria again as subcommander and thus we would be confronted with exactly the same ill-starred combination whose complete failure to act has cost us Nicosia."

"I think it is wrong to regard Admiral Colonna as a mere figurehead", the Pope interjected. "And I vouch for his excellent qualities in every respect. Of course, this time there must be no vacillation."

"Your Holiness," Cardinal Granvella said, "if it is permissible for Cardinal Morone to point out that a shipowner like Doria may not be inclined to take too many risks ..."

"... any risks at all", Surenzi growled.

"Then I must be permitted to state that the supreme command should not be given to an officer backed by too few ships. The papal fleet, unfortunately, is not as strong as I am sure we all would like it to be."

"There you are", Surenzi crowed. "Who is against Colonna now?"

Suriano seconded his colleague: "It would be interesting to hear whom His Eminence Cardinal Granvella would suggest as suitable. So far he has mentioned only Doria ..."

"... and Don Juan de Austria", Cardinal Pacheco interjected. "I think there is a memorandum about that in one of our meetings—was it in July?"

Suriano smiled politely. "No doubt, Your Eminence. And if I remember rightly, we appreciated the honor the suggestion conveyed, but we also felt that His Highness was much too young, a mere twenty-three years of age...."

"Of course," Surenzi said acidly, "if our conferences go on long enough, he may grow too old."

"Don Juan has done extremely well in the war against the Moriscos", the Pope said quickly. "We all feel great admiration for His Majesty's young brother. But he has had little experience at sea—and he is very young."

"A neutral personality would probably be the best solution", Suriano suggested. "For instance the Duke of Savoy."

"Or the Duke of Anjou", Surenzi added.

The three Spanish cardinals looked at each other.

"France has shown very little interest in the league—to put it mildly", Granvella pointed out. "And it is known that nothing happens there without the consent of a very formidable lady...."

"No doubt Queen Catherine de' Medici would like the idea of a French commander very much", Cardinal Pacheco said dryly. "France would not provide a single ship, not a single coin, and not a single man—except the commander in chief. And if we won, it would be a French victory."

"Neither the Duke of Anjou nor Duke Emanuel Filibert of Savoy have any experience at sea", Granvella joined in.

"We could refer the two suggestions to Madrid", Cardinal Zúñiga said. "But I have very little doubt that His Majesty will not agree to a commander from France ... or from Savoy."

Stonily the Pope said: "The matter must be decided. An agreement must be reached."

There was a pause.

Everybody was dead tired, after five hours of incessant but almost entirely fruitless debate, first about the different types of artillery to be used, then about the price of Sicilian wheat that the Spaniards were to sell to the papal administration, and now about the nomination of the supreme commander.

"I am willing to make every concession," the Pope said, "although I still believe that Admiral Colonna would be the best solution. Every concession." He was looking at the Spanish cardinals, then at the Venetians. But all eyes remained downcast and no one spoke.

The dullness of fatigue ruled the room. Surenzi, the most fiery of them all, stifled a yawn.

The Pope rose. "We shall adjourn until tomorrow", he said sadly. "And I implore you all to consider that you are not only Spaniards and Venetians, but also and first and foremost Christians."

One after the other they knelt and kissed the fisher-ring. Granvella was the last. As he rose again, he said, with a somewhat rueful smile: "Your Holiness knows, I am sure, that we all want only the best. . . ."

"Certainly, certainly . . ."

"We are not trying to fight Your Holiness", Granvella went on. "We are all fighting together as Laocoön and his sons fought the serpents . . . and I fervently hope with a better result."

The old man in white nodded. "Laocoön", he said, "did not have our Lord to support him." He walked away.

"We're all worn out", Zúñiga said. "He isn't. What is he made of?"

"Iron", Granvella replied.

The old man in white entered a strange room, small and triangular in shape. No architect had designed it. Formerly, it had been a corner of a reception room, from which it was now separated by a strong wall. All hangings, all tapestry had been removed and there was no carpet. The floor was stone.

From the ceiling, denuded of its original wood carvings, a silver lamp was hanging whose dim light shone upon the simplest of altars, made of some dark wood and bare of all ornaments, except for a silver tabernacle and above it a life-size picture of the Crucified.

Before that altar the old man in white collapsed.

There seemed to be no bone left in the small heap of white clothing, except in the dried-out, almost mummified hands and in the head. And hands and head were bones only, covered with thin, parchmentlike skin, loose and wrinkled over the large forehead, taut over the cheeks and the large, aquiline nose. The eyes were closed and the long, white beard trailed in the dust.

The old man began to pray, and King David's words became his own.

" 'Happy is he whose fault is taken away, whose sin is covered. Happy the man to whom the Lord imputes no guilt, in whose spirit there is no guile. As long as I would not speak, my bones wasted away with my groaning all day. For day and night your hand was heavy upon me; my strength was dried up as by the heat of summer. . . .' "

How could a man remain free of guilt, when because of his very office he had to deal with men of the world all the time? Cajoling them, flattering them, compromising with them in this and that and the other. . . .

How happy he had been as an ordinary friar in his monastery. Then he really had a well-founded assurance of salvation. He began to lose it when he was made a bishop. Perhaps he had lost it completely as the Pope.

He pulled himself back into the words of Psalm 31 [32]. He ploughed his way through it, verse after verse.

Only when talking to God could he forget the terrible, the unbearable burden he was carrying and had been carrying for almost five years. Only then were there moments when he could be Friar Michele Ghislieri again instead of Pius V.

This little room was his cell, his refuge from the splendor prescribed for his office. The splendor was God's and therefore never adequate. It would simply not do to try to diminish it. But a friar needed poverty when he wanted to empty his heart to God.

After Psalm 31 came Psalm 37 (38), "'O Lord, in your anger punish me not, in your wrath chastise me not....'"

Not me. And not them, poor creatures, always wrangling, always haggling, so keen on not missing the advantage of their own position, the favor of their worldly masters, at best the advantage of their states and nations and thus blind to the one thing that mattered: the cause of God's only begotten Son. Blind to the danger of the Half-Moon, steadily growing and stealthily moving toward the Cross, the deadly sickle, red with the blood of Rhodes and Malta and Cyprus.

They could not see it because they went on staring at their own grandeur, their own riches, their own power.

No wonder then that their fleet was powerless to stem the tide, that their commanders had failed to save Nicosia and avoided the enemy as if they were cowards. They were not cowards. But they cared only for their own countries, for their own grandeur, and not one of them, perhaps not even Colonna, had had the true spirit of the crusades, the spirit of self-sacrifice.

Lord, Lord, Lord! The way they argued with each other about the supreme commander of a league in thy service! The very fact that one faction was for one man was enough to make the other speak against him. And when a "neutral" man was suggested they were all against him lest he snatch the glory away for his own country.

As if any Christian leader could be neutral when the cause of Christ was at stake. Yet neutral they were, many of them, most of them. There was no Godfrey left, no Raymond and no Richard, no one of the lion-hearted breed. In England the cold daughter of Henry the Eighth; in France the wiles and intrigues of another woman; in Germany as in the Netherlands and in England they thought to serve Jesus Christ by hating his sweet Mother. . . .

The Emperor in Vienna—a weak, vacillating man, content to buy peace from the Sultan.

Emissaries had gone to Poland, even to Russia, but there was little to hope for from those countries.

Here he was, an old man, nearing the end of his life and a priest in the service of the Prince of Peace, and he had to talk about cannons and ships and troops; he had to try to move armies, nay, to raise them out of barren ground to defend his cause.

Psalm 51 [50] followed. "'I will teach transgressors your ways, and sinners shall return to you. Free me from blood guilt, O God, my saving God; then my tongue shall revel in your justice. . . .'"

And Psalm 102 [101]: "'For my days vanish like smoke, and my bones burn like fire. Withered and dried up like grass is my heart; I forget to eat my bread. Because of my insistent sighing I am reduced to skin and bone.'"

Aye, Lord. But I am insistent. I will not let thee go. . . .

Psalm 130 [129]: "Out of the depths I cry to you O Lord, Lord hear my voice!"

And the last of the seven penitential psalms, Psalm 143 [142], the most fervent of entreaties, wrestling with God as Jacob wrestled with the angel: "Hasten to answer me Lord, for my spirit fails me . . . at dawn let me hear of your kindness, for in you I trust. Show me the way in which I should walk. . . ."

The emaciated body was racked with sobs.

From the wall Christ crucified looked down on his servant with compassion.

Dawn came, but it was the dawn of November and there was little kindness in it.

The old man rose from the stone floor, tired and shivering. He made the sign of the cross. As always in the morning, and many a time during the day, he felt burning pains in his stomach, shooting up all the way to his throat, and he winced a little. "Lord," he prayed, "increase my pains, but increase also my patience."

He smoothed down his habit as best he could. Walking around the altar he passed through a narrow door almost at the back of it into the adjacent room.

The room was a beautiful, octagonal chapel. At the left of the altar, on the Gospel side was a canopy of gold cloth and under it a gilded chair, covered with gold brocade.

Four prelates, dressed in purple, with white rochets and embroidered stoles, rose from their prie-dieus and bowed deeply.

For a few moments the Pope prayed, kneeling before the chair under the canopy. Then he sat down, weak and exhausted.

Here also a single picture was hanging over the altar. A member of the Pope's own Order, a Dominican friar, had painted it, 125 years ago. Eugene IV was Pope then and he was much troubled, because the archepiscopal seat of Florence had fallen vacant and he did not know whom to appoint to it. For five long months he searched for the right man, without result. Walking through the Vatican in deep thought he came across the Dominican friar, painting, with infinite diligence, the picture of a Madonna. He did not know what made him talk to the friar about his problem, but talk he did. And the friar, still going on painting, said tranquilly: "That is easy, Holy Father. We have good and erudite men enough who could carry that burden and our brother Antonino is not the last of them. He is right here too, at the moment, being on his way to Naples...." "It isn't you who have spoken," Pope Eugene replied, "but the Holy Spirit has spoken through you. I have been searching for water in the midst of the ocean." The next day he made Antonino di Noccolo Perrozi, Little Antonino as everybody called him, Archbishop of Florence. And little Antonino died a saint.

Perhaps Fra Angelico, the painting son of St. Dominic, was a saint as well. One could well believe it, looking at his Madonna. *Salus infirmorum* she was, the Health of the Sick, Health of the Infirm.

Dear, loving, glorious world of Christ. The gates of hell would not prevail against it, not as long as there was a single Christian to defend it and there always would be, come pagans, Arabs, or Turks, or whatever other danger might lurk in the centuries to come.

Pius V felt a wave of strength filling him. Once more he knelt for a short prayer. Then he gave a sign to the four prelates, and they removed the vestments, draped over the mensa of the altar, and began to vest him.

He said Mass as always, in complete serenity, reading and speaking slowly. God, invoked by his own sacred Words, came down upon the altar and became Flesh and Blood and his servant thrice declared himself unworthy to receive him under his roof, in the words of a Roman officer whose name was forgotten by all, but whose faith was remembered by many across the centuries and always would be, as an example to mankind. The faith of a soldier, a leader of men in battle . . .

And Pius V partook of the Flesh and Blood of Christ, hoping like everyone else that the prayers of the great saints would help to make him less unworthy.

A few minutes later one of the prelates removed the missal from the Epistle side to the Gospel side and the Pope began to read the final prayer of the Mass, the "last Gospel", taken from the first chapter of St. John: "'In the beginning was the Word, and the Word was with God; and the Word was God. He was in the beginning with God. All things were made through him and without him was made nothing that has been made. In him was life, and the life was the light of men. And the light shines in the darkness; and the darkness grasped it not. There was a man, one sent from God, whose name was John.' "

The Pope stopped.

All the four prelates looked up, not because he stopped, but because the last short sentence was spoken in an entirely different voice, an entirely strange voice, deep and vibrant like a heavy bell.

The old man was trembling, but his face shone.

He's ill, Prelate Ruggiero thought, terrified. He can't go on. He's going to faint. He looked at Prelate Corri and saw that he was thinking the same thing. He could not see Duodo because he was on the Pope's other side, but Vanini, behind him, was gaping.

"'There was a man, one sent from God,' " said the Pope, "'whose name was John. . . .' "

This time his voice was again different, much lower, and strangely uncertain, almost that of a child, repeating a teacher's words. The old man was looking up. Was he looking at the Madonna? Was he looking through the painting at something or somebody else?

Prelate Ruggiero was a picture of confusion. Never, in five years, had he heard the Pope repeat a sentence of the Mass.

Pius V took a deep breath. "'There was a man, one sent from God, whose name was John'", he said for the third time, and now he was speaking in his usual voice—or was he? Tall and erect, no longer trembling, he went on with the sacred words, to the end of the Mass.

When they helped him to unvest, Ruggiero saw that Prelate Vanini's face was flooded with tears.

The Pope did not see it. His eyes seemed to be looking at something far away, and he was smiling like a child.

The members of the conference filed into the room and took their places as usual. They rose as the Pope entered, and they stood with their hands folded, as he spoke the short introductory prayer. Then they sat down again.

"Your Eminences," the Pope said, "Your Excellencies. The Supreme Commander of the fleet of the Holy League will be Don Juan de Austria."

There was a moment of stupefaction.

Granvella was the first to recover. "Despite his youth?" he asked. "Despite his—relative—lack of experience?"

"Despite anything that could be said by anybody", Pius V said. "It is the will of God."

"*Deus lo vult*", ejaculated Surenzi, and both Suriano and the Spanish cardinals stared at him in utter surprise. But no one was more surprised than Surenzi himself. Madonna, he thought, what made me say that? He looked at Suriano, whose mouth was open. He grinned sheepishly. "We had to come to some conclusion, didn't we?" he murmured.

"I suppose it could have been worse", Suriano said reluctantly, and Surenzi, relieved, laughed outright.

"I agree", said Cardinal Zúñiga.

"So do I", Granvella chimed in.

"*Deus lo vult*", repeated Cardinal Pacheco, looking at the Pope.

Suriano gulped. "If Your Holiness is willing—I would stipulate that two subcommanders be chosen and that Don Giovanni de Austria—Don John—Don Juan is to take their advice into consideration. I suggest admirals Sebastiano Veniero and Marc Antonio Colonna."

"We agree with pleasure", the Pope said. "Cardinal Granvella will set up the decrees. The session is adjourned." He rose and spoke the final prayer. It consisted of one sentence only.

"'There was a man, one sent from God, whose name was John.'"

CHAPTER 35

THE MESSAGE THAT Doña Magdalena de Ulloa y Quixada had arrived in Madrid and taken quarters at the town house of Doña Isabel de Guzmán was delivered to Don Juan as he came back from the palace in the early afternoon. He left at once and arrived at her address within a quarter of an hour.

She rose when he entered, and as he flew into her arms she made the sign of the cross on his forehead, just as she used to do when he was a child.

He was shocked to see how much she had aged in so short a time. Only fifteen months had passed since those black days at Caniles, when he had seen her last, but the difference was sad to see. Only part of it was due to the way she was dressed—she was still in black and her dress was of the simplest cut and made of ordinary cloth, the dress of a widow, fairly similar to that of a nun. Her hair— what was visible of it under the stiff white widow's hood— was gray; deep furrows went down from nose to mouth; and her hands, her lovely, cool hands, had aged, too.

"Don't look at me, my dear", she said with a rueful smile. "I'm an old woman now."

"Don't say that, Tía", he protested. "Just as you are, without a single jewel on you, you are more wonderful than all the ladies at court, the Queen included."

"The Queen . . ." She took no notice of his flattery. "She is not very beautiful, is she, our new Queen? Not when one thinks of poor Queen Isabella, God rest her. However, it's only right that the King should marry again, I suppose, and they tell me that she is very good and devout. He's still a young man, as men go—forty-four, isn't he? Just about twenty years older than you are. Ah well, it's as well poor Don Carlos is no longer alive to see his father married to another fiancée of his. First Isabelle of France, then Anne of Austria. But it speaks well for the King, in a way, doesn't it, that he chose the fiancées of his son after his own taste? I am sure he meant well in all things, and I am particularly glad to see how well he keeps his word to you!"

"To me?"

"Now you sit down and make yourself comfortable. Will you have some wine? Are you hungry? No? I am quite at home here. You know, Isabel de Guzmán is one of my closest friends, and anyway, you know she isn't here; she's in Sevilla at the moment, for the wedding of her younger daughter, such a good match too, Count Tendilla—you know him of course; he's the son of the Marquis of Mondéjar— but let's not talk about that now. Really no wine and nothing to eat?"

"I've only just come from a very sumptuous banquet at the palace, Tía. In honor of the papal legate."

"Cardinal Alessandrino—oh, yes, I know all about that. A very young man, isn't he?"

"Yes, but very intelligent and an excellent diplomat, they say. I only wish he wouldn't insist on calling me 'Highness' all the time. I'm still only what I used to be."

"Indeed you're not", Doña Magdalena exclaimed. "You're now also the victor in the war against the Moriscos and the supreme commander of the Holy League. The title Highness is nothing in comparison to that."

"Dear Tía. There is no one like you for always saying the right thing."

"The King once promised you the command of the fleet", she said firmly. "But even he could not foresee that it would not be the Spanish fleet only but the papal and the Venetian fleet as well. And at your age! You have no idea how proud we all are of you, in Villagarcía!"

Juan smiled. "How is the Abbess?" he asked. Both he and Doña Magdalena had come to call his daughter that in their correspondence, ever since Doña Magdalena wrote to him that after she had seen a baptism in the village, she toddled around "baptizing" everything within her reach, her dolls and other toys as well as cupboards, tables, and chairs.

"No further sign of a vocation yet", Doña Magdalena said gravely. "Except that she has baptized a cat. With ink, unfortunately."

He threw back his head, laughing. "Oh, Tía, if you only knew how much good it does me to be with you. For weeks and months I've had solemn conferences, discussions, war councils. The King has worked out everything for me in detail, as he always does, down to the smallest items. And all those compliments and the adulation, all this praise in advance. You—you are like a drink of fresh, cold water after a day's labor in a sticky atmosphere."

"I am glad you do not overrate compliments", she said, frowning a little. "I was just a little worried about . . . some things. Not everyone who praises you is your friend."

"Oh, I know that", he said casually. "I have made a few enemies—it was inevitable, I suppose. You mentioned one of them a short while ago . . ."

"The Marquis of Mondéjar, you mean?"

"Yes. No one likes to be replaced in office, in high office, for not being able to cope with the situation at hand. And what goes for Mondéjar, also goes for de los Vélez. I know they both launched complaints and tried to prove that their own measures would have been far more effective. But it's a little difficult for them, now that the war is over and won."

"What about State Secretary Pérez?" Doña Magdalena asked.

"Antonio Pérez?" Juan was surprised. "I have no reason to think that he is against me in any way. He is Don Ruy Gómez' man, of course, but the Ébolis both have been most kind to me since my return, although—" He broke off.

"I think he is a very, very ambitious man", she said slowly. "In fact, I know he is. And ambitious men are always afraid of the ambition of others—especially when the others are favored by birth as well as by success."

"Favored by birth . . .", Juan repeated bitterly.

"Juan! Remember, if you please, who his father was and whose son you are! You'll make me quite angry in a minute, me, an old woman, with the supreme commander of the Holy League. This will never do."

"Angel!" He kissed her hand. "You must never be angry with me; I couldn't bear it. Fancy your coming to me in Madrid, forestalling my visit to you. I have never been so honored. . . ."

"All right, all right. But don't forget what I said about Señor Pérez. I don't like him and I don't trust him. Don Luiz didn't either."

"Don Luiz ..." His eyes were moist. "How I wish he knew how I avenged him. And that he could give me his blessing on this new venture...."

"You have it", she said simply. "There isn't the slightest doubt about that in my mind."

"The crucifix," Juan said, "the one he saved from the Moors and gave to me when I was a boy—it's going with me. And I will have it fixed to the foremast of my ship, when I go into battle."

"Thank you", she said proudly. "You have become exactly what he hoped you would be. And what a wonderfully wise man the Pope must be! He was the one who insisted on you, I heard."

"He wrote me a personal letter", Juan told her.

She looked at him expectantly, but it was a little while before he went on.

"I scarcely dare repeat it, Tía, but he did not tell me that he wished me victory or good fortune or that he would pray for me—he said he *promised* me victory in the Name of God...."

She paled and began to tremble.

"Tía ... you are not well. Shall I ..."

She shook her head. "It is nothing—physical. You remember Friar Calahorra of Del Abrojo, don't you?"

"Of course I do. I should have asked you before about him. Is he ..."

"He has left us for a while to go to Medina el Campo, where they built a very large camp for the Moriscos expelled from Granada. He said in such cases there are always many hardships and it was his duty to try to help these unfortunate people."

"How like him."

"Oh, he has organized a great many things, first there, then in two other camps. He wrote to me several times and

412

said he was a great nuisance to the civil authorities, always demanding this or that for his Moriscos. 'But I always get it in the end', he said. A few weeks ago he returned to Del Abrojo and I saw him before I left for Madrid. He has charged me to tell you in the Name of God that your victory is certain."

Juan stared at her. "The same words as the Holy Father's . . ."

"Exactly."

After a while he said: "How can I fail?" His tone and expression were those of a small boy—a humble wondering that touched her deeply.

And yet there was a shadow.

"When are you leaving, my dear?"

"That's for the King to say, Tía, but it may be any day now. I may find a written order on my desk when I return to my house. The route was fixed some time ago. First to Guadalajara, then to Calatayud, Zaragoza, and from there to Barcelona. I shall stop for a day or two in Montserrat. Almost exactly the same route I took as a boy, when I wanted to join the fleet on the way to Malta. . . ."

"But this time you will not only join it, but command it."

He nodded absentmindedly. "How strange life is, Tía. The same way as then. And it's only six years ago. But what years, Tía, what years! So much has been compressed into them, a whole life. Sometimes I think God does not want me to live long. . . ."

"Juan!"

"And so he gives to every year of my life the content of seven ordinary years. There are lives like that, Tía. Surging up to success very early—and ending early, too. The pagans used to say: 'Whom the gods love, they call to themselves early.' "

"You are not a pagan."

"No. But pagans, too, were created by the one God, whatever foolish things they believed. Take Alexander, for instance . . ."

"Alexander?"

"Not Alexander Farnese, Tía. Alexander the Great. I always liked him. There is so much one can learn from him, too. The things he had achieved at my age! He was thirty-two when he died. Perhaps the span of life is of no importance, really. I— I cannot see myself as an old man, not even as a middle-aged man, ever."

"Few men can, at twenty-four, I should say", she said, smiling. But her heart was heavy. "Don Luiz, too, had a very full life. . . ."

"And a happy one," Juan said, "thanks to you, first and foremost. And you could never have loved another man, just as I could never—" He broke off and bit his lip.

Doña Magdalena rose. "You still love her, Juan?"

He said nothing. There was no need.

"And she still loves you", she said simply.

"She . . . how do you know?"

"She told me."

"When?"

"This morning."

"She is . . . here? In Madrid?"

"I asked her to come and she came."

"Where . . ."

"Come with me." She pretended not to see that he was shaking from head to foot. They left the room, crossed a broad corridor, and entered Doña Isabel de Guzmán's private chapel.

A young woman in black was kneeling before the beautiful small altar. She turned around.

"María . . .", Juan whispered.

Quietly, Doña Magdalena slipped out and closed the door behind her.

The two lovers stood motionless, spellbound, tongue-tied.

María de Mendoza's eyes filled with tears, but she smiled.

"María", he whispered again. "My love, my great love, will you wait for me? I must go and fight. Will you wait for me?"

"I will", she said almost inaudibly.

His eyes were shining. "Until this moment I believed, and believed firmly, that I would conquer. Now I know it. And when I return, I shall ask as my sole reward the King's permission to marry you. He will not be able to refuse."

"I will pray for you", she said, "as I did before I set eyes on you. But now all my love will be in my prayers."

"It is right and just that we should meet here, María, and that we should speak to each other in the presence of God and before his holy altar."

She made an effort to steady herself. "I will start praying— now", she said.

It was her farewell, and the end of the vision, the earthly vision he was allowed to have. He knew he was not allowed to approach her, to kiss her hand, not here. He bowed to her as one bowed to the Queen, and the last thing he saw of her was the movement with which she turned back to the altar.

He crossed himself and stumbled out of the chapel.

Steps approached, the steps of a woman and a man. The man must be a soldier; he was wearing spurs, clanking spurs.

"Here is Juan Galarza", Doña Magdalena said in an even voice. "He insists on coming with you, if you will have him. You'd better agree, or he'll fret so much that he'll be a nuisance to all Villagarcía."

The stocky old warrior, with the long scar on his cheek, gave him an anxious look. "I owe the heathens something ... for Don Luiz", he said. "And I haven't gone stiff yet, Your Excellency—or not much."

"Come with me, then", Juan said. He turned to Doña Magdalena. "I wish I also could pay my debts, but I'm afraid there is little hope for that. No son owes more to his mother than I owe to you."

As he kissed her she drew once more the sign of the cross on his forehead. And as he left, Galarza followed him, his shadow as he had been Don Luiz Quixada's shadow in so many campaigns of the past.

Doña Magdalena returned to the chapel, entered it, went up to the altar, and knelt down at María de Mendoza's side.

After a while María leaned her head on the older woman's shoulder. "When he comes back I shall be a Carmelite novice", she whispered. "Are you sure we did right?"

"Quite sure, my dear child. He needs all his strength now and only you could give it to him."

María gave a sobbing sigh. "It opened the wound again ..."

With a gesture of infinite tenderness Doña Magdalena pointed to the statue of another María, whose heart was pierced by a sword.


CHAPTER 36


THERE WAS SOMETHING strangely unreal about this journey into war.

In order to give battle to the most dangerous enemy not only of Spain, but of Europe and all Christendom, a young man of twenty-four set out with a suite of fifteen persons.

There was no official departure. Not even an escort had been provided. Juan himself insisted on that. At the final audience the King had been most gracious and kind. Even so, Juan did not want to create a stir that could be used by hostile critics.

The generalissimo of the combined forces of the Holy League on land and sea tried to steal out of Madrid.

He failed. A few wagging tongues sufficed to create a rumor that spread like wildfire through the city, and when the tiny cavalcade arrived at the Guadalajara Gate thousands of people were waiting, yelling, and shouting.

In Guadalajara, where Juan spent the night at the palace of the Duke of Infantado, his suite increased to 157 people, most of them young nobles with their retinues, volunteers for the fight against the infidels. Among them was Don Pedro Zapata, the young hero of Galera who declared that he wanted to find out which was harder: to guard the gate of a Moorish fortress or to board a Turkish galley.

"I'll take you with me on my flagship," Juan told him, "but I won't let you have a banner this time. You did extremely well when you carried it, fighting the Moors with one hand only. Now I want to know what you can do with two hands."

They left after dinner and rode all night over the naked plains of Old Castile, rested at dawn at Arcos, and proceeded to Calatayud, where couriers met them with a number of important messages, including a papal breve, in which the fierce old man in Rome called Juan his dear son and gave him his apostolic benediction, but exhorted him to hurry. Letters also came from Admiral Colonna; Cardinal Granvella, the acting Viceroy of Naples; Count Landriano,

Deputy Viceroy of Sicily; Don Juan de Zúñiga, Ambassador of Spain at the Vatican; and Don Antonio de Mendoza, Ambassador of Spain in Genoa.

At the frontier of Castile another fifty-odd nobles with their suites joined the cavalcade, and at Calatayud their number was tripled by young Aragonese nobles.

"If this goes on we'll arrive in Barcelona with an army of our own", Juan remarked to de Soto, who was to be his private secretary on this campaign. Poor Quiroga had died of a fever just before the end of the Morisco war.

"We won't have enough ships; they'll have to build their own", de Soto replied happily.

But they stopped jesting when whole swarms of fighting-mad young nobles joined them in Zaragoza.

"I had a sort of rehearsal of all this when I tried to reach the fleet in Barcelona six years ago", Juan said, overwhelmed. "But for every man who wanted to come with me then, there now seem to be three or four."

"Perhaps Your Excellency forgets that you won a little affair called the Morisco war between then and now", de Soto said. "And this is not a war—it's a crusade."

They rode up to Montserrat. In the huge church Juan knelt where he had six years ago, and Fray Juan de Calahorra's chubby, cherubic face smiled into his prayers: "Time is for mortals only. God lives out of time." And then, gravely: "I promise you victory in the Name of God."

When they descended and approached Barcelona, all the bells of the city began to ring.

"They are waking up the Occident", Juan heard himself say.

De Soto gave him a strange, oblique look, but said nothing.

The great city engulfed them; there was a solemn reception, headed by the Viceroy of Catalonia, now no longer the old Duke of Francavilla, but Don Hérnando de Toledo, and ... Don Luiz Requeséns.

Juan embraced his old comrade-at-arms and vice admiral. "This time I shall need you more than ever."

"Thinking of Don Luiz Quixada, eh?" Requeséns was moved and hated showing it. "Great man, fine man; fearful shame he's no longer with us. Wouldn't have been so much use to you this time, though; bad sailor, hated the sea, said so himself. Look what I've got here."

It was a letter addressed to Requeséns and Juan read it with deep emotion. The writer was Don García de Toledo, who had been captain general of the sea for so long, and it came from Poggio in Tuscany, where the veteran was taking the baths. Don García de Toledo ... he had been with Emperor Charles V at the glorious victory of Tunis and at the disaster of Algiers. He had been at Prevesa. He had relieved the gallant Grand Master of the Knights of St. John, Jean de la Valette, six years ago and driven the Turks from Malta.

"By the life of St. Peter," Don García wrote, "I swear that if I had but a little better health I would myself ship as a soldier or a sailor under Don Juan as gladly as I would under the King himself."

Juan wrote to him the same day, asking for his counsel.

Barcelona was throbbing with life. Every day new streams of soldiers, new loads of equipment and foodstuffs arrived. The huge arsenal was working day and night.

The very day of his arrival Juan sent orders to two leaders of the fleet, to proceed immediately to Barcelona: Admiral Don Álvaro Bazán, Marquis of Santa Cruz from Cartagena, and Admiral Sancho de Leiva from Mallorca.

De Leiva was the first to appear, and his squadron arrived at night, its masts and yards illuminated with hundreds of tiny lanterns.

With him came Juan's flagship. It was the same on which he had sailed on his Mediterranean exploit, but on Juan's orders the heavy statue of Hercules had been taken off and replaced by more guns. Instead of the one gilt lantern at the stern it now carried three, marking it as the flagship of the allied forces.

Don Lope de Figueroa and Don Miguel de Moncada arrived, each with a regiment of infantry.

New galleys were launched every day and for each a Solemn High Mass was said. Every soldier and sailor went to confession and received Holy Communion before going on board his vessel.

On the day after the arrival of the Marquis of Santa Cruz—received with a salvo of the harbor guns and musket salvos from all the ships in port—Juan gave a reception on his flagship.

It was more than a reception—it was a feast and an outburst of enthusiasm; it was a shout of pure joy and innocent pride.

A young man, with the laurels of victory still fresh around his temples, was setting out on the most dangerous venture of the century.

There was no more formidable enemy in the world than the Turk.

All the holy places, where Christianity was born and first proclaimed, were in Turkish hands, and now these hands stretched out across the summer blue Mediterranean, around which Christianity had spent its early youth and grown and conquered. They had torn down the Cross in the East, and Emperor Justinian's pride, the great Church of St. Sophia, had become a mosque. Now they were out to conquer the West as well, stage by stage, cunningly using the discord between the Christian powers.

No greater danger had threatened the West since the beginning of the eighth century, when Tarek ferried his wild Arabs across the straits and overran Spain. For a long time the Christian world fought back, and for a while even reconquered the holy places. But ever since the Turks had taken over instead of Arabs and Saracens, Islam displayed a fresh spirit of conquest. Islam! The very word meant "surrender". The very name of the faith was a program. Surrender to the Sultan's janizaries first, so that you may surrender to Allah and his prophet Muhammad afterward. And apart from the janizaries, most feared warriors of all, the Sultan commanded forces "countless as the grains of sand on the beaches, as the drops of water in the sea", not only regular soldiers, but the armed men of hundreds of nations and tribes, ivory white, yellow, brown, and coal black; men from the icy heights of the Caucasus and from the sun-baked sands of the deserts of Arabia, Egypt, and the long, arid coast of North Africa; men from the Black Sea and the Caspian; from the rugged mountains of the Kurds and the forests of the Lebanon; from the land of the Bulgars; and from the mountain fortresses at the Persian frontier, Mongolian hordes, descendants of the terrible Djengiz Khan, Uzbeks, Turkmenes, Kirgisians and Circassians, Nubians and Moors.

The Sultan beckoned and all over his gigantic empire imams and mullahs, fakirs and marabuts arose to proclaim that paradise was certain for anyone who fell in a jihad, in a holy war against the Christian infidels; among them first and foremost the Grand Mufti, who pronounced the war just and holy, although the Porte had a peace treaty with Venice. For no true believer need keep a promise or oath to an infidel.

So, like a man fighting with his fists, the Sultan drew back his right, his land armies, and struck the first blow with his left, across the sea, and under that blow the island of Cyprus crumbled and only one town, Famagusta, still offered desperate resistance.

Against this might, the like of which Europe had never seen since the days of the ancient Roman Empire, Don Juan de Austria went to war, the champion of the Christian cause, chosen by the Holy Father himself despite his youth and inexperience, chosen by the King of Spain and the great seignories of Venice and of Genoa despite the bar sinister on his escutcheon. And so when he went on board his flagship; he transformed his joy and pride into a feast and let all the great nobles and leaders and all the admirals and generals and captains join his company.

Flags were flying on masts and yards, a band was playing, and orderlies in liveries and caps of red damask served a sumptuous meal. The big ship was a floating garden: the girls and women of Barcelona had looted their gardens to provide that contribution.

The highlight of the evening was a dance of the sailors on all the three masts of the ship. In the exact rhythm of the music they moved along the yards, up and down mast-heads, flying through the air on rope ends, right over the heads of the enthusiastic guests.

Only old Requeséns grumbled: "Hope they'll fight as well as they dance."

Juan smiled. He thought of how he had left Madrid, with fewer followers than most nobles would take with them on a hunting trip; how that absurdly small suite had grown, because the sons of the proudest families of the proudest of all countries came streaming from all sides to serve under him. And all this was only the beginning. In half a dozen ports of Italy more men and more ships were massing.

I am building up my new body, he thought with a fierce joy.

The musicians played faster and faster; the flying dancers were shooting through space like fireflies.

They were all part of him, expressions of what he was feeling, waves and sparks of his own joy.

De Soto had turned up from nowhere; he was saying something, but his words were inaudible in the din of music and dance and the shouting of the guests.

A letter, he was holding out a letter to him—must it be, at this hour? But Juan caught sight of the seal, and at once he rose, took it, made his excuses to the guests at his table, and went to his cabin.

A letter with the King's own seal. He broke it open. It was in the King's own hand, too, and it was short.

In a few dry and bitter sentences the King reproached him for allowing an increasing number of personages to address him as Highness, and to accord him honors due only to an Infant of Spain. He was forbidden forthwith to accept such honors not in accordance with his rank. State Secretary Pérez would provide him with a copy of the instructions given to the authorities in Italy in connection with his reception in that country and the formalities involved; he, Don Juan, was commanded strictly to adhere to those instructions in every way.

The letter had been written immediately after his departure, no more than a day after the leave-taking in which the King had been at his most gracious and friendly.

Outside the musicians were playing fortissimo. The roof of the cabin shook under the feet of the dancers.

The smile of the King, it was said, was like the stab of a dagger.

Even the Grand Turk would not have written such a letter to the man he had sent out to fight and conquer.

Juan buried his face in his hands. But from afar a cherubic face was smiling through the darkness. "The blind beggar bewailing his fate." He found the strength to smile back at it and was instantly rewarded. The Grand Turk would not have sent such a letter. He would not dare. For neither he nor his general were Christians. The Muslim general might rebel against him. The Christian had to remain loyal in the face of royal injustice.

It was easy to think it. It was less easy to live up to it. Yet he knew he would have to. If he was to conquer in the cause of the One Crowned with Thorns, he could not afford to flinch at the first prick of a thorn. If he was to be the Lord's charger, he must respond to the Lord's spur.

Even so, it took a great effort, that night, to pray as usual for his brother, Philip, King of Spain.

The reception in Genoa was the most splendid Juan had ever received. The doge and the entire seigniory were assembled to conduct him to the palace, where the great Andrea Doria had so often entertained his master and friend Emperor Charles V. If the instructions of State Secretary Pérez had arrived, no one took much notice of them.

Juan protested half a dozen times against being called "Your Highness"—entirely in vain. Italians, much less formal and far more given to compliments and flatteries than Spaniards, simply did not accept what they regarded as a kind of exaggerated modesty. Besides, Don Juan was the brother of the King of Spain, so how could he be a mere Excellency?

Admiral Giovanni Andrea Doria smiled at Juan's protest. He was a tall, lean man with a strangely pointed head, deep-set eyes, and a snub nose. His voice was rough and loud, the voice of a man accustomed to being obeyed instantly and without questioning. "You will be called whatever you wish, Your Highness", he said, and Juan wondered whether he was joking or whether there was not a hidden meaning in the word "wish". The admiral was a difficult man, and few people could boast that they knew what he was thinking. Ruy Gómez' dossier about him was a document of over fifty pages.

At the palace a handsome young man of herculean build came up to Juan, laughing all over his face. "Welcome, Uncle", he said.

"Alexander!" Juan hugged his old friend. "What are you doing here?"

"Waiting for you, of course", Alexander Farnese replied. "And I'm coming with you, if you'll have me."

"If I'll have you? I need you!" Juan shouted.

"Good. Excellent. I have a small retinue with me here, and there are twenty of us who feel they cannot afford to let you sink the Turkish fleet without them."

"They're all very welcome."

"And here's the Prince of Urbino—he wants to come, too. I forget how many men he's taking with him."

"Only sixty", the young prince said modestly, bowing to the commander in chief. "But may I be permitted to present some of my relatives and friends who also want to join: my cousin Paolo Contarini . . . Ettore della Rovere . . . Lorenzo Alfieri . . ."

The introductions went on for hours. Eager, young faces, slim, well-trained bodies, the flower of Genoese, Florentine, Ferrarese youth, names that had made history through the centuries, swordsmen and riders of the highest repute.

Alexander never budged from Juan's side. "I wish I could come with you on the flagship", he said. "But Doria offered me shelter on one of his galleys—anticipating your permission—and he's a touchy devil."

"Wherever you'll be, I promise you a fair share in the fighting", Juan told him.

"Good. Remember how sorry you were when you couldn't go to save Malta? And that Hungarian place, I forgot the name now. . . ."

"Sziget", Juan said at once. "Count Zrinyi defended it and made his name immortal on earth as well as in heaven. Please God, we shall avenge his death."

"I told you then, there would be enough work left for us, didn't I? I'm a good prophet, it seems. If Queen Catherine de' Medici hears of it, she'll ask me to join her staff of seers and necromancers."

"I'm afraid you were right in your opinion about her too", Juan said grimly. "I'm told it was her influence that prevented Portugal from joining the Holy League."

"Of course. Horrible old lady. If you sprinkle her with holy water, she'll get blisters, I'm sure. Bound to hate the Holy League, naturally. That league now—it's well-nigh miraculous, you know. Imagine Genoese and Venetians fighting side by side—to say nothing of Spaniards and Venetians. I don't know how the Holy Father's done it. Can't help wondering how they'll get on, as allies, I mean."

"I had a certain amount of experience with that kind of thing in the Morisco war", Juan said quietly. "It will be my business to see that they get on together."

"You know, I suppose, what the name of Doria means to the Venetians. . . ."

"Yes, yes, but don't speak so loud, nephew. I've given a good deal of thought to the matter and I have my plans."

"Whatever they are, I venture to prophesy that . . ."

"No more prophecies, please." Unblinking blue eyes belied Juan's smile. "This is not an ordinary alliance. It is a crusade. It is God's way to force Christians to unity. And if anyone tries to upset it, he'll find himself hanging from the yardarm of my flagship."

When Juan had set out from Barcelona, his force consisted of forty-seven galleys. In Genoa the number swelled to eighty-four.

In Spezia strong contingents of German and Italian troops were taken on board, and still more at Port Ercole and Civita Vecchia.

On August 9 he landed in Naples. On August 14 he went in state to the conventual church of Santa Clara, where the Franciscan friars met him, chanting the Te Deum.

Flanked by the princes of Parma and Urbino he went up to the rails of the high altar. He was in full armor.

Cardinal Granvella celebrated Pontifical High Mass. At the end the commander in chief walked up to the stairs of the altar and knelt down. The cardinal, magnificent in his scarlet robes, gave him the threefold baton of the generalissimo, its handle ablaze with precious stones, and the banner of the Holy League; it was of blue damask and showed under the large image of Christ the Redeemer the escutcheon of the Pope—three red bars on a silver field—the lion shield of the Republic of St. Mark, and the shield of many quarterings of the Chief of the House of Austria. Still lower, the design ended in Don Juan de Austria's own arms.

"Take, fortunate prince," Granvella's voice rang out, "these emblems of the Word Made Flesh, these symbols of the true Faith, and may they give you a glorious victory over our impious enemy. And by your hand may his pride be laid low."

"Amen", said Don Juan, and, "Amen", thundered a thousand voices, each of which had uttered orders in battle on land or sea.

At one o'clock in the afternoon, a salvo thundered forth from the guns of the entire fleet and of the fortress, and the sacred banner majestically soared up the mast of the flagship.

A few days later the fleet left for Messina.


## CHAPTER 37


"ALL PRESENT, YOUR EXCELLENCY", Secretary de Soto reported.

Juan nodded absentmindedly. From the window of his cabin he could see all the papal and a few Venetian galleys. Colonna had his ships in excellent order, but the Venetians were badly undermanned, and it had taken days of persuasion before old Veniero agreed to take a few Spanish troops on board, to make up for that. The man could give a mule lessons in obstinacy, but at least he was honest in his likes and dislikes, which was more than could be said about Doria, and some others.

De Soto was nervous. "Shall I call the nuncio, Your Excellency?"

Monsignor Odescalchi, Bishop of Penna, had been sent to Messina by the Pope, to bestow on the entire fleet the Apostolic Blessing and to give its commander a capsula containing a splinter of the True Cross.

Juan promptly asked him to preside at the decisive war council—the last of many—and this was the appointed hour. Seventy leaders were assembled under a large awning on deck. Only the flagship's officers were on board. All sailors and soldiers had been put ashore for the duration of the council, not only to assure secrecy but also because there was not enough space.

"Let them wait a few minutes", Juan said. "I'll call you."

De Soto withdrew.

Three more boats were approaching that large Venetian galley—which was it?—the *Santa Maura*. If only Sforza would follow his instructions not to send a single Genoese on board a Venetian ship. Dogs and cats, and worse. Only three days ago fourteen men had to be hanged for murdering perfectly good Christians, instead of waiting until they could kill Turks.

How much credence could be given to the captain of that Calabrian bark who reported that there was a strong Turkish fleet near Corfu? Veniero believed him, Doria didn't, Colonna could not make up his mind. The Turks were still besieging Famagusta. Could they have a fleet there and another at Corfu? If so, this was the moment for attack. But perhaps Famagusta had fallen. Intelligence reports were difficult to come by in a naval war.

He could hear the subdued sound of the conversation on deck. Seventy leaders, seventy trained brains. He knew them all by now, and what was more he knew the thoughts of most of them, thanks to the most valuable piece of advice he had ever been given in this campaign. It had come from Brussels, and the sender was his old teacher, the Duke of Alba. Juan knew it by heart. "Before it comes to a debate in the war council," Alba wrote, "it will be advisable to discuss the matter in question with every single member secretly and to find out his real opinion. This is bound to lead to great advantages. The person thus consulted will feel extremely flattered and be grateful for Your Excellency's confidence. He is likely to give his opinion quite freely. At a general discussion military men will often seek to outdo each other for ambition's sake; but as they had the honor to give Your Excellency their opinion beforehand, they will then not commit such a mistake; also they will not use that well-known trick of contradicting others just to show that they have a strong opinion of their own; and everyone at the council will have made up his mind. When Your Excellency has heard each one, you will have time to consider his reasons for and against the matter in question. It is essential, however, that Your Excellency should not utter your own opinions in these secret preliminary talks— except toward those few, whose council His Majesty regards as important, or those you yourself may regard as worthy. Your Excellency should not tolerate any quarrel during the debate. A debate there should be, but no personalities, for this would be very bad for your own authority. Your Excellency will also find it useful to let a few simple colonels or ship's captains participate in the council of admirals. This will give much satisfaction to the body of officers as a whole."

Shrewd old Alba. Thanks to him one knew what to expect from those seventy men, each of whom had reason to regard himself as in the commander in chief's special confidence.

And now it was time to start. He called for de Soto, who had been fretting outside—he was the type of man who could never temporize—and together they went to fetch the nuncio in the cabin Juan had put at his disposal.

Monsignor Odescalchi was an energetic-looking man with grizzled hair, thick, black eyebrows, and the profile of a hawk. He looked much more like a military or naval man than many an officer. "Your Excellency has kept them waiting a bit", he said, smiling cheerfully. "I hope it hasn't dampened their enthusiasm for action."

"If it has," Juan said pleasantly, "*Your* Excellency's address will surely restore it. Shall we go?"

The buzz of general discussion ceased as the nuncio and the commander in chief appeared, and everybody shuffled to his feet.

Monsignor Odescalchi spoke a short prayer and then gave a ten-minute address, asking all those present, in the name of His Holiness, to remember that this was an issue of far greater importance than any that might affect this country or that; that the service of Christ came before all others; and that it was entrusted to the wisdom of their council. He ended by exhorting them to seek for and challenge the Turkish fleet, and in the name of the Holy Father promised them victory.

Seventy-six-year-old Count Priego, Don Juan's majordomo and master of ceremonies, jumped up. "Your Excellencies and Commanders: I have had the honor of being received in audience by His Holiness very recently. I was happy to see that the highest office in the world is now in the hands of a saint. If the Holy Father promises us victory, it would be rank impiety, it would be lunacy, not to do what he says."

There were a few cries of acclamation. The bulk of the assembly remained silent. Slowly old Priego sat down.

"The first thing to be considered from the point of view of military and naval warfare is our strength", Juan said, without rising. "Admiral de Santa Cruz will give us the figures for the Spanish fleet."

"The fleet of His Majesty the King of Spain", Santa Cruz said ponderously, "as present in this port of Messina consists of ninety galleys, twenty-four large ships, and fifty frigates and brigantines. Amongst the galleys there are three of Malta, three of the Duke of Savoy, and three of the Republic of Genoa."

"Thank you. Admiral Colonna?"

Marc Antonio Colonna, Duke of Pagliano, was a handsome man of no more than thirty-five. "The forces of His

Holiness, as present, consist of twelve galleys and six frigates", he said curtly. "And all ships are fully manned."

This, of course, was a thinly veiled attack against the Venetians.

Juan gave the crusty old Venetian admiral a dazzling smile and an almost imperceptible wink. "Now the Nestor of naval leaders, Admiral Sebastiano Veniero of the Most Serene Republic of Venice."

"One hundred and six galleys," Veniero growled, "six galleasses—there's nothing afloat in the Mediterranean that could stand up to them—two heavy ships, and twenty frigates."

"Added together", Juan said, "there are two hundred and eight galleys, thirty-two larger vessels, and seventy-six frigates and brigantines . . . all in all three hundred and sixteen sail." He paused to let the tremendous figure sink into the minds of the assembly. "The number of mariners and oarsmen is upward of fifty thousand," he went on, "and according to the lists given to me by the commanders of the land forces we have a little over twenty-nine thousand troops on board, of which eight thousand are Spaniards, ten thousand Italian, six thousand Germans, two thousand papal soldiers—including twenty-five Swiss of the Holy Father's bodyguard—and about three thousand noble volunteers."

Doria rose. "Numbers", he said in his rough, loud voice, "are pretty impressive things. But has anybody taken the trouble to count the numbers in the enemy's camp? My men got hold of a small ship only about two hours ago, and what its captain told them made me change my mind about the report of the Calabrian bark we received a little earlier. There are definitely two Turkish fleets at least and most likely three. One, the fleet of Mustapha Pasha, besieging Famagusta. Two, the fleet of Ali Pasha, the Sultan's high admiral. Three, the forces of Uluch Ali, Viceroy of Algiers.

The Turks are not only sailors of the highest quality; they are also past masters at strategy at sea. If we try to chase after those Turkish forces, alleged to have been seen near Corfu, they will avoid a head-on encounter and withdraw, in the hope that we will follow them. And within a few days we shall find ourselves in the middle of all three Turkish fleets."

"In the circumstances, what is your advice, Admiral?" Juan asked very gently.

"Not to play into the hands of the Turk", Doria replied instantly. "Uluch Ali is out and about. There could be no better opportunity for us to go and conquer those ports that are now denuded of naval defense: Algiers and Tunis. It will be a spectacular victory," he concluded, "yet it may not cost us much."

"And we all know that 'cost' and 'expense' are words written in very large letters in Admiral Doria's ledgers", old Veniero jeered. "By the Madonna, have I been waiting with all my ships and men for weeks and months on end, to hear that all the great fleet of the league will set out to do is to capture a few towns on the coast of North Africa?"

"Admiral Veniero is a very experienced seaman", Doria said affably. "But he has had little opportunity to fight against the Turk—the Most Serene Republic having been living in peace and harmony with the Porte for so long."

"I prefer that", Veniero replied hotly, "to being at war with them but carefully avoiding an encounter."

"Despite Admiral Veniero's age," Doria said, "I claim to be the man with the widest experience of naval warfare in this assembly. If I were in command of three ships I would not hesitate for a moment to attack an enemy of equal or even slightly greater strength. But here we are confronted by a very different situation. The forces of Christendom have assembled. There are few or no reserves left. The treasuries have been drained. This means that we cannot possibly afford to risk everything on one throw. As long as we are afloat, the Turk will think twice before attacking us. But if we are defeated, there will be nothing to stop him."

"I am still willing to risk it", Admiral Colonna said firmly.

Doria smiled. "Twelve galleys and six frigates", he said, and the papal admiral bit his lip.

"I entirely agree with Admiral Doria", said General Ascanio de la Corgnia, commander of the land forces. "Too much risk is too much risk."

Sforza, Count of Santa Fiore, seconded his chief.

Juan could not resist a look at the papal nuncio. Monsignor Odescalchi's eyes had lost some of their luster and his lips were forming a straight line. Juan thought of Fray Juan de Calahorra and what he had said about the spirit of the crusades and about the importance of laymen in spreading the Kingdom of Christ on earth.

Eighty thousand men and over three hundred ships, but they would not dare attack the enemy. . . .

Veniero, tugging at his shaggy, white beard, was spluttering protest after protest, aided and abetted by his two subcommanders, fat, good-natured Proveditore Barbarigo and sturdy, curly-haired Proveditore Quirini. Once he became so rude that Juan had to interfere.

"It is becoming more and more clear", Doria stated coldly, "that the commanders from Venice have only one object in mind: to have their Cypriot possessions saved for them with the help of the Spanish and papal fleet."

"I must forbid any remark likely to endanger the unity of the Holy League", Juan said, before Veniero could open fire.

Doria gave a slight bow to the commander in chief. "In that case", he said, "I will content myself by pointing out that the Turkish fleet is manned with experienced sailors, while many of our men are raw recruits—not excluding the Venetian galleys. The Turkish janizary is a soldier second to none, and Ali Pasha's fleet is bound to be full of janizaries. I have seen men on our ships who hardly know how to discharge their firelocks."

"Our artillery is superior to theirs, I believe", Juan said lightly, and Doria looked up in surprise.

"That is true, Your Excellency. But artillery is not everything, and despite our strength I very much fear we are no match for the combined strength of three Turkish fleets. Let us not forget that during our lifetime—not only Your Excellency's lifetime, but that of Admiral Veniero or Count Priego—the Turkish fleet has never been beaten at sea. And those who know me will know also that I do not say this out of lack of courage."

Suddenly Juan rose. Of slight build and very elegantly dressed, he looked as if he wished to present a toast in happy company. The tone of his voice, too, was amiable, almost soft.

"I have now heard your views and opinions, gentlemen, and I thank you all for voicing them. My decision is to leave this port with the entire fleet as soon as we have taken enough fresh water and food on board. We shall sail for Corfu."

Everybody sat up. From the benches of the younger officers came a ragged cheer. Veniero began to beam. Barbarigo, most unceremoniously, gave his thigh a resounding slap. De la Corgnia and the Count of Santa Fiore exchanged uneasy glances. Don Luiz Requeséns grinned openly at Count Priego.

"But Your Excellency ..." Doria, too, was on his feet now. "This may be inviting disaster. Ali Pasha ..."

"Enough, gentlemen." This time there was metal in Juan's voice. "You have heard my decision. I am resolved to bring the Turk to battle. Detailed instructions, including those for battle formation, will be given to every commander within two days. And with the help of God and with yours the end will be victory."

The nuncio, who had been praying desperately, suddenly awoke to find Juan's arm on his shoulder. "Amen", he said. Then only he remembered that he was presiding. "The council is closed", he added, enthusiastically.


CHAPTER 38


THE FLEET WAS on the move.

The vanguard consisted of three Sicilian and three Venetian galleys under the command of a particularly experienced fighting man, Don Juan de Cardona. At a distance of twenty miles in daytime and eight miles at night the right wing followed, under the command of Admiral Doria; then the left wing, sixty-three galleys under Proveditore Agostino Barbarigo; and the center of sixty-two galleys, under the generalissimo himself. The royal flagship was leading, with the flagship of Admiral Colonna keeping station on her starboard side and that of Admiral Veniero on her port.

At a distance of only one mile the Marquis of Santa Cruz brought up the rear—about thirty galleys.

Every squadron was a mixed unit, consisting of ships of all the allied nations, and each showed a pennant of different color instead of the national flag. Don Juan de Austria's pennant was blue, Doria's green, Barbarigo's yellow, and that of Santa Cruz white.

At a secret meeting with Juan, Don Luiz Requeséns pointed out that this idea of mingling the ships would hamper their movements. "Every admiral has trained his squadron, the ships know each other, they are accustomed to each other. Now you are giving everyone new neighbors whose character and temperament are unknown to him."

Juan nodded. "Exactly that was my intention, Don Luiz. You see, one or the other of my admirals may have trained his squadron too well—and if it should occur to him to order them out of the battle zone, they would obey instantly, especially if he happens to own the ships personally."

Don Luiz grinned. "I think I know whom you mean."

"I have mentioned no names", Juan said, blinking a little. "But this is not the only reason for my idea. The faults of captains are, on the whole, my own faults: that is, they are ambitious and vain. This is my way of making the best use of that. A Spanish captain wouldn't like to see a Venetian outdoing him in daring, or vice versa. There'll be a very healthy spirit of competition. I have been debating this matter with myself for weeks, and I don't think there is a better solution."

"And you didn't discuss it in the war council. . . ."

"Because there would have been protests from all sides, and I couldn't very well give them my real reasons, could I? Both Doria and Barbarigo came to see me about it, nevertheless. Barbarigo is a very reasonable man, and I like him. So I could point out to him that Doria was not likely to keep Venetian ships out of the firing line as he might his own, and that he, Barbarigo, now had the chance to see to it that the Genoese galleys under his command would fight. And as he wants to fight—he's a good man, Don Luiz—there was no further difficulty. Doria, of course, was as slippery as an eel. But I got around him by promising him that I would take care of most of his galleys myself, and after all, the King has hired them from him for this campaign, so he really had no leg to stand on. Not that an eel needs legs. . . ."

"If you are as good an admiral as you are a diplomat . . . or a general . . ."

"The Morisco war was nothing compared to this, Don Luiz. Sometimes that reminded me of the games I used to play as a boy: Moors and Christians. And every planned action had first to be submitted to Madrid and more often than not Madrid canceled it. This time no one and nothing will interfere—except God and the enemy. And unless God wishes to chastise his own cause on earth, as sometimes he does . . . I will beat the enemy."

Was it likely that God would chastise his own cause?

Before the fleet left Messina, every man, from the admiral down to the last oarsman, went to confession and received Holy Communion. A small army of chaplains had come on board—Franciscans, Jesuits, Dominicans, and Capuchins, both priests and lay brothers.

The last sight the fleet had had when leaving the straits was that of the nuncio, Monsignor Odescalchi, in his purple robes, surrounded by a cluster of priests in white surplices, blessing every ship and those who sailed in her as she passed by. He must have stood there for hours on end, giving one blessing after another to those who would defend Christ's cause. And these blessings were charged, in a mysterious fashion, by those of the frail, old man in white far away in the Vatican, the living saint on the throne of St. Peter who, in so many words, had promised victory.

I cannot fail, Juan thought. Or if I do, the Lord will take me away and put another man in charge who does not. The cause cannot fail. The gates of hell will not prevail. And in a kind of holy egoism he prayed: "Lord, let it not be I who fails you when the hour comes."

The fleet was on the move. Slowly it sailed up the Ionian, to Fossa di San Giovanni first, named after Juan's patron saint; and promptly he had tidings that the Turks had landed on Corfu, blockaded Cattaro, and then steered southward to Vellona.

On the eighteenth they anchored at Spartivento, on the nineteenth at La Pace. At night a giant falling star suddenly lighted the whole sky and burst into three meteors. Juan was told that the sailors regarded it as an excellent portent.

On the twentieth the fleet reached Cape Stilo, on the twenty-first Le Colonne. At Castello another five hundred men of Calabrian infantry were taken on board. The weather changed from fair to squally and then the feared Bora, the rough wind from the north, delayed departure for a few days. Juan sent out Gil de Andrade with some light ships, and one, returning, met the fleet again off Fano; the weather, still rough, had not permitted it to enter the harbor. Andrade reported that the Turk had sailed in the direction of Zante and that Uluch Ali with the Algerine squadron was supposed to have left for Coron. There was a rumor also that Ali Pasha was expecting fresh orders from the Sultan himself. Andrade was very obviously rather proud of having got hold of all this news, pieced together from the reports of the captains of a number of fishing vessels he had met.

On the twenty-sixth the dark peak of San Salvator was sighted, but so unfavorable were the winds that the fleet reached Corfu harbor only on the twenty-seventh.

The fortress fired a salute, and Juan with his chief officers went on shore to inspect the damage the Turks had done to the city. Ali Pasha had made no more than a desultory attack. Was it because he knew something about the imminent arrival of a large Christian fleet? Had he received fresh orders from the Sultan?

In any case he had lost three galleys in the attempt, and a couple of hundred men. But he had destroyed half a dozen villages, desecrated and pillaged several churches, and taken away 180 Christian men who were now galley slaves in some of his ships. Most of his galley slaves were Christian prisoners, in fact almost all of them, except for the usual contingent of criminals, more than paying off their various crimes by a life that was one prolonged torture lasting exactly as long as their physical strength would hold out.

Juan led his officers into one of the destroyed churches. He had seen this kind of thing before, in Granada and the Almanzora valley. Broken tabernacles, broken crucifixes, the pictures of saints slashed and their faces used for pistol practice, the vile stench of deliberate profanation. Many a mailed hand flew to the sword hilt.

"That, gentlemen, is what we are fighting", he said aloud.

His guides, old nobles from Corfu and Captain Domenico Barola, the commander of the harbor fortress, looked at each other.

"It is bad enough," Barola said, "but it must have been much worse in Famagusta."

"Famagusta?" Juan asked quickly. "What about Famagusta?"

Barola stared at him. "Is it possible, Your Excellency, that you don't yet know that Famagusta has fallen?"

Old Veniero pressed forward, purple in the face. "We don't know anything", he bellowed. "Talk, man, talk. What happened?"

"I most profoundly regret to have to tell you such sad news", Barola said gravely. "Famagusta capitulated after a siege of sixty-five days. Only about three thousand men were still alive in the fortress, and most of them were either wounded or ill. There was food left only for two days and no more than a hundred and twenty charges for the guns.

Mustapha Pasha offered fair enough terms. He promised to ship all officers and men to Candia. . . ."

Veniero had been Venetian governor of Candia before he took command of the fleet. "Bragadino", he said hoarsely. "Marc Antonio Bragadino, my old friend. What happened to him?"

"The brave commander is in heaven", Barola said. "His death . . ." The man's voice broke.

Veniero was crying unashamedly, and so were most of the Venetians present.

"He fell . . . in the defense of the city?" Veniero asked when he could speak again.

Barola shook his head.

"Murdered", Veniero groaned. "Murdered by the Turk, was he?"

"Cruelly murdered", Barola said.

Veniero's shaggy white beard twitched. The old man made a tremendous effort to steady himself and he succeeded. "Tell me everything", he said. "I have a right to know."

"As soon as the town had surrendered Mustapha broke his word. All Christian captives were chained to the galleys— those over age were killed. Bragadino was tortured for twelve days. . . ."

"Santa Madonna", Veniero said. He was as white as the chalked wall of the desecrated church.

"They cut off his nose and ears. Three times they led him to the execution place and three times they led him away again. Every morning he was scourged and then made to work on the broken walls. Whenever Mustapha passed by, Bragadino was forced to kiss his feet. In the end he was led into the cathedral, where Mustapha was sitting on the high altar, which he had desecrated. . . ."

A cry of fury went up.

"Mustapha told him that the cathedral would be transformed into a mosque. He also told him how he was going to die. He would have him flayed alive. Then he screamed at him: 'Where is your Christ? Why doesn't he free you, if he's so powerful?' They began to flay him then and there, and they started at his feet. He began to pray the Miserere. That was his whole answer. When they reached his thighs, his voice gave out. . . . Mustapha had his skin stuffed with straw and hung on the mast of a galley so that the Christian slaves could see it."

"He died a martyr", Juan said. He crossed himself, and the others followed his example. "I command that this story be told to every man in the fleet. I take it you are certain of your facts, Captain Barola?"

"Quite certain, Your Excellency, I am sorry to say."

As soon as Juan was back on board again, he made sure that his last order was obeyed. Within a few hours every man in the fleet knew about the fate of Famagusta and Marc Antonio Bragadino.

Throughout the twenty-eighth volunteers and foodstuff were taken on board. Juan conferred with Colonna. Veniero had excused himself and the commander in chief respected his grief.

"I'm having the espolones cut off my ships", Juan told the papal admiral. "We won't need spurs as much as we need accurate firing. The spurs are much too high anyway; they hamper the effective working of the guns on the forecastle and the gangway."

"The Turk is fond of ramming, though, Your Excellency."

"I know. That's where the netting comes in. I've had all the nets brought up that we could lay hands on, and we have been exercising with them. I'm cutting down all purely ornamental things, too. Room for more guns. Firing power is what we want, firing power."

"You didn't cut down those marvelous ornaments of Il Bergemasco's", Colonna said, aghast. "Why, they're priceless. . . ."

"They've gone. I had them stored on land. It gave me room for four more guns."

"But where did you get the guns?"

"The harbor fortress. I convinced those people that *we* are their fortress now, and a better one than they could ever hope to have. You can have two, if you wish."

Colonna accepted the present, not without a rueful look at his own beautifully ornamented poop deck.

"You seem to be very sure that we shall get hold of the Turk, Your Excellency."

"I am very sure. Wherever they are, I'm going to look for them until I find them."

Colonna led his commander in chief through the ship. Juan found the discipline on board faultless, equal, if not superior to that of the best Spanish ships. He particularly liked the admiral's bodyguard, twenty-five men of the Pope's own Swiss Guards under their young commander, a giant of a man, Hans Noelle by name.

"The sword of St. Peter", Juan said, smiling. "Mind you, Messer Noelle, this time it will have to cut off more than just an ear."

Noelle grinned cheerfully and said something in a Italian so grimly Swiss that Colonna had to translate it to Juan. "He says he wants a Turkish flag to send home to Switzerland. He comes from a place called Kriens, but most of the others are from Lucerne, I believe."

"Well, I hope he'll get his flag. Who is that man there?"

A tall, thin soldier was standing in the gangway and somebody was trying to drag him away by his coat. He resisted stoutly and at the same time saluted; his eyes fixed on the two great commanders.

"What's going on here?" Colonna barked.

The man behind the soldier emerged, saluting sheepishly. "Physician's mate, sir. This young gentleman is ill with fever and ought to be in his bed, sir."

"It isn't much of a fever, Your Grace", the soldier said eagerly. "And I just heard about what happened at Famagusta. I beg Your Grace's pardon for intruding like this—I would like to ask a favor of Your Grace."

"What's your name?" Colonna asked, frowning.

"Miguel de Cervantes Saavedra, at Your Grace's service."

"A Spaniard", Juan said. "Where from?"

"I was born in Alcalá, Your Excellency."

"I know it well. Where in Alcalá?"

"Our house was just next to the kitchen garden of the Capuchin monastery, Your Excellency. I was christened in Santa María Mayor. We went to Sevilla then and later to Madrid."

"You are a volunteer, I take it?"

"Yes, Your Excellency. That is to say, I am the kind of madman who still believes that nobility of heart, courage, and poetry are the three things that matter most, next to the grace of God."

"You are a poet, then?" Juan said with that grave charm that won the heart of every man.

"Yes, Your Excellency. I went to Rome in the retinue of the Most Reverend Giulio Acquaviva de Aragon. But what is life at the most magnificent court when the bugle calls for battle against the infidel? Poetry can remain poetry only so long as it is paired with courage and nobility of heart."

"I wish all Spaniards thought as you do", Juan said.

Miguel de Cervantes smiled deprecatingly. "There is need for the other type as well", he said. "Has it occurred to Your Excellency that there are two types of Spaniards and two only?"

Colonna cleared his throat impatiently, but Juan was not to be deflected. "Two types only? What are they, señor poet?"

"The first", Cervantes said, "is slim and dreamy and full of enthusiasm for all things great, sacred, and brilliant. The lady he loves is invariably the most beautiful in the world, and if she is not a queen she should be. He thinks the world is the field God gave him in which to perform shining deeds in the service of a great cause and so he is a hero and a fool, a poet and a knight."

"Like you." Juan smiled.

Cervantes bowed ceremoniously, but there was an expression of politely hidden irony in his dark eyes. "The second type", he said, "is intensely practical and knows exactly the value of a maravedí, a real and a ducat. A woman to him is a very useful creature, and if she is pretty too, so much the better. He thinks the world is a field in which he must find a small place where he can live with a minimum of discomfort. You only have to look at a Spaniard and you will always know to which of the two types he belongs."

Once more Colonna cleared his throat.

"Thank you, señor poet", Juan said, "I will certainly think about your theory. But what about the favor you were going to ask?"

"It is, Your Excellency, that I may be freed from the well-meaning but clumsy services of the physician's mate and permitted to command a dozen soldiers in battle—preferably at the bows."

"He'll be killed there, most likely", Colonna said.

"But if he isn't, he will reach Parnassus", Juan said, and Cervantes' eyes lit up. "Let him have his twelve men, Your Grace, as a favor to me."

"Very well, Your Excellency. You'd better go back to bed now, messer poet, and come out only when it's time to fight."

When Juan returned to his flagship, he was informed that a further report had arrived from Andrade. The Turkish fleet was in Lepanto harbor. It consisted, at a minimum, of 170; at a maximum, of a little over two hundred galleys. Former reports that Admiral Uluch Ali had left the main fleet were confirmed. He had left with the entire force of the Barbary coast, 110 galleys. Thus together the Turkish fleet would have considerably exceeded the Christian forces, as frigates, brigantines, and other small craft were not included in the report.

The wind was sharply adverse. There was no possibility of sailing for Lepanto immediately.

Juan decided to steer to Gomenizza on the Albanian coast, about thirty miles southeast of Corfu, and to approach the enemy by stages.

In Gomenizza also the six gigantic galleasses joined him, the pride of Venice, floating fortresses of vastly superior firing power, but hampered only too often by the fact that they had no rowers and therefore had to rely on their sails alone.

On October 2 there was a last review and inspection of all ships, and Juan had to settle a quarrel between the Venetian and the Genoese commanders. Doria was supposed to inspect a number of Venetian ships, and Veniero promptly refused to allow him on board. In the end Don Luiz Requeséns had to replace him, Doria sulked for a while, and Veniero was at his most testy and trying.

There was worse to come. Late in the afternoon Juan, talking to the young Prince of Urbino, suddenly heard several shots, followed by a diffused noise, coming from the direction of the Venetian ships. He sent off a boat to inquire into what was happening, but even before it returned another boat came alongside and Colonel Paolo Sforza came on board, requesting an immediate hearing. The man was so excited that for several minutes Juan could not make head or tail out of what he was trying to say. He gathered that on board the Venetian galley *L'Aquila*, commanded by Captain Andrea Calergi from Crete, a quarrel had started between some sailors and a few of the Spanish harquebusiers who had been put on board there to make up for the insufficient number of Venetian soldiers. This surely was no more than an ordinary police matter. But Sforza insisted that it was a dastardly offense committed by Admiral Veniero himself, who for some reason had interfered and, when Sforza tried to obtain permission to settle the dispute, threatened to have him thrown into the water and his galley sunk. . . .

Juan listened only with a small portion of his mind. He could see that some of the Venetian ships were moving about, including Veniero's flagship. From one of the papal galleys came a warning shot.

Sforza was still babbling away, when de Soto, who had heard what happened from the men in Sforza's boat, came up. The Venetian police chief had gone on board *L'Aquila* to arrest two Spanish harquebusiers, but their commander, Muzio Alticozzi, had shot him and wounded two Venetian officials. There was a general upheaval, and now Admiral Veniero had sent troops on board.

"He will hang them, Your Excellency", Sforza spluttered. "Hang them from his yardarm, he said so; he is mad, quite mad."

Juan gave orders to have the boat lowered. He was going to see for himself. But the order had not yet been executed, when on the foremast of Veniero's flagship three bodies were hoisted up. One of them was wearing the uniform of a Spanish commander.

A howl of rage went up from the Spanish flagship. No one but the commander in chief had jurisdiction over life and death. This was not only a crime; it was a deliberate insult to the Spanish flag, the commander in chief, the King of Spain. If this was not avenged and avenged at once, every Venetian would jeer when the fair name of Spain was mentioned.

Clusters of officers stormed up to the poop deck, shouting and clamoring; the entire flagship was a mass of wildly excited men.

But that was not all. As if touched by the invisible hands of demons all the ships in the bay began to move. The Spanish, papal, and Genoese ships gathered around the supreme commander's galley, the Venetian around Veniero's flagship. Sailors were picking up boat hooks and axes, soldiers their harquebuses and pikes.

Juan stood motionless, the nails of his fingers dug into his chest. More than anyone else he felt the insult offered to him and through him to his royal brother.

"Give the order, Excellency," Juan de Cardona roared, "and we'll sink the Venetian flagship and throw that infamous rogue of a Veniero into the water as food for the sharks."

"Down with Venice", howled a chorus of young officers from amidships. "To hell with all Venetians!"

A fast little brigantine came alongside, and a group of officers clambered up the ladder. The crowd recognized beside Admiral Colonna the large frame of the Venetian vice commander, Barbarigo, and broke into jeers. A cutlass swished through the air and stuck quivering in the bulwark of the brigantine.

A moment later Colonna and Barbarigo stood before Juan, both as pale as death and trembling.

Barbarigo apologized with folded hands for the action of his own chief. "He has been beside himself ever since he heard about the fall of Famagusta, Your Excellency. Marc

Antonio Bragadino was very dear to him. Oh, I know that's no excuse; there isn't any excuse for this act, and now it threatens us all with perdition. . . ."

"And not only us but also the cause of Christ", Colonna said. "Your Excellency, in the name of our Lord, I beseech you. . . . The Turk is only a few miles away and if you do not give the word, the Holy League will fall to pieces in this accursed bay and Christians will slaughter Christians by the thousand."

"Don't listen to them, Royal Spain", roared Cardona's voice, and somebody bellowed: "Hang all Venetians!"

One word . . . one word and a thousand guns would spout death on the Venetian galleys, sink the ship of the madman who thought he could hang a Spanish commander as if he were some lout picked up by a press gang on the Rialto or the Piazza San Marco. No blame could be attached to the commander in chief for giving that word. In fact, he might find himself sharply censured or even ignominiously dismissed for not giving it, for not defending to the last and utmost the honor of his monarch. Here was the perfect opportunity for Don Juan de Austria's enemies to spill their poison. "So when the King's sacred honor was besmirched, Don Juan did nothing about it. That comes from putting a bastard into a position of high command. . . ."

"Hang all Venetians!" the crowd roared. "Down with Veniero! Down with Barbarigo!"

But from afar, across land and sea and air, the voice of a man in a brown habit said: "Where is the man who still has the pure spirit of the crusades? The man who wants to fulfill a task not because he wants it but because God wants it? *Deus lo vult.* . . ."

And somewhere in one of the rooms of the Vatican an old man in a white habit was praying his heart out for the

victory of the Cross against the terrible power of the Crescent. . . .

Juan turned to the officers crowding the poop deck, the
stairs, and a good part of the deck below. He raised his
hand. "Quiet", he said. When the din subsided he added
in a clear, calm voice: "I know best what I owe to our Lord
and what I owe to my royal brother. This is my order to
the entire fleet: any man, be he soldier or sailor, and whatever his rank, who fires another shot will be hanged at once.
De Soto! See that this order is sent to every single ship
immediately." He turned back to the two admirals. "My
lord Colonna, I thank you for good advice. My lord Barbarigo: you will return to Admiral Veniero and tell him
that he will no longer be permitted to set foot on my flagship. In future war councils the Most Serene Republic will
be represented by the Proveditore Barbarigo. Admiral Veniero will at once start preparations for the departure. So, my
lord Colonna, will you. We are sailing this night for Lepanto."

CHAPTER 39

THE FLEET WAS on the move again.

Shortly after dawn it was off the town of Prevesa of terrible memory, Prevesa, where a previous Christian league
had found an inglorious end. And soon afterward it entered
the Gulf of Arta, the Ambracian gulf of old, where Octavius
defeated the combined fleet of Antony and Cleopatra in a
battle that decided the rulership of the Roman world.

Juan could still hear the mellifluous voice of Honoratus
Joannius as he explained what happened—when was it?

Eleven years before Christ? Fourteen before Christ? Much more than fifteen centuries, almost sixteen centuries ago in any case.

Were they looking at him from the land of shadows, to see how he would fight his battle where they had fought and lost?

Even in the hard light of the morning sun there was something ghostly and ominous about this slow, quiet progress of the ships, the progress of a forest of masts, very gently heaving, with no other noise than the clanking of the oars in the rowlocks and the very faint rattle of the rigging.

The Turks had triumphed in these waters, and perhaps some of Ali Pasha's officers had participated in that triumph, a little over thirty years ago.

Resolutely Juan shook off the specters of the past, both near and distant. I am standing where my father would like me to stand, he thought, and I am moving to where he would like me to move. As often before he felt comforted thinking of the old man of Yuste who had been the last great Christian emperor and who now was in heaven. If other ghosts of the past were watching him, so was the Emperor. And it was time that the shame of Prevesa was undone.

For the twentieth time Juan went over all the orders he had given.

Nothing was missing, nothing could be done to secure further advantage, to prevent further mishaps. They all behaved now, those big, bearded children of his, even that seventy-two-year-old child of a Veniero, though he had reports that the old man was sullen and dispirited. He probably always had been like that, either too full of optimism or deep in the dumps, and the change could come from one moment to the next. Some men were like that, and they never changed.

There had been no further unpleasantness since that last dangerous moment at Gomenizza, that last attempt of Satan to bring the effort of the Holy League to nought by playing on man's weaknesses, rousing man's obstinacy, man's rage, and, above all, man's pride. Why, he himself had had to exorcise his pride, with the help of Fray Juan de Calahorra's words and thinking of the old man in Rome who was praying for a victory then so desperately endangered. . . .

On the morning of October 4 the fleet anchored off Cape Blanco, the northern headland of Cephalonia. That same night sail was set again but the wind changed and fog came in so that the greater part of the next day had to be spent in the shelter of the harbor of Viscardo.

On October 6, too, the weather was unfavorable. The fleet crawled along the narrow channel. Orders were given once more that no one was to discharge a firearm under pain of death, but this time not because of any fear of fresh quarrels, but because the enemy was so near that he might well hear the report. The fleet anchored in Petala, seven miles off Cape Skropha.

At dawn of October 7 the first ships of the Christian fleet moved cautiously into the channel formed on one side by the Greek coast, on the other by the last of the Curzolarian islands, Oxia.

Juan ordered two frigates to land on Oxia and send a few lynx-eyed men up the rocks from which the entire Gulf of Lepanto could be seen.

It was Sunday, and Mass was said throughout the fleet.

A swift brigantine came back to report that from Cape Skropha two sails could be sighted, a lateen sail and a famula, obviously Turkish reconnaissance.

Only a quarter of an hour later one of the two frigates dispatched to Oxia came alongside the flagship and Juan gave orders that its officer should report to him personally in his cabin.

The man was a Genoese, Cecco Pizano. He was as pale as a sheet. "I've never seen anything like it, sir", he said in a quavering voice. "The whole gulf is full of them. I could count up to two hundred sail, but there were masses more too far away to be counted."

"Distance?" Juan asked calmly. "Speed?"

"They'll be at the cape in three hours, sir. And, sir—the report we had about the Algerine squadron having left—it wasn't true, or it isn't true anymore. I've seen dozens and dozens of Algerine ships; I know their rigging well, sir. That fellow Uluch Ali is back, sir—if he ever left, that is."

Juan nodded and said, "That will save us the trouble of going chasing after him."

De Soto announced Admiral Doria and General de la Corgnia's arrival alongside, and a minute later Colonna and Barbarigo also turned up.

Stony-faced, Juan listened to Doria's warning against giving battle to the entire Turkish fleet when it was backed by a good harbor like that of Lepanto, while the fleet of the league had no accessible port to fall back on; with an imperious gesture he silenced Barbarigo who was going to launch a protest.

"Gentlemen," he said icily, "the time for counsel is past and the time for fighting is at hand. Please return to your ships at once."

The commanders had only just stepped off the ladder when Juan gave orders to have the foresail hauled to the wind and one gun fired.

At the report of the gun every eye in the fleet turned toward the flagship, just in time to see the huge, blue banner of the Holy League hoisted. As it broke in the morning wind a cheer went up from every ship. Everybody knew what it meant: the end of the long, long period of waiting, of cruising about from one port to another, the end of the search; and strangely, it also meant the end of fear. For man is made in such a way that he fears most not what is but what might be.

It was all the difference between the danger in a nightmare, when one is beset by a terrible enemy and finds that one cannot move, that all one's limbs are like lead, and the danger of reality, when every muscle obeys the slightest effort of the will, when one's arms are good and trustworthy and all around one are friends to share one's own fate.

But the very first thing that the signal meant was the taking up of battle stations.

Always a complex maneuver it was made still more so by the fact that over three hundred ships were slowly coming out of a narrow channel to deploy all across the gulf.

The channel of Oxia was spouting galleys. As soon as each one came out into the open she took her appointed station, each captain knowing exactly which ship to follow.

Juan, with de Soto and Don Luiz de Córdoba, had gone on board his fastest frigate to inspect the galleys of the center and of the right wing, Don Luiz Requeséns performing the same task on the left. The commander in chief was wearing no armor as yet. His first order for every galley was that all oarsmen other than Muslim prisoners were to be freed of their chains and given arms, and he promised an amnesty for everyone who would do his duty in battle. Most of the men were crying with joy. And slaves and sailors, soldiers and commanders cheered alike when he told them: "My children, we are here to conquer or to die— and remember there is no place in heaven for a coward. Don't let the infidel ask us: 'Where is your God?' Fight in God's Holy Name and in death or in victory you will win immortality."

And such was the power of his personality that as soon as he sailed on, men vowed what they would do in battle and made up any quarrel they had with anybody else on board.

Juan himself did the same. Passing Veniero's flagship he saw the old man standing on the poop deck, already fully armored. He lifted his hat, smiling, and with his right hand made the sign of the cross as if blessing him; Veniero's answer was no more than a grave salute, but the incident restored his peace of mind, for when a quarter of an hour later Marc Antonio Colonna passed by, also on a swift frigate, Veniero hailed him, cheerfully punning, "Welcome to the stoutest column of the Church!"

In a dozen cases and more Juan went on board a galley for a few minutes, distributing medals, coins, rosaries, and souvenirs of all kinds. When he had nothing left, he gave one man his hat and to two others his gloves, which they proudly affixed to their caps. One of them was later offered fifty ducats for the glove by a young noble. He proudly refused to sell it.

When Juan returned to his flagship the battle array was almost complete: a number of light craft were tugging the six heavy galleasses to the front. The swimming fortresses were to serve as the buffers of the fleet; two took position in front of the center and of each wing.

The left wing—sixty-three galleys under Barbarigo— stretched out almost to the coastline, to make it impossible for the Turks to outflank the fleet.

The center also consisted of sixty-three galleys, grouped around the three flagships: left, that of Veniero, in the middle that of the commander in chief, with Colonna on the right. Don Luiz Requeséns was hovering just behind Juan, ready to assist him if necessary. On the outer left of the center was the galley of Captain Ettore Spinola, with Alexander Farnese on board; on the outer right the three ships of the Knights of St. John under Prior Giustiniani from Messina.

Doria, commanding the right wing with access to the open sea, had sixty-four galleys, and behind this triple front the Marquis of Santa Cruz commanded the rear with thirty-five galleys.

At eleven o'clock in the morning the entire Turkish fleet was fully visible, no more than a mile and a half away.

Juan was watching it on deck, while his valet was putting on his armor, black steel with silver clasps. Under it he wore the relic of the True Cross the Pope had sent him; over it the Golden Fleece, which, according to the statutes of that Order, had to be worn by a knight when he went into battle.

"De Soto", Juan said.

"Excellency?"

"See the form of the Turkish line? Both wings curved forward, the center farthest away? What's it remind you of?"

"The devil's head with two horns", de Soto said at once.

Juan smiled. "A crescent", he said. "The Muslim symbol. And our own line? Six galleasses in front with the small ships, the main line and Santa Cruz in the rear? If God looks down from high heaven he will see the Cross fighting the Crescent."

De Soto stared at him. He said nothing.

"De Soto, I want my own cross—the half-burned one; it's beside my bed in the cabin. Have it brought up and fixed to the foremast."

"Yes, sir."

As de Soto rushed down to the main deck Juan gave orders to hoist a white pennant and dip it. It was the agreed signal for every ship in the fleet to affix a large crucifix to its foremast.

De Soto came back with Padre Miguel Servia, Juan's father confessor, who was carrying the half-burned crucifix that Don Luiz Quixada once saved from Moorish hands. Juan kissed it reverently. Then the priest walked over to the foremast and, with the help of a carpenter's mate, nailed it on.

Six trumpeters gave a long-drawn signal.

Juan, his face toward the crucifix, fell on his knees, and so did everyone else. The sun, now almost at the zenith, shone on decks gleaming with prostrate men in armor. And thus it was in every Christian ship.

Another trumpet signal.

Eighty thousand Christians returned from a brief moment spent in the land of eternity to their immediate task. The oarsmen gripped their oars, the sailors took their positions, the gunners lit their linstocks. Officers supervised the throwing out of netting, the distribution of ammunition reserves, and the grouping of soldiers at all strategic points. Stewards placed baskets of food and small wineskins under the benches of the oarsmen, and at a number of points men with large oil cans stood in readiness to make the planking slippery in case the ship was boarded by the enemy.

The rash of white dots that was the Turkish fleet was becoming more compact now.

Don Felipe Heredia, standing next to Juan, said cheerfully: "The devil's drawing in his horns."

Juan gave no answer. Don Felipe was quoting de Soto, of course, but he was wrong. Ali Pasha was not pulling in

457

his wings; he was pushing his center, forward, and now he, too, was forming a clear-cut array, center, and two wings. There was little doubt that he was going to remain in the center and his left wing, facing Doria, consisted of the Algerine ships, so Doria's adversary would be Uluch Ali, disciple of the late Dragut, the most cunning of Muslim leaders. They called him the Ulcerous One, because of some loathsome skin disease he had. Uluch Ali and Doria—a duel between two foxes, where anything might happen.

Ali Pasha in the center, Uluch Ali opposite Doria—that meant that Barbarigo's opponent was Muhammid Pasha of Alexandria, whom they called Sirocco, after the devastating hot wind from Africa whose suffocating breath could be felt up to the northern coast of the Adriatic.

Both he and his commander in chief were known to be brave men, experienced and proud, leaders in the grand manner and, of course, fanatical Muslims. Even the Spanish dossiers, carefully kept by Don Ruy Gómez, could not say anything disparaging about either of them, or about Pertau Pasha, who was said to be in command of the Turkish troops.

"Masthead there", Juan shouted. "How many galleys in the rear of the enemy?"

"None, sir. Only frigates and brigantines, but many of them."

None. No reserve. That meant that they would try a breakthrough, using the light craft only as troop transports, which could come alongside the galleys at any given moment, to feed fresh troops into them.

Ali Pasha seemed determined to win this battle with one single gigantic punch. But if he was, Uluch Ali apparently had other ideas. He was thinning out his line toward the open sea, and so was Doria. This could mean a flanking attempt, and Doria, very sensibly, would have none of it.

The foxes had started trying to fox each other. If only the line was not stretched out too far.

"Don Bernardino."

"Excellency?"

"A frigate to Admiral Doria's flagship. My respects to the admiral, and will he please see to it that he keeps touch with my right?"

"Yes, Excellency."

There was always the chance that the Muslim fox was just feinting, trying to lure Doria away toward the open sea and then pouncing into the gap. Doria was much too shrewd not to think of such an eventuality, but he might rely on Santa Cruz for the closing of the gap, and there was no knowing how Santa Cruz was going to be engaged an hour from now.

Juan could see the Turkish flagship now, a huge galley, almost the size of a galleass. No netting. The spur rather high up. A large, green flag flying on the main mast. That would be their sacred flag, the flag of the prophet they called it, specially blessed in Mecca and embroidered with sayings from the Qur'an, their holy book.

A white disc suddenly protruded from the galley next to the Turkish flagship, and a few moments later a dull, growling thud wafted over.

"They're shooting at the galleasses", Don Felipe remarked.

Two more, then six more white discs, followed by thuds.

One of the light ships that had tugged the galleasses into position had its pennant shot away.

Juan noted with satisfaction that the galleasses were holding their fire, as they had been ordered to do.

On the whole it seemed as if the intelligence reports Gil de Andrade provided were correct, except for the presence of the strong Algerine squadron. The Turkish vessels appeared to be somewhat lighter than the Spanish, about equal to the Venetians. But what they lacked in weight and therefore also in artillery, they made up in numbers. Their right wing, opposing Barbarigo, was about as strong as their opponent's but the center seemed to consist of almost a hundred ships and the left wing was as strong as the center.

The sun was right overhead now, noon and very little wind; the Turkish ships were hull-up, forming what appeared one enormous solid front of prows, jibs, sails, and flags. Every Turkish ship was showing bunting all over the place, including long streamers in various colors and the white discs, soon dissolving in the wind, were no longer the only sign that they were still firing their forecastle guns. . . . Water was splashing at a number of places, all around the two galleasses in front of the Christian center.

A flurry of smoke came from one of them and for a moment Juan thought that she had been hit. But the deep, metallic thud that followed showed that she had opened fire, and almost immediately the second galleass followed suit.

From Veniero's flagship, near enough for a line to be thrown over to it, came the strains of music. The Venetians had their band playing, not a bad idea at all, at least as long as there was no need for orders to be shouted. Well, there soon enough would be.

The galleasses seemed to have hit something; there was a commotion going on in the broad Turkish front—a galley, no, two galleys were being withdrawn from the front line and replaced at once.

Now the moment was coming when they would have to show how they wanted to deal with the buffers, whether they were going to attack them or—they were not going to attack them, they were trying to bypass them, have them surrounded, probably, by a ring of firing galleys to prevent them from causing havoc in their rear. A breakthrough, that was the idea. A breakthrough in the center, while trying to lure the right Christian wing farther and farther away. That frigate must have reached Doria by now, but so far he had not done anything to close the gap, in fact it was getting wider.

Should he send for Santa Cruz; let him advance a little?

No, not yet. Santa Cruz was a very experienced man; he could see the situation as it was and act accordingly, if he thought fit.

The Turks opened fire at Barbarigo now, still hopelessly out of range. Juan could see the splashes. That would become a holding battle, no doubt, with the Turkish right wing being their weakest and its end so near to the shore, where the water was full of shoals and shallows. If it weren't for that, he might have considered ordering Santa Cruz to join up with the left wing and attempt a breakthrough there, to roll up the Turkish center. As it was it would be inviting disaster, with a dozen galleys stuck on reefs and the others hampered in their maneuvers by the wrecks.

The thing that had to be done was for once the obvious: a headlong clash with the Turkish center; and by Almighty God, it was the fulfillment of all dreams.

Juan gave one more look at the enemy line. Evading the galleasses was not an easy maneuver for Ali Pasha, especially as the heavy ships were now firing for all they were worth. Damage was visible on three, no four, Turkish ships and at least two were in imminent danger of colliding.

"Mother of Christ", somebody said at his elbow. "The wind's changing."

Juan looked up. The man was right. The wind, so far slightly adverse, was now favoring his fleet. It was as if the very breath of God had come to speed them on. Was there not some passage in the Old Testament, saying that the Lord was coming in the heart of a gentle wind?

Juan crossed himself. Then he raised his right hand high. It was the signal for one gun to be fired—and that again was the signal for the general advance of the center.

The gun went off instantly. No doubt the gunnery officer and his men had been awaiting the signal for several minutes.

Half a mile ahead Ali Pasha's flagship came swooping past the galleass on the left, Andrea da Pezaro's galleass, and Pezaro gave her a greeting with his starboard guns; the Turks responded and there was so much smoke that it was impossible to see the effect.

There . . . the flagship was coming out of it. No damage visible. Her decks were crowded with soldiers, dressed in all the colors of the rainbow, and on some vantage point on the forecastle a lonely figure was dancing madly.

"A dervish", Luiz de Córdoba said. "That's what they call their monks." "Santísima, how they're howling", Don Bernardino said.

"They always do when they attack. It's supposed to frighten us."

There was laughter among the young nobles standing in a group behind the officers.

Half a dozen galleys came hurtling after the Turkish flagship, each braving the fire from Pezaro's galleass and all but one escaping it. The one that was hit was listing badly to port and Pezaro sent some more metal over. He had two sixty-pounders, which could finish off a galley in a few minutes.

Farther back the whole Turkish line was coming on, rowing as fast as they could, but no longer in real formation. The buffers had done exactly what had been asked of them. . . .

Again Juan raised his arm, this time pointing straight to the Turkish flagship.

462

"Helm one point astarboard."

There was heavy gunfire on the left wing now, and yet one could hear the infernal din the Turks were making on Ali Pasha's ship.

Don Luiz de Córdoba, who was in charge of the gunnery, looked at his commander in chief.

"Wait", Juan said coldly.

The Turkish flagship loomed up, filling a third, filling almost half of the horizon.

"Don Luiz . . . the forecastle and portside guns must be ready."

"Yes, Your Excellency."

"Sul-ta-na", Don Bernardino read out. He was one of the few on board who could read Turkish writing.

The dervish was still dancing, a tall, thin fellow in white with a conical hat. Harquebusiers by the hundreds, a number of men with bows and arrows.

"Don Luiz . . . the forecastle guns will fire on the soldiers on deck as soon as I give the sign."

"Yes, Excellency. Gunners on the forecastle: take your aim on the soldiers on deck. . . ."

"Don Bernardino—have the boarding parties ready."

There was a shot from the *Sultana* and a crash on the prow. Somebody screamed. Another shot and another crash. The esquife, the boat of Juan's ship, became a madly dancing heap of splinters. A third shot went high up over their heads.

Hampered by their own jib, Juan thought, and at the same time he commanded: "Fire the forecastle guns."

Don Luiz barked out the command, but only the first word was audible, the rest was drowned by the thunder of the forecastle guns, four altogether with the two that were added at Corfu.

463

A huge black cloud of smoke was enveloping the ship.

"Helm hard astarboard", Juan shouted at the top of his voice.

The ship swung away.

"Don Luiz ... the portside guns will fire."

Don Luiz bellowed into the smoke and ten guns shot their metal into the *Sultana*, their muzzles almost touching its board.

"Shields up and hold tight", Juan commanded, gripping the iron rail.

Another crash, and this time it seemed as if the world were going to pieces. Out of the fumes of hell a huge apparition loomed up, high above the royal flagship's forecastle. The whole ship seemed to rear like a horse.

"The horn of the devil", Don Bernardino said, struggling to his feet.

"No, the next worst thing", Don Luiz de Córdoba said furiously. "The prow of the Turk. He's rammed us."

"But of course", Juan said, and now only it dawned on Don Luiz that this was part of the commander in chief's plan, and he gasped.

Around them was a pandemonium of shrieks and curses, acrid smoke, splinters flying in all directions, oars, most of them, but iron parts as well and a few shapeless things that once were parts of human beings.

Then a moment of uncanny silence.

"Stand by, boarders", Juan yelled.

If only this smoke would disperse just a little. There was no use firing the portside guns again, not with the ships interlocked as they were and rolling wildly, like wrestlers come to grips and trying to throw each other.

"Don Miguel! Get a hundred harquebusiers ready to cover the boarders. Fire as you see fit."

"Yes, Excellency."

A gust of wind blew part of the smoke away, and for a few moments the decks of the *Sultana* became visible, grotesquely oblique, and strewn with what might well be a hundred and more bodies. The forecastle guns, with their sights unhindered, had done their duty.

Muskets were fired wildly on both sides.

"Boarders away", Juan shouted. "Christ and the King!"

There was ragged cheering. The topmen ran out along the yards to lash the ships together; they were performing their flying dance again, but this time in grim earnest.

A horrible, gulping noise made Juan turn around. Don Bernardino de Cardenas was falling at his feet with a long arrow sticking out from his throat. He was dead.

"Up shields", Juan repeated. He remembered that two of Don Bernardino's sons were serving on another ship, and gritted his teeth.

The boarders climbed up the *Sultana*'s sides like cats, their cutlasses flashing between their teeth. Picked men with muskets and harquebuses were spraying the enemy deck. There was little fire from the enemy, thanks to that salvo of the forecastle guns that had raked his decks, but that would not last long.

Now Don Miguel de Moncada was going over and with him Don Pedro de Zapata, this time with no banner to hamper him.

"Masthead", Juan called, but there was no answer. "Two men up the masthead. I must have reports."

There was fighting on the deck of the *Sultana*, but he could only see part of it, now that the ships no longer rolled as much as before.

"Don Rodrigo, form a second wave of boarders, a hundred men. Masthead, what do you see?"

"Our men are almost at their mainmast, sir, but the fighting's heavy. There are Turks coming out from down below. They're two to one against us, sir."

"Second wave of boarders, away!" Juan shouted.

A volley of arrows came singing over their heads and one of the two men Juan had sent up to the masthead came hurtling down, landing with a crash on one of the deck guns. The mast looked like a hedgehog.

The second wave of boarders went over.

"Don Luiz, have those harquebusiers armed with cutlasses and swords and form a third wave. More men; I must have more men."

A shout came from the masthead. "Three galleys approaching the enemy with reinforcements, sir."

"Don Pablo, signal to Don Luiz Requeséns, reinforcements required at once."

But the signal was never given. There was a heavy thud and a moment later a stream of Spanish soldiers came over. Requeséns had not waited for the order; he was there already.

"We are being driven back", came the voice from the masthead. "Two more galleys approaching the *Sultana*, sir."

"Gentlemen," Juan said cheerfully, "this is what we have been waiting for. Follow me, if you please."

The young nobles cheered as they clanked after him along the deck, and toward the plank thrown over the side of the *Sultana*.

The two ships, locked together, were a battlefield surrounded by water, and that battlefield was growing all the time. There were six galleys now either alongside or at the stern of the *Sultana* and two more at the stern of the royal flagship, all of them feeding troops into the battle.

Old Requeséns on his own poop deck was dancing with excitement, as he saw the group of officers in armor climbing on board the Turkish ship.

"He's with them", he shouted. "I'm sure of it. Told him a thousand times he mustn't, but will he listen? Christ Almighty, it's just as it was at Galera and Serón. Get another boat off to Santa Cruz! Vásquez, see to it yourself. Gónzalez, lead your men over. If anything happens to the commander in chief, I'll split your bellies, if it's the last thing I do. Off, I say!"

Half a dozen young nobles scrambled madly over the *Sultana*'s bulwark and Juan followed them. There was no way of getting over the plank; it was all congested with bodies, dead, wounded, and whole. It was an athletic feat to swing over in full armor, and he only just managed it. He landed with both feet on a crouching Spanish harquebusier and the man swore in no uncertain terms, until he saw who the "kicking son of a misbegotten mule driver" was, and his jaw dropped.

Somehow Juan kept his footing and here was a grinning young man handing him his shield, and he seized it and looked about. Never in his life had he seen so many men on the deck of one ship, but only a third were Spaniards, fighting against a forest of plumed warriors who were shrieking like lost souls, janizaries, the soldiers who had never been beaten—we'll see about that.

On the poop, agleam with ornaments, a group of picked men was shielding a handful of officers who seemed to be dressed completely in gold  maybe Ali Pasha was among them. That's where we'll have to go, but how?

Short of falling on their heads there was no way of reaching them. Once more he remembered the flying dance.

"Don Jaime!"

467

"Excellency?"

Juan whispered his orders into the young man's ear, and Don Jaime looked up at the *Sultana*'s shrouds, all entangled in the rigging of the royal flagship.

"Stop staring in that direction", Juan snapped. "Did you understand everything? Jump to it, friend."

Don Jaime disappeared the way he had come, over the bulwark.

Juan saw Pedro Zapata trying to drive a wedge into the thick Turkish front; the boy was right, that way the heavier armor paid off. Don Miguel de Moncada was wounded; they were pushing him back to some corner where he could sit down. Somebody was pummeling his shield, arrows, at least a dozen of them; he brushed them off with a few strokes of his sword. By now Don Jaime must have reached Don Luiz de Córdoba, and something had to be done to distract the attention of the Turks.

Juan raised his sword. "Christ and the King", he shouted into the din. The young men with him took up the battlecry and pressed forward.

The ladder to the upper forecastle was slippery with blood. Sand—let somebody get some sand as they did in the arena. He hacked away at a Turkish leg, saw a turbaned head fall right at his feet, and pushed it out of the way with his foot as he mounted. A janizary officer with a beautifully worked shield and a long scimitar barred his way, smiling; the man was finely built.

Juan lunged at him and the Turk parried—lunge, parry, lunge, parry, an excellent fencer that man; that's why he was smiling. What about this double feint, nice, friend, now a circular blow, feint again, lunge—and a gash right across the face; I thought that would wipe that smile off, lunge, and there he falls. . . .

"Kilidj Hussein", somebody shrieked. "Kilidj Hussein!" And the Turkish line seemed to waver.

"Beautiful, Excellency, beautiful ..."

Who was that? Galarza, Juan Galarza, grinning all over his face and pushing the dead Turk out of the way. "He was one of their best", he said. "They call him Sword, Sword Hussein. Stop it, you!" He clubbed an all too bold Turk over the head.

Don Lope de Figueroa mowed his way toward Juan. "They have twelve ships all around this one, sir, ten galleys and two galliots. What are your orders, sir?"

"Fight them", Juan said, lunging. "There'll soon be—ah, here they come."

His flying dancers were in the Turkish shrouds now, twenty, thirty, fifty of them; some armed with muskets, some with harquebuses, and the Turks found themselves attacked from above.

"Get that flag down", Juan yelled at them. "Get the green flag down."

A number of Turks began to climb the rigging.

Shots were beginning to crack from the shrouds, and there were screams from the poop deck, which seemed to cause consternation in the Turkish ranks, although it was not possible to see what was going on there.

Juan went on fighting his way up the ladder, covered by Galarza on one side and Lope de Figueroa on the other. He felt a jar up his leg and a burning pain in his ankle and saw Galarza stab the janizary who had wounded him—the man had been playing dead; now he was dead.

"You are wounded, Excellency. . . ." Lope de Figueroa was beside himself.

"Be quiet, Don Lope. . . . It's nothing. And no one must know."

He pressed on, smashing his shield into the next Turkish face.

"The pasha is wounded", Don Pedro de Zapata roared.

They could see him now, hacking their way past the mainmast, a tall man, bearded, in magnificent armor, covered by a cloak of gold brocade, held upright by two officers. He was bleeding from a wound in the forehead.

Something large and green came floating down and fell on a group of Spanish harquebusiers: the flag, the sacred flag of the prophet.

With a cry of rage the Turks surged forward to save it.

"Back with it", Juan yelled, "as far back as possible. Get it on board our ship."

Just then a new, formidable apparition loomed up on the flank of the *Sultana*; there was a crash like a thunderbolt, and half the fighting men were thrown to the deck.

Juan, too, had fallen, but was helped to his feet instantly by half a dozen hands.

"Colonna!" roared Don Lope de Figueroa. "You're lost now, you dogs!"

The papal flagship had rammed the *Sultana* amidships.

Right and left Turkish soldiers were jumping overboard by the dozens. Some of the galleys at the stern tried to shear off as fast as they could.

"The pasha", Juan shouted. "Get the pasha. Don't let him escape."

"I'll get him", said Don Pedro de Zapata, leaping to his feet. He had been knocked senseless for a few moments by the shock of the ramming.

Ali Pasha saw his men waver, as the first men from Colonna's ship were boarding the *Sultana*. The papal flagship was packed with soldiers. The gold-shimmering officers around him tried to make him use the ladder by which reinforcements had come on board and which now was almost empty; but he shook his head, and seizing a jeweled bow he sent an arrow into the mass of on-rushing Spanish soldiers.

More and more Turkish soldiers were jumping overboard, trying to reach the galleys at the stern.

There was a wild tussle around the poop deck; Spanish helmets were moving up the ladder. Pedro de Zapata only reached the foot when thirty Spaniards were already up, butchering everybody in sight. One of them turned toward the main deck, holding something round and bleeding in his hand. It was a head—Ali Pasha's head.

At that sight the Turks still alive threw away their arms and fell on their knees. They were killed before Juan could stop it, and the soldier who had killed Ali Pasha planted the head on a pike and swung it around so that it could be seen by other ships.

Spaniards and Italians roared their Viva's as Juan mounted the poop deck. Despite his pain he managed not to limp.

"Hoist the flag of the Holy League", he ordered.

It was two o'clock in the afternoon.


Monsignor Busotti de Bibiana, treasurer of the Vatican, was making his report as usual, and the Pope, as usual, received it walking up and down, because that way he did not suffer so much from his stones.

After about a quarter of an hour of reading figures and giving explanations the good monsignor had a vague feeling that the Holy Father was not listening.

Looking up he saw that he was listening ... but not to the treasurer's report.

Pius V was staring out the window, his head held obliquely, his expression one of the most intense expectation.

"W-what is it, Your Highness?" the monsignor quavered.

The Pope beckoned him to be quiet. He walked over to the window, and opened it. He still appeared to be listening to something or someone.

To the monsignor it seemed as if his face were shining; his hands were folded and now he was raising them and he kept them raised.

A minute passed, and another, and the monsignor began to wonder how the old man could stand it, plagued as he was by rheumatism in his arms and shoulders. Only after another minute and a half did the Pope let his arms drop and turn away from the window. He was smiling.

"This is no day for business affairs", he said. "What we have to do is to thank God for our great victory over the Turks."

He gave his treasurer a friendly nod and walked away to his private chapel.

Once more Fra Angelico's Madonna looked down on him as he prayed before the crucifix on the altar.

When he had given praise to God he looked at God's Mother. "'*Salus infirmorum*'", he whispered. "'*Refugium peccatorum . . . Consolatrix afflictorum . . .*'" All that she was: Help of the sick . . . Refuge of sinners . . . Comforter of the afflicted. All that and more. Through her mankind had become akin with the Creator, through her Christianity received her Son, and her help was never ending.

"'*Auxilium christianorum*'", he murmured. "'Help of Christians pray for us.'" And he decided there and then to add this new title to the beautiful song in her honor.

Monsignor Busotti de Bibiana in the meantime buttonholed everyone he could get hold of and told him about what had happened in the Pope's study—Cardinal Rusticucci, prelates Vannini and Ruggiero.

Prelate Ruggiero was an intensely practical man. "Very well," he said, "let's put this incident down on paper at once and deposit it with our signatures in a notary's chancellery. Then we shall see what happens, or rather what happened at the time ... if anything. What was the exact time when the Holy Father began to look out of the window?"

"It was about a quarter of an hour ago", Monsignor Busotti said. "What is the time now?"

Prelate Ruggiero pointed to the clock on the mantelpiece. He took a quill and a piece of official notepaper and began to write: "On the seventh day of October A.D. 1571, at two o'clock in the afternoon ..."

## CHAPTER 40

THE SIGHT FROM the *Sultana's* poop deck was one never to be forgotten.

Colonna had a few light guns trained on the galleys and brigantines still hovering near, and the two nearest surrendered without a shot, the first Turkish warships ever to do so. The flag from holy Mecca in the hands of the Christians and Ali Pasha's head on a Spanish pike seemed to be more than they could bear.

Colonna started firing at the others. His ship, too, showed a good deal of damage.

Juan thought of the young man on board there, what was his name? Cervas or Cervantes. Good luck, señor poet, he thought.

There was a large Venetian galley sinking, blocking the view toward Barbarigo's wing. Half a dozen frigates were alongside it, taking on its soldiers and crew, unhampered, at least for the moment, by the enemy. It was not Veniero's flagship, that was over there on the right, firing away at an invisible opponent and surrounded by wreckage.

The frigates around the large Venetian dispersed hastily as the galley was going down, she was the *Veglia* and now he could see half a dozen Turkish ships rowing toward Lepanto harbor; fleeing, by God, they were fleeing—Barbarigo must have been performing magnificently.

Don Miguel de Moncada came up, one arm in a sling and with him a group of officers, Rodrigo de Mendoza, Juan de Guzmán, and Ruy Díaz among them, faces wreathed in smiles; the fools seemed to think that the battle was won.

Juan cut off their felicitations at once. "Have this ship cleared of Turks at once, gentlemen", he ordered. "See to it that we get makeshift crews for all workable guns. Don Miguel, my respects to Don Luiz Córdoba and will he please provide a crew for the sails also and organize everything to get my flagship free. Don Rodrigo, my respects to Admiral Colonna, many thanks for his timely help, but would he please get his spur out of this ship. This is only the beginning, gentlemen."

They were speeding off in all directions.

Juan could see Colonna now; the admiral was standing on his forecastle, inspecting the damage the ramming had done. He waved at him and Colonna waved back, grinning delightedly.

A fast Venetian brigantine was coming alongside, with a blue-white streamer on its mast, showing that she was carrying important reports.

A moment later a handsome young Venetian noble bowed to his commander in chief.

"Almoro Morosini, of Admiral Sebastiano Veniero's staff, at Your Highness' service", he said in a silky voice. "The admiral most regretfully reports that the Proveditore Barbarigo was gravely wounded by an arrow in the left eye and is not likely to survive."

Barbarigo, florid, good-natured Barbarigo, whose decency had done so much to save the situation at Gomenizza . . .

"Further losses are: Captain Giovanni de Loredano and Captain Caterino Malipieri with their vessels sunk by the enemy. Command over the wing is now in the hands of Commissary Canale and the commander of Proveditore Barbarigo's galleys is Captain Nani. Commissary Canale most respectfully reports that he has engaged and sunk the vessel of Mohammed Sirocco, Pasha of Alexandria."

"Excellent", Juan said, brightening. "What happened to the pasha?"

"We fished him out of the water, Highness", the young Venetian said, beaming. "He was taken on board the commissary's galley, but he was rather badly wounded, so the commissary had his head cut off."

Juan raised his brows, but abstained from a word of criticism. Unlike Ali Pasha the man had been a prisoner of war, but fine distinctions could not be demanded of a Venetian commissary, still smarting from what had happened to his compatriots on Cyprus and especially to Bragadino. What mattered very much was that two of the three highest Turkish commanders were dead and that would have a strongly discouraging effect on the entire Turkish fleet. He remembered how at Sziget Mehmed Sokolli kept the death of Sultan Süleyman a secret to ensure an orderly withdrawal.

"Attention", shouted Don Lope de Figueroa. He pointed to the starboard side of the *Sultana*, where four Turkish galleys were approaching at full speed.

"Pass the word to the gunnery captain: fire as you see fit", Juan said quickly. "They should be ready by now." The one thing the Turks were not likely to expect was to be fired on by the guns of their own flagship. By now there was no living Turk left on board. Even so it was a struggle of one against four, unless Don Luiz de Córdoba succeeded in getting the royal flagship free. Colonna was hard at it to disentangle his spur, but his batteries could not yet reach the attackers and the papal flagship had only two traversing guns on the forecastle. Colonna had seen the new enemy, but seemed to be quite unruffled.

An instant later Juan saw the reason for his calm. Two, three, four, five Spanish galleys were rushing up, so close together that their spars almost touched. Santa Cruz! And if Santa Cruz could afford to send them, that gap between center and left wing must either be closed or Uluch Ali was not as foxy as his reputation.

Colonna was making tremendous efforts to get off.

The *Sultana's* guns began to fire, but only a few of them, and that was not surprising. Don Luiz de Córdoba could not afford to denude his own batteries, and the men were not accustomed to the Turkish guns. Even so, the effect might tell on the Turkish morale. There was nothing a soldier or sailor hated more than to be fired on by his own guns.

The Turks were firing too, now.

"We have sunk six galleys so far, and I saw one more sinking on my way out here, Highness." Young Morosini was going on with his report as if nothing had happened.

"Excellent", Juan said again. "My respects to Commissary Canale, and will he please carry on with the good work.

476

Tell him how sorry I am about Proveditore Barbarigo. I'll send my own physician to him as soon as it is possible."

There was a crash and a second and a third.

"I am sorry, but your report back to your ship will be somewhat delayed", Juan told the young Venetian affably. "I'm afraid your ship's been hit." He turned away: "Fish the men of that frigate out of the water", he ordered. "Don Lope ... better collect your men to repel boarders, if necessary."

It was not necessary. Santa Cruz' reinforcements sank two of the galleys approaching and the other two turned tail. At the same time Don Luiz sent a message that he was going to get the royal flagship free in a few minutes.

"Very well. I'm coming."

Juan left Don Rodrigo de Mendoza in charge of the *Sultana* and returned with Don Lope, Don Miguel, and the other nobles including Don Pedro de Zapata, who was in a foul temper because somebody else had been able to get the pasha before him, "and a simple soldier, too."

"Did you get his name?" Juan asked.

"Yes, Highness. One José Gómez, impudent rascal."

"The impudent rascal's going to get a thousand ducats from me", Juan said. "Take a note, Don Francisco, and pass it on to de Soto."

"I gave him everything I had in *my* pockets." Don Pedro laughed.

Don Luiz de Córdoba was in a state of sheer exultation. "Whoever built that ship of ours knew his business, Excellency. We cut the Turk's spur and all we lost is a couple of spars now replaced and the boat, of course. I had the sails replaced, too."

"No report from Admiral Doria?" Juan asked.

"No, Excellency."

"Get us off then, Don Luiz."

"Oars!" Don Luiz bellowed.

The rowing masters were ready with trumpet and whips. The men rowed as if they were trying to escape from hell itself. There was no need to apply the whip to their backs, not this time, when their chains were off and they were rowing for their liberty.

"Sails", Don Luiz roared, and a naval captain took over from there, using his own nautical language, which to a noble was of no interest. The royal flagship began to move.

The prize crew they had left on board the *Sultana* cheered madly, and a few minutes later Admiral Colonna, too, extricated his ship, an excellent feat of seamanship, as he did not cut his spur but took it out of the *Sultana*'s boards as neatly as if he were extracting a loose tooth.

Young Morosini was staring in fascination at the flagship of his admiral. Old Veniero, chasing after a huge Turkish galley, was literally running over a number of light enemy craft, filled with soldiers.

Juan caught a glimpse of the old man, standing on the poop and gesticulating wildly. Everywhere on the left wing, two or three galleys were forming little battlefields of their own, but a great number of Turkish vessels were in flight toward the harbor and all of them were being pursued. Canale was doing well. Juan remembered him from the war councils, a spare, bald-headed man, as cold as Veniero was peppery.

The other wing, Doria's wing, disappeared completely in a pall of smoke hanging over the sea like ground fog. Trouble was brewing there—at least two or three ships must be burning; that was not just the smoke of gunfire.

Another frigate came up, swooping elegantly past the wreckage of a Turkish vessel. The blue-white streamer . . . news again. This time it came from Santa Cruz. The young officer who came on board was one of his nephews. "The respects of my ... of Admiral the Marquis of Santa Cruz, Highness, and here is a report for Your Highness' most urgent attention."

A written report! This was sure to be bad news. Santa Cruz obviously did not want the boy to blurt it out in front of the whole staff.

Juan opened the note. Uluch Ali had broken through after all. After a long-drawn maneuver that made it look as if he were leaving the battle altogether he had gone on the other tack and sailed through what by now was no longer a gap but almost a gulf, and with no less than sixty galleys, Algerine galleys, the fastest of them all. He had got into the rear of the entire Christian line and Santa Cruz had to turn about to face him and to turn again, as Uluch Ali avoided an engagement and raced on toward the outer right of the center where he was causing havoc. Santa Cruz had followed but came too late to save the three galleys of Prior Giustiniani and his Knights of St. John.

Juan forced himself to read on without showing what he felt. They were all staring at him, trying to guess what the news was.

The whole thing had happened apparently just after Santa Cruz had sent those five galleys to help him out, and by now it was to be hoped that Doria, whose ships were fobbed off by a mere thirty to forty of Uluch Ali's galleys, had seen what happened and was underway to catch the Algerine fox. "I am attacking," Santa Cruz wrote, "but I have only twenty-three vessels left and some of them damaged."

"Another frigate alongside, Excellency. News from Admiral Colonna."

"Take the messenger on board. I want fifteen galleys to follow the flagship."

They were looking at each other. The battle had dissolved into dozens of single combats; the left wing was in full pursuit of the Turks—from where were they going to get fifteen galleys?

Juan looked about. Two vessels were towing off Turkish prizes at a distance. "Get those two to start with", he ordered. "A prize crew on the Turkish ships is quite enough. Send a frigate over."

Colonna's messenger came on board. "Highness, the three ships of the Knights of St. John ..."

"I know all about that. How many ships has your admiral at my immediate disposal?"

"I don't know, Highness. He has just taken the *Mihrmah*, and we found it's old flagship of Pope Pius the Fourth that we lost at Yerba. It's the Turkish paymaster's ship now, and full of gold."

"I congratulate the admiral, but I must have at least a dozen galleys to clean up what's happening over there." Juan pointed to the pall of smoke, still as dense and foglike as before. "Off with you and tell him to send me every ship he can spare. The battle is more important than loot. We'll have all the loot we want later, and none at all if we hesitate now. Tell him it's just one more strong effort."

He caught three Venetian ships with Turkish vessels in tow. Their captains hated to part with them, fearing that their precious conquest might easily be snapped up by somebody else, but Juan broke the tow of one of them by sailing right through, and there were no more protests.

He picked up another five ships, Spaniards this time, and Colonna sent him three papal galleys, including the *Toscana* and the *Eleugina*, which had conquered a Rhodian galley half an hour earlier.

480

Thirteen in all, fourteen with the royal flagship. It was not much but it would have to do. He raced with them toward the fog and arrived just in time to control the decision in half a dozen fierce combats, in which each Christian galley fought two and even three of the lighter Algerine ships. At a distance of at least three miles Doria was battling with Uluch Ali's rear, if one could call it a rear, with the crafty leader changing his position five times in the course of an hour.

At long last Doria broke through and Uluch Ali's ships changed tack once more and fled to the open sea.

Juan pursued them with his thirteen vessels, but desisted when he saw that there was no chance of keeping up with them. They were built for speed, and Uluch Ali was a past master at making the most of that advantage.

Returning from the chase the commander in chief's squadron by its very appearance ended the fighting still going on between Doria and the rest of the Algerine ships.

Juan saw Doria saluting him jauntily as their ships passed each other, and he reciprocated a little stiffly.

The Genoese was covered with blood from helmet to shoe, but as he was able to move about with his usual feline elegance the blood was not likely to be his own. Juan found out later that it had originally flowed in the veins of a Genoese sailing master who was hit full in the chest by a Turkish cannon ball two yards away from his admiral.

Juan's own wound began to hurt badly. Several times he felt faint. But this was not the day when he could afford to give in to what St. Francis used to call Brother Ass, to that limitation that was his body. He had enjoyed it many a time in his life; he had enjoyed it even this very day, when he was fighting the man the Turks called Kilidj

Hussein. But apart from those moments this day more than any other proved the body's limitations. In a battle involving more than six hundred ships the commander in chief needed several hundred bodies to cope with all the situations that evolved. It had been impossible to decline the challenge of the *Sultana*. But it had been also impossible to fight a duel with her and still supervise what was going on on the right wing of the center, or on the front commanded by Doria.

Twelve, fifteen, seventeen Algerine ships surrendered; ah well, he had come in time and that was what mattered; now back, back to the gulf to see what still had to be done.

The panorama of the Gulf of Lepanto was overwhelming. The very sea around the fleet was reddened in large, dark patches, with wreckage floating all over it, empty boats, boats strewn with corpses, the charred remains of masts, spars, and cabin furniture. An armada of light craft was picking up survivors, barrels, chests, anything afloat.

Fighting was still going on in some places, with about thirty-odd Turkish ships trying to save the day against impossible odds.

Here again everything stopped when the Turks saw the royal flagship arriving as the vanguard of what seemed to be another and formidable Christian fleet—Juan's thirteen galleys, followed by Doria's and the remnant of Santa Cruz' vessels. The Turks surrendered.

The royal flagship did not have to fire a single shot in this last phase of the battle.

Old Galarza came up to Juan. "If Your Excellency will permit," he said in a low voice, "there is no more need for armor." Without waiting for a reply he began to undo the buckles of the heavy steel plates.

Juan saw that his fingers were trembling and his eyes shining with admiration. Who was the man with him? Dr. Martínez, of course, the physician. He should really go to his cabin for this, but the cabin would be hot and stuffy—it was hot enough even on deck. Somebody came with a chair, and he sat down and closed his eyes. Strange that he should feel so tired now that they were taking all that steel off him; now that God had taken all that burden from him. . . .

Dr. Martínez, crouching at his feet, made clucking noises.

Juan grinned. "Well, how bad is it?" he asked. He winced a little as the doctor's fingers touched his ankle.

"Bad? It isn't bad, Highness, only painful." He burst into a torrent of scientific explanations, ending with the assurance that mortification was most unlikely in such cases, and proceeded to apply a dressing.

Don Pedro de Zapata announced that a frigate with Admiral Colonna on board was coming alongside.

The papal admiral seemed to be walking on clouds. He bowed deeply, and so did the gentlemen of his suite. He tried to say something and could not. Large tears were trickling down his face.

Juan embraced him and he began to stammer incoherently, sobbing on Juan's shoulder. All around them Spanish officers pressed forward, and behind them soldiers and sailors came up from the forecastle, the gangways, and the prow.

"God give me strength", Colonna said breathlessly. "God bless my soul. There has never been anything like it, never."

Juan said nothing.

"Salamis," Colonna spluttered, "Actium . . . Prevesa . . . all nothing in comparison." He began to recover. "Do you realize, Highness, that this is the end, the absolute end of Turkish sea power?"

"I hope so", Juan said, strangely unmoved.

"Of course we don't know how many of Uluch Ali's ships have escaped. . . ."

"A little over thirty", Juan replied promptly.

"We sank about ninety", Colonna told him triumphantly. "All the rest we captured. It's unbelievable. It's beyond my capacity to grasp. All the rest we captured. That means a hundred and sixty and more—a hundred and eighty is probably nearer the mark. Dear God, don't let me wake up and find it's all a dream. What's the Holy Father going to say, when he hears about it? And your royal brother? Oh God, don't let me wake up."

"What do we know about our losses?" Juan asked.

Colonna beamed at him. "That also is unbelievable. I lost one galley—one! Veniero lost eight. . . ."

"And we another six," Juan added, "including the three ships of the Knights of St. John and one belonging to the Duke of Savoy."

"Fifteen ships in all," Colonna said, "and the enemy lost three hundred. Holy Mother of God, how can they believe us when we tell them . . ."

He was right, Juan thought. There was something dream-like, something unfathomable about it all.

"The Cross against the Crescent", he said softly, and his hand went up to the relic of the True Cross. Galarza had not dared to take it off when he helped him out of his armor. "This is our Lord's victory, not ours." As he spoke he saw the cloud. It was not a large cloud, not much bigger than a man's hand, but it was lead-colored and the air was heavy.

Colonna was talking to him, something about the casualties being estimated at four or five Turks to one Christian. "We'll have more accurate figures in a day or two, but my estimate . . ."

The cloud was growing, Juan thought. Very slowly growing. He felt strangely uneasy, and he wished that Colonna would stop gabbing at him.

But Colonna was going on and on, he certainly had found his voice again. "Easy to make up our losses. There are more than ten thousand Christian galley slaves on board their ships, and if they'll behave the way the ones did that I met on board some of my prizes, I shall be hugged to death or torn to pieces—they'll make relics out of me, and of you too, if you're not careful. . . ."

Relic? Had he said something about a relic? There was a thunderstorm coming, of course, it often happened in these waters and at this time of the year.

A thunderstorm. Great Lord in heaven, a thunderstorm, and half a thousand ships in the open sea. Collisions, galleys sunk, Turkish ships making a dash for freedom. All pursuit stopped by mountainous waves, impossible to fire guns. . . .

"Don Luiz!" Juan shouted, and Colonna was so baffled, he recoiled as if he had been hit. "Don Luiz de Córdoba!"

"Excellency?"

"Have one gun fired, if you please, and the storm signal hoisted on the mainmast."

"Yes-yes, Excellency."

"Storm, by God", Colonna said, scanning the horizon. "Where were my eyes? How are we going to watch all those Turks. . . ."

"Exactly, my lord Colonna. We must sail at once—back to Petala. And we'll be lucky if we get through the channel of Oxia before the storm breaks."

## CHAPTER 41

THE FLEET REACHED the harbor of Petala half an hour before the storm, without having lost a single ship or even a single prisoner, although it was not exactly easy for the leaders to get back into formation.

The men felt they had done enough for the day; they wanted to eat and drink and count their loot; they wanted to brag to each other about their individual feats of bravery. In a number of cases their officers had to force them to their places, and the flagships had to rush about like shepherds' dogs to herd their sheep together and drive them back to their fold.

Darkness fell long before they had sailed around Cape Skropha, and the gathering clouds first dimmed and then extinguished the stars. But there were lanterns on every mast. Thirty Christian galleys were the vanguard, followed by a long, double line—Christian ships on one side, Turkish prizes on the other, hugging the coast—and the light craft bringing up the rear.

There was almost no need for oars. The winds blew the fleet into harbor.

Then and only then the first long zigzag lightning split the heavens, and the thunder as of a thousand cannon crashed down on victors and vanquished alike.

Juan was alone in his cabin.

Nobles and officers had come to felicitate him; he had shaken a number of hands and spent all the smiles he had left. Then de Soto came, somewhat embarrassed, to announce that everybody was very hungry but that one of the *Sultana's* shots had damaged the galley beyond repair, at least for that evening, so there could be no dinner.

"It doesn't matter", Juan said wearily. "Are the wounded being looked after?"

"The physicians are doing all they can, Your Excellency."

Juan nodded. He knew how little they could do, except in the case of light wounds like his own. All men who had lost a limb were likely to die. All men who had been shot in the chest or the abdomen were likely to die. There was talk also that at least some of the Turks had been using poisoned arrows.

Outside the thunder was firing one salvo after the other.

"If Your Excellency will permit . . ."

The fellow was still there. "Yes, de Soto?"

"Don Luiz de Córdoba would like to take some of the gentlemen with him on board the *San Felipe*, where they can get something to eat."

"By all means, de Soto. You may join them if you wish."

"Thank you very much, Your Excellency, but . . ."

"What more do you want, de Soto?"

"Don Luiz thought—we all thought—wouldn't you come with us yourself? All you've had during the day was a few biscuits and a goblet of wine. . . ."

"I'm not the least bit hungry, de Soto. You go, all of you."

The secretary withdrew, in his eyes the same expression as in those of Galarza, of the nobles and officers, an expression of admiration bordering on veneration.

At last he was alone and God's thunder was rolling overhead, now like cannon, now like a million hooves. The wind howled in the rigging of the fleet. The biggest fleet the Mediterranean had ever seen, yet it was hiding here, in a miserable little harbor, the King's men, the Sultan's men, the Pope's men, all hiding like frightened children.

487

There was little difference now between victor and vanquished.

And he, the conqueror, whom they all stared at as if he were a holy image, he was sitting in his little cabin, with nothing to eat.

Five hundred ships. Five hundred nutshells. A hundred and fifty thousand men, all crowded together like so many ants in an ant heap.

What was it that God wanted to show him? That he was still no more than a little boy, playing Moors and Christians in the dirty streets of Leganés?

That victory and defeat were brothers under the skin, and that neither could be trusted?

That every man born of woman was a poor devil? Riches and power were skin-deep only; four or five hours of battle and the great pasha was a galley slave, chained to an oar. Beauty was skin-deep only; a single slash with sword or scimitar and every woman turned her head away from the man without a nose, from the man with the ugly scar across his face.

But then, all life on earth only went skin-deep. Honoratus Joannius had explained it well enough, about the thin, the absurdly thin crust around an earth filled with fire, and the fire breaking through in many places, for what else were volcanoes but warnings that life on earth only went skin-deep?

The great sea cared little about the nutshells warring against each other; the proud galleys lost all dignity as they fled like so many frightened chicks to the nearest corner where they were safe.

What of this day, then? They would make much of it in many countries, to be sure, there would be receptions and banquets, solemn speeches and fulsome addresses. But the

Mediterranean had seen so many battles, and it mattered little, surely, how many ships and men were involved? There were always enough for mothers to weep because their sons would not come back. And a generation or two later the battle would be no more than a date, to be remembered by scholars.

On October 7, A.D. 1571, the fleet of the Holy League under the command of one Don Juan de Austria defeated the Turkish fleet in the Gulf of Lepanto.

That was how they would put it; that was how they would teach it to their children.

And it was wrong. For what really happened was that God made use of a number of his servants to stop the progress of the Crescent in the holy name of the Cross.

They would say that the commander of the Christians was a great man, the son of a great emperor, a genius in naval and military matters, another Alexander the Great.

But in reality the commander of the Christians was a noble only on his father's side; his mother a woman who just once aroused the senses of the Emperor, a lowborn woman and of doubtful repute. He was born out of wedlock; and as for his gifts, who gave them to him but God?

They would say that it was marvelous how a young man, not much more than twenty-four years old, made the right decisions over the heads of men double his age and with ten times his experience, and they would not see that it was God's way of showing that he could inspire even such a one to do his holy will.

They would say that it was his victory, when in reality it was Christ's victory, already won when his sacred Body was hanging on the Cross. *In hoc signo vinces....*

And for that reason alone the victory was decisive and final. Never again would the Turks have the hegemony on sea. Indeed, from now on their power would dwindle and vanish and with them the power of Islam.

He could see it. That was what God was writing with his lightnings in the sky.

And with the same luminous and terrible clarity he saw that there would be no reward for him on earth. He would not rule on earth, he might not even be made an Infant of Spain, and with a searing pain in his heart he felt that María also was not for him. Of all his cherished dreams not one would be fulfilled. Not here, not on earth.

Once again, as a few times before, he felt that he would not live long and perhaps this was a blessing.

This day, October 7, 1571, was what he had been born for. This was what God decided to draw from him.

He knew he would not always think so. He would try to banish these thoughts, to forget them and chase again after rank and honor and power; he would try to find María again; he would tell himself that God wanted more of him—the conquest of Constantinople, perhaps, or of the holy places in Palestine.

But he knew also that he would never be able to banish and to forget what he had learned today, that in his heart of hearts he would always know that it was true, and that the very fact that he had learned it was due to the mercy of God, steeling him against disappointment and despair.

All of a sudden thunder and lightning ceased, and into the stillness came the rustle of the rain.

On October 8, in the early afternoon, a meeting of the commanders took place on board the papal flagship; it was to be followed by a review of the entire fleet.

The weather was perfect.

When Don Juan de Austria came on board he was greeted by a fanfare of silver trumpets and the rumble of copper kettledrums, both spoils of yesterday's battle.

Admiral Colonna received the commander in chief on the gangway and led him to his cabin, where all the leaders were waiting.

Juan shook hands with Doria, warmly greeted Requeséns and Santa Cruz, and then found himself in front of old Veniero. He embraced him. "You have done admirably, padre mio", he said, and the irascible old man's eyes filled with tears.

"Thank you, Your Excellency", he said in an unsteady voice. "I am unhappy only to have to report the death of Proveditore Agostino Barbarigo. He regained consciousness for a few moments, just before the end, and I was able to tell him how great our victory was. He could no longer speak but he raised his hands to heaven and smiled. Then he died."

"Enviable Barbarigo", Juan said. "God rest him."

"Amen", they all said.

Alexander Farnese stepped up. "This is better than Malta and Sziget together . . . Uncle", he whispered, grinning like a little boy. "I wish I could have been with you when you took the *Sultana*."

"Somebody told me this morning that you didn't waste your time either", Juan said. "You took a Turkish galley singlehandedly, which is more than anybody in the fleet can say of himself. I want all the details, of course."

"It isn't true, Uncle", Alexander said. "I wasn't alone. Davalos was with me, yes, a Spaniard, and if it weren't for him, I'd be dead now. I jumped on board the silly ship and so did he, and then our galley broke loose and there we were, the two of us. So we decided to make the best of it and laid about, and the Turks must have thought we were djinns or afreets or whatever they call their demons, because they were absurdly frightened, especially when I killed the captain and Davalos the helmsman. After a while our galley managed to get close again and blew all the Turks on the prow into the water; the boarders came over and there we were. Believe it or not, neither Davalos nor I have a scratch! It's miraculous, really, but then the whole day was."

"Yes", Juan said. "A thousand ducats for that man Davalos. Make a note of it, de Soto! As for you, my redoubtable nephew...."

"All I want is the privilege of calling you uncle", Alexander said, grinning. "Madonna, I wish I could see Queen Catherine's face when she hears about all this. She'll burst, and so will her necromancers. Mind you, if you're interested in details, I have a nice one for you. We had a Roman chaplain on board, that is, he was sent to us from Rome, an Irishman with a name that sounds like an invocation: Odonel or something like that; I've never been very good at outlandish names. Well, when we boarded another Turk we found her full of janizaries, and they are fighters, as you know, and things didn't look too good at one point. So Padre Odonel—he's all of six feet tall and has fire red hair—Padre Odonel seized a pike, yelled, 'Christ Himself would fight in this battle', and went to work like Samson among the Philistines. He slew seven of them and made a dozen prisoners—I never laughed so much in all my life."

"Five chaplains were killed in battle", Veniero interposed. "Four Venetian priests and one of His Holiness' friars."

"And all priests and brothers remained on deck during the battle", Colonna added. "I have the final figures now, Excellency. We lost fifteen ships and a little over seven thousand, six hundred men, and we have about fifteen thousand wounded. We sank ninety-two galleys and captured one hundred and seventy-eight. We made almost ten thousand prisoners. According to the lists we found, the Turks must have had between thirty and thirty-five thousand dead. And we liberated about fifteen thousand Christian galley slaves. All of them have volunteered to serve in our fleet until we reach home."

"There has never been anything like it", Doria said. "And if I hadn't seen with it my own eyes, I would never believe it."

"Courage is better than vacillation", said the irrepressible Veniero to nobody in particular.

"Pray, let me go on, gentlemen", Colonna said hastily. "We have taken one hundred and fifteen heavy cannon and two hundred and ninety-four light cannon. Among our prisoners are the two sons of Ali Pasha, Ahmed Bey, aged sixteen, and Muhammad Bey, aged thirteen, with their teacher El Hamed. Their mother is a sister of the Sultan himself. We have Pertau Pasha among our prisoners and no less than thirty governors of provinces. The amount of gold, silver, and jewels taken could not be counted as yet; we have teams working at it. Among the flags, standards, and banners taken is the Sandjack, the green standard of the prophet from Mecca and the imperial flag of the Sultan."

"I hope that Swiss officer of yours has got the banner he wanted", Juan said, smiling.

"The Swiss Guards captured several banners", Colonna told him. "They've done honor to their country and to the Holy Father. There is one more fact I wish to mention, Your Excellency. You gave the order that every Christian ship should have a crucifix tied to the mast. Very many of our ships were damaged, of course. But not a single crucifix came to harm in all the ships afloat."

A number of officers gasped.

Juan just nodded, as if he had not expected anything else. He was looking at the sea's calm, blue majesty. I shall send Tía the relic of the True Cross, he thought, and a Turkish banner, too.

He wondered a little whether they were expecting him to address them, although that was not part of the agenda de Soto had given him.

If they did expect something of the sort, they must have felt that he was not in the mood for it, but most likely they were not thinking of an official address at all.

They were all still looking a little dazed, understandably enough. He would meet them again tonight, on board his own flagship—the galley would be repaired by then—and soon after dinner they would quarrel with each other over the distribution of the spoils.

One of Colonna's aides came in to report that the frigate *Madrileña* had come alongside.

That was the next point on the program: sailing along the line of all the ships. Colonna, Veniero, Doria, Requeséns, and Santa Cruz would do the same, each in his own frigate.

Colonna accompanied the commander in chief to the gangway.

A tall, thin soldier appeared on it, his left arm bandaged and in a sling. Somebody, a physician's mate, was trying to drag him away by his coat, but he resisted stoutly and at the same time saluted, his eye fixed on Don Juan.

"Señor poet", Juan exclaimed, smiling. "Leave him alone, you there! I am glad to see you still alive, although it looks as if you've been fighting as you said you would."

"He did, Your Excellency", Colonna affirmed. "And very bravely."

"I lost the movement of my left hand for the glory of the right", said Miguel de Cervantes. "And I want to thank you, Your Excellency. Yesterday was the most beautiful day of the century."

So he knows, too, that there will not be another, Juan thought. "I thought of you once", he said, "during the battle."

Deeply moved, Cervantes said: "With or without a crown—you, sir, are a true king."

There was no answer. Instead, the silver trumpets sounded again and the huge copper kettledrums rumbled.

Don Juan de Austria went on board his frigate, and his standard rose at once on its only remaining mast.

The vessel began to move toward the endless line of ships, all proud with flags.

The soldiers, the sailors, the liberated slaves started cheering.

A true king, Cervantes thought. A magnificent young king. A crusader. Perhaps . . . the last crusader.

But those who were shouting "Hosanna" today might well be shouting "Crucify" tomorrow. Yesterday's conquerer was today's victim and tomorrow's fool.

The thing was done, though.

Glorious fool! Glorious folly! Was not there someone who had spoken even of the Folly of the Cross?

St. Paul, of course.

To whatever heights a poet soared, to whatever depths he plumbed, always a saint had been there before. . . .